Metternich

AMONG OTHER BOOKS BY THE SAME AUTHOR

The Hundred Years War

Richard III

Napoleon's Family

Henry V

Napoleon and Hitler

DESMOND SEWARD

Metternich

THE FIRST EUROPEAN

VIKING

VIKING
Published by the Penguin Group
Viking Penguin, a division of Penguin Books USA Inc.,
375 Hudson Street, New York, New York 10014, U.S.A.
Penguin Books Ltd, 27 Wrights Lane, London W8 5TZ, England
Penguin Books Australia Ltd, Ringwood, Victoria, Australia
Penguin Books Canada Ltd, 10 Alcorn Avenue, Suite 300,
Toronto, Ontario, Canada M4V 3B2
Penguin Books (N.Z.) Ltd, 182–190 Wairau Road, Auckland 10, New Zealand

Penguin Books Ltd, Registered Offices: Harmondsworth, Middlesex, England

First published in 1991 by Viking Penguin, a division of Penguin Books USA Inc.

1 3 5 7 9 10 8 6 4 2

LIBRARY OF CONGRESS CATALOGING IN PUBLICATION DATA
Seward, Desmond, 1935–
Metternich: the first European / by Desmond Seward.
p. cm.
Includes bibliographical references and index.
ISBN 0 670 82600 6
1. Metternich, Clemens Wenzel Lothar, Fürst von, 1773–1859.
2. Statesmen—Austria—Biography. 3. Austria—Foreign
relations—1792–1835. 4. Austria—Foreign relations—1815–1848.
5. Europe—Politics and government—1789–1815. 6. Europe—Politics
and government—1815–1848. I. Title.
DB80.8.M57S49 1991
943.6'04'092—dc20 91-50175

Printed in the United States of America
Set in Caslon 540

For Karl Eibenschütz

For a long time now, Europe has had
for me the value of a mother country.

METTERNICH in 1824

Contents

Acknowledgements

My first debt is to Dr Karl Eibenschütz, to whom this book is dedicated. It owes its origin to many discussions with him over the years.

I have benefited from the criticisms of Dr A. S. Ciechanowiecki, who read the typescript. I am also grateful to Susan, Viscountess Mountgarret, for help at every stage, including some very useful suggestions. I owe a particular debt to Comte Christian and Comte Hadelin de Liedekerke Beaufort for presenting me with a copy of their ancestor's invaluable memoirs, privately printed and not in the British Library or the Bibliothèque Nationale; they contain a wealth of information about Metternich's visit to England in 1794 which has been available to no previous biographer.

As so often before, I must thank the staffs of the British and London Libraries for their courteous and patient assistance. Also Mrs Joanna Barnes, who found the pictures.

Family Tree: The Metternichs

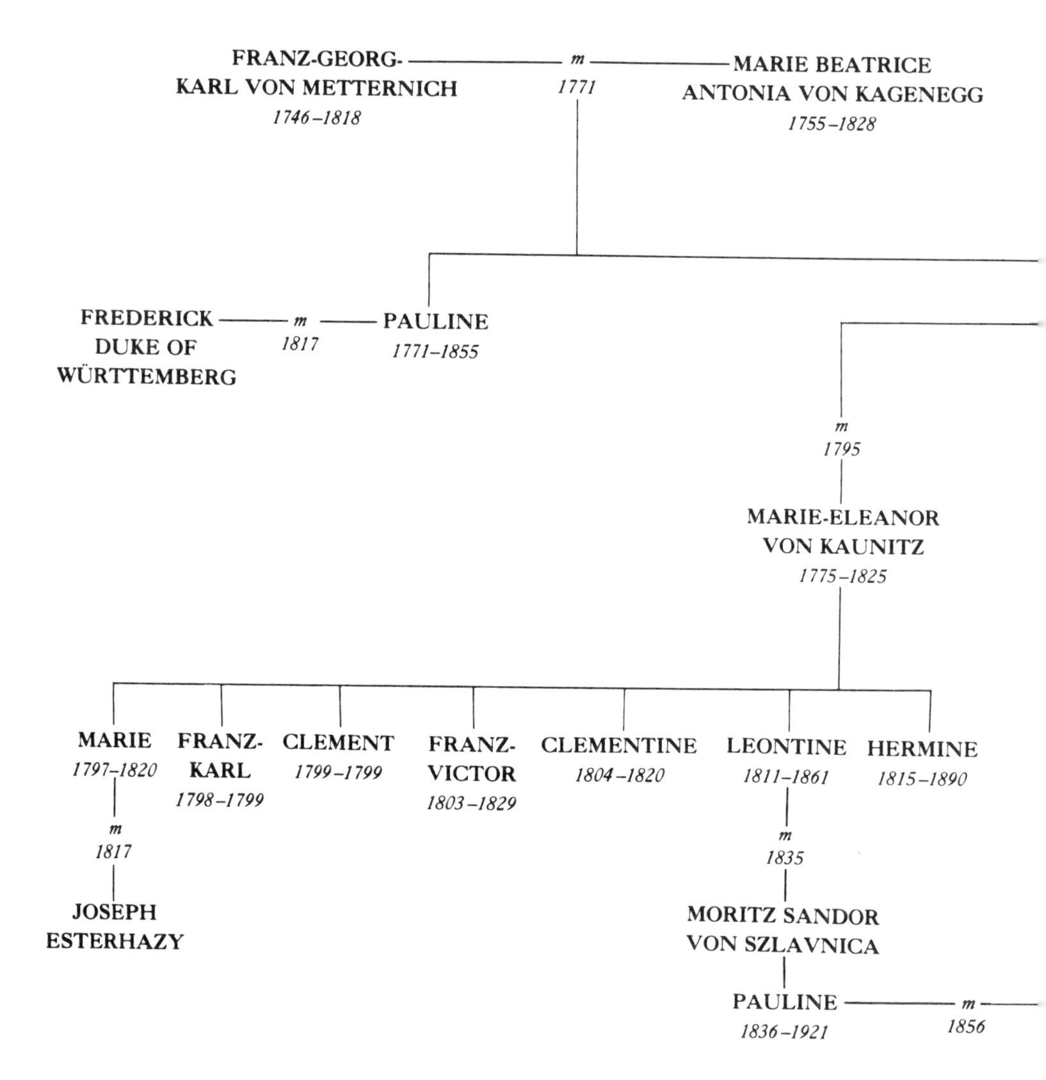

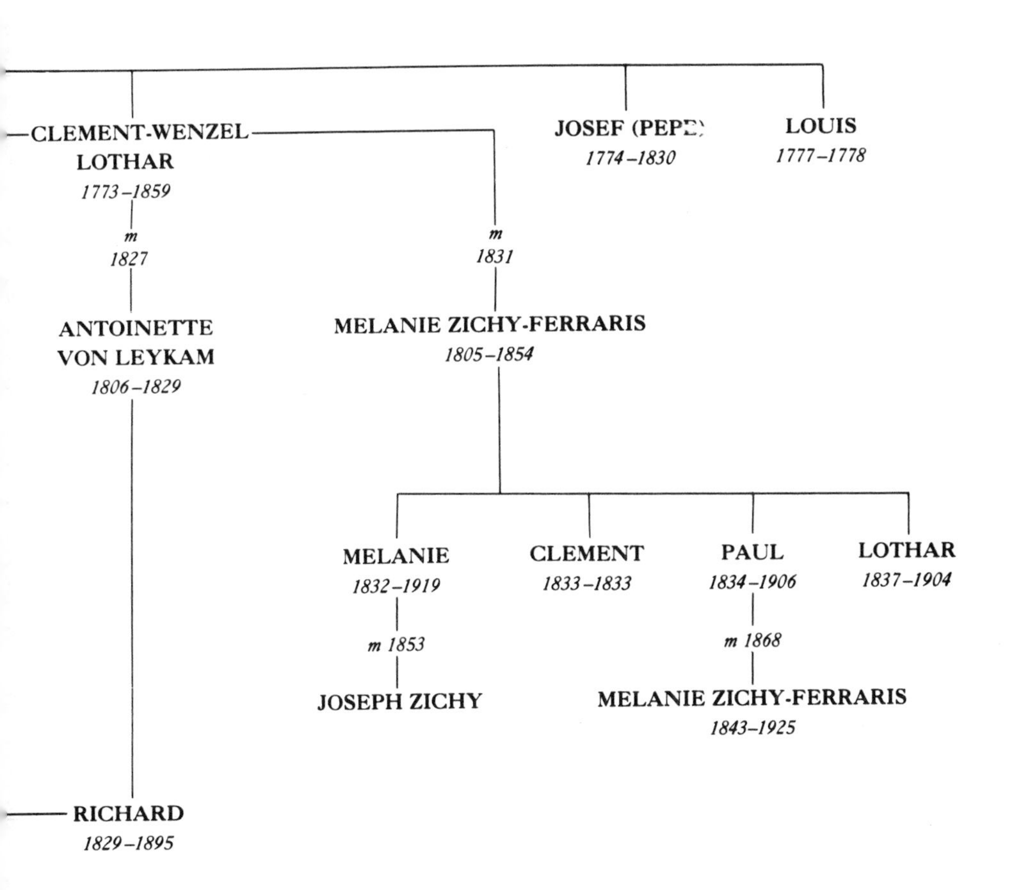

CLEMENT-WENZEL LOTHAR
1773–1859
m
1827
ANTOINETTE VON LEYKAM
1806–1829
RICHARD
1829–1895
m
1831
MELANIE ZICHY-FERRARIS
1805–1854
JOSEF (PEPE)
1774–1830
LOUIS
1777–1778
MELANIE
1832–1919
m 1853
JOSEPH ZICHY
CLEMENT
1833–1833
PAUL
1834–1906
m 1868
MELANIE ZICHY-FERRARIS
1843–1925
LOTHAR
1837–1904

Introduction

> A man who came to dominate every coalition in which he participated, who was considered by two foreign monarchs as more trustworthy than their own ministers, who for three years was in effect Prime Minister of Europe, such a man could not be of mean consequence.
>
> HENRY KISSINGER, *A World Restored*

> Looking back, converted though we cannot be to the *ancien régime,* to the 'system Metternich' or to Tsarism, we no longer exult over the age of nationality and democracy and its victories. All past social superiorities have been wiped out behind the Iron Curtain, and most of the cultural values which the educated classes had created. Anti-Socialist, clerical peasant communities may yet arise in States now satellites of Russia.
>
> SIR LEWIS NAMIER in 1955

In 1992 Western Europe takes a gigantic step towards unity. Yet at the same time the peoples of Central Europe are reemerging, and a new age of nationalism looms. In the last century a great Central European statesman tried to make the entire continent act as one in working for peace. If Clemens von Metternich's battle with liberalism does not endear him, his struggle to preserve the frontiers of 1815 should be remembered, by the Community and by a *Mitteleuropa* which will be in turmoil should the 1945 frontiers be questioned—a nightmare which may well come true.

The elegant patrician who smiles sardonically from Lawrence's portrait is not everyone's image of a master of Europe. Yet he brought Austria through the Napoleonic wars in such a way as to dominate Russia and Prussia and make her seem the greatest of the powers. In 1822 Lord Castlereagh declared that 'Austria is the pivot of Europe'.

His hostility to liberalism must be put in context if his good qualities are to be appreciated. He opposed it because for him it meant revolution and war. A philosopher of the right, Louis de Bonald, points out that behind all the seductive grace of the Enlightenment which created it, there had lurked the mentality of the Terror and the guillotine. In our own century, J. L. Talmon stressed (in *The Origins of Totalitarian Democracy*) that the French Revolution gave birth to two forms of democracy, the liberal and the totalitarian. In Prince Metternich's time Europe had seen democracy only in France—Britain was an oligarchy—where liberal turned into totalitarian very quickly.

Metternich's adopted country was Central Europe, the Habsburg Monarchy, the only state which ever brought lasting order to the Danubian lands. Not an easy empire to understand in retrospect, it was more than a group of territories inherited accidentally by a single family, as is often suggested. In varying degrees its Germans, Magyars and Czechs, its Croats, Poles, Romanians and Italians were united by loyalty to their Emperor and King which, despite its people's sense of its own identity, made for a feeling indistinguishable from patriotism; in 1795 Heinrich vom Stein thought the Monarchy a far more cohesive state than Prussia. As Alan Sked has recently reminded us, it was able to survive the 1848 Revolution, only disappearing because it lost the Great War. Nowadays it can be regarded more sympathetically, as a supranational association.

Metternich's insistence on Austria's European role, not just in Central Europe, Germany or Italy, but in Europe as a whole, has been interpreted as cynical opportunism. Yet this sort of self-interest, if self-interest it can be called, is precisely why so many nations are committing themselves to the European Community.

Few men have been more hated. '*Metternich, mitternacht über Mitteleuropa*' was how some liberals thought of him. Enemies were baffled by his many masks, his flippancy and his weakness for women. (His friend Gentz said that he knew how to love women, not how to rule them.) On the other hand, Disraeli's verdict was, 'A profound head and an affectionate heart.'

British historians tend to dislike him. A. J. P. Taylor showed an extraordinary aversion for this 'dessicated aristocrat'. In *The Habsburg Monarchy* he contrasted Tito's Yugoslavia with obvious admiration:

> Only time will show whether social revolution and economic betterment can appease national conflicts and whether Marxism can do better than Counter-Revolution dynasticism in supplying central Europe with a common loyalty.

Almost half a century later one is entitled to ask if Metternich's way was so ineffectual after all. In the opinion of Alan Sked, a more modern historian (1989), it would be mistaken to see his domestic policy as a failure—the greatest of his achievements being that the Monarchy avoided revolution for thirty-three years.

In a shrewd analysis of Metternich's diplomacy, Henry Kissinger has written:

> Metternich's policy was . . . one of status quo *par excellence*, and conducted, not by marshalling a superior force, but by obtaining a voluntary submission to his version of legitimacy. Its achievement was a period of peace lasting for over a generation without armament races or even the threat of a major war.

Although one of the most conservative statesmen in European history, Metternich was never static, never an apostle of reaction. 'Stability is not immobility,' he told Tsar Alexander I. He detested fanaticism. 'The red and white doctrinaires shun me like the plague,' he wrote proudly in 1825. He looked forward to a Europe whose countries would live in peace and harmony, instead of a continent of rival, aggressively nationalist states, though he thought it could only evolve at some future date. He knew that his own Europe was doomed; he warned a Russian foreign minister that 'between the old order and the new there lies a long period of chaos'.

In the words of his greatest biographer, Heinrich von Srbik, 'He raised Austria from the lowest depths to the proudest heights, and for decades directed its foreign policy with the utmost success, despite enormous obstacles.' The quality of his statesmanship is evident when the peace settlement of 1815 is compared with Versailles or Yalta. The social order which he defended has passed away, but not the need for international solidarity he defended with no less conviction—which is why he is of such interest to Europe during the last decade of the twentieth century.

This book tries to understand the man by seeing the world as he saw it. If at times it may seem partisan, that is not the intention. Its aim is to provide fresh insights into his personality and career.

Metternich

1

On the Edge of the Abyss

The wild *gas*, the fixed air, is plainly broke loose . . .

EDMUND BURKE,
Reflections on the French Revolution

The French Revolution . . . that monstrous social catastrophe . . .

METTERNICH, *Memoirs*

Many people consider the world of their youth superior to that of their middle or old age. Metternich is famous for his attempt to rebuild the world which he had known as a young man. It is essential to realize what it had been and what it meant to him.

On 9 October 1790 the seventeen-year-old Clemens von Metternich attended the coronation at Frankfurt am Main of the Holy Roman Emperor of the German nation, successor to the Roman Emperors of the West and the Sword Temporal of Christendom. Leopold II had made his solemn entry into the city on the previous day. First came the Frankfurt cavalry, then the envoys of the six lay Electors with their escorts, then, amid their bodyguards the three ecclesiastical Electors of Cologne, Trier and Mainz, bareheaded and riding sidesaddle—the suite of the first occupying ten state carriages, that of the last, twenty. Behind them marched ten Imperial footmen, forty lackeys and ten hayduks in Hungarian dress. These preceded a gilded, red-roofed glass coach, topped by a crowned double-headed eagle, in which sat the Emperor and his son and heir, the twenty-two-year-old Archduke Francis, who had just returned from fighting the Turks; its coachmen and outriders were in black and yellow, Swiss pikemen marching at each side. Behind rode the Marshal of the Empire bearing the Saxon sword, at the head of the Field Marshals, after whom came the Imperial Guard in gold-braided surcoats over red tunics. The aldermen of Frankfurt brought up the rear, in smaller coaches, the city clerk carrying golden keys on a red cushion.

Metternich rode with his father. Their suite filled not less than ninety-eight carriages whose coachmen and footmen wore a splendid red livery. 'Count Metternich's . . . retinue was the most brilliant among those of the Austrian court', recalled a spectator, the Comte de Bray.

On the coronation day fountains in the shape of double-headed eagles poured wine from their beaks—red from one, white from the other. In the cathedral the Archbishop-Duke of Salzburg anointed Leopold, then placed the crown on his head. The air rang with '*Vivat Imperator!*' On either side of the altar sat mitred prelates together with Knights of Malta in black cloaks and Teutonic Knights in white; beneath the altar steps were the Knights of the Golden Fleece in purple and gold. In a Knight of Malta's red uniform, the young Metternich had an excellent view of the ceremony, in his capacity as a Marshal of the College of Westphalian Counts. 'Everything down to the smallest detail pulled at the heartstrings, by appealing to one's instinct for tradition and by the sheer splendour of the spectacle,' he wrote many years later. After his crowning, Leopold rode to the banqueting hall beneath a jewelled canopy, 'like the ghost of Charlemagne'. Metternich was one of the noblemen who waited on the Emperor's table. (Among the crowd outside was Mozart, who had come to Frankfurt hoping to find a commission for a new opera.)

Clemens-Wenzel-Lothar-Nepomuk von Metternich-Winneburg-Beilstein had been born on 15 May at the family residence in the Münz Platz at Coblenz. His father, Count Franz-Georg, is dismissed by some historians as a garrulous fop, 'an old-time courtier in opera bouffe'. In reality he was an extremely professional diplomatist, of whom Prince Kaunitz—the greatest Imperial statesman of the eighteenth century—had a very high opinion.

Metternich's mother, Maria Beatrix von Kagenegg, came from

Freiburg in the Breisgau, in those days a Habsburg enclave. She was a protégée of Empress Maria Theresa, who always chose amusing and intelligent girls for her ladies-in-waiting, and who had arranged the marriage with Kaunitz's aid. Metternich inherited her handsome, curiously masculine features. She had two other children who survived infancy, Pauline—the eldest—and a younger boy, Josef or 'Pepi'.

'You nobles merely take the trouble to be born,' Figaro tells the count in *The Marriage of Figaro*, and by any reckoning Metternich was a very great nobleman indeed. His father was a *Reichsgraf* or Count of the Empire, a member of the Council of Counts of the Westphalian 'Circle'. (The many states of what is now Germany were grouped in ten Circles.) His family claimed to have been noble since Carolingian times and had certainly been so since the thirteenth century. Both parents possessed *seize quartiers*, all their sixteen great-great-grandparents having been noble, so that it was impossible for them to have a commoner relation nearer than a fifth cousin. German society was stratified almost geologically, in a system far more rigid than that of *ancien régime* France, the *Bürgertum* or middle class accepting its inferiority in a way which no French bourgeois would have tolerated; a merchant's daughter did not dare presume to the aristocratic '*Fräulein*' but was content to be styled '*Jungfer*'. Only the higher nobility could aspire to senior posts in the army or the Church. The Metternichs belonged to the *Reichsunmittelbar*, the sovereign aristocracy.

He wrote an account of his family for the *Almanach de Gotha* of 1836:

> The ancient princely house of Metternich descends from a very old noble family of the Juliers region. Lothar [Metternich] was Archbishop Elector of Trier from 1599–1623. The branch of the Barons of Winneburg and Beilstein became extinct in 1616 whereupon its lordships of Winneburg and Beilstein (on the Hundsrück and the Moselle) reverted to the Emperor as Imperial fiefs. Lothar bought part of them, acquiring a seat in the College of Westphalian Counts and the right to speak in it; he then transferred them to his

> cousins, the Barons Karl Heinrich (Elector of Mainz from 1679) and Phillip Emmanuel, whom the Emperor raised to the rank of Count on 20 March 1679.

Clemens descended from Phillip Emmanuel.

The Metternichs owned estates all over the Rhineland, amounting to seventy-three square miles of farmland and vineyards which produced an income of £25,000 a year, even if Winneburg and Beilstein were crumbling feudal keeps. Despite its Baroque palaces and churches, the Germany into which Metternich was born was still all but medieval, the world of the *Tales of Hoffmann* (whose author was three years younger), a sleepy country of ruined castles, rich abbeys and walled towns with narrow, crooked streets and timbered houses, where custom and tradition meant everything. This ancient, wine-drinking southern Germany was untouched by the Emperor Joseph II's reforms, let alone by Spartan innovations from Prussia.

Three Rhineland cities, each the capital of an archbishop-elector, loomed large in the family's life during Metternich's early years, even if he seldom visited them. His father was Imperial envoy to the courts of Cologne, Mainz and Trier, whose rulers, together with six lay princes, elected the Emperor. Cologne flourished as a river port for the barges which plied between Frankfurt and Holland, though the Elector only visited his capital on great festivals to say Mass in the cathedral; the citizens would not let him stay for more than three days a year and normally he lived at Bonn, a few miles away. Outwardly Mainz too seemed prosperous, as it was where all merchandise along the Rhine was transferred to fresh barges, yet in the year before Metternich's birth the Elector had to buy grain from Poland to avert famine while one in three of its women was said to be a beggar or a prostitute. The third, and in some ways most distinguished, electoral city was Trier on the Moselle, whose imposing palace had been built by Archbishop Lothar von Metternich. (All male Metternichs were hereditary chamberlains to the Electors of Mainz.) These three little states formed the heart of the Rhineland, the proximity of France giving them considerable strategic importance. Count Metternich's post as envoy was one of some eminence; in 1777 he received the additional appointment of Minister to the Circle of Westphalia, becoming the Emperor's personal representative in the greater part of western and southern Germany.

There was also a Metternich estate in Bohemia, won 130 years before by a soldier ancestor. The family seem to have looked on it much as eighteenth-century English peers did their lands in Ireland. Clemens visited Königswart for the first time in 1786, very briefly. Like the Irish, apart from a few great families who had been absorbed by their conquerors, the Czechs were a subject race speaking a despised tongue. Mozart's Prague was a German city where only servants spoke Czech, if one or two intellectuals dreamt of reviving the language. Bohemia was very much a part of the 'Roman Empire of the German Nation'.

Eighteenth-century Germany was (as Metternich would one day say of another land) a geographical expression rather than a country, its myriad states ranging from the Habsburg domains down to the estate of a *Reichsritter* (Imperial Knight) no larger than an English manor. There were duchies, margravates, principalities, counties, baronies, bishoprics, abbacies, free cities, each a sovereign domain—Kaunitz referred to their rulers as 'the humming-bird kings'. Yet though the Emperor held only nominal sway, no one ever forgot that he was Emperor of the German nation. In the Habsburg lands, in what are now Slovenia and Croatia as well as Austria, in his Hungarian and Bohemian realms, in Belgium and Lombardy, he ruled directly. Vienna was the spiritual capital of Germany, every great German nobleman learning to speak the language of the Austrian court, *Schönbrunner Deutsch*.

Even so, there was considerable distrust and resentment of Vienna throughout the Reich, especially when the Emperor was a tactless innovator such as Joseph II. Count Franz-Georg's embassy was far from being a rococo sinecure. In 1778 Joseph attempted to annex Bavaria but was deterred by Prussia. When he tried again in 1785 Prussia formed a League of Princes to stop him, consisting of seventeen states. Among them was Mainz, normally a staunch ally of Vienna. The Count cannot have had an easy task soothing him down.

Meanwhile the young Metternichs were given tutors. Religion was unfashionable but the Abbé Bertrand, a member of the Piarist Order which specialised in education, instilled a basic Catholicism even if the young Clemens was scarcely fervent. The other tutor, Jean-François Simon, who joined the family in 1785, was an Alsatian, a Lutheran schoolmaster from Strasbourg whose academy for girls at Dessau had failed. A kindly soul, he got on well with his pupils. As an intellectual, a follower of Johann-Bernhard Basedow—the 'German Rousseau'—and the *philosophaillerie*, he found the household congenial, since Count Franz-Georg was vaguely Voltairean and a discreet freemason. However the only taste which this keen peruser of the *Encyclopédie* communicated to Clemens was a lifelong interest in medicine. While the boy's mother insisted on his speaking and writing French to her, his father made him polish his German.

In the summer of 1788 they were sent to the university of Strasbourg, accompanied by Simon. It was always full of young German noblemen trying to improve their French, though the Strasbourgeois spoke German and seemingly the students talked nothing else. Moreover, the city contained many gaming houses and brothels, if good company was to be found among the officers of the garrison. (A Lieutenant Buonaparte had left just before the Metternichs arrived and they employed his fencing master.) They stayed with a family friend, Prince Maximilian of Zweibrücken, the future King of Bavaria, who was then in the French army as Colonel of the Royal Regiment of Alsace. Among the lectures attended by the boys were those of the famous Christoph-Wilhelm Koch, a specialist in international law.

The French Revolution began and in July 1789 Metternich watched a rabble storm the town hall. As he puts it, 'I had been present at the plundering of the *Stadthaus* at Strasbourg, perpetrated by a drunken mob which considered itself the people.' It was his first contact with the movement he would fight for the rest of his life—'The doctrines of the Jacobins and their appeal to the passions of the people excited in me an aversion which age and experience have only strengthened.' He said goodbye to Simon, who went to

Paris, where he became a notorious Jacobin and president of a revolutionary tribunal during the Terror; his former pupil ascribed his career to bad judgement rather than innate evil. But from the start Metternich never doubted the wickedness of the Revolution.

He left Strasbourg to study law at Mainz university, lodging with a new tutor. Here he came into contact with professors and students in whom 'the spirit of innovation' was making fast progress; lecturers alluded to 'the emancipation of the human race, so well begun by Robespierre and Marat'. He met the historian Nicolas Vogt, who told him, 'However long your career may be, it won't let you see the end of the explosion which is destroying the great neighbour kingdom.' There were many French refugees:

> Meeting the élite of this society, I learnt to see the defects of the *ancien régime;* what was happening every day [in France] showed me too the crimes and absurdities into which a nation inevitably falls when it undermines the foundations of the social structure. I learnt to appreciate the difficulty of establishing a society on new foundations when the old ones have been destroyed. This was also how I came to know the French; I learnt to understand them and be understood by them.

Ironically, if he was to outwit them on more than one occasion, the French were the one race which he would never really succeed in understanding.

One reason why he thought that he had fathomed the French was his romance with the beautiful Duchesse de Caumont la Force. Only nineteen, she was living off her jewels. Later he seems to have seen a good deal of her at Brussels. Apparently she spent the nights with her husband while sharing the days between Metternich and a Marquis de Bouillé, a threefold division of favours which in no way diminished his affection. Long after, he described her as 'a delightful creature, full of charm, sound sense and wit', writing,

'I loved her as only a young man can.' Undoubtedly he always thought of her as his first love, continuing to write to her for over three decades.

In the meantime the Revolution was beginning to threaten all Europe, together with the entire world of Clemens von Metternich.

2

From Attaché to Ambassador

> It appears to me as if I were in a great crisis, not of the affairs of France alone, but of all Europe, perhaps of more than Europe.
>
> EDMUND BURKE,
> *Reflections on the Revolution in France*

> England . . . a part of Europe cut off not just by sea but by language and peculiar manners . . .
>
> METTERNICH, *Memoirs*

Far too little attention has been paid to Metternich's time in Brussels between 1790 and 1794. Yet it was here that he received his training in diplomacy. It was from the Austrian Netherlands too that he first visited England, a visit of which little has been known until recently.

Joseph II had died in February 1790, not yet fifty, aware that he had failed in his self-imposed mission to unite the Habsburg lands in a centralised German state, an *Einheitstaat.* 'Since I am Emperor of the German Reich, all other states which I possess must be part of it,' he had declared. Hungarians, Slavs and Italians must become Germans, any barriers of language, race or creed be removed. Class distinction before the law was ended. Serfdom was abolished together with compulsory labour service on manorial land (the *robot*). The civil disabilities of Jews and Protestants were removed. Welfare services were introduced, including lunatic asylums, homes for the aged, blind and deaf and dumb, maternity hospitals, and a medical service for the poor. (By 1785 the Vienna General Hospital had 2,500 beds and was admitting paupers free of charge.) Many of the reforms were excellent, but they were implemented by a new and heartily disliked bureaucracy with a total disregard for custom, tradition or nationality. By the time Joseph died, Hungary was in open revolt while the Austrian Netherlands had already seceded.

Joseph's successor, Leopold II, was no less progressive. He had abolished the death penalty when Grand Duke of Tuscany and admired the American Constitution. But he had been horrified by his brother's 'arbitrary and brutal principles, his most severe, brutal and violent despotism'. He turned for advice to Prince Kaunitz.

Wenzel Anton von Kaunitz was nearly eighty, notorious for his use of cosmetics and fear of open windows, yet still possessed a mind of great flexibility. He had created the famous 'diplomatic revolution' during the Seven Years' War, Austria fighting by the side of her traditional enemy France—a realignment which prevented confrontation between Austria and France for over thirty years. He had also secured Galicia during the first partition of Poland. Deeply alarmed by the way Joseph had made enemies at home and abroad, Kaunitz advised Leopold to restore representative institutions throughout his lands. 'You must try to regain the friendship and affection of all your subjects of every nationality,' he told Leopold. The Emperor must also convince every foreign government of his friendly intentions.

Leopold took the advice and was astonishingly successful. He soon regained the loyalty of landowners by restoring the *robot*, though not serfdom, while keeping the best of Joseph's other social reforms. He placated Hungary by calculated concessions, soothed Austria and Bohemia by cancelling new taxes. His conciliatory attitude persuaded Prussia to withdraw her agents from Hungary. He welcomed the Polish constitution of 1791, believing that it would prevent revolution in Central Europe. He was even inclined to welcome the French Constitution of the following year and did his best to avoid any worsening of relations with France, to such an extent that Edmund Burke accused him of 'folly and perfidy'.

However, the Belgians proved intractable. Joseph had alienated them by suppressing the three councils by which they were governed. The States of Brabant refused to register the edict, so in

January 1789 the Austrian Minister told them that if they would not obey, his orders were to 'turn Brussels into a desert and let grass grow in the streets'; in June the States were abolished. Two main opposition parties emerged: a group of liberals led by François Vonck and a conservative group under Henri van der Noot. An armed revolt in November made Noot dictator of the 'United States of Belgium', whereupon he outlawed the Vonckists.

Leopold offered an amnesty, but Noot refused it, recruiting 20,000 volunteers. When Leopold renewed his offer, Noot directed the States to elect the Emperor's younger son Charles 'Grand Duke of Belgium'. In December 1790 Austrian troops crossed the Meuse and occupied the entire country. The Archduchess Maria Christina was reinstated as Governor-General while Count Mercy-Argenteau was appointed Minister, with orders to show scrupulous respect for the Belgians and their institutions. However, Mercy soon resigned in disgust, reporting to Vienna that there seemed to be 'no Belgian nation as such, each of the ten provinces being totally different'. He was replaced by Franz-Georg von Metternich.

Clemens Metternich recalls, 'Following the advice of Prince Kaunitz, who knew his calm wisdom and conciliatory character, my father had been chosen by the Emperor to pacify the Provinces, which he managed to do, helped by the repeal of the reforms so unwisely introduced by the Emperor Joseph II.' The new Minister arrived in 1792 and tried to play one party against another, making what concessions he could. His task was made nearly impossible by the Archduchess opposing all progress towards self-government and by the States refusing to grant subsidies.

The younger Metternich spent his university vacations working in Franz-Georg's office at Brussels, reading dispatches, and learning to draft them. He tells us that his father's post required grinding hard work:

> The Minister united in one man the direction of every government department. There was full-scale diplomatic representation at Brussels and the Minister headed a political cabinet . . . I watched and studied two countries at the same time, one undergoing the horrors of a revolution, the other

showing the scars of what it had just been through. I have never forgotten the experience nor its lessons.

The premature death of Leopold II in March 1792 was a tragedy. He had dismantled Joseph II's centralised machinery because he believed in representative institutions, and not because of pressure by the nobility. He might well have averted war with France. His son Francis II listened to new advisers, hypnotised by French émigrés, who urged him to invade France and crush the Revolution. Kaunitz resigned when he heard of the plan; in his view France would stay weak and divided if left alone.

In July the Metternichs attended Francis's coronation. At Prince Esterházy's ball after the ceremony the younger Metternich opened the dancing with a childhood friend, Louise of Mecklenburg-Strelitz—the future Queen of Prussia. He remembered that 'the contrast between what was taking place at Frankfurt and what was happening in the neighbouring realm was too shocking to go unremarked, and everyone was painfully aware of it.'

Shortly after, an Austro-Prussian army marched out from Coblenz under the Duke of Brunswick. Most observers expected the French to bolt at the first shot, but in September they halted the invasion during the 'Cannonade of Valmy'. In Metternich's opinion, even had Brunswick occupied Paris he could not have crushed the Revolution—'the evil had spread to such an extent that it could not be halted by a mere military operation.'

In October the French occupied Mainz, in November Brussels. The Metternichs took refuge at Coblenz. At first the Belgians welcomed their new masters but soon came to regret the old. The French imported the Terror, erecting a guillotine in the Grande Place; thirty commissioners arrived to hunt down aristocrats, priests and those insufficiently committed to the Revolution, while châteaux and abbeys were sacked, churches closed and young men conscripted.

However, in March the French were routed at Neerwinden and the Austrians returned to Belgium. Franz-Georg now saw excellent prospects of winning over the Belgians. He secured the replacement of Archduchess Maria Christina by Archduke Charles and summoned the States of Brabant, who willingly voted subsidies to pay for the war. He then persuaded the Emperor to visit Brussels in the spring of 1794, to be invested as Duke of Brabant. The welcome was so enthusiastic that Francis stayed there for two months.

'I spent the winter of 1793–94 in the Netherlands, continuing to study for the service I would enter, working on Cabinet affairs,' Metternich tells us. 'Brussels was packed with foreigners, émigrés still dreaming of an end to exile with a confidence I could not share.' When the French General Dumouriez defected in April 1793 he interrogated the Jacobin commissaries handed over by Dumouriez. 'Outside France, and especially among our troops, the execution of Louis XVI and Marie Antoinette aroused a horror which swiftly turned into implacable hatred,' he recalls. 'In spite of everything their officers could do, for some weeks our soldiers gave no quarter.' He drafted an *Appeal to the Imperial Army* which, as he admits, shows 'youthful zeal' in such phrases as 'The blood of Austria herself, spilled upon a scaffold . . . summons you to vengeance.'

Having heard how the Catholic peasants of the Vendée had struck terror into the French Republic, Franz-Georg decided to arm 20,000 Belgian peasants. His Treasurer-General, Vicomte Desandrouin, was highly critical: 'Each time M de Metternich spoke to me about it I attempted the impossible in arguing against this disastrous idea and his deplorable resolution to persuade the Emperor to agree to it.' The younger Metternich wrote a pamphlet, *On the Need for a general Arming of the People on the French Frontier*, the 'people' being yeomen-farmers as opposed to city rabble.

The pamphlet foreshadows many dispatches of later years:

> The French Revolution has reached a stage when it threatens to ruin every European state. It plans to create universal anarchy and is immensely strong. Four years of internal chaos and three of war against the great powers have not weakened it. Without money, without stable government, without a disciplined army, without even unity, the Revolution is supported by no class inside France but simply

> threatens other countries . . . from the start even the most obtuse could see consequences lasting for centuries.

The Revolution's armies were planning 'to destroy the social framework, obliterate principle and steal everyone's property'.

In the spring of 1794 Metternich went on his first diplomatic mission, accompanying Desandrouin to England to negotiate a loan. (And to sell Mme de Caumont's last remaining jewels for her.) Until recently, knowledge of the visit had been restricted to Metternich's memoir, written thirty years after. However, the journal of Desandrouin's son-in-law, Hilarion de Liedekerke Beaufort, who was among the party, has become available. It reveals that Metternich's brother Josef came too.

They sailed from Ostend on 27 March, on board a little vessel about sixty feet long and twelve in the beam, which mounted six cannon. 'We left at half-past five in the evening,' Liedekerke Beaufort tells us. 'Next day, at half-past seven in the morning we could already see Albion's cliffs emerging, growing white. My three companions were much sicker than I during the night.' Two hours later they landed at Dover.

At London they took lodgings in Panton Square near Coventry Street, not far from Covent Garden, in a house kept by a Swiss called Danthan. Their bedrooms were small but clean and cost three shillings a day; there was a common table at which one paid half a crown for a lavish dinner said to be among the best that could be bought. They were given cards of introduction to various important personages, 'notably to Mr Pitt, the real ruler of proud Albion'.

Soon after their arrival they were presented at St James's Palace to George III, who said a few amiable words to each in turn. The following day they were presented to Queen Charlotte and the Princesses, the King being again very pleasant. At a masked ball they saw the Prince of Wales and Mrs Fitzherbert—without their masks. Metternich thought that the Prince in those days was 'one of the handsomest men I ever saw, and to an agreeable exterior he added the most charming manners'. 'Mme Fitzherbert is a little plump though with a very good figure,' says Liedekerke Beaufort. 'She has a superb face but is already a ripe beauty of thirty-four.'

On 7 April the party had dinner with Messrs Boyd and Benfield, the bankers with whom Desandrouin was to do business, a colourful pair. Walter Boyd had owned a banking house in Paris but its assets were confiscated when he fled for his life. He had set up the London firm of Boyd, Benfield & Co. and, as Mr Pitt's trusted friend, was engaged in government loans of up to £30 million. Paul Benfield, an East India 'nabob', had amassed a fortune estimated at half a million in sterling by shady dealings with the Nawab of the Carnatic—Edmund Burke called him 'a criminal who long since ought to have fattened the region's kites with his offal'.

After the bankers' dinner, the young men went to the Hanover Square Rooms to hear Salomon, 'one of the best violinists in London'. There was a large orchestra which he led. There were also some songs, sung perfectly by Mme Mara. Then Haydn appeared, 'conducting himself a symphony for full orchestra which he had composed expressly and performed on that evening so that his Austrian fellow countrymen should be the first to hear it'. Clearly the great composer was not above a little flattery; this was not quite the first performance of symphony no. 100, the 'Military'. According to the *Morning Chronicle* of 9 April 1794:

> Another new Symphony, by Haydn, was performed for the second time; and the middle movement was again received with absolute shouts of applause; Encore! encore! encore! resounded from every seat: the Ladies themselves could not forebear.

Liedekerke Beaufort adds that Haydn 'as a Viennese often came to see us and sometimes dined with us, the simplest, most modest and best man in the world'.

The young men had humbler pleasures. Sometimes, after leaving the theatre at midnight, they would go to a tavern for a glass of punch, walking back to Panton Square at two in the morning. They had a few grumbles, notably the terrible food, the contempt for foreigners, the frumpish way in which ladies dressed, and English Sundays. They were unimpressed by 10 Downing Street. Liedekerke Beaufort recorded that 'the famous Pitt . . . is lodged in a scurvy house in a cul de sac, with only three windows facing onto the street, which looks just like the abode of some lawyer in a little provincial town.'

'I frequented the sittings of Parliament as much as possible, and followed with particular attention the famous trial of Mr Hastings,' Metternich tells us in his memoir. On 10 April he went to Westminster to watch the marathon prosecution of the former Governor-General of Bengal for corruption. According to Liedekerke Beaufort, Lord Cornwallis was being cross-examined. 'Lord Cornwallis did not accuse Mr Hastings but he didn't excuse him either.' He adds that Fox, Grey and Stanhope spoke, and how Warren Hastings was hard put to keep his composure 'during a terrible diatribe which Burke threw at him, with unbelievable heat, lasting more than half an hour'. Burke ended by denouncing the administration in India as 'drinkers of blood and butchers of the people'.

On 20 April they drove down to Portsmouth, to see the East India merchantmen set sail. A fleet of men-of-war was there to guard against a French attack. Admiral Sir Hyde Parker sent two officers to show them the arsenal, the shipyards and the fleet. They went on board the *Caesar* of a hundred guns, the captain entertaining them in his cabin, where they drank a great deal of wine, toasting the King and the fleet. Next day a skiff manned by a single sailor took them through the fleet, 'passing beneath vessels which seemed like mountains', to a signal station on the Isle of Wight from where they watched the merchantmen weigh anchor. Metternich thought it 'the most beautiful sight I ever beheld'. They were rowed out to the flagship, the *Queen Charlotte,* where they were Lord Howe's guests till evening. A cutter brought news that the French had put to sea, and Metternich asked the Admiral if he could sail with him and see the battle, but 'Black Dick' replied, 'I have to send you back alive and can't let you face the dangers of an engagement.'

The party returned to London, to a further round of balls and plays. One evening 'Messieurs de Metternich dined early at the hotel in order to go to Drury Lane to see the tragedy of *Henry VIII*, in which Mrs Siddons acted to perfection.' They also saw *Macbeth* at Drury Lane and *Hamlet* at Covent Garden. On 1 May they went to their friend Haydn's benefit concert, at which he conducted two new symphonies. 'Viotti [a famous violinist] played marvellously a concerto specially composed for the occasion. Dussek performed at the piano as perfectly as ever, while a Miss Park sang very well.'

As soon as the news of Lord Howe's great naval victory over the French off Ushant—the 'Glorious 1st of June'—reached London at night, the city was illuminated with bonfires and torches in celebration. 'Black Dick' had dismasted ten enemy vessels and captured seven others. Metternich rushed down to Portsmouth to see the fleet return with its prizes. 'The admiral's ship, which I had left a few days before in the most perfect condition was one of those which had suffered most damage,' he recalls. 'She had engaged the French admiral's flagship and looked like a ruin, most of her crew having been killed or disabled.'

Desandrouin and the Metternichs stayed at London for several months more, although Liedekerke Beaufort went home at the end of May. Further doors opened when Metternich was appointed Ambassador to the Hague, Kaunitz having recommended him to the Emperor. He was presented to the Prince of Wales and became sufficiently intimate to warn him against his Whig friends. (Thirty years later the Prince Regent reminded him, 'You were very right then!')

'I got to know William Pitt, Charles Fox, Burke, Sheridan, Charles Grey and many others who, both at the time and later, played an important part in public life,' he writes. However, it seems unlikely that he knew them very well, even if he may have been introduced. It is more probable that he heard them speak a good deal, since he tells us he frequented the sittings of Parliament as much as possible.

Burke had criticised Leopold II's policy in Belgium. 'Their great object being now, as in his brother's time, at any rate to destroy the higher orders,' he had written of the Emperor's advisers. 'They would make him desirous of doing, in his own dominions, by a royal despotism, what had been done in France by a democratic.' Metternich cannot have enjoyed such comments. It is probable that he had already read Burke's *Thoughts on French Affairs*, since it was published in 1791 and appeared almost immediately in a French translation, though less likely that he had had discussions with the author.

Metternich developed a sincere if qualified admiration for England, even praising the Revolution of 1688. 'Not a single law was broken, not a constitutional form violated, not one individual right destroyed,' he would write in 1821. 'It was not one of those upheavals brought about by violence and revolt.' In his view (as Bertier de Sauvigny puts it), England had been 'vaccinated' against revolutions, while her institutions were a basis of strength for each government, as was the separation of political parties. He preferred the Tories as more practical, considering the Whigs to be 'tainted by ideology'. But the system was only suited to England—it could not be exported.

News came that the French had invaded the Netherlands. Metternich sailed for Holland from Harwich in September 1794. His ship was caught by a gale which almost ran her aground off Dunkirk when the port was being shelled by the English; for over two hours the vessel was caught in the crossfire and was only saved by the wind changing. Eventually he landed in Holland and presented his credentials, though not at The Hague, since the Dutch government had fled across the Rhine. He rejoined Count Franz-Georg, who had also taken refuge in the Rhineland. The invaders were not going to be evicted for another twenty years, and neither father nor son could return to their posts. He recalls accepting the situation with resignation 'but with a feeling of bitterness towards the Revolution . . .'

3

A Back Seat

> I had withdrawn entirely from public affairs and observed them purely as a spectator.
>
> METTERNICH, *Memoirs*

> When I was five-and-twenty years old, I foresaw nothing but change and trouble in my time; and I sometimes thought then that I would leave Europe and go to America, or somewhere else, out of the reach of it.
>
> METTERNICH to George Ticknor in 1836

The new Imperial foreign minister Baron Thugut blamed Count Franz-Georg for the loss of the Austrian Netherlands, accusing him of excessive leniency, of paving the way for the French by arming the peasants. In his memoir Metternich, while conceding that Thugut was not untalented, calls his ministry 'an unbroken series of mistakes and miscalculations'. He claims that Thugut owed his prominence to subtlety and dexterity, 'qualities which, if accompanied by deep dissimulation and a love of intrigue, can only too easily be mistaken for talent'.

Meanwhile the Rhineland fell to the armies of the Revolution. The Metternich estates were confiscated, and though the Emperor gave Franz-Georg a pension, the family was ruined—becoming what in the twentieth century would be known as 'displaced persons'. Only the Bohemian estate was left. Till now it had brought in little income, so the young Metternich was sent to make it more profitable. He spent the last two months of 1794 at Königswart, managing the property. He had a facility for languages and it was probably then that he first acquired his knowledge of what he called 'Slavonic', picking up some Czech from the servants.

He had visited Vienna for the first time in October 1794, with his father. Although its population was over 200,000, behind its medieval walls (the site of today's *Ringstrasse*) it was curiously small and compact. There were a few suburbs, yet the setting was still essentially rural. It contained many palaces, not just the Hofburg but those of great magnates from all over Central Europe, each with its own art gallery and even opera house, not to mention ballrooms or riding schools. According to Josef Pezzl, writing in 1789 in *Skizze von Wien*, a well-to-do count numbered among his servants a secretary, two valets, a lackey, a huntsman, messengers and footmen. (This was only for personal needs; his household required a majordomo, a chef and a master of the horse, each with his own staff.) The middle class was comparatively small. Yet in some ways Vienna was also a very modern city, such vast new buildings as the General Hospital and the Academy of Military Surgery being scarcely a decade old. Moreover, lavish expenditure by the privileged classes put enormous sums of money into circulation besides providing employment.

When Metternich rejoined his parents here early in 1795 they solved the family's financial problems by finding him a rich bride. Eleanor von Kaunitz, granddaughter and heiress of the great foreign minister, was nineteen and a famous catch on account of her enormous dowry; she had had many other suitors. Small and plain, save for curly dark hair and large brown eyes, she was scarcely pretty. But she was levelheaded and very affectionate, while Metternich recognised her intelligence.

On meeting the handsome young Count in the summer of 1795, 'Laure' fell in love at once. He did not. 'I was only twenty-one and the thought of marrying so early simply hadn't occurred to me.' The wedding took place on 27 September 1795 in the church next to the Kaunitz *Schloss* at Austerlitz (now Slavkov near Brno) in Moravia—in Metternich's words, 'a place which became wretchedly famous ten years later'. The occasion was something of a fête champêtre, six peasant couples being married at the same time. Weeks of hunting parties and banquets followed at the Kaunitz house, which was built like a French château with two wings on each side of the courtyard. Eleanor's father, a widower who had no other children, insisted that she must go on living with him. He obligingly died two years after the wedding.

Eleanor presented Metternich with a daughter, Marie, in 1797, the first of seven children. Judging from Metternich's later taste in wives—and mistresses—sometimes Laure must have bored him profoundly, but he became a kind and considerate husband, writing almost every day when he was away from her during the early years of their marriage and afterwards seldom less than once a week.

This was the quietest period of Metternich's life. He attended lectures on geology, chemistry and physics, above all on medical science. He records that there had been numerous distinguished physicians at Vienna for many years, commenting, 'Man and his life seemed worth studying.' He overcame any squeamishness, spending long hours in hospitals and anatomy theatres—which meant witnessing operations without anaesthetics. He even claims that he thought of becoming a doctor. This is usually dismissed as affectation, yet noblemen who practised medicine for the benefit of their tenants were not unknown in the eighteenth century.

He always insisted that 'public service' had never attracted him as a young man. He tells us, unconvincingly, 'A diplomatic career appeals to ambition but I have never been moved by such a feeling.' However, the real reason why he spent so much time in his library or in the hospitals was that Thugut would not employ his father, who in consequence could not make the younger Metternich an attaché.

During 1796 General Bonaparte's army swept like a whirlwind through northern Italy. By 7 April 1797 his cavalry were within seventy miles of Vienna. The Emperor's ministers hastily negotiated an armistice. A formal peace was signed at Campo Formio in October by which France gained among other territories the left bank of the Rhine. The treaty (perhaps the most profitable ever secured by the French) meant the end of *ancien régime* Westphalia and the Rhineland. A congress was summoned to Rastatt in Baden to discuss compensation for all those counts and princes who, like the Metternichs, had been dispossessed. Even Thugut accepted that Franz-Georg was the best man to be the Imperial plenipotentiary, while his son represented the Westphalian College of Counts. They arrived in December 1797 and stayed until March 1799.

The realities of the situation were recalled by Napoleon on St Helena. 'Old Count Metternich represented the Emperor at the Congress as head of the German confederation, while Count Cobenzl represented him as head of the House of Austria, forming two legations with opposite aims and instructions.' He adds that Count Metternich's party was 'merely one of parade', which explains Franz-Georg's behaviour.

The elder Metternich's pomposity at Rastatt has been derided by Metternich's biographers. As representative of the Holy Roman Emperor, Franz-Georg insisted on a canopied chair of state in the conference hall, adopting the stiffest of manners. But he had precious little else to bargain with. Outwardly the representatives of the new France laughed; inwardly they felt a certain inferiority. Metternich copied his father, assuming a frozen hauteur which aroused painful resentment—his mocking wit must have made it peculiarly effective. Privately he was in despair. 'I can't bear the thought of leaving my home in the hands of these criminals,' he lamented. 'I don't want to be quoted, but in my opinion everything is going to the Devil, and it's high time for everyone to save what he can from the general shipwreck.'

All hoped that Bonaparte would return to settle matters. He had left Rastatt a few hours before the Metternichs' arrival but never came back, going to Egypt instead. The congress dragged on. Thugut took little interest in it, save as a means of buying time while he built up a new coalition against a France weakened by Bonaparte's absence. The French envoys were even less interested. The younger Metternich called it 'a congress which from beginning to end was never more than a phantom'.

He was horrified by the French, 'ill-conditioned animals' who made a sad contrast with the émigrés he had known at Mainz and Brussels. 'The highest polish and an elegance one could scarcely hope to emulate have been replaced by the utmost slovenliness, extreme amiabiality by a dull, sinister air,' he comments. Some were sullen and tongue-tied, others had uncouth accents—'one speaks the most beautiful Gascon', and all wore dirty boots, workmen's neck cloths and long greasy hair. 'You would die of fright if you met the best dressed of them in a wood.' They looked thoroughly disgruntled 'as much with themselves as with anybody else'. One should remember that most Europeans regarded such people much as they do the Khmer Rouge in our own day. 'I think I see traces of the men of September in them, men of the guillotine,' he wrote to his wife.

He grew bored. 'I have absolutely nothing new to tell you,' he complained to Eleanor at the end of the first month. 'Our business here goes very slowly—I wish it had no further to go,' he grumbled at the close of April the following year. In those days he seems to have been genuinely in love with her. 'I can't tell you how much I'm going to enjoy coming back to Vienna at the most beautiful time of the year, to our little garden of which I'm so fond, and to you and my loved ones. You will be so happy and we shan't be separated again, ever. We will give the sort of parties you like and spend months in the country.' He wrote once a week, sometimes daily, until she joined him at Rastatt in the summer of 1798.

During her absence he explored the Baden countryside. With his father he visited the Margrave Charles Frederick's court at Karlsruhe, where he was so well received that he fancied the heir's consort had fallen in love with him. He enjoyed the Comédie Française when it came to Rastatt, admiring the actresses' dresses, and went to balls. 'There is not under the roof of heaven anything more dreary than a ball at Rastatt; there are almost a hundred men, nearly all envoys or their deputies, and eight or ten women, half of them over fifty.' He conducted a symphony concert and played the violin in a quartet—'the most pleasant evening I've spent in Rastatt, since I like playing very much.' But usually he refers to 'this miserable Rastatt'. In April he wrote to Eleanor that as it was Holy Week he was staying away from the theatre and would take Communion. (His atheism seems to have been short-lived.) He was moved by the number of peasants who crossed the Rhine to attend the Holy Week services; they told him that their churches were closed and that they dared not ring the bells. They also told him they were paying twice as much tax as they had under the *ancien régime*. 'Fine regeneration, fine liberty!' he observed. 'Everyone jeers or weeps when the word "liberty" is mentioned or "equality", at which they mock even more.'

He complained of his work load. 'I work all day,' he told Eleanor in May 1798. To make matters worse, 'I have had to let my secretary go away on leave. His wife is so ill that it would have been cruel to stop him, but I'm left alone with a mass of papers.' He suspected, correctly, that Bonaparte had no intention of returning to bring the congress to a successful conclusion—'It all looks like a trick'—and was far from surprised on being definitely informed that Bonaparte would not come.

French resentment of his aristocratic airs and graces burst out in slanders that he patronised brothels. He was even said to have met his father in one (a not entirely inconceivable meeting). One Paris newspaper accused him of mistaking haughtiness for dignity and demanded that he stop treating better men than himself with such offensive disdain.

The congress came to an end when another war broke out between Austria and France in the spring of 1799. As soon as the French plenipotentiaries left Rastatt they were ambushed and murdered by a troop of Hungarian hussars. Their papers were stolen; although proof was never found, it was rumoured that these contained information about Austrian plans to annex part of Bavaria. However, there was no suggestion that the Metternichs were implicated, unpopular as they were with the French.

The younger Metternich was only too pleased to go back to Vienna. He claims that Rastatt made him dislike still more the very idea of a diplomatic career. 'The French Revolution had reached and passed the culmination of its barbarous follies; the Directory was only the miserable dregs of it; and a disunited Germany was paralysed by the peace which the Prussians had signed separately with France at Basel and by the North German princes' policy of neutrality whatever the price. Only Austria went on fighting and the war was badly managed.'

He went back to his books, but did not shut himself off from the world. 'I led the life of a man who enjoys the best society,' he says, adding that he went only to drawing rooms where there was good conversation; they were also those where he was sure of meeting people with influence. The house he visited most was that of his wife's aunt, Princess Carl Liechtenstein, who had been a close friend of Joseph II and was one of the great Viennese hostesses. He could be seen too in the *salon* of Countess Rombec, sister of Count Ludwig Cobenzl, the Imperial ambassador at St Petersburg; it was always full of French émigrés, very different from the new men with whom he had been dealing at Rastatt. He made the acquaintance of a Corsican, Carlo Pozzo di Borgo, at that time an English agent, who would later enter the Russian service.

He even paid occasional visits to Thugut. Sometimes he appeared at court, in the Hofburg or Schönbrunn. One day the Emperor told Metternich, 'Be ready for my orders.'

After ten years of warfare and many defeats, Austria was exhausted. In December 1800 General Moreau smashed the Imperial army at Hohenlinden and invaded Austrian territory, capturing Linz. At the peace of Luneville two months later Francis II recognised France's right to her conquests, including the Rhineland and Northern Italy. Thugut resigned, to be succeeded by Count Trauttmansdorff and then by Ludwig Cobenzl.

In Metternich's opinion, 'the Austrian cabinet's weakness and indecision came to a head with the peace of Luneville'. He considered it a disastrous settlement, resulting from the sheer mediocrity of the ministers who had followed Kaunitz—'that great statesman who presided over the cabinet at Vienna for over forty years, though suffering from the infirmities of old age during his last days'. He had as low an opinion of Trauttmansdorff and Cobenzl as he did of Thugut. He particularly blamed Thugut for his lack of professionalism, for concentrating on the war with France to the exclusion of all else and for not even bothering to read, let alone answer, dispatches from minor embassies. (When he left a special commission had to be set up to deal with hundreds of unopened letters and reports.) It was Thugut's hostility which had so far prevented young Count Metternich from receiving a diplomatic post.

4

Kaunitz's Man

> The great comedy of the world, the grand intrigue of the European scene, never had so fertile an author or so consummate an actor.
>
> ALBERT SOREL,
> *Essais d'Histoire et de Critique*

> Europe was in a state of extreme tension, the natural result of the uncertainty hanging over the whole world.
>
> METTERNICH looking back on 1801,
> *Memoirs*

A few days after taking office, Trauttmansdorff informed Metternich that the Emperor Francis wished to appoint him ambassador to either Dresden or Copenhagen. Metternich claims that he told Francis he had no vocation for a diplomatic career but would accept Dresden from a sense of duty. He tells us that it was close enough to Berlin and St Petersburg to make a good listening post. 'As I was forced to enter the service I wanted some chance of at least being useful. I have never done anything by halves and since I had to become a diplomatist I was going to do it properly.'

The Emperor realised belatedly that Kaunitz had been right and Thugut had made a terrible mistake in committing Austria to a decade of war. Not only was Metternich the son of Kaunitz's protégé and married to his granddaughter, but one of the old minister's last official acts had been to commend him to Francis—'a likeable young man, good company and amusing, suitable for some important embassy'. It cannot be too much emphasised that Metternich was the heir of Kaunitz.

Eighteenth-century diplomacy is too often seen as the amateurish preserve of dilettante noblemen. In *The Marriage of Figaro*

Beaumarchais caricatures how a diplomat of the period was expected to behave: 'Pretend to be ignorant of what everyone knows, and to know what others don't, seem to understand what no-one understands, not to hear what all are hearing, and, in particular, appear able to do the impossible. Seem profound when one is only empty' (behaviour not entirely unknown today). Admittedly noblemen monopolised the career and differed from modern diplomats in many ways. However, the real differences were that in Metternich's time ambassadors were servants of the monarch rather than of the state, men who were on close terms with him, and that they were accustomed to taking decisions which might affect the fate of nations.

Before taking up his post at Dresden, Metternich drafted a paper on the state of Europe at the end of 1801, a paper so practised and mature that his father must have helped him. (A Baron Daiser von Sylbach has also been suggested, implausibly, as his mentor.) Much of it was pure Kaunitz. While Metternich agreed that the upheavals caused by the Revolution far exceeded changes brought about by eighteenth-century wars—'any attempt to create a lasting system of European states out of the present chaos is impossible for the near future'—he was more distrustful of Prussia than he was of France: 'Her entire policy has been designed to increase her territory with a total disregard for accepted international and moral principles.' He deplored the fate of the Poles: 'Only the Berlin government's blind desire for aggrandisement, and the revolutionary period which enabled the Empress Catherine to put her long prepared plans into action, brought about the partition of Poland, contrary to all sound policy.' Summing up, he stressed how remote was the prospect of 'restoring the European balance of power and a general peace'.

He defined his task at Dresden as the reduction of Prussian influence, attributing 'hideous designs' to Prussia in the past, 'designs whose sole aim was to bring the Empire's affairs under her own despotic control and make most of Germany subservient'. He also stressed Dresden's value as a listening post, since the international situation prevented direct communication with St Petersburg—and that the many influential Russians and Poles living in the Saxon capital should provide important information, though this would have to be checked.

Dresden was one of the pleasantest capitals in Europe. A Baroque city famous for palaces, gardens and theatres, as well as for its musical tradition, it had a deserved reputation for elegant amusement. The new ambassador called it an oasis amid the recent horrors—'one might have thought the world was standing still.' He admired the manners—'just as they might have been in the middle of the eighteenth century.' The Elector Frederick Augustus III has gone down to history as an amiable incompetent, fond of the arts and landscape gardening. Yet Metternich recalled 'a prince of sound abilities whose government might have remained a happy memory to his quiet, hard working country but for the storms of later years'. Even so, Frederick Augustus was a dissatisfied man, with dreams of becoming King of Poland like his grandfather and great-grandfather before him.

Metternich made friends with the British minister in Dresden, Hugh Elliot. A Scot from the Border and a brother of the Earl of Minto, he had led a life which even Metternich considered colourful. As a boy he had been educated in Paris with Mirabeau, who dominated the early stages of the Revolution, and contacted him in 1790 as the British government's secret envoy; when a young man he had fought in the Russian army against the Turks; as minister in Copenhagen he had declared war on Denmark on his own responsibility; at Berlin, refusing to be snubbed by the King, he had displayed an arrogance which staggered the Prussians. According to Metternich he had quieted down by the time he came to Dresden. 'A pleasanter man in society I have never known . . . I consider my friendship with him one of my pleasantest memories.' He remembered with amusement Elliot's advice on how to seem useful, by sending two dispatches a week. 'If I have nothing I invent some news and then contradict it by the next courier.'

In the summer, after he arrived at Dresden, he met one of the Revolution's most formidable foes, a Prussian intellectual of obscure origin called Friedrich Gentz. Once a minor civil servant, Gentz had become what would now be called a political journalist, specialising in foreign affairs—to such effect that he was being paid for advice by nearly every government in Europe save the French. An odd figure in a red wig and dark glasses, he was always in debt because of his weakness for actresses, gambling and amazingly expensive chocolate, yet his mind—he had been a pupil of Kant at Königsberg—was as sharp as a diamond. Treitschke admitted that Gentz had been the outstanding German publicist of his day, commenting on 'the classic beauty of his style, coupled with the compressed power of his logic'.

The second time that Metternich met Gentz he lent him £100 to visit England with Hugh Elliot. He at once realised that this strange man could be a valuable ally. For years Gentz had been waging his own war of ideas. In 1793 he had published a translation of Burke's *Thoughts on French Affairs;* he admired its emphasis on historical tradition and saw that it was a superb weapon with which to counterattack the Revolution. In 1802 he considered translating Châteaubriand's *Génie du Christianisme,* recognising that it marked the beginning of a Catholic revival in France with political implications. In 1799 he had begun to publish a little magazine, written entirely by himself, the *Historisches Journal;* a commentary on current affairs, its message was that the new French ideas threatened all Europe. It was read throughout the world—in Philadelphia John Quincy Adams approved highly of the author's argument that the American Revolution in no way resembled that of France. The journal was widely read in England, since Gentz was a vociferous Anglophile. His semi-official visit was a triumphant success; he was praised by the *Times*, presented to George III and met Castlereagh and Canning.

Almost as soon as he took up his post, Metternich embarked on a love affair. Princess Catherine Bagration was the wife of one of Russia's most distinguished generals. Twenty years old, born a Countess Skavronskaya, she had married her husband because of his reputation for bravery but then refused to sleep with the future hero of Borodino, embarking instead on a career of wild promiscuity. Dark-haired, with a perfect figure, her small size, pale face and shortsightedness gave her a deceptively timid air. The susceptible Comte de la Garde credited her with 'a touch of Oriental languor to which is added a soupçon of Andalusian allure'. She was so outrageously dressed that her low neckline earned her the name of 'naked angel'. She was not unintelligent, developing an interest in politics, but she was shallow and jealous. In September 1802 she gave birth to Metternich's one acknowledged bastard, a daughter whom she christened Clémentine. He had the baby brought up at a village outside Vienna.

He met a much more dangerous woman, Wilhelmine, Duchess of Sagan, with whom he would eventually have a long and unhappy liaison. About the same age as Catherine, she was a daughter of the last Duke of Courland on the Baltic and had recently married a young émigré general in the Austrian service, the Prince de Rohan-Guéménée—shortly after bearing a child by another lover. Totally amoral, tall and willowy, with black eyes and blond hair, speaking German in a seductively husky voice, she enthralled Metternich to the extent that he credited her with more intelligence than she possessed. But it is unlikely that she became his mistress for several years.

Extramarital amusements did not stop him being an attentive husband. Eleanor bore a third child, Victor, in 1800, and a fourth, another Clementine, in 1804. There were unfounded rumours that he was not the father. He continued to sleep with his wife intermittently for many years and they remained firm friends, writing constantly to each other even during his most torrid infidelities.

His premonition at Rastatt that the family estates in the Rhineland had gone forever was justified. However, there was compensation. Franz-Georg was created an hereditary Prince of the Empire and given an estate near Ulm, the former abbey of Ochsenhausen.

In February 1803 Metternich was made ambassador to Prussia, though he did not take up his appointment till the end of the year. Amid sandy wastes and pine forests, Berlin was very different from Dresden, its grim court pompous and dull. But despite Frederick William III's preoccupation with military uniforms and normal haughty reserve towards the diplomatic corps, he received the Austrian ambassador as an old friend. So did his queen, the same Princess Louise with whom Metternich had opened the Esterházy ball at Frankfurt in 1792. He noticed that since then she had acquired great dignity and grace. However, for all his pleasant reception, his task at Berlin was an extremely difficult one.

As Metternich wrote at the end of September 1804, the interests of Prussia and Austria were inextricably involved. But the two leading Prussian ministers, Haugwitz and Lombard, dreaded war with France. He describes the former as 'unprincipled, perfidious and false', the latter as 'a man devoted to France's interests, and . . . Bonaparte's spy'. They wanted the French to buy neutrality from Prussia. Metternich records that 'the year 1804 went by in that unhappy condition which is neither peace nor war'.

Meanwhile, he acquired a new mistress in Berlin, Princess Catherine Dolgoroukaya, wife of one of the Tsar's aides-de-camp. It does not seem to have been a very serious affair. He was pursued unsuccessfully by that voracious bluestocking Mme de Staël. While enjoying her *salon*, he disliked intensely its ugly, mannish, overbearing hostess.

Every Prussian as well as Austrian had been outraged by Napoleon's kidnap and murder of the Duc d'Enghien in March 1804, and they regarded his assumption of the title of Emperor in the following May as an insult to the thousand-year-old Reich. Gentz wrote that to recognise it would be to accept the sovereignty of the people and the Revolution, and undermine every legitimate throne. The situation was complicated by no one at Berlin or Vienna being able to fathom Napoleon's intentions, or what he was going to do next. Most observers thought his primary objective was the invasion of England, though Metternich afterwards claimed that he had always suspected that the great army concentrated at Boulogne was really being held in readiness for an attack across the Rhine. In January 1805 he suggested to Karl von Hardenberg of the Prussian Foreign Office that the 'restorer of the Empire of Charlemagne' was aiming at 'a universal monarchy'.

Austria had made peace in 1801 because she was exhausted, her army decimated and demoralised, her treasury empty. When Britain too gave up in 1802, it had seemed for a moment that Europe had accepted the new France. But after only a year, hostilities recommenced, the official *casus belli* being Britain's refusal to return

Malta to its Knights. British diplomacy, and British money, set about building another coalition against the 'Corsican demon'. By 1805 Austria had recovered, her army's losses made good, her treasury replenished. Even so, Metternich was still having difficulty in convincing Vienna that Napoleon meant to extend his hegemony over all Europe, even if it was a view well known to be shared by the Tsar. Eventually, Austria and Russia agreed on an alliance. The armies of Sweden and Naples, who joined them, were scarcely a substitute for what was still seen as the might of Prussia.

In Metternich's opinion, however, 'The Prussian monarchy, which is three times bigger than it was when Frederick the Great died, is far weaker in real terms.' Its government was 'a conspiracy of mediocrities . . . united solely by a dread of taking a single decisive step'. Not only ministers such as Haugwitz but the King himself were terrified by the international situation. Yet if Prussia had benefitted by not opposing France, securing a species of protectorate over north Germany, Metternich was nonetheless convinced that an alliance with Berlin was possible. His diplomacy was so persuasive that Tsar Alexander massed troops on the Prussian border, demanding peace or war. But Frederick William was more frightened of the French than he was of the Russians.

Napoleon struck with devastating speed, attacking General Mack from behind and finally annihilating Mack's entire army at Ulm on 26 September 1805. Six weeks later he marched into Vienna. Then, unexpectedly, Prussia joined the coalition. The Tsar came to Berlin, telling Metternich that he already knew all about him—'You've steered the ship perfectly.' 'Had the allied armies kept their distance, instead of insisting on fighting at Austerlitz, the French would have been forced to fall back on Vienna,' wrote Metternich later. 'Napoleon was in grave danger. Archduke Karl was advancing by forced marches through Styria with his army of Italy, while the Prussians were advancing from Regensburg.' But the Tsar wanted a battle.

On 1 December 1805 Napoleon won the greatest victory of his career, routing the Austrians and Russians at Austerlitz—and then spent the night at Metternich's *Schloss*. At Berlin its owner begged the Prussians to send troops, arguing that together the allies still outnumbered Napoleon and now was the time to counterattack. Metternich may have been right, but Haugwitz had the ear of Frederick William; Napoleon bought Prussia's neutrality with Hanover, which he had seized from George III. The Russians withdrew into Poland. At the Treaty of Pressburg, only three weeks after Austerlitz, Austria had to surrender Venice and Dalmatia to France besides ceding the Tyrol to Bavaria. She also had to pay eight million francs in gold as the first instalment of a crushing indemnity.

Metternich was so desperate that in January 1806 he proposed a species of Iron Curtain. Three lines of fortresses would stretch from the mouth of the river Weser to the Adriatic, making use of the Thuringian forests. It would separate an 'Eastern Alliance' of Austria, Prussia and Russia from the Napoleonic Empire, quarantining what was left of *ancien régime* Europe from the French contagion. But he was overtaken by events.

5

'In the Lion's Den'

I do not think it was a good idea on Napoleon's part to summon me to a post which, while giving me the chance to appreciate his brilliant qualities, also gave me the opportunity to discover the weaknesses which in the end ruined him and freed Europe.

METTERNICH

I spent with Napoleon, or near him, the best years of my life.

METTERNICH

In 1806 Napoleon established the Confederation of the Rhine, with himself as Protector. Instead of a state for every day in the year it consisted of sixteen kingdoms and principalities, whose rulers obeyed France. In August Francis II relinquished his ancient title of Holy Roman Emperor for that of 'Emperor of Austria'. The Habsburg lands in Italy became part of Napoleon's new Italian realm, while French bayonets placed Joseph Bonaparte on the throne of Naples. Metternich saw little future for Austria in this new Europe. He had written in January:

> Whose side does Russia mean to take? What will happen to the Ottoman Empire, placed in direct contact with France on its most vulnerable frontier? How will negotiations with Prussia turn out? Peace, and the Austrian monarchy's very existence, depends on these three questions.

Immediately after Prussia joined the coalition in November 1805 Haugwitz had gone to Napoleon's headquarters, on the pretext of a courtesy call, to assure him that Prussian participation was merely a diplomatic manoeuvre. Yet there was also a powerful war party at Berlin. And, as has been seen, Metternich suspected that Prussia might be destroyed in a confrontation with France.

Cobenzl resigned, Count Philip Stadion (formerly ambassador at St Petersburg) becoming responsible for foreign affairs. Metternich expected to replace Stadion in Russia, since the Tsar had asked for him, but on returning to Vienna in April, he was told that he was going to Paris. The news 'struck me like a thunderbolt'. He believed that it was because during his time at Berlin he had made a point of getting on with the French ambassador, M de Laforest. 'It was always my policy to avoid mixing official life with private so I tried to stay on good terms with my French colleague, being as courteous as possible.' The French foreign minister, Talleyrand, had noticed this and thought he might do business with such a man. Metternich was nervous at the prospect of representing a defeated country at Paris, but Francis insisted. As he says, 'it was the start of my public life . . . fate placed me face to face with the man who ruled the world.' It was also the beginning of a personal duel.

In August Metternich presented his credentials to the Emperor of the French, who rudely kept his hat on throughout the audience. Determined not to be overawed, the ambassador made a brief, concise speech of a sort which he knew to be quite unlike the grandiloquent orations customary, referring to his sovereign simply as 'Emperor of Austria': 'I shall strive at all times to strengthen good relations between the two empires since only on that basis can lasting peace be established between independent states.' The speech seemed to surprise and even embarrass Napoleon, who replied with equal brevity. Metternich recalls that the Emperor's 'short, broad figure, untidy clothes and obvious attempts to impress' made him think less of the man before whom the world trembled. He noticed that Napoleon walked on tiptoe. 'I am certain that he would have given a lot to be taller and add dignity to his appearance, which grew even commoner as he put on weight.' Nonetheless, Metternich was aware that he was in the presence of one of the most fascinating men in history.

In after years the Duke of Wellington summed up the Emperor

and decided he 'wasn't a gentleman'. Metternich not only shared this opinion but turned it to account. He discerned early on Napoleon's secret reverence for blue blood and exploited his sole asset, his aristocratic bearing, just as he and his father had done at Rastatt. The Duchesse d'Abrantès recaptures the impression he made on the flashy court of Imperial France: 'M le Comte de Metternich, who powdered his blonde head (although he did not have a single white hair) to give himself a more dignified air, in his Knight of Malta's red coat with black facings and with his courtesy and easy nobility of bearing was truly the *grand seigneur* at his most elegant.' The red coat's significance has been overlooked. It was the uniform of an organisation detested by Napoleon—in treaty after treaty he insisted on confiscating its European estates—and a reminder of why war had broken out in 1803. There could have been no more arrogant gesture.

War between France and Prussia was imminent. The Prussians had been infuriated at the revelation that the Emperor Napoleon, having given Hanover to them in March, was now offering it to Britain as part of a peace package. Haugwitz was replaced by Hardenberg, and what Metternich calls 'the feeble élite of the army' forced their timid King to declare war. He did so on 8 August, with an ultimatum that all French troops must withdraw behind the Rhine by 8 October. On 14 October Napoleon destroyed half his army at Jena while Marshal Davout routed the other half at Auerstadt. Its operational commander-in-chief, the Duke of Brunswick, was mortally wounded, and twenty-six generals were captured together with the entire artillery.

In Metternich's view, Jena was the summit of Napoleon's power. Had he been satisfied with making a weakened Prussia join the Confederation of the Rhine, Napoleon's position would have become unassailable. Instead, he indulged in overkill, mercilessly pursuing Prussia's troops and riding into Berlin. The Hohenzollern realm and its army ceased to exist, the country being occupied by the French and split into four departments; Frederick William fled to Königsberg, where he was protected by Russian bayonets.

Despite horrifying casualties, Napoleon defeated the Russians at Eylau in February 1807 and at Friedland in June. During the interview at Tilsit, on a barge in the Niemen River, the fickle Tsar succumbed to the Emperor's magnetism and agreed to join him in a war against England which would bring about a general peace. At a treaty signed on 8 July 1807 between France, Russia and Prussia, Russia took Finland from Sweden, Danubian Roumania from Turkey; Prussia lost half her territory, the lands west of the Elbe going to Jerome Bonaparte's Kingdom of Westphalia; while Prussian Poland became the Grand Duchy of Warsaw under the King of Saxony.

In a dispatch from Paris at the end of July, Metternich said that the Parisians had thought France and Russia were going to divide the world between them, and that Austria would be broken up into small kingdoms; they were surprised that this had not happened at Tilsit. Prussia was now a third-rate power: 'We no longer have a powerful enemy on our right but neither could we ever find an ally there.' Metternich made a prophecy:

> The condition of Europe contains the seeds of its own destruction. Shrewd policy on our government's part should create a situation in which 300,000 men, directed by a single will and with the same objective, would take the leading role in Europe during a period of universal anarchy—one of those phases which always follow large scale seizures of power, and all but obliterates any trace of the usurper; a phase whose date nobody can foretell but which nothing can delay save the life of one man.

He added how odd it was that the childless Napoleon had never taken steps to provide himself with a successor.

He suspected, with some justice, that the Emperor regarded Austria as a rival. 'Undoubtedly we are first on the list of victims whom he believes he must sacrifice to his insane ambition.'

Nevertheless the ambassador enjoyed Paris. He had an excellent staff, especially Baron Vincent, a Lorrainer who acted as Chargé when he was away, and Engelbert de Floret, the Belgian First Secretary who became almost his shadow. He found the Imperial court ludicrously pretentious, observing that even Napoleon's new nobles laughed at their titles. He thought the French 'a people degraded below all others . . . worn out and demoralised, with any trace of the national character destroyed by eighteen years of revolution and crime'. However, they admired Metternich's patrician manners and superb stable, while his good looks and love of feminine company—he wrote appreciatively to Eleanor about the Paris fashions—enabled him to indulge in his favourite recreation, the seduction of high-born women. He was undeterred by the arrival of his wife and children.

Caroline Murat, Napoleon's sister, could scarcely be called high-born, even if she was the future Queen of Naples. Her head and bust were too big, her legs too short, but she had a pretty face and was both charming and promiscuous. Metternich was surprised by her intelligence, struck by her premonition that her brother would overreach himself. A short affair began in 1806, lasting for some months; he wore a bracelet made from her hair. After their first night together, he was able to inform Stadion that Napoleon had a mistress at Warsaw (Maria Walewska) and a little later that he might divorce the Empress Josephine. After the end of the liaison he retained a certain affection for this peculiarly unloveable Bonaparte. For her it was merely an interlude in her long romance with General Junot, Duc d'Abrantès.

It was rumoured that Napoleon had encouraged the affair to make the ambassador malleable in negotiations to adjust Austria's frontiers with Germany and Italy. But France already held all the cards, the Emperor agreeing to withdraw a garrison from Braunau-on-the-Inn (on the Austro-Bavarian border) but no more. A treaty was signed at Fontainebleau on 10 October 1807 after a month of preparation and eight days of argument. An exhausted Metternich reported to Stadion that he had never met with 'more bad faith or sheer impertinence'. Moreover, 'My efforts to secure any improvements for Austria have been in vain.'

'There has been a total change in Napoleon's manner recently; he seems to think that he has reached a position in which moderation simply exposes him to needless annoyance,' Metternich wrote a few days afterwards. 'The peace of Tilsit is responsible.' He warned that Austria was in the greatest danger. Some of his apprehension was due to Talleyrand, who had ceased to be Foreign Minister in August. Both were men of the *ancien régime,* practitioners of the '*haute diplomatie*'. But the Frenchman was known to be dangerous; Metternich once compared him to a double-edged sword which might turn in the hand. Yet Talleyrand was telling the truth when he wrote that he had resigned his ministry when he realized that the Emperor's megalomania was leading to ruin.

As has been seen, Metternich guessed very early that Napoleon meant to establish a universal monarchy, reducing other kingdoms to administrative departments. He was also aware that many Frenchmen were nervous about the Emperor's ambition, especially those who had done well out of the Revolution, the *Notables*. They were terrified that his foreign adventures might end in the collapse of France and a second breakdown of society. 'An immeasurable feeling of uneasiness was present amidst all the rejoicings at any victory by the French army, because everyone knew that such victories made new ones necessary, to complete the work.'

He himself always thought that a second French Revolution was far from impossible, that 'the revolutionary elements were merely smothered for the time being'. His interpretation of what had happened in 1789 went as follows: A discontented middle class had used the doctrines of the Enlightenment, above all Rousseau's theory of the Social Contract, to destabilise society and overthrow the existing order. Those who benefitted had turned to a strong man to preserve their gains, but the saviour became a tyrant who, because his power rested on no firm foundation, had to make conquests abroad. War was the inevitable result of revolution. (In modern terms, liberal democracy always becomes totalitarian democracy, which invariably seeks to extend its territory by force.)

'M de Talleyrand who now makes profession of attachment to the court of Austria', Metternich reported to Stadion at the end of January 1808, had talked to him for two days, explaining that there were two plans in the Emperor's mind. One was an expedition to India, the other partition of the Ottoman Empire. Soon Napoleon himself raised the topic of Turkey's future. Neither Metternich nor Talleyrand realised that he had done so in order to conceal his designs on Spain.

Metternich did not share the awe in which contemporaries held the ex-bishop. 'His whole character makes him better suited to destroy than to build . . . always placing obstacles in the path of any positive course of action.' He quotes the Emperor's opinion: 'If I want anything done, I don't employ the Prince of Benevento. I use him if I wish something undone while appearing to want it.' Metternich's unflattering assessment did not stem from any antipathy—'In private life Talleyrand was as trustworthy as he was agreeable.'

In March 1808, Charles IV of Spain abdicated in favour of his son Ferdinand VII, an abdication which he swiftly withdrew. Napoleon offered to arbitrate, inviting the entire Spanish royal family to Bayonne; as soon as they arrived, both father and son were bullied into abdicating. On 24 April a bulletin in the *Moniteur* announced that the Bourbons had ceased to reign in Spain, and in March Joseph Bonaparte was proclaimed King. Metternich was genuinely shocked. The Bourbon monarchy had been a loyal ally of the Emperor. 'Peace does not exist with a revolutionary system,' he commented, predicting that Turkey would go next.

Yet his attitude towards Napoleon was never inflexible. He did not share Stadion's blind hatred of the Emperor. Loathing what the man stood for, despising certain aspects of his personality, Metternich was nonetheless fascinated by Napoleon's genius, by the wonderful clarity of his mind. 'Conversation with him always had a charm for me difficult to define.'

His suspicion that Napoleon was overreaching himself was confirmed by the break with the Pope. Pius VII had refused to enforce the 'Continental Blockade' within his territory, an embargo on trade with Britain. French troops marched into Rome in April 1808.

The Emperor gave the customary reception for the diplomatic corps on his birthday, 15 August 1808. Suddenly he asked Metternich, 'How far has Austria rearmed?' He then launched into a tirade, sneering at Austrian weakness. 'Just what do you think you can do against France and Russia? The next war against Austria will be war to the death—either you reach Paris or I conquer your entire empire!' (He had known since May that Austria was rearming, while Metternich had been sending details of French troop movements to Vienna.) The ambassador replied, untruthfully, that his country was rearming to save Turkey from dissolution. Neither he nor Austria's Emperor Francis I were invited to the meeting between Napoleon and the Tsar at Erfurt in September, its purpose being to show that Napoleon was supreme ruler of Germany. Yet Napoleon failed to secure a guarantee of Russian support in the event of war with Austria, whom he called 'my real enemy'. Talleyrand took the opportunity to warn the Tsar that he must save Europe from Napoleon's insane ambition.

On 29 October the Emperor left Paris with the cream of his army, to put down a national uprising in Spain. Talleyrand and Fouché, his police minister, were convinced that there was going to be a disaster. No two men knew better what France was thinking and they were in close touch with Metternich. Unfortunately, they gave Metternich an exaggerated impression of French weakness, which he communicated to Vienna.

The ambassador's mistress after Caroline Murat was the Duchesse d' Abrantès, the wife of Caroline's lover. Her *Journal Intime*, written twenty years later when she was an opium addict, reads like a novelette, with secret assignations and declarations of love, Metternich appearing as a wildly romantic figure. On one occasion her husband, crazed by jealousy at finding a letter from Metternich, tried to kill her with a pair of golden scissors; if she is to be believed, she was rescued by none other than Mme Metternich, who accused Abrantès of trying to play Othello. Admittedly she was a great beauty, small, dark-eyed and vivacious, very intelligent and well informed—though the Emperor called her 'a little pest'.

Metternich took advantage of Napoleon's absence in Spain to go to Vienna. He found Stadion demanding war but Francis and Archduke Karl opposing it, saying that Austria's finances were insufficient, her army too weak. Metternich was convinced the Monarchy's very existence depended on fighting. He argued that the French were tired of Napoleon, who after his Spanish adventure would have far fewer troops—half of them German or Italian and supposed less loyal: 'Austria's forces, inferior to those of France before the [Spanish] rising, will at least become equal to them.' Francis and the Archduke let themselves be convinced that it would be possible to drive the French out of Germany and Italy. The offensive would begin in the spring of 1809.

Napoleon restored the situation in Spain more quickly than anyone expected, replacing 'King Joseph' on his throne. In January 1809, he hastened back to Paris at news of Austria's preparations for war. Metternich was there to greet the Emperor, who treated him with ostentatious reserve, merely inquiring about 'Mme de Metternich's health'. Talleyrand advised Austria to wait until May before declaring war, since France should then be much weaker —'All Germany will be on your side and you will have supporters in Italy too, if not so many.'

Metternich overestimated the extent of French war-weariness, even hoping for a coup against Napoleon. On 17 January, just before the Emperor's return, he grumbled to Stadion that Talleyrand and Fouché were not going to risk their necks, although well aware that 'the helm is in the hands of a mad pilot cheerfully steering their ship onto the rocks'. Yet the sheer magnitude of the prize made the gamble attractive; after freeing Germany and Italy the Habsburgs should be able to rule over them as never before, becoming the strongest power in Europe.

The strain began to tell on Metternich, who informed Stadion that he expected to end at Vincennes like the Duc d'Enghien—shot in the moat at midnight. He sold his wine and his carriages. In those days diplomats caught in a war could not fly out or take a train; they had to go across country in a coach, at risk from trigger-happy troops. On 15 April the foreign minister Champagny informed Metternich that hostilities had begun and he might leave Paris; his family would be perfectly safe. His departure was delayed by the French insisting on his being exchanged against their own embassy personnel in Vienna, so that he could not go until 25 May. Ominously, at Châlons-sur-Marne Metternich encountered Austrian prisoners—including officers whom he knew. It took him ten days to reach Vienna, with a cortège of half a dozen carriages containing his staff. The Imperial capital had already been occupied by the enemy, but on 18 June, after being interned for over three weeks, Metternich was allowed to join the Emperor Francis at Wolkersdorf.

The war was still undecided. Despite Talleyrand's advice, war had begun too soon; Austria's hand had been forced by Andreas Hofer's rising in the Tyrol. Napoleon had halted the Austrian advance into Bavaria at Eckmühl, forcing Karl to retreat and occupying Vienna. Even so, Karl and his brother Archduke Johann had done wonders with their troops, supplementing the regulars with volunteers whose morale was excellent; they knew that every German was praying for their success, even Prussians. On 21–22 May, Karl fought the Emperor to a standstill at Aspern-Essling near Vienna, defeating him for the first time, and though Archduke Johann had been defeated in Italy, Johann's army still remained intact.

However, on 5 July, Napoleon defeated Archduke Karl decisively at Wagram, driving the Austrians back in full retreat. Francis's comment to Metternich, 'We shall have much to retrieve', was a gigantic understatement—everyone knew that the French Emperor had threatened to make separate kingdoms out of Austria, Hungary and Bohemia. Metternich wished to continue the war, but an armistice was signed at Znaim on 11 July.

Metternich must share some of the blame for this terrible disaster—he had completely misjudged the situation in France.

6

'Tacking and Turning, and Flattering,' 1809–12

I did not make the peace of 1809, for I did not choose to make it.

METTERNICH to George Ticknor in 1836

To co-operate without losing one's soul, to assist without sacrificing one's identity, to work for deliverance in the guise of bondage and under enforced silence, what harder test of moral toughness exists?

HENRY KISSINGER, *A World Restored*

A remarkable partnership was about to begin, between the Emperor Francis and Clemens von Metternich. Francis I has had a bad press. Treitschke depicts him as 'a heartless and mistrustful despot' who only granted pardons to condemned men if they hoped to be executed. Historians emphasise his suspicious nature, uninquiring mind and narrow piety. His portraits are unattractive; the face is that of an immensely well bred horse, the eyes guarded, the pose stiff. His reputation is lowest among those American historians of Metternich who in the 1950s and 1960s, as Alan Sked puts it, 'admired his [Metternich's] defence of Europe against the Left and who envisaged him as some sort of nineteenth century John Foster Dulles stemming the tide of red revolution.' They saw the Emperor as the man blocking Metternich's plans to reform the Monarchy. Others are less dismissive. 'Francis does not altogether deserve the very harsh judgements which have been passed on him by many later Austrian historians and adopted by their superficial foreign copyists,' says C. A. Macartney. 'He was neither a bad man nor a stupid one.' Sked thinks that the Emperor had much more in common with Metternich than is generally appreciated, and that Metternich had more influence than he admitted over his 'August Master.'

Personally Francis was a very decent man, simple and unassuming, an Austrian George III (George as perceived by the British, not by Americans). He had to work far harder but did not complain and was popular throughout his long reign, especially with the Viennese; plain-mannered, speaking broad Viennese dialect, walking round his capital unescorted, he was always ready to give his humblest subjects an audience. The Imperial anthem which commemorates him, '*Gotterhalte Franz den Kaiser*', was sung (to what later became the tune for '*Deutschland über Alles*') until 1918. He was a skilful political tactician, though scarcely a political strategist, a good judge of character. He was fully aware of Metternich's calibre, if he did not invariably take Metternich's advice and may sometimes have felt a certain jealousy.

On the morning of 8 July 1809, Francis sent for Metternich. 'Count Stadion has just resigned,' he told him. 'I'm giving the department of foreign affairs to you.' Metternich prevaricated: 'I don't think I'm capable of steering such a big empire's ship of state.' He did not want to be blamed for making what was obviously going to be a humiliating peace, persuading Francis that Stadion's abrupt departure might convey the impression that Austria was so broken she would accept any terms. Stadion stayed on as foreign minister in name until the treaty had been signed, Metternich directing negotiations from the background. The plenipotentiary dealing with the French was Prince Liechtenstein, who had succeeded Archduke Karl as commander-in-chief.

Metternich swiftly accepted the need for a peace, as long as he was not blamed for it. He almost lost Francis's confidence by suggesting that Galicia (Austrian Poland) should be surrendered and the Polish kingdom restored, his object being to weaken the Franco-Russian alliance; the Tsar would have seen the restoration as a threat to his own Polish provinces. Fortunately he convinced the Emperor that another lost battle would be the end of the Monarchy. In a memorandum of 10 August Metternich told Francis bluntly, 'Whatever the peace terms, the outcome means that our sole security lies in adapting to the French system.'

Peace was signed on 14 October 1809. Predictably, Napoleon imposed harsh terms. The Monarchy lost a third of its territory, Galicia going to the Grand Duchy of Warsaw while what is now northwestern and coastal Yugoslavia became the French province of Illyria—cutting Austria off from access to the sea and threatening Hungary. There was also a crippling financial indemnity.

Stadion left office a week before the signing and Metternich became foreign minister. In November he described himself as 'caught in a maelstrom'. Even so, Gentz was shocked by his obvious confidence. Yet he had reason not to despair. At least the Monarchy had been saved. Napoleon would have been much wiser to split it up into several states. The new minister had outlined the road forward in a memorandum of 10 August:

> From the moment peace is signed we have to limit our activities to tacking and turning, and flattering. It is the only way we can survive until the hour of deliverance. Without Russian aid any opposition to such pressure from all sides is unthinkable. Their vacillating court will wake up sooner if it sees that it can gain nothing more from its wretched policy. Always contradicting itself and the principles it held yesterday, it may yet join us when it finds its aggressive rival crossing its path. There is only one way forward, to build up our strength for better times, working very quietly to ensure our survival . . .

His conviction that France and Russia would eventually fall out was strengthened by the Tsar's failure to help Napoleon during the war.

He intended to collaborate, on a scale which would not be seen again until the Second World War, and soon found a means to remove French suspicion of Austria's long-term objectives. The new ambassador in France, Prince Schwarzenberg, reported that Napoleon was going to divorce Josephine. At once Metternich told the prince, untruthfully, that the Emperor Francis had authorised him to encourage overtures towards Napoleon for the hand of an Archduchess. He added, 'You will also try to identify what advantages Austria might gain from a family alliance.'

On 29 November he asked a French agent in Vienna, Alexandre de Laborde, whether Napoleon had ever thought of marrying an Archduchess, but admitted that he had not discussed the idea with Emperor Francis. In December Floret wrote from Paris to say there was a good chance that Napoleon might seek an Austrian bride.

The foreign minister was shaken momentarily by rumours that Tsar Alexander was giving sympathetic consideration to a French request for a Grand Duchess, but they turned out to be without foundation.

According to Metternich, Napoleon approached Eleanor—who had never left Paris—at a masked ball in January 1810 to ask if the Archduchess Marie Louise would accept him. Shortly after, Josephine confided in Eleanor that she hoped he would marry an Archduchess. Metternich told his wife to let Josephine know there was no obstacle. He swiftly persuaded the Emperor Francis to order his daughter to marry the Corsican ogre, telling Prince Schwarzenberg with some satisfaction that the Russian ambassador to Vienna, Count Schuvalov, had been 'terrified by the news'.

In the previous century Kaunitz had instigated a 'diplomatic revolution' of which the most unpopular feature in Austria had been the ensuing marriage of an Archduchess (Marie Antoinette) to the Dauphin. But in those days the two dynasties had at least been equals, and their countries had not fought so bitter a war. It is hard to exaggerate the revulsion felt by the ruling circles of the defeated, humiliated Austria of 1810; they regarded the sacrifice of their Emperor's daughter almost as a blasphemy. (One can imagine the horror in Britain if George III had let Napoleon marry a British princess.) It took great courage for a newly appointed minister to commit the Habsburg Monarchy to such a step. Yet he cannot have anticipated that it would contribute so much, and quite so rapidly, to Napoleon's destruction.

Two years before, when the French Emperor had been trying to secure a Russian Grand Duchess, Metternich had commented, 'If Alexander refuses his sister [to him], we're going to see some extraordinary developments', implying that any rupture between the two powers must inevitably lead to war because there was no buffer state between them. When the at first incredulous Tsar heard of Napoleon's Austrian marriage, his reaction was that the Emperor intended to invade Russia—he muttered, 'The next step will be to drive us back into our forests.'

Metternich decided that he must revisit Paris at once, not only for reasons of diplomacy. His wife and family were still there, while he had continued to write to Mme d'Abrantès, assuring her, 'I cannot live without you.' (This flattering declaration occurs in letters to a number of ladies.) He arrived at the Tuileries on 4 April 1810, just after the great nuptial Mass at Nôtre Dame, attending the wedding banquet in the palace; he appeared on a balcony, raised his glass to the crowd and shouted cheerfully, '*Au roi de Rome*'—the title destined for Napoleon's unborn son.

He had been much more frightened by the Franco-Russian axis than is generally appreciated. In March 1810, shortly after the marriage was announced, he explained to the Prussian ambassador Finckenstein that had Napoleon decided to marry a Grand Duchess instead of Marie Louise, the closer alliance with Russia might have meant the end of Austria.

He spent five months in Paris, taking a considerable risk. Not everyone in Vienna liked him and he was criticised. However, the Emperor Francis supported him, approving the choice of Franz-Georg as *locum tenens* foreign minister. No doubt Metternich expected concessions from Napoleon; he also dreamt of a general European peace which would include Britain, and Gentz was asked to prepare a paper on how to persuade the British to take part in negotiations. And he wanted to learn what was in the French Emperor's mind, what would be his next move. In the event, he obtained nothing save more time in which to pay the indemnity. For Napoleon had got all he wanted—legitimisation of his parvenu empire.

Even so, the French Emperor was unusually amiable, offering Metternich a German principality, which he declined. Years later, he claimed that no one who was not a Frenchman had seen so much of Napoleon. Some consider that the Emperor was merely playing with him; if so, Napoleon confided in him as he did in no other envoy. Metternich had the distinct impression that war between France and Russia might break out in the summer of 1812.

Metternich lived with his family in the house which he had inhabited as ambassador. He and Eleanor went to the ill-fated ball given by the Schwarzenbergs in July, where the curtains caught fire and many guest were burnt to death, including the ambassador's sister-in-law. Eleanor had to tolerate a brief revival of Metternich's affair with Caroline Murat, now Queen of Naples. However, Mme d'Abrantès was in Spain with her husband.

When Metternich returned to Vienna in October 1810 he reported to the Emperor Francis that Austria's only hope of survival was to avoid another war. In his absence an influential group had emerged to oppose him: the former foreign minister Stadion, the finance minister Count Wallis, the Archdukes Karl and Joseph, and the Empress Maria Ludovica of Modena, who hated Metternich for allying with the man who had stolen her little country—she complained that he was frivolous. But the group could do nothing, since he had Francis's unwavering support.

'He has held and still holds the monstrous idea of ruling alone over all Europe,' Metternich wrote in January 1811. 'Napoleon has reached such great heights that only he can decide the limits of his ambition.' Later he recalled of the year 1811: 'Napoleon's power oppressed the entire continent . . . It was the edge of catastrophe but, to thoughtful observers, looked not so much like the calm before a storm as a gloomy vista of rulers and peoples humiliated by the *diktat* of inescapable destiny.'

In the same report he warns the Emperor Francis, 'We are on the brink of total financial collapse.' The enormous cost of the recent war, together with the savage indemnity, resulted in state bankruptcy and draconian inflation. Too much paper money had been in circulation; all bank notes were called in and devalued by 80 per cent, 500 gulden in paper buying only 100 in gold. A succession of bad harvests came to a head, causing an exaggerated demand for credit and a bank rate of 60 per cent. The crisis dragged on until 1816, many people being ruined.

Yet the Emperor of the French had problems too. The 'Continental Blockade', refusing admission to British goods, meant bankruptcy for Russia, which withdrew from the system at the end of 1811. (Ironically, Napoleon had freed Austria from such a burden by removing its coastline.) The war in Spain was going badly for the French. No less damaging were the French Emperor's attempts to control the Church by bullying Pius VII.

Throughout Metternich's reports there still ran the theme of European concert. Time and again he refers to 'all the European Powers', implying the survival of the old international structure from before the revolutionary wars. This tallies with his views as a young envoy at Dresden and anticipates his vision of Europe in the years ahead.

So far he had not established contact with the British government. They knew where he stood from Gentz, who was now living in Vienna and was the boon companion of the British agents there, John Harcourt King and John Mordaunt Johnson. Downing Street learnt that the Austrian foreign minister was not so attached to the Napoleonic system as might appear. In May 1811 Johnson reported that Gentz was 'on the most intimate footing with Count Metternich'. The odd, slightly disreputable little man, loose-living and debt-ridden yet indomitable in his lonely crusade against the ideas of the French Revolution, was becoming indispensable.

Nevertheless, Metternich believed that French hegemony over Europe would continue for the rest of Napoleon's life. Only after his death might a France ruled by a half-Habsburg Emperor allow the continent to return to normal. But at least Austria was free from the interference suffered by states within the Confederation of the Rhine.

Metternich has seldom been congratulated on the marriage of Marie Louise. At the time and after, there were jokes about the sacrifice of a virgin to a minotaur. It may well have saved the Monarchy.

7

Statesman against Soldier, 1812–13

> Napoleon and I spent years together as though we were playing chess, watching each other carefully—I in order to checkmate him, he so that he could crush me and all the chess pieces.
>
> METTERNICH

> Prince Metternich behaved like a skilled minister. He is the one statesman who has appeared in Europe since the Revolution. He has destroyed me systematically and I have helped him by my mistakes.
>
> NAPOLEON

Metternich's diplomacy before, during and above all after Napoleon's Russian campaign was a *bravura* performance. He saved Austria from an involvement which could well have proved ruinous. Only when he was certain that Napoleon would be beaten did he commit himself.

As has been seen, he knew that war was coming. He was far from displeased at the prospect of Russia suffering as Austria had done, and when Count Schuvalov proposed a secret Austro-Russian alliance he declined smoothly, explaining to the Emperor Francis that 'Russia's sole object in these negotiations is her own security'. Since he was convinced that Russia was going to fight a defensive war and be defeated, he could see little point in allying with her. Even so, he was seriously alarmed when Berlin made overtures to the Tsar, but Alexander would not accept the terms and Prussia signed a new treaty with France in February 1812. Austria followed suit in March, agreeing to supply the French with an 'auxiliary army' of 30,000 men; her territorial integrity was guaranteed, while there was also a secret clause that should the Kingdom of Poland be restored, Austria would be given Illyria in exchange for Galicia. What really mattered was that Napoleon's father-in-law did not have to declare war on Russia. Metternich himself called it one of the oddest compromises in diplomatic history. 'I was satisfied because what I wanted more than anything else was to ensure Austria's political freedom of action when the time came to decide what to do about the approaching war.'

In May 1812 Napoleon summoned his client kings and princes to meet him at Dresden, where he had assembled 600,000 troops from all over Europe. Not only the 'sovereigns' of the Confederation of the Rhine had to attend but the Austrian Emperor—who grumbled 'I cannot stand the creature' when referring to his son-in-law. His foreign minister came too, meeting the French Emperor daily. He records their discussion of the forthcoming campaign. Napoleon was convinced that the Russians would eventually advance to meet him, explaining that he would invade only as far as Smolensk during 1812 but that, if this failed to draw the Tsar, he would thrust deeper in 1813. 'I have to admit that neither I nor anyone else thought Napoleon would try to complete so difficult an enterprise in a single campaign' is Metternich's comment.

The subject monarchs crept away from Dresden, back to capitals whose citizens despised them. The Archdukes and the Empress argued furiously that a policy of collaboration humiliated both the dynasty and Austria, while the Hungarians refused to grant subsidies, so that Francis had to suspend the Diet and levy taxes arbitrarily; Archduke Joseph, the Palatine (or Viceroy), protested, much to the Emperor's anger. Metternich saw an opportunity to eliminate his principal opponents when the Austrian police intercepted sympathetic letters from the Empress to the Archduke; he promptly showed them to Francis with the warning that his wife and brother were about to start an affair. He would have no more trouble from Maria Ludovica or from Joseph.

Napoleon launched his invasion in June and Metternich waited for Russia to collapse. In March he had observed that Alexander did not have enough soldiers; a single defeat would destroy him utterly. His opinion was endorsed by Prince Schwarzenberg—until recently ambassador in Paris—whose troops were on the Grande Armée's extreme right wing, where they did not see any serious fighting.

An old friend arrived in Vienna in September, Hilarion de Liedekerke Beaufort, whom he had not seen since their visit to England in 1794. He stayed for two months and Metternich entertained him frequently. On 11 September he noted:

> At half-past three I went to Clément de Metternich's, where he received me in his office, filled with fine furniture and prints with which I entertained myself while he finished his work. Then I got into his barouche and off we went to dine at his villa [on the Rennweg], very prettily done up and surrounded by a really large garden. It is only a few steps from Vienna but one might think oneself a hundred leagues away. Clément . . . has planted the garden, and built hothouses, conservatories and a ménagerie, all in fourteen months, in such a way that it looks as though it has been there for years.

Liedekerke Beaufort was with Metternich's parents on 27 September when news came that Napoleon had entered Moscow on the 12th [actually the 14th]. After dining with him on 7 October he recorded,

> High politicians assure us that peace will be made in a month. Details of the battle of the Moskva [Borodino], very glorious for France, arrived in the *Moniteur* . . .

At his hotel he and fellow guests discussed the burning of Moscow:

> Some approved, and others disapproved, of the action taken by the Russians. I was among the latter. To me it seems barbarous and more harmful to themselves than to their enemy.

For some weeks there would be no more news, only rumours.

If Metternich was staggered by the Grande Armée's disaster, he showed no sign of concern on receiving the news in the first week of December. He sent a dispatch to Floret at Vilno ordering him to inform Napoleon that Austria was ready to arbitrate, and that Emperor Francis had declared, 'The hour has come for me to show the Emperor of the French who I am.' For the moment Austria could make a bid to be the peace broker. Prussia was still a broken land, Frederick William being too frightened of Napoleon to contemplate opposing him, even if a number of Prussian generals went over to the Russians at the end of 1812. 'There ensued a contest as stylized as a Japanese play and with rules as intricate,' writes Henry Kissinger, who stresses that Napoleon remained convinced that Austria was on his side but did not wish to be involved in another armed conflict. 'Because the parvenu from Corsica identified obligation with personal relations, he could not conceive that a father might make war on the husband of his daughter.' He did not grasp till too late that Austria had always been determined to profit from his defeat in Russia.

As usual, Metternich was criticised by those in Vienna who understood neither his aims nor his methods. People of the highest rank, forming a party who called themselves the 'Napoleon Haters', they clamoured for Austria to declare war on France without delay. In March 1813 Metternich had to stop Archduke Johann's raising the Tyrol. Meanwhile, 'we implemented a plan known only to ourselves, unobtrusively and in secret,' he recalls. 'Building up our armament . . . in the conviction, which grew stronger every day, that Napoleon would begin a new campaign in Germany during 1813.' The defence minister, Count Bellegarde, worked at breakneck speed, recruiting and rearming—with French approval.

In January 1813, before breaking openly with France, Prussia asked Austria for an alliance. She proposed that in the event of victory north Germany should be ruled from Berlin, south Germany from Vienna. While insisting that Prussian and Austrian interests were identical, Metternich refused, but at the same time urged Prussia to ally with Russia. He told Berlin that Austria was in an exceptionally difficult position because of Marie Louise's marriage.

By waiting and refusing to commit himself to either side, he was able to obtain just what he wanted from Tsar Alexander. He needed strong nerves. It was only too clear from the Treaty of Kalisch of February 1813 between Russia and Prussia that they intended to remake the map of Europe—Russia meant to have all Poland and to compensate Prussia with Saxony and other German territories. The implication was that Prussia was determined to dominate all north Germany. However, at the end of March Russia offered Metternich the liberation of Germany, the restoration of the Holy Roman Empire under a Habsburg Emperor and the return of all Austria's former possessions, including those in Poland.

In consequence Austria had effortlessly secured her recognition as mediator by Russia and Prussia on the one hand, by France on the other, all of whom hoped that she would bring her army into the approaching war on their side. 'It is a tribute to his [Metternich's] skill and patient preparation that what might have been considered a declaration of Austrian self-interest came to be seen as the expression of simple justice' is Kissinger's comment. As always, Metternich was aiming at the restoration of a political equilibrium in Europe. He did not see the future of Germany in terms of a revived Empire, in which the Kaiser and the Princes would be constantly at loggerheads with each other, but as a confederation dominated by Austria, whose position would be buttressed by the member states' fear of Prussian aggrandisement. He believed that stability in Central Europe must depend on a strong Austria and on Prussia. He was not so much intent on the destruction of Napoleon as on ending the Napoleonic hegemony and on confining the Emperor behind the frontiers of France. If at all possible he wanted to do so by peaceful means. He manoeuvred to such effect that in March Austria ceased to be a French satellite and became what Kissinger calls the 'pivotal power of Europe', wooed by everybody.

By the spring of 1813 the Emperor of the French found himself facing a new coalition—Russia, Prussia and Britain, soon to be joined by Sweden. He was still convinced that his father-in-law would support him, and offered Silesia, Illyria and all Galicia to Francis as inducement. In April he requested Austria to concentrate her army, now 100,000 strong, in Bohemia. This was exactly what Metternich wanted, since it would provide an ideal position from which to attack the French should the moment come, as well as increase his bargaining power. In the meantime, he encouraged the Tsar to invade. Metternich assured him that Austria would come in on the Allies' side but in her own time—though we know that privately he still hoped to avoid her being involved in the war.

During these nerve-racking months he spent much of his time at Ratiborzitz in Bohemia, the country house of the Duchess of Sagan, with whom he recommenced their old affair. He nonetheless continued to write to his wife and family almost every day. He also went frequently to the castle of Gitschin for discussions with his friend from Berlin days, Baron Karl August von Hardenberg, the Prussian Chancellor. The Russian envoy Count Karl Nesselrode was there too, a German who had once been a midshipman in the Tsar's navy but still spoke Russian badly. Both men tried to persuade Metternich to bring Austria into the war on the Allies' side, without success. Nesselrode reported disconsolately, 'Count Metternich has conceived the plan of proposing to Napoleon moderate conditions for a European peace.'

Conditions acceptable to Russia and Prussia were communicated to Count Stadion by Nesselrode and Hardenberg on 16 May: Austria and Prussia must recover their 1805 frontiers; the Confederation of the Rhine must be dissolved; France must give up northwestern Germany, Holland and northern Italy; and Spain must be restored to the Bourbons. But four days later Napoleon followed an earlier victory at Lützen (on 1 May) with another at Bautzen; if the French had had more cavalry the Allied armies would have been totally destroyed. The Tsar and Frederick William were badly shaken. So was the Emperor Francis, convinced that his son-in-law was going to win again and Austria must join him while there was still time. However, an armistice was signed on 4 June; the French needed new cavalry and the Allies wanted to mobilise more men. Some 'Napoleon Haters' were angered by the halt in hostilities. 'People will shout at the armistice,' Metternich wrote to his wife. 'Such as it is, it will save the world.'

He visited the other belligerents. On 19 June he went to the

Tsar and Frederick William at the castle of Opocno in eastern Bohemia. In his memoirs he tries to give a false impression that he had planned to destroy Napoleon from the very beginning. He claims that the Tsar asked what would happen should the French Emperor accept mediation. ' "If he refuses', I answered, "the truce will end and you'll have Austria as an ally. If he agrees, the negotiations will show beyond doubt that he possesses neither judgement nor honesty, so the result is going to be exactly the same. Whatever happens, we'll gain enough to position our armies in such a way that we shall never again be exposed to separate attacks on any of them, and we can take the offensive ourselves." '

(Metternich was also trying to take credit for the strategy devised a month later by Bernadotte, the Swedish Crown Prince, and Radetzky, the Austrian chief-of-staff; this was that the Allies should disengage when they faced the Emperor in person, only attacking his flanks or his isolated corps.)

Whatever Metternich may have actually said to the Tsar, it had the desired effect, enabling him to keep his options open till the very last moment, and offering a chance of peace. Gentz—by now accompanying Metternich everywhere—had a three-hour conversation with the Tsar, who confessed that previously he had distrusted the Austrian foreign minister but was completely reassured. In consequence, during Metternich's visit to Opocno the Treaty of Reichenbach was drafted, to be signed with his approval after he left. It allowed Austria to mediate with Napoleon for a preliminary peace but committed her to joining Russia and Prussia in fighting France if by 20 July (a dateline later extended by three weeks) the French Emperor had not agreed to surrender the Grand Duchy of Warsaw, Illyria and northwestern Germany, and to a vast increase in Prussian territory. These terms were for only a preliminary, not a comprehensive, peace; by accepting them, Napoleon would obtain no more than the Allies' agreement to negotiate—they were going to insist on nothing less than the end of the Confederation of the Rhine, of Napoleonic Germany.

After a week at Opocno Metternich set off to see the Emperor of the French. The night before, he wrote to Eleanor, 'I leave for Dresden tomorrow evening. I shall stay for twenty-four hours.

Those twenty-four hours are going to be the hardest in my life—they will decide the fate of the world.' He says in his memoirs—and in this case there is no need to doubt his sincerity—that he felt he represented all Europe. He was not over optimistic, telling Stadion in a letter, 'The conversation will lead nowhere.' But Kissinger goes too far in arguing that 'the final step in Metternich's diplomacy was to show that peaceable arrangements were incapable of setting limits to Napoleon'. Metternich certainly hoped to avoid war.

During the extraordinary six-hour meeting on 26 June, at the Marcolini Palace in Dresden—in which Napoleon raged, 'swearing like a devil' and hurling insults, even throwing his hat on the floor—Metternich remained unmoved, urging peace again and again. The Emperor accused him of taking advantage of France's misfortunes, of wanting Austria's lost territories returned without having to pay for them—'You wish me to surrender more than I would after losing four battles'—and asked him how much he had been paid by the British. Throughout, Metternich begged his host to accept Austrian mediation, pointing out that at the worst France would keep her 'natural' frontiers—the Rhine and the Alps.

'Between Europe and the aims you have hitherto pursued there is absolute contradiction,' he warned Napoleon, according to his own version of the meeting. 'The world requires peace. In order to secure this peace you must reduce your power within bounds compatible with the general tranquillity, or you will fall . . . The moment has arrived when you and Europe both throw down the gauntlet; you will take it up, you and Europe; and it will not be Europe that will be defeated.' He told Napoleon, 'I have seen your soldiers; they are mere children.' This provoked the response, 'A man such as I does not concern himself much about the lives of a million men.'

The most cynical exchange came when the Emperor enquired, 'So I have perpetrated a very stupid piece of folly in marrying an Archduchess of Austria?' The foreign minister replied blandly, as if agreeing that Napoleon had been duped, 'Since your Majesty desires to know my opinion, I will candidly say that Napoleon, the conqueror, has made a mistake.'

If Metternich did not warn, 'Sire, you are lost!' as he claims, he made clear that he thought it. After the meeting he wandered round the shabby city he had once known as a last bastion of eighteenth-century civilisation but which was now an armed camp. He estimated that it contained at least 25,000 wounded, countless houses having been turned into military hospitals. 'I could weep for these unending upheavals they call the history of empires,' he wrote to Eleanor.

Meanwhile, Napoleon was telling his confidant Caulaincourt that Metternich had spoken nothing but 'peace'. The word was 'just a pretext and will later be used to disguise his treachery'. He (of all men) even accused Metternich of bullying. Yet just as Metternich was about to leave Dresden on 30 June there was another, briefer, meeting. The Emperor agreed to a peace conference at Prague and to accept Austrian mediation. 'Tell your mother I'm coming back from Dresden very pleased with myself,' Metternich wrote to his daughter Marie on 2 July. 'Soon we shall have either peace or a really frightful war.' One surmises that the reason for being so pleased with himself was that he expected it was going to be peace.

He had contacted the British government in the spring, urging it to take part in the peace talks which he anticipated, but his invitation had been rejected out of hand. However, in mid-July the foreign secretary Lord Castlereagh wrote to the British ambassador at the Tsar's headquarters, Lord Cathcart, to inform him that the government was ready to accept Austrian mediation.

The Prague conference never materialised, apart from a few vague diplomatic formalities. Afterwards, on St Helena, Napoleon admitted that he had agreed to the conference solely to buy time and never had any intention of making peace. Yet he had had every reason to do so. Two days after the meeting Joseph Bonaparte fled from Spain, his troops having been defeated beyond all hope of recovery by Wellington at Vitoria a week previously. Even Francis could see that his son-in-law was doomed. On the other hand, it is plainly untrue that Metternich's offer to mediate (as he himself later suggested) was a deliberate deception, whose sole object was buying time. He genuinely wanted peace with a French empire cut down to size.

On 6 August the French Emperor made a last-minute bid to persuade Austria to fight on his side, sending Caulaincourt to Metternich to ask Austria's price. Six days later Caulaincourt tried again, but the foreign minister informed him that 'the fate of Europe is once more being decided by force of arms'. On 11 August Austrian troops entered the conflict on the Allies' side; a manifesto drafted by Gentz stated that Austria's policies since 1809 had been designed to persuade Napoleon to make peace, but she had finally been forced to fight for reasons of self-preservation and to save the social order. Not only did she become the Allies' military leader at once, Prince Schwarzenberg being appointed supreme commander despite Russian protests, but henceforward Metternich was to be virtually their spokesman. Only a few months before, Austria had been the weakest of the great powers, without even a proper army.

8

The Colossus Falls, 1814

> For Metternich belongs to the favoured few who achieve both the highest peaks of human destiny and of culture.
>
> GOETHE, October 1813

> I now believe in Your Excellency as in the Delphic Oracle, even when I don't quite understand everything that you say.
>
> GENTZ to Metternich, October 1813

The next nine months were to be, physically, the hardest of Metternich's entire life—spent not in the Ballhausplatz or some elegant château but with the Allied armies. They were no less exhausting diplomatically. He had to dance attendance constantly on the sovereigns, their accompanying ministers and their commanders-in-chief, to prevent them from falling out. The Tsar was vain, wilful and vacillating; Frederick William III did just what Alexander told him; while Bernadotte, not content with Sweden, wanted the throne of Imperial France. The very size of the armies involved was against them. The problem was to hold the Alliance together, not just until it defeated Napoleon but until it finally destroyed him. The French Emperor was waiting for it to collapse, as well it might—especially after a major victory.

By the end of August the Allies had won three minor victories and Metternich severed all communications with Napoleon. Undoubtedly he thought of the struggle as a duel. When the French forces withdrew to Leipzig, awaiting the final, decisive battle, he wrote to his daughter on 1 October, 'Everything indicates that the hour is striking and that Providence has blessed my mission to destroy this great evil. I am sure Napoleon thinks of me constantly.' The bloodiest fighting to be seen in Europe until the twentieth century took place at Leipzig on 16–18 October, the 'Battle of the Nations'. (Schwarzenberg wrote that he had never known a more horrible battlefield.) The Allies had 360,000 troops, the French 185,000. The French lost 40,000 killed while another 20,000 of them were taken prisoner, including 27 generals. Napoleon led what was left of his army in headlong retreat. Metternich wrote triumphantly to Wilhelmine de Sagan, 'We have won the battle for the world.'

'If the Count has won a battle, then we shall have to worship his star like the one which led the Three Kings of Orient to Bethlehem,' wrote Gentz while waiting for news. He too saw it as a duel. Of the glorious outcome, he told Metternich, 'I now believe in Your Excellency as in the Delphic Oracle, even when I don't quite understand everything you are saying.' It was a personal triumph, a vindication of Metternich's entire policy since his appointment in 1809.

When the Emperor Francis bestowed the Grand Cross of the Maria Theresa Order on Schwarzenberg, that loyal friend suggested that the foreign minister should also be rewarded. Accordingly, Metternich was made a Prince. Next morning his valet, Giroux, came into his bedroom and asked, 'Will His Serene Highness wear the same suit that His Excellency wore yesterday?' Metternich told this story for the rest of his life.

He may have had a valet, but he was living in great discomfort, perpetually on the move, visiting other diplomats, reporting to the Emperor and, after Leipzig, following in the wake of the advancing Allied armies. For long periods he seldom slept under the same roof for two nights running. Usually he travelled in a light carriage with a secretary and a portable desk, Giroux and his baggage in another carriage close behind, followed by still more carriages containing his staff—a mobile chancellery. When they went westward after Leipzig it was through a devastated land. The roads were muddy tracks, churned into deep ruts by the retreating French artillery, which had then frozen hard in the autumn frosts, breaking horses' legs and smashing carriage wheels; the verges were strewn with dead or dying Frenchmen. Metternich and his party had to sleep in the verminous public rooms of filthy village inns and, despite bringing provisions with them, suffered real hardship. Often the foreign minister rode ahead of his carriage, sometimes spending ten hours a day in the saddle, or else walked beside it. As he journeyed west he was accompanied throughout by General Merveldt and Lord Aberdeen.

Max von Merveldt, the former Teutonic Knight from Westphalia and a much-decorated cavalryman, had by now become one of Metternich's right-hand men, a soldier-diplomat of the same mould as Schwarzenberg. A veteran negotiator, his diplomatic experience went back to Leoben in 1797, where he had impudently tried to persuade Bonaparte to change sides and enter the Austrian service.

Aberdeen was the British ambassador to Austria, a priggish and conceited young Scot of twenty-nine who had joined Metternich at Teplitz (and who would one day be Britain's Prime Minister during the Crimean War). After presenting credentials to Francis I, Aberdeen wrote to his sister-in-law, 'I have had every reason to be satisfied with him.' He was completely taken in by Count Metternich, overwhelmed by flattery; in his opinion the Austrian foreign minister was vain and somewhat stupid but open and trustworthy: 'In such good society one forgets the horrors that are past,' he wrote of him. Metternich never let the Scot out of his sight, referring to Aberdeen behind his back as that 'dear simpleton of diplomacy'.

Not everyone was so easy to deal with. Less than a fortnight after the victory at Leipzig the coalition was showing signs of falling apart. The Tsar was especially difficult. He had been enraged by Austria's refusal to let him become commander-in-chief instead of Schwarzenberg. Knowing that Francis wished to be the first to enter Frankfurt where he and his ancestors had been crowned, Alexander deliberately marched in two days before the Austrians. Although he had hitherto assumed a most friendly manner, at Weimar he had a noisy argument with Metternich which lasted for three hours, 'a terrible scene' according to Metternich. The Prussians, intoxicated by victory, were behaving with characteristic arrogance. There was a furious row at Frankfurt between Generals Blücher and Schwarzenberg, in which Metternich had to intervene.

Far more worrying than Alexander's vanity or Prussian bullying were Allied plans to divide up the spoils. The Tsar wanted the Grand Duchy of Warsaw in its entirety while enlarging Prussia so as to make her a more useful ally in future. Understandably, the Prussians concurred wholeheartedly, regarding Saxony and the Saxon duchies as their share of the booty at the very least, treating the Saxons as a conquered people. What particularly alarmed Metternich was Alexander's insistence that Heinrich vom Stein should direct the administration of all liberated German territories. Stein's liberal and nationalist views, his wish for a unified Germany under Prussian rule, were only too well known. 'The revolutionary spirit', Metternich recalled, 'appeared among those advising the Russian Emperor in 1812, in Baron Stein, General Gneisenau and other Prussian and German fugitives.' There is no doubt that Stein wanted a radical, not to say revolutionary, solution; in November 1812 he had told the Tsar that German Princes should be treated as enemies who were at the disposal of the advancing Allied armies; fortunately Alexander rejected his suggestion. Gentz was so horrified by the spread of 'Jacobinical' sentiment that he began to argue that Napoleon's survival was necessary as a counterweight to Prussian ambition.

The Allies paused at Frankfurt for six weeks. Metternich persuaded them to offer terms which would leave Napoleon France's 'natural' frontiers. No satisfactory reply was received, so the Allies prepared to invade, disregarding the convention that campaigning should cease in the winter. In December Metternich accompanied them to Freiburg, staying at the Kagenegg house, where his mother had been born. During the same month, against Alexander's wishes, Austrian troops entered Switzerland and occupied Basel. 'Harmony has never returned since that moment,' Gentz was to record in a memoir of February 1815. 'Angry and bitter discussions [between the Tsar and Metternich] took place almost every day during the latter part of the campaign.' Even so, Metternich rode by Alexander's side to watch the Cossacks crossing the Rhine on 13 January 1814. Three days later, Alexander announced that he would not rest 'until he reached Paris and could proclaim Bernadotte Emperor of France'. Even Frederick William of Prussia was horrified, begging him to wait for the arrival of the British foreign secretary. Metternich instructed Schwarzenberg to halt the advance unobtrusively—'Peace will have to be made in three weeks at most.' A Russian puppet on the French throne was a nightmare beyond Metternich's worst imaginings.

A strange figure arrived at Allied headquarters in Basel on 18 January, a tall, unsmiling, pompous man in bright red breeches and a gold-braided fur bonnet—Metternich joked that he looked like a bishop on his travels. Coldly good-looking, frigidly formal, Robert Stewart, Viscount Castlereagh, was undeniably impressive; a contemporary referred to 'that splendid summit of bright and polished frost'. Few realized the strain of maintaining so stiff a manner, how highly strung he was beneath. He had earned a grim name in Ireland, as a member of the Dublin Parliament who played a key role in the bloody repression of the 1798 rebellion and in forcing through the union with England. Four years older than Metternich, he had been the British foreign secretary since February 1812.

However, Castlereagh's daunting exterior concealed great talent and, although he spoke no German and very poor French, he and the Austrian foreign minister took to each other immediately. No two men could have been less alike. Yet both wanted a stable Europe before all else, if from different motives, and a Europe which would not be dominated by any one power. 'A few hours conversation was quite enough to create a feeling of trust between this upright and enlightened statesman and myself,' wrote Metternich. He informed Schwarzenberg that 'we concur on the stupidity of a certain person' [the Tsar]. Both were in seeming agreement that Napoleon and his son must go and that the only man to replace them was Louis XVI's brother—even if Metternich was not telling the truth. Before the end of the month he was comparing Castlereagh to an angel.

On 25 January Metternich and Castlereagh moved with the headquarters to Langres, on the edge of the flat plain of Champagne. It was the coldest winter in living memory and wolves attacked an Austrian courier's coach horses just outside the town. Secretly, Metternich contacted Napoleon—whatever he may have told his new British friend, he was trying to save the half-Habsburg dynasty at Paris. On 5 February a conference met at Chatillon. Caulaincourt asked for the terms offered at Frankfurt, France's 'natural' frontiers. Metternich, by then at Troyes, would have agreed, but Castlereagh was adamant that France must revert to her frontiers of 1792, surrendering Belgium, the left bank of the Rhine, Savoy and Nice. At first the French Emperor took the conference seriously, since the combined Austrian and Prussian forces had recently defeated him at La Rothière. However, on 9 February the Tsar suddenly withdrew from the talks, recalling Razumovsky. The next day, Alexander informed Metternich at Troyes that he intended to march on Paris without further delay, where he would summon an assembly to elect a new ruler in place of Napoleon.

In mid-January Metternich had written to Gentz that 'the Emperor Alexander believes that he owes it to Moscow to blow up the Tuileries'. He was determined to avoid both this scenario and the summoning of a such an assembly, arguing forcefully that the only alternative to Napoleon—if he had to go—was Louis XVIII, since were the French people allowed to choose their ruler for themselves it would undermine the foundations of every throne in Europe; it might also end in another social revolution. And he dreaded the prospect of an overmighty Prussia, backed by an even stronger Russia in Eastern Europe, an axis which could well dominate the entire continent. Kaunitz's disciple as always, he wanted France as a counterweight, not to crush her or leave her in anarchy.

In the days before radio communications it was very difficult for such large armies as those of the Allies to achieve coordination; to some extent their enormous superiority in numbers worked to Napoleon's advantage. In the second week of February Napoleon won five amazing victories against huge odds, defeating separately Russians, Prussians and Austrians. He was intoxicated by his success, writing to Emperor Francis after winning what was really only a skirmish at Montereau in the same tone he had used in the wake of some great victory. He broke off negotiations at Chatillon, still hoping to drive the Allies out of France.

A sudden change in the fortunes of war had a profund effect

on the unstable Alexander. 'But it is the characteristic of a policy which bases itself on purely military considerations to be immoderate in triumph and panicky in adversity,' observes Henry Kissinger when discussing the Tsar's behaviour during the campaign. So horrified was Alexander by Napoleon's apparent recovery that he joined the Austrians in offering the French an armistice.

The Chatillon conference began all over again. The Allies were only too anxious for peace but Caulaincourt was instructed by the French Emperor to hold out for the natural frontiers. The run of French victories had been halted by the end of February. Even so, Napoleon still believed that he could force his opponents to accept his terms. Metternich tried hard to make him see reason. 'Has he placed beyond recall his destiny and that of his son on his last gun-carriage?' he asked Caulaincourt in a letter of 30 March. If Francis I had been able to surrender the Tyrol in 1809, why could not the French Emperor surrender Belgium in 1814?

Allied morale recovered. At Chaumont on 4 March, Austria, Russia, Prussia and Britain signed a treaty which formally committed each of them for twenty years, to put 60,000 troops in the field should France ever again threaten European harmony. They pledged themselves not to make peace separately with Napoleon. It was a treaty of general alliance against the Emperor, the brainchild of Castlereagh, who was able to secure the Allies' agreement by promising a subsidy of five million pounds to be divided among them. Yet above all it was a triumph for the Austrian foreign minister; there was an additional clause guaranteeing the establishment of a Germanic confederation of independent states—he had outwitted both the Prussians and the Tsar, thwarting their designs on Germany, while securing at the same time a foundation on which to build European cooperation. Those who signed did so at a whist table, observing (according to Castlereagh) that no whist party had ever seen such high stakes. They were referring to the outcome of the war, not to Metternich's gains.

Until the very last moment Metternich hoped to secure much more, even if on 17 March he drafted a proclamation, promptly issued by the Allies, that they were no longer prepared to negotiate with the French Emperor. But on the same day, Metternich wrote to Caulaincourt begging him to persuade his master to give up Belgium and the left bank of the Rhine, pointing out they would rise in revolt if France tried to keep them. 'Austria still wishes to preserve a dynasty with which it is so closely connected.' It was the first time he had shown his hand clearly, revealing that he really wanted Napoleon to survive—if on a limited scale. Yet Castlereagh would not have allowed peace at this late stage; British public opinion had grown increasingly opposed to it. In any case, the French Emperor would never have agreed. Metternich, essentially a rationalist committed to equilibrium, did not understand that Napoleon could not permit himself to be tamed into becoming just another Louis XVI.

The Allies had been contacted by the French opposition to Napoleon. In mid-March Talleyrand's envoy, the royalist Baron de Vitrolles, reached Allied headquarters disguised as a Swiss merchant, bringing a letter in invisible ink dictated by Talleyrand; this advised the Allies to march on Paris at once. Vitrolles's own message was that the French wanted to be freed: 'There can be no peace with Bonaparte and there can be no peace without the Bourbons.' Metternich seemed sceptical. The baron had several conversations with him, being impressed by 'his handsome, amiable face, his noble and indeed elegant carriage, his engaging, natural and most attractive manner.' He never guessed that Metternich would have preferred the Bonapartes to the Bourbons, though he noticed Metternich was evasive. 'He knew how to wait for events to unfold and take them as they came, rather than try to make them happen.' The baron was impressed by Metternich's loathing of war and lack of any desire for revenge, by his wish to end the destruction and save France from further misery.

Clearly the French Emperor was doomed, even if he would not admit it. On 9 March he had been defeated by the Prussians at Laon, as he was again ten days later by the Austrians at Arcis-sur-Aube. He had only 30,000 troops left, exhausted scarecrows. He withdrew to the east, intending to find reinforcements, after which he meant to attack the Allies when they turned to pursue him. Their missions' headquarters lay in his path, their members fleeing before him. Metternich went with Francis, they and their suites travelling in two post-chaises, taking refuge at Dijon on 25 March. News came that Bordeaux had declared for the Bourbons. By now everyone, including Metternich, saw that the only possible ruler for France was the late king's brother, Louis XVIII. On 28 March Allied leaders drank his health at a dinner given by Castlereagh.

Freiherr von Wessenberg, Austrian envoy in London, arrived unexpectedly, dirty and unshaven; trying to reach Metternich, he had been caught by French partisans and taken to the Emperor's headquarters, where he was recognised. Napoleon sent him to Francis at Dijon with a message that he was ready to accept the Allies' peace terms and would leave the arrangements to Austria —'If the Austrians don't save me, I'm lost!' He even hinted at a regency. He also sent a warning to Metternich, telling him to beware of Russia and Prussia.

Metternich wrote ruefully to his wife that if only the Emperor had realized he was beaten a fortnight earlier he could have had peace. 'But now his last army is destroyed, negotiations are broken off and the Bourbons have been proclaimed at one of the Empire's principal towns.' He added, 'How many chances has he had of staying in the saddle, of remaining at the head of the most beautiful country in the world . . .'

Napoleon's ruse to decoy the Allies eastward failed. Instead they marched on Paris. After a short but bloody resistance at Montmartre by 13,000 weary and outnumbered troops, Marshal Marmont surrendered the city to save it from destruction. The Allies rode in on 31 March, led by the Tsar and the King of Prussia. On 3 April, Talleyrand, recognised by the Allies as head of a provisional government, secured the Emperor's deposition by the Senate. On the following day Napoleon abdicated at Fontainebleau and was promised the island of Elba for his new domain. On 6 April the Senate proclaimed the accession of Louis XVIII.

At Dijon Metternich did not learn of the fall of Paris until 4 April. He and Castlereagh took three days and nights to reach Paris. He was horrified by the cession of Elba; not only was it too near the European mainland, but it had belonged to Habsburg Tuscany. The result 'will be to bring us back onto the field of battle in under two years', he prophesied (no one can say he was wrong). Not only

Schwarzenberg but Castlereagh were inclined to agree with him. In the end he gave way reluctantly, after securing Parma for Marie Louise.

He was in low spirits. He believed that Napoleon would have been better at containing the revolutionary currents which lurked beneath the surface in France. From a window in the Rue Montmartre he watched Louis XVIII's entry into Paris. 'It made a most painful impression,' he recalled. He noted the gloomy faces of the Imperial Guard who escorted the King, the sullen silence of all too many in the crowd. He was given a private audience by Louis in his study at the Tuileries, the King joking that Napoleon had been a very good tenant who had left everything in excellent order.

Metternich was amazed by the city's peaceful appearance. No one would have thought there had been a war. 'The boulevards are full of people,' he reported to Wilhelmine de Sagan, 'dandies, hussars, ladies in masks, cossacks . . . everybody seeming to know everyone else and greeting each other in the friendliest way'. He also marvelled at such extraordinary contradictions as the King's brother, the Comte d'Artois, in the uniform of the National Guard or Napoleonic marshals wearing the royalist white cockade. He grew more cheerful. He refused to renew his friendship with Mme d'Abrantès, but Wilhelmine arrived early in May. There was an orgy of balls and receptions, most of which he seems to have attended. He saw much of the Duke of Wellington, to whom, with his undoubted flair for getting on with the British, he took a great liking; he wrote to Eleanor that the Duke was 'Austrian in his soul'. He took the Emperor Francis and General Bubna on a tour of demimondaine Paris, including the Palais-Royal, which they thoroughly enjoyed. He sent dresses and hats in the latest Parisian fashion to his wife at Vienna. They were chosen for her by Wilhelmine, though their affair was beginning to make him very unhappy; Wilhelmine was sleeping with a young man from the British Embassy, Frederick Lamb (Lord Melbourne's brother). He laughed at the female Anglo-Saxons who flocked over the Channel, writing to Eleanor, 'You should see the Englishwomen's unbelievable appearance and clothes'.

Meanwhile, supported by Castlereagh on most questions, he

achieved a good deal. If he could not have a Habsburg-Bonaparte France, then at least he was able to ensure that the new Bourbon France was not crushed out of existence. As he wrote afterwards, the Peace of Paris signed on 30 May 1814 bore the unmistakeable stamp of moderation, 'a moderation which did not stem from weakness but from a resolve to secure lasting peace in Europe'. France lost its 'natural' frontiers, returning to those of 1792, but regained most of its colonial empire. There was no crushing indemnity of the sort inflicted on Austria in 1809, no army of occupation. The French were not even asked to disarm what was left of the Grande Armée. 'The treaty of Paris was thus a peace of equilibrium,' comments Henry Kissinger. 'In this manner the war against Napoleon ended, not in a paean of hatred but in a spirit of reconciliation, with a recognition that the stability of an international order depends on the degree to which its components feel committed to its defence.' In view of Russia's and Prussia's thirst for revenge, this was a far from modest achievement.

Much to Metternich's satisfaction, the fate of Saxony and Poland was postponed. At the end of April, Hardenberg had proposed that Prussia should annex Saxony while most of Poland should go to Russia. However, the Tsar insisted on delaying any decision about these states; he wished to wait for a full discussion at the congress which, as stipulated by the Peace of Paris, was shortly to take place in Vienna to determine the future balance of power. In Gentz's view, Alexander, though determined to have the Grand Duchy of Warsaw, wanted to cut a figure at the congress as 'arbiter of Europe's destiny'.

Austria had done more than join in the invasion of France. Her troops had overrun all northern and central Italy, which they now occupied, besides reinstating the Pope at Rome. Of all the Bonaparte family, only Napoleon's brother-in-law Murat remained on an Italian throne, at Naples. He had reached a secret agreement with the Allies before Leipzig, helping in the attack on French Italy; the Allies guaranteed his kingdom and promised to try to persuade the exiled Bourbons to abandon their claim to Naples, if he would recognise theirs to Sicily. Metternich was always well disposed towards an old mistress such as Caroline Murat and did his best to save the couple; they might have had a place in his plans for Italy. However, as 1814 went by, it grew increasingly obvious that post-Napoleonic Europe was not going to tolerate them. In the meantime, Austria had no other rivals in Italy and waited for the congress to confirm her position. Hopes of an independent Lombardy under a Habsburg Archduke were ill-founded. The Emperor Francis regarded the northern Italian lands as his, either by inheritance or, as in the case of Venice, by right of conquest.

Early in June, Metternich accompanied the Tsar and the King of Prussia to England, which he had not seen since 1794. The Emperor Francis returned to Vienna. His foreign minister's object was not so much to share in the glory as to stop the Russians and Prussians from securing more support from the British government, while strengthening his own links with it and his working relationship with Castlereagh. He crossed the Channel in a frigate, to be welcomed at Dover with the honours normally given to a sovereign. At first it looked as if Tsar Alexander would carry all before him, since he had been a popular hero in Britain since the Retreat from Moscow, but he played into Metternich's hands by infuriating the Prince Regent by his arrogance and tactlessness; after a very few days, according to Creevey, Prinny was 'worn out with fuss, fatigue and *rage*'. The Tsar angered ministers by making a point of consulting the Opposition, though the Whigs too were disenchanted —'a vain, silly fellow' was Lord Grey's verdict. Alexander's favourite sister, the temperamental Grand Duchess Catherine, insulted the Regent to his face, threatened to vomit if music was played at banquets and called on his detested wife, Caroline of Brunswick.

In contrast, the Austrian foreign minister endeared himself to all he met. As he put it, he was 'nearly killed' when leaving a reception at midnight by a mob shouting 'Hurrah! Prince Metternich for ever!' and thrusting their arms into his carriage to '*sheck hands*' [sic]. He knew exactly how to please the Regent, investing him with the Austrian Golden Fleece; this was tact of the subtlest sort, since Wellington had been the first Protestant to receive the Spanish Golden Fleece. Metternich also brought the Regent the honorary colonelcy of an Austrian cavalry regiment, with the right to wear its white tunic and red breeches. He then piled compliment upon compliment till the delighted Regent called him 'the wisest of ministers'. The government admitted that much of what Castlereagh said in praise of Metternich seemed to be true; he was never seen with a Whig, let alone to talk politics with one. If he and the foreign secretary were able to do little work, his bravura performance deepened Castlereagh's respect.

Metternich enjoyed himself, amused by such celebrations as a Guildhall dinner in honour of the triumph of Allied arms, and flattered by the bestowal of an honorary doctorate at Oxford. Wilhelmine de Sagan had followed him to England, although their affair was growing unhappier every day. Luckily she was invited to very few receptions, so that he could flirt with other pretty women.

He left England early in July, visiting Paris for a brief stay with Wilhelmine. He returned to Vienna on 19 July, to a hero's welcome. Prince Palffy, once a rival for Eleanor's hand, had arranged a concert in Metternich's honour in the Ballhausplatz, with an orchestra and chorus recruited from the combined resources of the court theatre and the *Wiener Theater*. It began with Beethoven's *Prometheus* and ended with a cantata which opened, 'Hail to thee, great Prince!' The cantata's dedication spoke of 'the illustrious statesman whose insight and tireless patience, whose moderation and caution, have gained rewards of which no man would have dared to dream a year ago'. It was no more than the truth.

9

Rebuilding Europe, 1814–15

> If ever the powers meet again to establish a political system under which wars of conquest would be made impossible and the rights of all would be guaranteed, then the Congress of Vienna may not have been in vain in preparing the way.
>
> FRIEDRICH VON GENTZ

> The European policy of Metternich had taken form at a moment of general weariness after a long war; this policy was no less than an attempt to 'federalise' Europe as Germany had been 'federalised'.
>
> SIR LLYWELLYN WOODWARD, *Three Studies in European Conservatism*

The Congress of Vienna is often seen as a triumph of reaction over progress. Yet if those who took part looked back to the old order of things before 1789, their overriding concern was to secure lasting peace. They succeeded and no general war broke out in Europe for a century. As Alan Sked stresses, the resulting settlement 'left no major power with a major grievance'.

At the time, Gentz, the congress's secretary, was cynical about its motives and its effectiveness. 'The grand phrases of "reconstruction of social order", "regeneration of the political system of Europe", "a lasting peace founded on a just division of strength" and etc, were uttered to tranquilise the public and give an air of dignity and grandeur to so solemn an assembly,' he wrote in February 1815, 'but the real purpose of the congress was to divide amongst the conquerors the spoils taken from the vanquished.' He was convinced that another European war would break out within five years. Castlereagh, with a less vivid imagination, thought it would do well if it kept the peace for a decade.

An air of almost frenzied frivolity made it hard for many observers to take the congress seriously. It opened officially on 3 November 1814 and among guests staying at the Hofburg were the Tsar, the King of Prussia, the King and Queen of Bavaria, the King of Denmark, and a host of lesser Princes. Most of the great nobles of Germany, Central Europe and Russia were in Vienna. They were celebrating the end of twenty years of war and upheaval, the like of which (so they believed) had not been seen since the Middle Ages. The Habsburg Monarchy was determined to provide suitable entertainment, to demonstrate that Vienna was the capital of Europe. The famous *mot* of the Prince de Ligne, '*Le Congrés danse mais il ne marche pas*,' was at once taken up, passing into legend and ensuring its reputation for lighthearted pleasure.

'Metternich swam as happily as a fish in this glittering whirlpool,' says Treitschke. His enjoyment of the festivities was noted with disapproval in certain quarters. 'He spends three-quarters of his time at dances or other entertainments,' sneered Talleyrand. Castlereagh's secretary considered him 'most intolerably loose and giddy with women'. Yet he was not the only one to enjoy himself. The British ambassador got fighting drunk more than once while Lady Castlereagh danced at a ball with her husband's garter in her hair.

A rumour was to circulate that Metternich forfeited Austria's chance of acquiring Bavaria because he was too exhausted to attend to business after a night with Wilhelmine de Sagan. Admittedly the collapse of their affair occurred during these vital weeks; on one occasion he could speak of nothing else to Gentz and was incapable of concentrating on matters of state, yet it was an isolated instance. The ill-informed called him the 'butterfly minister', but his abandonment to pleasure during the congress has been wildly exaggerated; sometimes he worked through the night. As Treitschke puts it, 'He was not all upset by his Prussian comrades thinking him more frivolous than he really was.' Behind the festivities Metternich was fighting a ferocious diplomatic battle.

When the talks began, he wrote to his wife (on 19 September),

'I am going to have from four to six weeks of hell.' His opponent was the Tsar, feebly seconded by the King of Prussia—in reality by Hardenberg. Gentz says that Alexander came to the congress convinced that Prince Metternich intended to thwart him on every issue; in the latter stages of the French campaign there had been 'bitter and angry exchanges almost every day'. At Vienna he was to grow increasingly jealous of the foreign minister's success, political and social, to the point that irritation turned into hatred and resulted in 'daily explosions of rage and frenzy'. Metternich was forced to regard the Tsar as 'a declared enemy'.

There were unpleasant undertones. When he arrived in October, Talleyrand reported to Louis XVIII that the German 'mediatised' Princes who had lost their lands resented the prospect of being ruled by such new masters as the Kings of Bavaria or Württemberg and would have preferred a single unified Germany. Intoxicated by Napoleon's defeat, they had become German nationalists. 'Jacobinism holds sway here, not as it did in France twenty-five years ago, in the middle and lower classes but among the highest and richest members of the nobility,' Talleyrand explained, adding that many university professors and students shared their views. 'United Germany is their slogan, their dogma; it is a religion carried to extreme fanaticism, a fanaticism which infects even reigning princes.'

Anti-Semitism had revived. One undoubted benefit of the Napoleonic régime in Germany had been the emancipation of the Jews, who now feared that their ancient disabilities might be revived. The 'Israelites' of Frankfurt sent representatives to Vienna, Messrs Baruch and Gumprecht, to plead their case. Metternich had many Jewish acquaintances, such as Baron Eskele (the first Jew to be ennobled in Austria) and Leopold von Herz, a banker whose skills had helped to save the Monarchy. Learning that the police were about to expel Baruch and Gumprecht from Vienna, he intervened and gave them visas. Shortly afterwards, he asked all the free cities not to penalise Jews when restoring the old constitutions. Throughout the congress he tried to secure equality for them, but there was such fierce opposition that he had to defer his efforts.

The Tsar nearly wrecked the congress. Influenced by his Polish friend Adam Czartoryski, who had accompanied him, he wanted a Russo-Polish dual monarchy with himself as King of a restored Poland. He meant to have the entire Grand Duchy of Warsaw, including its former Prussian provinces; Prussia was to be compensated with Saxony. But although he had half a million men in Poland, his bargaining position was weaker than he realized; Austria had secured all the territory she coveted, Britain had regained Hanover. If Metternich was ready to see a Polish kingdom in the east, he would never accept a revival of the old western frontiers under a Russian ruler who could threaten *Mitteleuropa*. Castlereagh agreed with him.

Castlereagh reminded Alexander of the Treaty of Reichenbach in 1813, when Russia had agreed to divide the Grand Duchy with Prussia and Austria, but made no impression. He had even less success in urging the restoration of a fully independent Poland. Talleyrand, trying to divide the Allies, goaded the Tsar into shouting, 'I will go to war rather than surrender what is mine!' The Frenchman argued that the only legitimate states were those whose monarch's claim to his throne was beyond question; accordingly, Saxony was inviolable. Metternich recognised an ally, of sorts, besides appropriating Talleyrand's theory of legitimacy. Alexander was unmoved. It was the Congress's most dangerous moment.

On 22 October Metternich informed Hardenberg that Austria would not oppose Prussia's annexation of Saxony if Russia was resisted over Poland. With his agreement he presented Alexander with an ultimatum demanding a public debate. The enraged Tsar threw his sword on the table and challenged Metternich to a duel, shouting, 'You're the only man in Austria who dares speak rebelliously to me!' The situation had to be defused by the Emperor Francis, who explained to Alexander 'how very strange such a proceeding would seem'. Frederick William ordered Hardenberg to make no more separate agreements with Austria or Britain.

In a series of intricate manoeuvres Metternich widened the gap between Prussia and Russia, attracting support from smaller German states such as Bavaria, who were fearful of suffering Saxony's fate. Aware that he was being outmanoeuvred, Hardenberg became infuriated; in December he threatened to declare war, hastily withdrawing the threat in the face of Castlereagh's icy disapproval. Then, unexpectedly, Alexander's mood changed from sabre-rattling to mild benevolence.

The settlement of the Polish and Saxon question finally agreed by the congress in the second week of February 1815 accepted the division of Poland first suggested in the Treaty of Reichenbach, Russia securing the centre and east, the remainder being shared between Prussia and Austria; Austria obtained Galicia while Cracow became a free city. Against all odds, the Kingdom of Saxony survived, keeping two-fifths of its territory. Prussia was compensated with Westphalia and a large part of the Rhineland, to establish a bulwark against the French. Some historians give Talleyrand the credit for breaking the impasse, but in reality it was a triumph for Metternich diplomacy—even if Castlereagh contributed.

Castlereagh returned to London. The mutual understanding between the British foreign secretary and the Austrian foreign minister had continued, and while their objectives may have been slightly different they were never at serious variance. Metternich also got on well with the Duke of Wellington, who took Castlereagh's place.

The congress still had much to settle, especially in Italy, the outstanding problem being Murat. Louis XVIII, anxious for his Bourbon cousins to regain their Neapolitan throne, was exasperated by Metternich's predilection for Caroline Murat; he compared the Emperor Francis to Mark Anthony, grumbling that at least the latter had been ruled by his own mistress and not by a mistress of his minister. But Murat antagonised the Austrians with inept attempts to stir up trouble in northern Italy and an ill-concealed plan of conquering the entire peninsula. By the end of 1814 Metternich and Wellington had agreed that he had no right to his throne and to get rid of him at the earliest opportunity.

There was a rude interruption. Metternich's account has often been given, but is worth repeating. He went to bed at 4.00 a.m. on 7 March, after a long conference, leaving instructions that he was not to be disturbed. However, a servant woke him at 6.00 a.m. with a despatch from the Austrian consul at Genoa marked URGENT.

He tried to go back to sleep but, failing, opened it at 7.30 a.m. The despatch informed him that Napoleon had disappeared from Elba. In less than half an hour he was with the Emperor Francis, who instructed him to tell the Tsar and the Prussian King without delay that he was ready to order the Austrian army to march back to France. Before 8.30 a.m. Metternich received similar assurances from these two sovereigns. (The Tsar, on whom he had not called for three months, insisted on embracing him and promised to forget any previous differences.) Metternich records, not without satisfaction, M de Talleyrand's prophecy, 'He [Napoleon] is going to land somewhere on the Italian coast and go directly to Switzerland'—to which Metternich had retorted that Napoleon would make straight for Paris.

In Metternich's words, 'The Hundred Days were only an episode.' Yet at the time he was not so confident. By 20 March Napoleon was back at the Tuileries with an army far more formidable than it had been in 1814. Even if he were beaten, it was by no means certain that the Bourbons could be restored. Metternich contacted Fouché, the Emperor's Minister of Police, suggesting that the Allies might accept a regency for Napoleon's son if his father would leave France. But there was no way of getting rid of the French Emperor without war.

During this trying period Metternich nonetheless found time to tease Gentz, who had very little sense of humour. The latter was drinking his morning coffee when a poster printed in French arrived—Napoleon was offering 10,000 ducats in gold to anyone who apprehended Friedrich von Gentz, or could prove he had killed him. Gentz was prostrate with terror until he realized that it was 1 April.

Metternich insisted that the congress must continue. In Italy Austria's possession of Milan and Venice was confirmed, as was Marie Louise's right to Parma. A Habsburg Grand Duke was restored in Tuscany, a Habsburg Duke in Modena. Joachim Murat solved the problem of Naples by attempting to invade northern Italy and meeting with total defeat at Tolentino in May; he fled into exile, returning to be court-martialled and shot, and the Neapolitan Bourbons regained their mainland realm. The Kingdom of Piedmont was given Genoa, in the hope that it would become a bulwark against French aggression.

Metternich's provision for Napoleon's Empress was both ingenious and delicate. Although Parma had been promised to Marie Louise in the Treaty of Fontainebleau, the head of its former ruling family, the Bourbon-Parma, possessed an undeniable claim to be legitimate Duke; Metternich fobbed him off with the minuscule Duchy of Lucca until her death. He ensured that there would be no question of her son inheriting Parma, let alone of Napoleon joining her, by appointing the dashing General von Neipperg, a noted lady-killer, as master of her household with instructions to use 'any means whatever' to stop her seeing her husband—in effect to seduce her. Neipperg obeyed his orders so zealously that she married him when Napoleon died. Until Marie Louise's death Parma remained a Habsburg bastion.

The last business to be concluded was the structure of the new Germanic confederation. Austria and Prussia were among the thirty-eight members of a loose league of kingdoms, duchies and free cities, whose only link was the federal Diet. Metternich saw no object in reviving the Holy Roman Empire, since the Emperor would have had little authority. The small, independent states of the confederation would live in fear of Prussian absorption or French invasion and look to Austria.

Metternich presided over the official closure of the congress on 9 June. One reason for its success had been his exceptionally able staff. Gentz had proved a tireless and resourceful secretary, while diplomats such as Josef von Hudelist, Franz von Binder and Johann von Wessenberg (the 'worker bee') were invaluable, as was the military adviser, General Radetzky—Schwarzenberg's chief of staff. Public relations were well organised by Josef-Anton von Pilat, once the foreign minister's secretary but now editor of the *Österreichischer Beobachter*.

Only the British troops in Belgium and the Prussian in the Rhineland were available, but on 18 June Napoleon was beaten at Waterloo. 'Even if the battle had not been the success it was, owing to the English commander's iron resolution and Marshal Blücher's gallant assistance, Napoleon's cause would have been doomed,' wrote Metternich in 1853. 'The Austrian and Russian armies, together with troops from the Germanic Confederation, were advancing towards the Rhine and would have overrun all France.' Britain was ready to finance an Allied army of a million men.

Nevertheless, the speed of Wellington's victory came as a relief. Admittedly the four Allied powers, supported by Spain, Portugal and Sweden, had promised to help Louis XVIII help restore order, but since then he had been driven into exile. The Tsar began to talk again of an alternative régime in France, perhaps a republic. It had looked very much as though the Allies would not merely be divided, as they had been in the previous year, but that the harmony established at Vienna would be lost, together with the vital principle of legitimacy. Fortunately, Castlereagh stood firm on the need to bring back Louis XVIII, and Wellington and Blücher reached Paris before Alexander. The National Assembly restored Louis to the throne for a second time.

The Austrian army crossed the Rhine only a week after Waterloo, Metternich following. 'When one is on horseback seven or eight hours a day, under a burning sun, on a perfectly white road in the midst of 25,000 men and 6000 cannon etc, one has a foretaste of the delights of one of Lucifer's courtyards,' he wrote from Saarburg on 2 July to his daughter Marie. 'Every moment a man or horse falls, dead or dying, one from apoplexy and the other from that noble spirit which makes a horse go on pulling till he dies.' Ten days later he was in Paris and went to the Opera, where he was amused to hear the King cheered. He felt a certain nostalgia —'I was back in my box as if I had been eight years younger.' Blücher gave him dinner at St Cloud; strolling through the palace afterwards, old 'Marshal Vorwärts' commented, 'That man must have been a regular fool to leave all this and go running off to Moscow.'

If Metternich was no admirer of the French at this moment, he did not go as far as the Prussians, who tried to blow up the Pont de Jena because it commemorated their defeat. Blücher and Hardenberg wanted not just Alsace-Lorraine and the Saarland, but Burgundy and Franche Comté. To be fair, the war was not over until the last Napoleonic garrison, Longwy, surrendered in September after 400 Prussians were killed during the siege.

Despite the 'ravings of the Prussians' (a phrase of their former compatriot Gentz), the imperturbable Castlereagh talked them into a reasonable peace settlement, warmly supported by Metternich. The Tsar, 'in a cordial, contented, and reasonable disposition' according to the British foreign secretary, was now 'disposed to keep the Jacobins at arm's length'. This was due to the influence of a pious lady from Livonia, Lord Castlereagh reporting to his prime minister, Lord Liverpool, that since the Autocrat of all the Russians had come to Paris 'he has passed a part of every evening with Madame de Krüdener, an old fanatic'. The second Treaty of Paris was signed in November. France was reduced to the frontiers of 1790, losing Savoy, and was to be occupied for three years besides paying the Allies an indemnity of 700 million francs; in addition she had to restore the art treasures looted during Napoleon's campaigns.

In acknowledgement of Metternich's services the Allies presented him with the former abbey of Johannisberg on the Rhine, which grew the best hock in the Rheingau. It was a graceful recompense for the loss of his ancestral patrimony. Emperor Francis gave him the right to quarter the arms of Austria-Lorraine, together with a large sum from Austria's share of the French indemnity, and Alexander presented him with an annuity of 50,000 francs.

On 26 September, two months before Metternich left France, the Tsar had held a great review of the Russian army on the plain of Vertus near Épernay, at which 150,000 troops marched past. 'That day was the finest of my life,' Alexander told Baroness Krüdener. It was also the day on which the Tsar proclaimed his brainchild, the 'Act of the Holy Alliance'. Signed by Russia, Austria and Prussia a fortnight before, it stated that 'the three consenting monarchs will remain united by the bonds of a true and indivisible fraternity and, regarding each other as fellow-countrymen, will, on all occasions and in all places, lend each other aid and assistance.' Soon it was signed by every European ruler save for the Pope, the Sultan of Turkey and the Prince Regent—though the latter wrote to express his entire sympathy.

At first Metternich saw little practical use in the agreement, persuading his Emperor to sign it only to avoid upsetting the Tsar. He told Francis that the act was no more than an 'empty, echoing monument'. Both were convinced that Alexander was quite mad; he invited the Austrian foreign minister to dine, together with Mme Krudener and one other—the fourth place being laid 'for our Lord Jesus Christ'. Castlereagh too thought it a 'piece of sublime mysticism and nonsense'. Yet behind the act lay the Tsar's not unworthy dream of a united Europe.

More important was the renewal of the Grand Alliance of Chaumont by the second Treaty of Paris. This bound the four great powers to take joint action should France restore Napoleon or try to enlarge her frontiers, committing them to intervention if there was a revolution. The 'High Contracting Powers' agreed to meet regularly to discuss measures for preserving peace.

Few observers (except Gentz) realized quite how much the Vienna settlement of 1814–15 had been shaped by Metternich. At one level it reflected his vision of a united Europe whose five great powers lived in constructive harmony; at another level it reflected his concept of Central Europe as a community of states, German and Italian, grouped around two powers, Austria and Prussia—a firm alliance between Vienna and Berlin would discourage any aggression by France or Russia. Instead of the old *Reich* he had created a federal union, to hinder the emergence of a new, warlike world power. As Srbik stresses, the *Deutsche Bund* appeared to most contemporaries as 'the start of a new brotherhood of nations, a lasting union for peace between states'. (A plan for a '*Lega Italica*', modelled on the Germanic Confederation, on which Metternich is known to have been working in autumn 1814, was rejected by the Italian Princes.)

The settlement's overriding concern was peace—unlike that of Versailles in 1919, when thirst for revenge ensured a Second World War. It was this absence of any hint of retribution, demonstrated by refusal to take Alsace-Lorraine from France, which makes it so impressive.

10

Saviour of Europe

> Kings have to calculate the chances of their very existence in the immediate future; passions are let loose, and league together to overthrow everything which society respects as the basis of its existence; religion, public morality, laws, customs, rights, and duties, are all attacked, confounded, overthrown, or called in question.
>
> METTERNICH to the Tsar, 15 December 1820

> Kings will be tyrants from policy, when subjects are rebels from principle.
>
> EDMUND BURKE,
> *Reflections on the Revolution in France*

The months immediately after the second Treaty of Paris were the zenith of Metternich's career. So far he had achieved almost everything for which he had hoped and was the most admired man in Christendom. Yet, as he saw it, his life's work was only just beginning, a challenge bewildering in its complexity—the preservation of Restoration Europe.

At forty-eight his once plump face had grown long and narrow, due to the extraction of his molars, while his hair had receded, turning grey, almost white. In the portrait painted by Lawrence in 1818 the impression is of a languid, amiable aristocrat, but he had instructed the painter to remove his sardonic expression; also absent are tired blue eyes—he suffered regularly from eye strain. The glossy self-satisfaction remarked on by hostile critics may not have been so obvious in real life, since Lawrence invariably gave sitters the same glossiness.

Admittedly Metternich had much to be pleased about. He had

built his powerful Central Europe. Austria now ruled more territory than she had in 1792. She had secured all Galicia, her borders extending as far as Russia. Not only had she recovered Trieste, formerly her sole port, but Venice as well, together with the entire Dalmatian coast, so that she was free to expand down the Adriatic. She dominated all Germany outside Prussia; the federal *Bundestag* was little more than an assembly of diplomats whose president was invariably the Austrian ambassador, while Austrian influence was asserted by envoys in every German capital. The relationship with Berlin was excellent. Besides controlling the Habsburg territories in Italy, Austrian troops garrisoned a string of fortresses in the Papal States and occupied Naples.

However, Austria's armed might was an illusion. 'She has reduced her military resources even beyond the limits that prudence allows,' wrote Gentz. 'She has neglected her army in all respects.' He adds that the Monarchy possessed insufficient funds or sources of credit to wage a full-scale war—'Everything conspires to fasten Austria to systematic peace.'

Accompanied by Floret, Metternich left Paris on 20 November for a working holiday in Italy, where they were to join the Emperor at Venice. During the journey, which took a fortnight, he had time to reflect on his plans. His carefully thought out strategy is worth examining in detail.

He was determined that a French Revolution and a Napoleon should never plague Europe again. The former was 'the volcano which must be extinguished, the gangrene which must be burnt out, the hydra with jaws open to swallow the social order'. He had seen it arouse hysterical expectations drowned in blood, and the ensuing 'saviour' turn into a tyrant whose ambition had caused the death of millions.

Srbik supplies a basic definition of Metternich's political creed:

> a world doctrine which saw the new century and its forces as hostile, a doctrine heir to the international attitude of pre-Revolutionary days, which was at the same time a classic expression of the ultra-conservative thought of the Restoration era.

Henry Kissinger qualifies this by stressing that Metternich was a conservative, not a reactionary.

However, Kissinger goes too far in portraying Metternich as a survivor of the Enlightenment waging a lonely battle in an uncomprehending new century, as 'an intellectual contemporary of Kant and Voltaire'. He ignores the mental climate of the Restoration, dismissing his Catholicism. 'Metternich was not irreligious,' he writes, 'but he admired the Church more for its utility and its civilising influence than for its "truth".' He turns Metternich into a political philosopher, although Metternich's pretensions to treat politics as a science and references to 'immutable laws' must never be taken too seriously. Above all, Kissinger's excessive emphasis on Metternich's rationalism obscures a natural affinity with Edmund Burke. His conservatism was based no less on history than the Irishman's, if it was European rather than British history. He agreed wholeheartedly with such Burkian maxims as 'People will not look forward to posterity who have no time for their ancestors' and 'You can never shape the future by the present.' Metternich adopted many of Burke's ideas reformed; where Burke had seen revolution as violating Britain's historical constitution, the Austrian saw it as destroying the traditional structure of Christian Europe.

From 1815 until the late 1820s, Metternich's views were very fashionable. Tradition and the past had become a popular craze, fuelled by the novels of Sir Walter Scott, which were translated into every European language. Catholicism revived, the upper classes abandoning Voltairean free-thinking and rediscovering a religion which was fiercely antagonistic towards the new doctrines. The liberals (to use a later term) hated the Church even more than monarchy because of its belief in original sin, that human nature was flawed and no moral progress could be achieved without clerical guidance. The liberal version of legitimacy was the sovereignty of the people, who had the right—indeed, duty—to rebel against monarchs who would not give them constitutions.

Chateaubriand's *Génie du Christianisme,* harnessing something very like Rousseau's appeal to emotion, made religion attractive to Romantics. Two formidable if eccentric political thinkers, the Vicomte de Bonald and the Comte de Maistre, were widely read as 'prophets of the past' who argued fluently for a traditional and hierarchical society, their ideological base being ultramontane Catholicism, their solution partnership between 'Throne and Altar'. Joseph de Maistre condemned both the Enlightenment and the Revolution as Satanic. If many German writers were nationalists, others were attracted by the Holy Alliance, such as Adam Müller, a convert to Catholicism who advocated a neomedievalist society buttressed by Church and aristocracy, championing traditional as opposed to natural rights. A close friend of Gentz, he was a keen supporter of Metternich, who made him consul at Leipzig. Müller's friend, the literary historian Friedrich von Schlegel, was appointed editor of the semi-official *Österreichischer Beobachter* besides serving as counsellor at the Austrian embassy at Frankfurt. Another supporter was the Swiss Carl Ludwig von Haller, a Catholic convert and former professor of law at Bern, whose *Restauration der Staatswissenschaft* (1824) gave the period its name. A disciple of Bonald, he wrote to refute Rousseau's social doctrines and to 'crush the Jacobin reptile'. However, he never belonged to what has been called 'Metternich's stable of conservative ideologues', since he was not entirely trusted—he had implied that governments might be resisted in certain circumstances.

Müller and Schlegel joined forces with Gentz and the Austrian foreign minister in contributing articles not only to the *Beobachter* but to the *Wiener Jahrbücher der Literatur* and the *Augsburger Allgemeine Zeitung*. Metternich took ideas from all three men, many of them communicated by Gentz. However, he regarded religion as the ultimate ally in his battle against revolution. 'I read one or two chapters of the Bible every day and discover new beauties daily,' he wrote to Nesselrode in 1817. He confessed to having once been an atheist, but 'now I believe and make no more criticisms'. (He added that the Bible he used was Luther's translation, 'the best done in any country into a living language'.)

Having reconstructed Europe, he hoped to do the same with the Monarchy. For many years it was assumed that he meant to build a federal Austria, but recently Dr Alan Sked, after examining Metternich's notes for 1817, has concluded that he wanted to centralise it, behind 'a constitutional façade which would have appeared to give a voice to local interests'; he had been 'tempted to balance appearance against reality in domestic affairs'. Sked cites the view of the Hungarian historian Erzsébet Andics that 'one of the fundamental aims . . . of Metternich's proposals was in reality to take away from Hungary her ancient rights; not, however, to endow other peoples with similar rights'. Yet it has to be said that Metternich learnt to live with Hungary's ancient rights, while his outburst to Count Hübner in 1848 (see p 222–224) seems to argue against Sked's interpretation; Metternich would have had to be very optimistic indeed to hope to 'balance appearance against reality' during that year. He was to tell Hübner in 1850 '*Zentralisation ohne Despotismus ist eine Fantasmagorie*' and he did not believe in despotism.

Metternich accepted that all the Monarchy's peoples were entitled to keep their languages and traditions. He wished to preserve the local Diets, which embodied 'reasonable, long-existing differences sanctioned by speech, climate, manners and customs in the various regions of the Monarchy'. It may be, as Sked argues, that originally he intended to give them institutional personalities without political powers. Even so, as he himself suggested in 1848, such a structure could have been developed politically. Had his proposals been implemented, a Danubian confederation might exist today in place of the chaos which looms in Central Europe.

When he reached Mestre in the early morning of 4 December, it was raining and the boat taking him into the city was caught in one of the frightening little storms which strike the lagoon in winter. Depression provoked the comment, 'Venice resembles one vast ruin.' He found Francis delighted at being welcomed so warmly; what the Venetians were really cheering was the revival of seaborne trade. Francis's courtiers were bored—'There is nothing to do'—but his foreign minister was busy with the fate of northern Italy. 'These lands must be ruled from here and their government must be . . . represented at Vienna,' Metternich urged Francis in a memorandum of 29 December, when they were at Milan proposing a semi-independent state under a Habsburg Viceroy. The police minister Count Saurau opposed the idea, arguing that Lombardy-Venetia should be Germanised; even Gentz wrote from Vienna to disagree with his patron. The Emperor listened to Saurau and made him civil governor of Milan. Some observers thought that the foreign minister was facing dismissal. However, Francis then appointed a Viceroy, Archduke Anton, with very limited powers.

When Metternich returned to Vienna in May after spending the winter in Italy with the Emperor, he was exhausted and collapsed with a 'fever'. His eyes were so inflamed that the doctors feared he might lose his sight. Gentz informed Wessenberg that 'Metternich is said to be very badly run down indeed and thoroughly depressed. He does not dare to read, to write, to go out into the sunlight, to drink, to make love . . .' His eyes continued to give cause for alarm until he found an excellent occulist, Dr Friedrich Jäger.

He had further cause for misery in 1816 at the death of the young Countess Julie Zichy. A Hungarian and the wife of one of Metternich's closest friends, she was one of Vienna's leading hostesses and known as 'The Celestial Beauty'. Metternich had fallen in love with her during the last wretched stages of his affair with Wilhelmine de Sagan; she converted him to her own ardent Catholicism and the romance remained chaste. 'She died the death of a saint,' he wrote two years later. 'She left me a little sealed box; opening it, I found the ashes of my letters, with a ring she had broken . . . My life ended then, I had no wish to go on living.'

He had to go on working. There were alarming reports from Italy, where the liberal secret society known as the *Carbonari* was plunging Naples into anarchy and spreading northward fast. In Germany nationalist student fraternities known as *Burschenschaften* were causing concern. The Monarchy's finances were still thoroughly unhealthy; English subsidies had stopped, but not the need for an expensive defense budget. He had take part in the work on currency reform, going through column after column of figures despite his poor eyesight.

His grasp of foreign affairs remained as wide and vigorous as ever. His proposal in 1817 that the Knights of Malta be given Tangiers for their new headquarters and entrusted with policing the Mediterranean shows his ability to baffle both contemporaries and historians. Russia was seeking a naval base in the western

Mediterranean, while Britain wanted a free hand to deal with North African pirates. Gentz refused to believe that Metternich was serious, suspecting that the proposal was a smokescreen. 'He would deliberately arrange for everything to be swallowed up in a discussion which was deliberately made complex and interminable' is the comment of Bertier de Sauvigny, one of the best among Metternich's modern historians. But was he really being insincere? Admittedly at the Congress of Vienna he had ignored the Knights' envoys, Commendatore Berlinghieri and Cavaliere Miari, when they pleaded for another Mediterranean island on which to build a hospital and from where they could continue the crusade against the infidel. Yet in 1816 he was promoted Bailiff Grand Cross by Lieutenant-Master de Giovanni and he always encouraged his family to join the Order of Malta. As for the idea being fanciful, it is said that as late as the 1950s General Franco contemplated offering Ibiza to the Knights.

Metternich paid a second visit to Italy in June 1817, still far from well; Dr Jäger went with him. The ostensible reason for the trip was to escort Francis's daughter Archduchess Leopoldine, to Leghorn, where she would take ship to join her husband, the future Emperor of Brazil, but his real purpose was to inspect Italy. This time, like so many Germans, he fell in love with its landscape and climate though not its inhabitants. He wrote to Eleanor that while a Tuscan afternoon was too hot, 'the morning, the evening and the night are like what a day in Paradise will probably be'. Everywhere he went—Venice, Florence, Lucca—he was in raptures. Dr Jäger made him take a course of baths at Lucca, which seemed to do some good. Then he visited the little Habsburg capitals of Parma and Modena; at the former the Duchess Marie Louise gave a memorable banquet in his honour.

On returning to Vienna, however, Metternich again collapsed. He had come home for the marriage in September of his favourite daughter Marie to Count Josef Esterházy, brother of the Austrian ambassador in London. During the wedding breakfast at the Kaunitz, he fainted.

Nonetheless, on 27 October he began to send the Emperor a scheme for reforming the Monarchy's entire system of government.

He wished to replace the *Kabinettsweg* system, by which Francis consulted ministers haphazardly, with a *Staatsrat* or advisory council, the decisions to be taken by the Emperor with his *Ministerkonferenz* or council of ministers. Metternich also proposed the establishment of a Ministry of the Interior and a Ministry of Justice. Most important of all was the proposal to set up four new chancelleries—for Austria, Bohemia-Moravia and Galicia, Illyria-Dalmatia and Italy—which would join those for Hungary and Transylvania, already in existence. He also suggested the creation of a *Reichsrat*, composed of delegates from the regional Diets, with a consultative function. Francis appointed three of the chancelleries and a Ministry of Justice, in the person of the unloved Count Saurau, but ignored most of the scheme—notably the *Reichsrat.*

A week later Metternich handed in his report on the condition of Italy, which expressed concern about the secret societies, though adding that they had no effective leaders. He spoke bluntly in the report of northern Italy's fear that the Emperor wished to Germanise it: 'Italians see daily the appointment of German magistrates.' Even so, the province could easily be conciliated by appointing Italians to official posts and by winning over influential writers and clerics. Francis acted on some though not all of Metternich's suggestions. Archduke Anton (the Grand Master of the Teutonic Knights, who had no interest in Italy) was replaced as Viceroy by Archduke Rainer, who possessed a Piedmontese wife and undertook to hold court at Milan and Venice alternately; a Lombard, Count Mellerio, was appointed to head the Italian chancellery at Vienna; and Italian remained the official language.

Metternich was convinced that the rest of the peninsula should stay divided into small states, though not until 1847 did he comment, '*Italien ist einer geographischer Begriff.*' (Ironically, the Italy of autonomous regions which has developed since 1945 is much nearer Metternich's concept than the Italy of the Risorgimento.) Italians needed disunity 'to plunge their hands into public funds, and take what salaries and pensions they want'. In 1833 Metternich observed, 'The régime which still corresponds most closely to the opinions of today's Italians is general administrative disorder.' Their rulers stubbornly opposed his call to join in an Italian confederation on the German model, so that he had to fall back on military alliances with Tuscany and Naples. The Neapolitans were not entirely well disposed. Given to understand that His Highness Prince Metternich would not be averse to a Neapolitan dukedom, after much delay they announced that King Ferdinand had bestowed on him the title 'Ducca de Macaroni'. It took months of angry remonstrance before the name was changed to Portella.

It has been suggested that Metternich regarded Germany too as no more than a geographical expression; admittedly he saw the Germanic confederation as an association of European rather than German states. Yet he was perfectly sincere when referring to 'the Fatherland'. Beyond question, he thought of Germany as a nation, but in cultural, not political, terms, fully accepting the unity imposed by the cultural and artistic heritage. For him political unification implied the triumph of Prussian values, which in his day meant liberalism as well as militarism, besides the end of Austrian hegemony. He encouraged the Princes to revive the old consultative 'estates' of local nobles, clergy and burghers, while fiercely resisting the granting of constitutions based on popular sovereignty.

In practise Vienna and Berlin ran the Germanic confederation between them, though the Monarchy, with thirty million subjects as opposed to Prussia's ten million, was very much the senior partner. Nevertheless, Metternich always treated Prussia's envoy to the confederation with the utmost tact; before every meeting to the federal Diet (*Bundestag*) he arranged with him what business should be discussed. Even so, to begin with, Metternich did not entirely trust King Frederick William, fearing that he might replace the eight Prussian *Landtage* (regional estates) by a single national assembly.

Meanwhile, the student fraternities, the *Burschenschaften,* had spread from the University of Jena in Saxe-Weimar to fifteen other universities. Their inspiration was the heady nationalism which Germany had known during the War of Liberation, and their members duelled, drank and sang—harmless enough activities. But in October 1817, on the anniversary of Luther posting up his theses and of the battle of Leipzig, 30 professors and 800 students marched in procession to the Wartburg. A student made a fiery speech, claiming that after the defeat of the French, a 'meeting of despots' had established 'a system of brigandage and injustice', urging his hearers to swear that they would die rather than suffer tyranny. The crowd responded with shouts of 'Long live liberty!' and 'Down with the tyrants and their traitor ministers!' A bonfire was lit and, thrown onto it with manure forks as symbols of reaction, were the acts of the Congress of Vienna with 'Legitimist books', a police manual, a corporal's swagger stick, and a pigtail.

Not only university students but Princes were giving cause for alarm, above all the septuagenarian Charles Augustus, Grand Duke of Saxe-Weimar—once Goethe's patron. Besides granting a constitution based on popular sovereignty in 1816, he allowed freedom of the press. King Maximilian of Bavaria followed suit in 1818, as did the King of Württemberg the year after.

In 1818 Gentz put on paper the fear which inspired his patron until the very end:

> All European countries, without exception, are tormented by a burning fever, the companion or forerunner of the most violent convulsions which the civilised world has seen since the fall of the Roman Empire. It is a struggle, it is war to the death between old and new principles, and between the old and a new social order . . . the equilibrium of authority is threatened; the most solid institutions are threatened, like the buildings in a city trembling from the first shocks of an earthquake which in a few instants will destroy it. If in this dreadful crisis, the principle sovereigns of Europe were disunited in principles and intentions; if one approved what the others condemned; if but one among them looked on the embarrassments of his neighbours as a means of advancing his own interests, or if he regarded the whole prospect with blind or criminal indifference; if in short, the eyes of all were not open to the revolutions which are preparing, and the means which remain to them for preventing or retarding the explosion, we should all be carried away in a very few years.

The Tsar, exceptionally complex even by Russian standards, gave constant cause for concern. He possessed great intelligence and even greater imagination, together with a well-attested personal magnetism; none of his contemporaries ever made the error of taking him for a mediocrity, let alone a fool. Yet his many talents were undermined by an inherent indiscipline and instability—he never quite knew what he wanted. The fact that he had nearly a million men under arms (in theory) made him particularly alarming. Gentz declared in 1818 that nothing could stand up to the first onslaught of such an army.

Alexander's vain and unpredictable character was reflected in his foreign policy. In Germany his agents encouraged the liberal Princes and the Jacobin students, but in Spain they supported the bigoted tyranny of Ferdinand VII. They offered to sell Russian warships to the Spanish navy for use against the South American rebels; in part this was done to provoke Britain, who was most anxious that Spain should not recover her colonies and once more challenge British commerce in the New World. The Tsar's policies produced deep and widespread uneasiness. In a memorandum of 10 June 1818 the Austrian ambassador to Paris, Baron Vincent, wrote (in terms anticipating the Cold War) that St Petersburg was seeking to dominate all Europe

> by affecting the language of moderation, by veiling the preparation of a great permanent military force under a display of evangelical abnegation, and by employing in turn the language of mysticism and of inspiration for the support of its maxims of government.

A month later Metternich was disturbed by Alexander's announcement that he intended to improve the lives of his Polish peasants—the Austrians feared the Tsar might cause an uprising which could spread to Galicia.

Alexander's assistant foreign minister, Gian Antonio Capo d'Istria, was seen as a very dangerous man. By origin an Italian from Dalmatia, he had been born in Corfu, where his father was a doctor, and he had studied medicine at Padua, after which he became a minister in the short-lived Ionian Republic of the Seven Islands. When it was occupied by the French he had entered the Russian diplomatic service, where his abilities so impressed the Tsar that he began to supplant Nesselrode, whom Alexander thought too close to the Austrians. His earlier career had committed him to constitutionalism and Greek nationalism, and he was a friend of Prince Ypsilanti, a Graeco-Roumanian officer in the Russian army. As soon as Capo d'Istria's appointment as assistant foreign minister was announced, the Hetaeria, the Greek patriot society, began to make overtures to him.

Metternich was increasingly anxious for another congress. Fortunately, the second Treaty of Paris had provided for a review of France's situation by the Quadruple Alliance after three years. In the summer of 1817 the Tsar agreed that a meeting should take place in the following autumn, at Aix-la-Chapelle.

Castlereagh was just as concerned. He had been receiving dispatches from the British Embassy at St Petersburg, which spoke of Russian xenophobia and feelings of inferiority, especially towards Britain. In May 1817 he nonetheless politely rejected Metternich's offer of a secret pact between Austria and Britain against Russia, arguing that it would only be necessary to take action against the Russians if they became 'a real and obvious danger'. Although most British politicians distrusted Metternich and disliked what they considered to be meddling abroad, the Duke of Wellington, commander-in-chief of the army of occupation, had reported growing bitterness in France, together with rumours of a projected Franco-Russian alliance.

Still not fully restored to health, Metternich took a short holiday in preparation for the congress. In July 1818 he went to Carlsbad in Bohemia, accompanied by Dr Staudenheim, a strict disciplinarian who made him go to bed supperless. However, the patient was in excellent spirits. He informed Eleanor that Mme Catalani, a diva whose singing he much admired, was at the spa and was going to give a concert; the orchestra's leader had been there for three years curing a liver complaint, while Prince Biron, who played the clavichord, invariably told lies except when he said he played it badly; a Saxon colonel was first violin, a Prussian captain second violin and a Prussian general cello.

Then he drove to Königswart, where he learnt of his father's death; in a letter to his mother he claims that he had never given Franz-Georg a moment's unhappiness.

At the end of July he set out for his new estate of Johannisberg. En route he visited the Prince of Hesse Homburg, who consulted Staudenheim about 'a disease which Staudenheim says is flying gout, but which in the Prince's case looks like almost anything—meaning that it strongly resembles insanity'. He adds,

> The point on which negotiations between doctor and sick man broke down was the sick man's breakfast. The Prince did not want to forego the half-yard of sausage on which he normally starts the day. Then Staudenheim flew into a rage, the Prince began to swear, and they appeared to have the sausage by both ends, each struggling to wrest it from the other. Staudenheim ended by carrying off the sausage and the cure is about to commence . . .

Johannisberg delighted him when he arrived there in the evening.

> I came early enough to see from my balcony twenty leagues along the Rhine, eight or ten towns, a hundred villages, and vineyards which this year will yield twenty millions of wine, interspersed by meadows and fields like gardens, beautiful oak woods, and an immense plain covered with trees which bend beneath the weight of delicious fruit.

The abbey could be made into a fine château. He was charmed by the priest who managed the estate and did not drink, judging the wine entirely by his nose. He spent a day at Johannisberg nearby, writing to his mother that their old house was dilapidated and filthy, its riding school demolished and the garden a field; almost all their old friends had gone. He was consoled by Johannisberg, and sorry to have to leave it so soon.

When he entered Cologne on his way to Aix-la-Chapelle (once the Imperial capital), he was mistaken for the Emperor. Bells rang and the crowd attempted to take the horses out of the carriage shafts. 'I was furious and Gentz trembled in every limb.' (Gentz had joined him at Bonn.) At the house where he was staying the women insisted on kissing him, crying how they hated being ruled by Prussians. 'I realized that my efforts were futile in the face of such determination, and delivered myself up to their kisses with heroic abandon.' At last, however, the Emperor arrived at his own house, two doors away, and the crowd and the kissing moved farther on.

Metternich's relationship with Francis has baffled many historians. Viktor Bibl argued fluently but mistakenly that the Emperor was the author of Metternich's policies; in reality Francis never had an original idea in his life. He admired his foreign minister until the day he died and would never have allowed him to resign. Yet if he usually agreed with Metternich on foreign affairs, his attitude towards internal affairs was often obstructive; sometimes he tried to steer a middle course between his advice and that of other ministers or else he simply ignored the issue. Srbik quotes an instance of the foreign minister's irritation with his 'august master': the Emperor, Metternich wrote, 'handles matters as though he were a drill, penetrating deeper and deeper, till suddenly, to his immense surprise, he comes through on the other side having done nothing except bore a hole in the memorandum'. However, Metternich fully accepted that his survival in office depended on Francis: 'If he overwhelms me with kindnesses, if he has confidence in me, it's because I go along the road he wants. Should I have the misfortune to stray away from that road, then Prince Metternich would not be foreign minister of Austria for another twenty-four hours.'

The two men genuinely liked each other. In old age Metternich would recall how on some evenings the Emperor had played the cello while he himself played the violin. 'At times the joint performance was somewhat halting and would not exactly have been a feast for the ear had anyone else been there to listen.'

When monarch and minister rode together to Aix-la-Chapelle in the autumn of 1818, it must still have seemed that everyone agreed with Metternich in believing that what Europe needed was '*le plus grand des bien-faits, le répos*'.

11

Europe United: The Congress System, 1818–22

What characterises the modern world, and distinguishes it fundamentally from the ancient, is the tendency of nations to grow closer to each other and enter into a league of some form.

METTERNICH, *Memoirs*

Perhaps never again has European unity been so much a reality as between 1815 and 1821 . . .

HENRY KISSINGER, *A World Restored*

Metternich's capture of what became known as the Congress System was arguably an even greater triumph than outwitting Napoleon Bonaparte. He did so almost imperceptibly at Aix, transforming the system into a weapon against revolution. For the next five years he more or less kept control of the system.

The Congress System was the first true attempt at European unity. It had emerged partly from the military alliance forged at Teplitz in 1813 and partly from the mystical dreaming of the Tsar in 1815. Its real foundation, however, was the sixth article of the second Treaty of Paris:

> The High Contracting Powers have agreed to renew at fixed intervals, either under their own auspices or by their representative minister, meetings consecrated to great common objects . . . and for the maintenance of peace in Europe.

In Gentz's words, the system was 'the last attempt to provide the transparent soul of the Holy Alliance with a body.' Its functions were to prevent wars and revolutions, and it was based on a general recognition that no state's survival should ever be threatened even if small, local wars of a fire-brigade nature might sometimes be needed to quell disorders or adjust minor disputes. But everyone hoped that all quarrels could be settled by negotiation at the periodic meetings by foreign ministers of the great powers.

Admittedly any comparison between the European unity of the first quarter of the nineteenth century and that of the last decade of the twentieth must not be taken too far. As Henry Kissinger stresses,

> When the unity of Europe came to pass it was not because of the self evidence of its necessity, as Castlereagh had imagined, but through a cynical use of the conference machinery to defend a legitimising principle of social repression; not through Castlereagh's good faith, but through Metternich's manipulation.

Even so, whatever reservations must be made, it was a remarkable achievement, a landmark in European history.

The little city of Aix, normally a quiet watering place, had never seen so many distinguished visitors, even in Carolingian times. They included the Emperor, the Tsar, the King of Prussia and an army of German Princes, every one of whom had brought his minister for foreign affairs. In addition there was the French prime minister, the Duc de Richelieu, together with the British foreign secretary Lord Castlereagh, the Duke of Wellington and Mr George Canning—who would one day destroy the entire system. In emulation of Vienna there were balls, fireworks displays, balloon ascents and concerts by Metternich's favourite soprano, Angelica Catalini. There was also, he grumbled to Eleanor, an infant prodigy—a boy of four and a half who played the double bass excruciatingly. There were numerous balls at which his daughter Marie Esterházy had a dazzling success; the Emperor, the Tsar and the Prussian King all danced with her. Castlereagh's fat wife gave receptions once a week. 'I can't avoid mentioning the unimaginable sense of boredom inflicted by visiting that establishment,' the Austrian foreign minister observed unkindly of poor Lady Castlereagh's soirées. 'Everybody spurns milady's charms and has established themselves in my drawing room.' He himself gave a party every evening, but his letters give the impression that he took little interest in the congress's social life.

He could not help laughing at the fascinated interest which he aroused. When his sovereign and he were confined to bed by colds he suspected that 'the whole city thinks the Kaiser and I have avoided a party [given by the King of Prussia] for political reasons of the most profound nature. We must see that they go on believing this and to keep the delusion I am going to behave today as though I were perfectly well.' He was no less diverted by a report that he had been seriously injured in a coach accident, remaining unconscious for many hours. 'All the English papers have correspondents here; they must write something and, having nothing to say about the progress of affairs, they amuse themselves by killing off the ministers.'

He had not come for amusement. The congress's principal business was to discuss 'the internal state of France'. The French government had paid off most of the indemnity and borrowed the remainder from Baring, Hope and other British bankers. The four great powers swiftly agreed that all Allied troops should leave French soil by 30 November. A protocol was signed by which Austria, Britain, Russia and Prussia admitted France to 'the System which has given Peace to Europe and which alone can insure its duration'. In consequence the Quadruple Alliance became the 'Concert of Five'.

Tsar Alexander behaved with his usual bewildering unpredictability. He was losing his Jacobin sympathies. He told the Duc de Richelieu, the French prime minister, that nine tenths of the French were violent revolutionaries and that with France in so precarious a condition it was stupid for her to join the Alliance. Yet he made no opposition to her doing so. His request that Spain too be admitted to the Concert was rejected, as were nearly all his other suggestions—including the offer of his army to put down revolution. He also proposed the creation of a European army, with its headquarters at Brussels and the Duke of Wellington as commander-in-chief. However, this remarkable foreshadowing of NATO was rejected, being seen as an attempt to establish a Russian military presence in Western Europe. Despite these refusals, he remained full of goodwill, enthusiastically committed to European unity.

Ironically, the system was undermined by the very success of the Aix problem. With the French problem solved, few Englishmen could see any point in England being represented at such meetings. Only Castlereagh was convinced of their value. 'It really appears to me to be a new discovery in the European Government, at once extinguishing the cobwebs with which diplomacy obscures the horizon' was his view. The meetings gave to the counsels of the great powers 'the efficiency and almost the simplicity of a single state'.

Castlereagh's opinion was born out by the way in which so many lesser questions were settled at Aix. Mediatised German Princes recovered some of their privileges, rulings were given on disputed successions, the Elector of Hesse was not allowed to turn himself into a King. The rights of German and Austrian Jews were confirmed. A plea from Napoleon's mother for the release of her son from St Helena was rejected on the grounds that he must have dictated the letter. Negatively, there was failure to secure cooperation on measures to suppress the slave trade or to deal with the pirates of North Africa. Even so, the congress acted as a species of European supreme court, so much so that the King of Sweden accused it of 'dictatorship'. On 15 November the five powers affirmed 'their invariable resolution never to depart, either among themselves or in their relations with other states, from the strictest observation of the principles of the law of nations; principles, which, in their application to a state of permanent peace, can alone effectually guarantee the independence of each government, and the stability of the general association'.

The Austrian foreign minister's verdict was that 'a prettier little congress never met'. He had begun to rebuild his bridges with the Tsar, by adroit flattery. 'We have found one another again, as in 1813,' he told Eleanor. Observers were astonished to see the two former enemies strolling arm-in-arm. (Marie, who understood her father perfectly, found it very funny.) Metternich sent King Frederick William two secret memoranda warning him of the spread of revolutionary activities in Prussia and dissuading him from granting a constitution. He intended to enlist both monarchs in his counterrevolutionary crusade, whose principal weapon was to be the Congress System.

He was certainly not the 'Robespierre of Conservatism', as more than one modern historian has called him. There was nothing of the zealot in his makeup, and he resigned himself to losing a good deal of the past. 'A new régime can only be made out of new materials, even if they include re-shaped or adapted elements from previous régimes, but it can never take their shape,' he once wrote. For him conservatism meant a strategy of carefully planned actions in defence of the traditional order. The enemy were 'financiers who stop at nothing to ensure their profits, bureaucrats, writers, and the persons who run public education', he told the Tsar in 1820. He added that they recruited very few members of the working class but a fair number of misfits from the upper. The slogan of all these people was, 'Get out, so we can take your place.' Consciously or unconsciously, he was echoing Babeouf, who defined the purpose of the Revolution as '*ôte-toi de là que je m'y mette*'.

He thought much in the same way as Edmund Burke. 'Is our monarchy to be annihilated, with all the laws, all the tribunals, and all the ancient corporations of the kingdom?' Burke had asked. 'Is every landmark of the country to be done away in favour of a geometrical and arithmetical constitution? Is the House of Lords to be voted useless?' Metternich's distrust of capitalists and intellectuals had been encapsulated by Burke. 'They felt with resentment an inferiority, the grounds of which they did not acknowledge,' Burke had written of 'the monied interest' in 1790. 'There was no measure to which they were not willing to lend themselves, in order to be revenged of the outrages of this rival pride, and to exalt their wealth to what they considered as its natural rank and estimation.' Burke prophesied, not altogether accurately, that the new constitutions would exclude landowners from government, replacing them by 'the money manager'. Like Burke,

Metternich saw the landowning aristocracy not only as society's natural rulers but as a buffer between the state and the people. (Nevertheless, he believed that if an aristocracy lost power, as it would in France, then a strongly based, propertied urban middle class might take its place as both hierarchy and buffer.) 'Along with the monied interest, a new description of men had grown up, with whom that interest soon formed a close and marked union; I mean the political men of letters,' Burke had also observed. 'Men of letters, fond of distinguishing themselves, are rarely averse to innovation . . . They become a sort of demagogue. They served as a link to unite, in favour of one object, obnoxious wealth to restless and desperate poverty.' This is how Metternich saw them as well.

Metternich was even more pessimistic than Burke. 'In revolutions those who demand everything always get the better of those ready to bargain,' he remarked in 1831. Extremists must invariably triumph over moderates, totalitarians over liberals. He knew that his world was going to die, and sooner rather than later. 'Our society is on a downward slope,' he acknowledged, writing in 1830 that 'the old Europe is nearing its end'. He thought that its true successor would take a long time to emerge.

There was nothing rigid in the way Metternich used the new in defence of the old, even new men of 'obnoxious wealth'. During the congress at Aix, prompted by Gentz, he invited Karl and Salomon Rothschild to dinner. At that date no Frankfurt burgher would deign to sit down to a meal with the Rothschilds, while even Gentz referred to them as 'vulgar, ignorant Jews, outwardly presentable', but it was in the Monarchy's interest to be on good terms with M. A. Rothschild & Sons. Metternich encouraged them to set up a branch at Vienna, making a friend of Salomon Rothschild—who soon endeared himself by lending the impresario Domenico Barbaia 50,000 gulden with which to lease the *Kärntnertor Theater* and bring Italian opera to the capital. Metternich was responsible for all five brothers being created barons, an excellent investment. Not only did they ensure Austria's financial viability, but more than once they helped Metternich personally; in 1822 they were to lend him nearly a million gulden, though there was never any hint of bribery. He had little sense of money, in matters of state or his own affairs; more than one historian has observed that he placed foreign policy above any considerations of finance.

He responded to Salomon's plea that he should encourage Jewish emancipation, ordering Count Buol, ambassador to the *Bundestag,* to tell the notoriously anti-Semitic Frankfurt senate that it must improve the conditions of Israelites. He also made a point of dining at Amschel Rothschild's house at Frankfurt. In 1822 the senate bowed to his wishes, abolishing the ghetto and giving Jews full municipal rights.

The connection did not go unnoticed by Metternich's enemies, who tried to beat the anti-Semitic drum. Articles attacking the Rothschilds began to appear in the *Frankfurter Allgemeine Zeitung.* After an especially vicious piece in 1822, Metternich banned the paper in Austrian territory. Gentz wrote angrily to the editor that 'the constant attacks on the firm of Rothschild invariably, and sometimes outrageously, reflect on the Austrian government by necessary implication, since everyone knows it is transacting important financial business with the firm, which is not only unimpeachable but honourable and thoroughly respectable'. Eventually the foreign minister's link with the Rothschilds grew so strong that they called him 'Uncle Metternich'.

At Aix Metternich began the strangest romance of his entire life. On 22 October he was introduced to the wife of the Russian ambassador at London, Countess (later Princess) Lieven, at a reception given by Mme Nesselrode. Thirty-four, born Dorothea Benckendorff, she was a Baltic German whose mother came from Württemberg. However, her family had served the Tsars for a century and she had been educated at the Smolny Institute in St Petersburg, while both she and her husband were close to the Imperial family. In England Mme Lieven was a friend of everyone, from the Prince Regent—who was half in love with her—to Castlereagh and the Duke of Wellington, even of the Whig leader Lord Grey. Lawrence (who invariably flattered his sitters) immortalised her as a delicate, gazellelike creature with huge dark eyes; in real life she was a hard-looking woman, thin and bony, with ugly red arms. Yet she clearly possessed enormous charm, a compound of vivacity, intelligence and wit; she had made herself popular in London by introducing the waltz. Her consuming passion was power politics, and her only other great love was to be the French Prime Minister Guizot. For Darya Lieven, Metternich's supreme attraction lay in his being one of the most powerful men in the world.

Metternich must have realized immediately that she was extremely dangerous. In modern language (or the language of yesterday), Darya was a top-level Russian agent, always seeking to influence politicians in favour of Russia, always looking out for vital information; she specialised in being on close terms with world leaders. Yet the foreign minister met a woman who, besides possessing a brilliant mind, shared his interests; to a middle-aged man her understanding of his work and her enthusiasm for it was flattery of an intoxicating sort. Moreover, he knew how to handle women in the enemy camp, as he had shown with Caroline Murat; he was able to distrust without disliking. He would give away nothing which would be of use to St Petersburg.

Until their meeting on 22 October he seems to have known her by sight but ignored her, while she had thought him cold and haughty. The ice was broken three days later when he accompanied the Nesselrodes and the Lievens on an excursion to Spa, where the party spent the night; on the way back he insisted on riding in the same carriage. Later he remembered, 'I began to see why those who described you as "an agreeable woman" were quite right.' The next day he called on her at Aix, spending an hour sitting on the carpet at her feet. On 13 November she found a pretext to return his call without impropriety at the house where he was staying. Saying that she felt feverish, she asked if she might lie down, and they became lovers. The affair was interrupted after a few days, when she had to go to Brussels with her husband. Metternich soon joined her there, on the pretence of 'official business', and they spent four days together. On 27 November the Lievens returned to London. Darya told her family that the Congress at Aix-la-Chapelle had been a great success and that 'I made some interesting acquaintances, of whom I shall always retain a pleasant memory'.

The affair was to be resumed briefly on only two occasions, yet they wrote to each other regularly for nearly eight years. He tells 'Dorothée' in one of his letters that he has had two other 'liaisons' and many affairs. 'I've never been unfaithful; the woman I love is the only woman in the world for me. When I'm not in love I take a pretty woman who wants anything but love.' He writes with passion—'I've found you only to lose you again' . . . 'a man of ice melted when he touched you.' He wishes that she was sitting on his knee. (A vision of the Russian ambassadress sitting on the Austrian minister's lap is irresistible.) On 1 December he sent her his autobiography in miniature in which he describes Eleanor:

> My wife has never been pretty; she is loveable only to those who know her well. Everyone who does loves her; the world finds her disagreeable [*maussade*], which is just what she wants. There is nothing in the world which I would not do for her.

He told Darya that after Julie Zichy's death 'I reached a stage in my life when I thought that I would never be able to fall in love again.'

One wonders what this cold, hard woman made of the frivolous side of the great man's nature. In February 1819 he reports that the burgomaster of Judenburg in Upper Styria had complained to him that mice had been ravaging the fields about the town ever since the French occupation; it was because the troops had dropped bread over the entire countryside. 'I believe that never since the world began has a plague of mice been explained in this way,' Metternich informed Darya. 'There must have been a French camp in Egypt in Pharaoh's day.'

Throughout his affair with Mme Lieven he continued to send his weekly letter to Eleanor. Three days after the affair had begun, he wrote, 'I spend my days working and all I can tell you is that I am wonderfully well and not yet driven out of my mind.' When he was reunited with his children at Vienna he was so exhausted that he confused his two youngest daughters, forgetting who was who.

In March 1819 Metternich set out for Italy again, where he was to join the Emperor Francis on a series of state visits. He took his daughter Marie and Dr Staudenheim with him. He was overwhelmed by Rome—'I was literally terrified at the first glimpse of my accommodation. It is twenty-five magnificent rooms.' He had a long, pleasant audience with the aged Pius VII, discussing the battles they had had with Bonaparte and making the old pontiff laugh. He saw much of Cardinal Consalvi, the secretary of state, whose brilliant diplomacy at the Congress of Vienna had secured the restoration of the Papal States, whom Metternich found most congenial. Yet he told Gentz that now he understood how Martin Luther must have felt. 'As a botanist, you would find great happiness here,' he said, adding, 'What glorious plants! The flowers compare with ours as Rome does with Vienna as a city. I'm bringing a lot back with me and am sending you some beautiful seeds.' As will be seen, there was more to this amiable letter than meets the eye.

Then he travelled down to Naples with the Emperor. The Bay of Naples enchanted him, though not the Neapolitans. He went to the San Carlo every night, hearing eight Rossini operas in succession. Pompei fascinated him, but the fiery crater of Vesuvius pleased him best—'I could scarcely tear myself away from a spectacle so full of indescribable beauty, awesome in a way it is impossible to describe.

Amidst the sightseeing, revolution was never far from Metternich's thoughts. After the conference at Aix, Capo d'Istria had visited Naples, horrifying the royal ministers by the 'Jacobin' tone of his conversation and remarks 'highly abusive of the Austrian Government'; undoubtedly Russians were encouraging the Carbonari to demand a constitution. However, the British envoy to Tuscany, Sir Robert Gordon, met Metternich in Rome and reported that Metternich was much too worried about Russian agents. In Gordon's view, shared by many British observers until the Risorgimento, Italy was in a thoroughly peaceful condition.

The Tsar's conversion to conservatism had not gone unnoticed in Germany. At Mannheim on 23 March August von Kotzebue, a mediocre playwright known to be a Russian agent, was stabbed to death by a theology student, Karl Sand, from the University of Jena. The entire faculty, professors and students alike, was suspected. Gentz wrote frantically to Metternich that 'the revolutionary rabble's hatred of Kotzebue was of long standing, had many causes, and was fostered with devilish art'. The foreign minister was calmer, if accepting that Gentz's fears were 'more reasonable than many others he has had during the last few years'. Metternich agreed that 'Kotzebue's assassination is more than an isolated instance. Gradually this is going to be recognised on all sides, and I won't be the last to make use of it.' Gentz and Adam Müller bombarded Metternich with letters advising that strong action was indispensable, such as stricter control over every university faculty in Germany. But he would not be hurried, waiting to see how the German sovereigns would react. His letter about the Roman flowers had been to stop Gentz from losing his head.

Metternich's instinct was amply justified. Everyone in authority began to fear they might be murdered—even the Grand Duke of Weimar panicked, proposing that all German universities should be supervised, much as Gentz and Müller had proposed. Nothing could be wider of the mark than to suggest, as have some historians, that Metternich wavered. He waited calmly while alarm grew. In June he explained to Gentz that there was no immediate danger from the German universities, the threat from the press being far more serious. What was needed was a conference of the principal German states to discuss measures to deal with the situation; informality was everything. Gentz was ecstatic in his relief—'I see the only man in Germany who can still act freely and firmly.'

As soon as Metternich left Italy in July he went to Teplitz, to meet the King of Prussia. After the Kotzebue affair Frederick William III accepted his views totally. 'Six years ago we could fight the enemy out in the open,' the King admitted. 'Now he sneaks and hides. You know what confidence I have in your opinions. You have been warning me for a long admitted time and everything which you said has come true.' The admission was a triumph for Metternich, as the King had been toying with the idea of granting his subjects a constitution since 1815. In addition, the foreign minister had been well aware that while the 'revolution' was organised openly in Weimar alone, the men behind it were operating from Berlin.

Frederick William agreed that the federal Diet should be used to combat the Jacobins, while on 1 August the Prussian chancellor Prince Hardenberg and the Austrian foreign minister signed the Convention of Teplitz, pledging their countries to joint action. When ministers of the German states assembled at Carlsbad five days later, they were presented with an antirevolutionary programme, which included stricter censorship of books and newspapers, a ban on all political meetings, a purge of professors and students, and surveillance of universities. The *Burschenschaften* were dissolved, Gentz having advised that they were so dangerous that no trace of them must be left. In October the 'Carlsbad Decrees' were approved by the federal Diet. However repressive the decrees may seem, Metternich was undoubtedly justified when, referring to the universities, he warned his Emperor, 'A whole class of future officials, professors and would-be literary men is there, which is ripening for revolution'. He completed his counteroffensive in December with the '*Schlussakte*' (Final Acts), which stressed the power of sovereigns throughout the Confederation and insisted that no parliament must ever be permitted to endanger public order in any German state. Gentz described the *Bund*'s acceptance of these new articles as 'a victory greater than the battle of Leipzig'.

It is only justice to stress that Metternich's dislike of German liberalism stemmed from more than fear that constitutional monarchies might take power away from the aristocracy. He genuinely believed that they were merely preludes to revolution. He was also convinced that they would increase the likelihood of war, especially in Germany—he foresaw nationalist fanatics in these assemblies thundering out demands for the return of Alsace.

Among the liberal 'martyrs' of the Carlsbad Decrees was Ludwig Jahn, a pioneer of group calisthenics and founder of the gymnast movement who believed fervently in the overwhelming worth of the ordinary German *Volk* and detested noblemen and foreigners. Dr Pieter Viereck was among the first to argue (in 1941) that the liberalism of men like Jahn was not quite the same creed as the gentle Anglo-Saxon variety:

> Jahn—and later, Richard Wagner—are the two nineteenth century Germans in whose writings the entire Nazi ideology appears point by point, long before any Treaty of Versailles.

Jahn was the first to use the word '*Volkstum*' (folkdom) so beloved by Hitler and was much admired by Alfred Rosenberg. 'Germany needs a war of her own in order to feel her own power; she needs a feud with Frenchmen to develop her national way of life in all its fullness,' he ranted. 'This occasion will not fail to come.' He was one of the earliest German racialists, writing, 'A state without a *Volk* is nothing, a lifeless frivolous phantom like the vagabond gypsies and Jews.' Anticipating the Führer, he wished to absorb into Germany such blood brothers as the Danes, Dutch and Swiss. His 'gymnasts'—many of whom had been members of the *Freikorps* he had helped to raise in 1813—roamed the streets of their local towns like storm troopers, beating up those who looked 'Un-German'. He was to be lionised by nationalists during the Revolution of 1848, and he would be virtually canonised under the Third Reich.

Jahn had organised and led the Wartburg demonstration in 1817, foreshadowing a more infamous 'burning of the books'. Metternich had complained to Berlin about Jahn's activities in 1818. 'The gymnastic institution is the real training ground for the university mischief,' he wrote. 'The inventor, the invention and the execution come from Prussia.' Another such 'martyr' was a popular professor at Bonn University, Ernst Arndt. Besides the need for constitutions, he preached hatred of the French in his lectures, composing savage songs of vengeance which were roared out by his students. The chancellor was well aware that what he called 'National Jacobins' were different animals from the Carbonari.

A peculiarly unpleasant aspect of German nationalism was its anti-Semitism. In August 1819 news of what was being debated at Carlsbad resulted in riots, during which mobs attacked the Jews of Würzburg, Bamberg, Frankfurt and other cities, looting their houses. Metternich complained to the Frankfurt senate, not for the last time.

Gentz, who possessed a keen nose for political danger, had

been certain the situation was very serious. In July he had warned that the unity of the German confederation might be at stake and that a frightful revolution was threatening all Europe. His master shared his apprehension up to a point—'an entire class of future civil servants, dons and literary men are being trained for revolution'—but was confident that he could handle the crisis. 'By God's help I hope to defeat the German Revolution just as I vanquished the conqueror of the world. The German revolutionaries thought me far away because I was a hundred miles off [in Italy]. They deceive themselves. I shall be back in the middle of them, dealing out blows.' His blows proved so effective that he would have no more trouble from German revolutionaries for a generation.

In a mere three weeks Metternich had secured the adoption throughout Germany of measures he had hoped to bring in since 1813. He succeeded because of the absence of the man whom he privately termed 'that infernal Tsar'. He wrote to Eleanor, 'If the Kaiser thinks he's no longer Emperor of Germany, he's mistaken.' Francis I had more power over the German confederation than ever Joseph II had over the Holy Roman Empire.

Britain was highly critical of the Carlsbad Decrees. Admittedly the cabinet had introduced the 'Six Acts' to put down disturbances of the sort which had recently erupted at Peterloo—including restrictions on political meetings and mild censorship. But the British disapproved of other countries bringing in such measures. Secretly Castlereagh thought that the decrees were justified, but he dared not say so in public. A realist, he accepted that British public opinion was vehemently opposed to putting down revolution in other countries, even if he sympathised with Metternich's position. In May 1820 he drafted a state paper which was redrafted by the cabinet. An ominous sentence declared that the Alliance had never been 'intended as a Union for the government of the world, or for the superintendence of the internal affairs of other states'.

Tsar Alexander's reaction was bewildering. He told Lebzeltern, Austrian ambassador at St Petersburg, that the decrees were needed because of 'the spirit of corruption and immorality which exists in Germany'. Yet almost simultaneously, Capo d'Istria circulated a memorandum in the Tsar's name attacking the decrees as a bid to impose 'the ridiculous pretensions of absolute power'. There was ample reason for Austria to fear Capo d'Istria's influence over Alexander; as a Greek nationalist, he had the ear of an absolute ruler who saw himself as heir to the Byzantine Emperors and dreamt of riding into Constantinople. Metternich believed that if ever the Ottoman Empire disappeared, the Monarchy would soon follow it—which in the end was precisely what happened.

Events seemed to justify Metternich's warnings of danger throughout Europe. Even before the Teplitz meeting with Frederick William, the first minister of Nassau (ironically enough a German state granted a constitution) had been assassinated. In February 1820 the Duc de Berry, Louis XVIII's nephew, was stabbed to death in Paris; shortly after came the discovery of a Bonapartist plot by discontented officers. England was not immune; in February the Cato Street conspirators were caught plotting to murder the cabinet and set up a republic. Southern Europe erupted in the spring; when Ferdinand VII was forced to give the Spaniards a constitution, the Portuguese and Neapolitans followed suit. 'We have come to one of those fatal epochs when one can't count on anything,' observed Gentz grimly.

After his exertions at Carlsbad and Frankfurt, Metternich opened a conference at Vienna to complete the 'great German business'. It lasted until the following May. Its principal achievements were to give to each of the confederation's sovereigns a right of appeal to the Diet for help against a rebellious assembly, and to forbid assemblies to discuss public security. No other German state could hope to defy the Austro-Prussian partnership. As Metternich reminded the Emperor, Austria's word was law throughout Germany.

For much of the Vienna conference Metternich knew that his sixteen-year-old daughter, Clémentine, was dying. 'Nothing breaks me down like a sick child,' he wrote after she had been suffering from bouts of fever for two months. In April he realized, 'We can no longer to hope to save her.' He attended lengthy meetings every day, though occasionally he rebelled—when someone asked him about the 'Rhine tolls' just as he was about to see the doctors, 'I insisted on going, even if the Rhine flowed back to its source.' She died on 11 May 1820. 'Fortunately I have the gift of concealing my feelings even when my heart is half broken,' he confessed in a letter the next day. 'The thirty men with whom I sit at the conference table every day can certainly never have guessed just what I was going through.'

He went off to Königswart by himself. 'It rains here as it always does.' He had gone to arrange for the building of a new family vault, and was grateful for the company of Prince Schönburg, 'a keen sportsman and a cheerful young fellow—a very agreeable guest in a lonely house'. Unusually for a man of his class and time, Metternich himself neither shot nor hunted; he was sorry for the dead game when it was brought in, wondering how people could kill such beautiful creatures. He was so fond of animals that he placed lumps of sugar next to the mouse holes in his library.

On the way back, news reached him from England of Queen Caroline's divorce. 'A really horrible woman,' he remarked. 'If people knew what I do about her they would be amazed by her audacity.' He added that her trial was 'a piece of dirt which one can't touch without defiling oneself'. He thought that 'Castlereagh and company have not behaved very cleverly'.

He returned to Vienna to find another tragedy. Ten weeks after Clémentine's death, Marie—his favourite daughter—died of consumption at twenty-three. 'For many years she has been my best friend' was his epitaph for her. 'Even on the day of my daughter's death I had to sit for six hours in a ministerial meeting and then for another eight at my desk.' Perhaps he was grateful for it. When Clémentine died he had written, 'I soon return to my work which builds a barrier between me and myself.'

Five days before Marie's death on 20 July he had been called away from her bedside by news of 'the Neapolitan catastrophe'. He expected, wrongly, that much blood would flow. 'A semi-barbarous people, of absolute ignorance and boundless credulity, hot blooded as the Africans, a people who can neither read nor write, whose last word is the dagger—such a people offer fine material for constitutional principles!' he observed. Even if he did not understand the Neapolitans and there was little bloodshed, he had reason to worry. He had counted on controlling Italy as he controlled Germany; when her sovereigns refused to join with Lombardy-Venetia in an Italian confederation on the German model, fearing for their independence, he had embarked on a programme of close links with each court individually—the reason for the Emperor's state visits in 1819. If the new Neapolitan ministers were former supporters of Murat, they posed no military threat. Nor was their chaotic régime in any sense a Terror, although some of the Carbonari leaders were murderous enough. However, they detested Austria, removing half of the peninsula from her control. Worse still, the Carbonari began to spread all over Italy and even into France. As Metternich put it at the end of the year, 'The Naples affair threatened Italy, Austria and Europe equally.'

On 21 July Darya Lieven reported what the Duke of Wellington had said to her:

> Devil take me, Prince Metternich must march. He must advance all his troops against Naples. It will be five or six weeks before they are in a position to act. Meanwhile he will warn his allies of what he is going to do. They will give their consent. He must crush this Italian revolution; but he must come out of it with clean hands, do you understand. He can play a splendid part.

However, as Metternich admitted later, 'Our fire-engines were not full in July, otherwise we should have set to work immediately.'

Amid this crisis which required such delicate handling, Metternich remained shattered by the loss of his daughters. He wrote:

> I sit at my desk like some bankrupt in a tavern. *He* drinks to forget the loss of his goods. *I* work to drown my distress of mind . . . I am more of a stranger to myself than the people who pass my window. In the evening, looking at the work I've done, I realize that life is still in me yet in no way do I feel alive.

He suffered from a sense of hopelessness. 'I have to spend my life propping up a mouldering building,' he told Darya. (By 'mouldering building' he meant the Europe restored in 1815, not the Habsburg monarchy—as suggested by some historians.)

At the beginning of September it was agreed that there should be another congress at the end of October, at Troppau in Austrian Silesia (now Czech Opava). 'The issue at Troppau is who is stronger, Alexander or Capo d'Istria' was how Gentz summed up what was at stake. Capo d'Istria still hoped to persuade his employer to use collective intervention to introduce liberal constitutions all over Europe. Arguing that if any revolution were suppressed it must be replaced by 'national independence and political liberty', he was so eloquent that Metternich grew seriously alarmed. Then on 9 November news reached Alexander that the Semenovsky Guards had mutinied at St Petersburg. It was in fact a rebellion against a brutal colonel, but Metternich convinced the Tsar that it was the work of liberal agitators. He noted smugly that Alexander suspected they were trying to panic him into abandoning the congress.

The mutiny was the start of the Tsar's conversion. 'I am on the same footing with him as in 1813, going to see him whenever I want, and we talk for hours together without ever disagreeing,' Metternich reported. They drank tea endlessly. 'If only that aromatic beverage could cure Capo d'Istria's brains!' he joked. 'Good heavens, what a cargo of tea I would have sent from China!' Every day he showed Alexander fresh evidence of underground activity in Italy, warning him that Europe was menaced by a new French Revolution: 'It is in Paris, Sire, that the great furnace exists for the most vast conspiracy that ever threatened society.'

Metternich asserted, indirectly, Austria's right to invade Naples, by declaring that there should be no intervention in another country unless it was in such disorder as to endanger others in close proximity. Capo d'Istria argued that it could only be justified if needed to preserve the 1815 settlement and must take place in the name of all the Allies. He would sanction Austrian occupation of Naples if it upheld political liberty; he commended the French constitution of 1814 in place of the unworkable Spanish model adopted by the Neapolitans. However, there must first be mediation, perhaps by the Papacy.

Austria then insisted that the real question was how to restore King Ferdinand to his rightful powers. Capo d'Istria had to abandon any idea of reconstructing the Neapolitan constitution, outmanoeuvred by Metternich's proposal that Ferdinand should come in person and, as the legitimate ruler of Naples, decide what to do. Lebzeltern, the Austrian ambassador to Russia, succeeded in winning over the Tsar, partly by convincing him that Capo d'Istria's plan was unworkable. Prussia was firmly on Austria's side. A 'Preliminary Protocol' was signed by Austria, Prussia and Russia in which they recognised the need to intervene in any country where a revolution threatened others. The Austrians were authorised to occupy Naples, though their troops must be accompanied by observers from the other powers.

Castlereagh was not at Troppau, Britain being represented only by her ambassador to Vienna, Sir Charles Stewart. Knowing how much his government opposed intervention, he refused to sign the protocol. In London, Castlereagh objected that Britain could not belong to an alliance 'with the moral responsibility of administering a general European police'. For he always saw the alliance purely as a mechanism for ensuring harmonious relations between the nations of Europe. In any case, historically he was in no position to commit Great Britain to upholding dynastic legitimacy, that keystone of Metternichian foreign policy; as he pointed out, 'the House of Hanover could not well maintain the principles upon which the House of Stuart forfeited the throne.' Nevertheless, Castlereagh did not anticipate Britain abandoning the Concert of Five; rather, he forecast that the new triple alliance would drift away from Britain.

No stickler for the truth himself, Metternich clung to the belief that Castlereagh's objection to intervention was a political ploy, a sop to British public opinion. He cannot be blamed for thinking that secretly Castlereagh supported him when he was assured that this was so by the Austrian ambassador in London, when the Duke of Wellington had said he should invade Naples. And he was right in supposing that Castlereagh had no wish to destroy the rapport built up over the last eight years.

Despite British disapproval, the Congress of Troppau was one of Metternich's greatest achievements. Not only did he get what he wanted in Italy, but he established an extraordinary psychological ascendancy over the Tsar. The latter's conversion—one historian calls it seduction—from liberal sympathies was in part due to a 'Confession of Faith' which Metternich drafted in the evenings at Troppau and presented to Alexander at the end of the congress. Poorly written, verbose, it is often dismissed; the claim that middle class 'presumption' is the root cause of revolution attracts ridicule. Yet Metternich identified just the same dichotomy in democracy that Talmon was to do a century later in *The Rise of Totalitarian Democracy*. Metternich wrote:

> The enemy is divided into two sharply distinct parties. One is the Levellers, the other the Doctrinaires. . . . Among Levellers one finds strong-willed, determined men. Doctrinaires have no-one like this. But if the former are more to be feared during a revolution, the latter are more dangerous in the period of deceptive calm which precedes it.

In his view Girondin must inevitably give way to Jacobin, plebeian liberal to plebeian tyrant. However, the real purpose of the 'Confession' was not so much to write political philosophy as to frighten and win over the Tsar. Metternich struck exactly the right note of apocalyptic indignation:

> Drag through the mud the name of God and the powers instituted by His divine decrees, and the revolution will be prepared! Speak of a social contract and the revolution is accomplished. The revolution was already completed in the palaces of Kings, in the drawing-rooms and boudoirs of certain cities, when among the great mass of the people it was still only in a state of preparation.

Shaken by the mutiny of his favourite regiment, Alexander had already blurted out, 'In the year 1820 I would not do what I did in 1813 for anything in the world. You have not changed but I have!' Metternich had noted complacently. ' "As is the master, so is the servant" I said to myself. Now we will wait. Nesselrode is to come.'

Metternich had also destroyed any chance of a Franco-Russian alignment. The French had hoped to revive the Bourbon family pact. Encouraged discreetly by Metternich, their envoy the Marquis de Caraman offered to mediate between the Neapolitan government and King Ferdinand. Recognition of the régime infuriated the Tsar—as everyone had known it would. The French angered him even more by refusing to sign the Preliminary Protocol. Still hoping fatuously to mediate, they then joined in inviting Ferdinand to come to Laibach and seek their help, upsetting Britain as well.

The Austrian foreign minister's summing up on 11 December was, 'We have come to the end of the first act of the play.'

The King of Naples was expected at Laibach (Ljubljana) in January 1821. All the other Italian sovereigns came too. Metternich drove from Troppau along icy roads, spending New Year's Day with his family in Vienna. He was pleased with his accommodation, even if 'the mistress of the house is as ugly as the seven deadly sins, and has seven children who each resemble one of the said sins'. There was a theatre where he could hear Rossini's latest operas. The congress was a success before it opened officially on 11 January. On the previous day he had written 'we have won the battle', implying that Tsar Alexander's cooperation was working wonders—'Here again tea makes its astonishing power felt.' Prince Ruffo, the ambassador of Naples at Vienna, read aloud on his King's behalf speeches drafted by Gentz and Metternich in which Ferdinand bemoaned his subjects' wickedness. The Austrian foreign minister assured the King that his oath to uphold the Neapolitan constitution was invalid, since it had been taken under duress. Ferdinand sent a letter to the Neapolitans—written for him by Gentz—to say that he was coming home with a large Austrian army and warning them not to resist. Even the normally pessimistic Gentz confided in a friend, 'Really, things aren't going badly.'

The trump card was the Tsar. Full of a convert's zeal, he agreed to everything Metternich wanted as soon as he arrived. Delighted by the decision to invade Naples, Alexander wrote to Princess Mestcherski, 'Our purpose is to counteract the empire of evil, which is spreading rapidly through all the occult means at the disposal of the Satanic spirit which directs it.' He was finding much comfort in the Bible, especially in the stories of Nebuchadnezzar and of Judith and Holofernes. 'Capo d'Istria twists and turns like the Devil in Holy Water,' Metternich observed complacently. A month later he noted, 'The breach between Capo d'Istria and the Tsar grows steadily.'

The British were angered by attempts to associate them with the congress's decision to intervene. Stewart protested ineffectually, insisting it be put on record that Great Britain had not agreed. He reported to his brother how Troppau had created a 'Triple Alliance'—the three courts 'have now, I consider, hermetically sealed their treaty before Europe'. Yet he accepted Metternich's statement that 'he had conducted the Austrian monarchy, under the greatest peril with which it has ever been threatened, to a secure and creditable triumph'. In addition Castlereagh assured the three Allies that he respected the purity of their motives and believed profoundly in 'the cordiality and harmony of the Alliance'. He defended them vigorously in the House of Commons, arguing that if they had made mistakes they had been provoked by the Carbonari. As for the Alliance, 'I am far from being disposed to shrink from its defence.' He hoped it would 'long continue to cement the peace of Europe'. Few of his hearers shared his vision. Even so, as long as he lived, the British foreign secretary would do his best to save the European Alliance.

On 7 March at Rieti the Austrian army engaged the Neapolitan troops, who were unenthusiastic for their new government and badly led. 'Dress them in blue, in green or red, but whatever you do they always run,' their King observed of his soldiers. 'Our army has not lost one drop of blood,' Metternich recorded. 'They did not fire because their fire could not be returned.' On 23 March the Austrians entered Naples in triumph after a campaign of less than a fortnight. The Carbonari fled, the constitution was abolished and King Ferdinand was restored to his old powers. Russia had been ready to send in 90,000 troops, but there was no need.

'I am in the strangest position I have ever been in,' Metternich wrote on 3 April 1821. 'I have one revolution extinguished on my hands with two others blazing away.' When told on 12 March of the rising in Piedmont and how the garrisons at Turin and Alessandria had mutinied, he said that it was what he had been expecting. It was set off by Carbonari officers, who demanded a Spanish-style constitution. They found a leader in Prince Charles Albert, later to be a source of infinite vexation to Metternich. Eighty thousand Austrians marched down, brushed aside the rebel army at Novara on 8 April and restored the King.

The Piedmontese monarch, Victor Emanuel, King of Sardinia, was summoned to Laibach, where Metternich rebuked him to such effect that he abdicated in favour of his brother Charles Felix. Their young kinsman and ultimate heir, Charles Albert, received an equally fierce reprimand.

The third revolution was potentially the most dangerous. In February Prince Alexander Ypsilanti had crossed the Prut River, invading Moldavia with a handful of Greek nationalists and Christian Albanians. They intended to recruit a Romanian army and liberate Greece. News of the plan had been discovered by the Austrian secret police, who had warned the Sultan's government. On 1 May Metternich wrote:

> What may happen in the East is incalculable. Perhaps it won't be so bad—three or four hundred thousand hanged, strangled or impaled beyond our Eastern frontier doesn't amount to much. Ypsilanti, that masked liberal, that Hellenist, is going to put me in a dilemma.

It was bound to arouse Russian sympathy, even if Alexander condemned it. The Turks made matters worse by hanging the Patriarch of Constantinople over the door of his own palace.

Although the congress ended on 28 February, the Austrians and Russians stayed on at Laibach until 2 May. As a Romantic, Metternich enjoyed the wild mountain scenery—'beautiful in the truest sense, with everything a lovely green and the tall snowy peaks of the Alps on the far horizon'. He went to good performances of *Cenerentola* and of a forgotten opera, *Eduardo e Cristina*, which he considered one of Rossini's best. He cultivated Nesselrode, showing him the mountains. Above all, he worked on the Tsar—'If ever anyone changed from black to white, he has.' He was sorry to leave Laibach on 21 May. 'We accomplished great good things.' The boast can best be understood in the light of Burke's dictum that a man has an interest in putting out the flames when the house next door is on fire. The Congress System seemed the best of fire engines.

Dominating the three congresses between 1818 and 1821 was as much a tour de force as outwitting Napoleon. Metternich captured each one, making it do exactly what he wanted, dictating the foreign policy of Russia and Prussia—whose rulers trusted him more than they did their own ministers. Britain and France might disagree with him, yet they did not abandon the Alliance. Europe would not see such unity again for a century. And Metternich was the mainspring.

12

The End of European Unity: The Congress of Verona, 1822

Things are getting back to a wholesome state again. Every nation for itself, and God for us all!'

GEORGE CANNING

He has in common with most English ministers the defect of not appreciating the viewpoints and needs of Continental Powers.

METTERNICH on Lord Liverpool

Metternich saw George Canning as the destroyer of the first attempt at European unity. It can be argued that Canning took to its logical conclusion a policy mapped out by Castlereagh. Yet Castlereagh not only worked hard to maintain friendly relations with Austria, but he refused to despair of the Alliance; when he said that it might drift away from Britain, he meant that the Triple Alliance might do so over certain questions but never the full-scale Concert of European Powers. This is why Metternich was to be so appalled at Castlereagh's death in 1822 and replacement by Canning, who was a politician of the most insular sort, whom Castlereagh had described as 'a charlatan'.

For the Alliance was unpopular with those Englishmen who took an interest in politics, including Prime Minister Lord Liverpool. They disliked 'despotism' and were disinclined to interfere in other countries' politics; in any case, they had an instinctive, xenophobic, distrust of all foreigners. Unlike continental Europeans living in close proximity to one another under a perennial threat of war, the British were able to shelter behind their Channel. They believed, quite wrongly, that their country was in no danger of revolution.

Metternich could not understand their hostility. He thought that Austria was the happiest country in Europe. 'Of all the world's régimes, ours is the one which most respects rights and guarantees,' he told Darya Lieven. 'Individual freedom is complete, the equality of all classes before the law absolute; there are titles but no privileges.' In many ways it was a fairer society than was early nineteenth-century Britain, where a peer could only be tried by the House of Lords, where no Jew or Catholic might sit in the House of Lords. Nor were the Emperor and his ministers ever hooted in the street like George IV and his cabinet.

The '*Biedermeyer*' epoch (so named later after a mythical Viennese burgher), which coincided with Metternich's heyday, was a period of great prosperity for many parts of the Monarchy, especially Austria, Bohemia and northern Italy. An industrial revolution began after 1814, machinery being imported from England and Englishmen engaged to build factories; Austria grew famous for cotton textiles, Bohemia for cloth. If the police were a little too much in evidence, the force was smaller than that established at London by Sir Robert Peel. Admittedly much of Hungary and Galicia was a barbarous waste, but no more so than the Scottish Highlands or Connacht.

When Metternich returned from Laibach, the Emperor appointed him *Haus, Hof und Staatskanzler*—chancellor for household, court and state. 'A bomb exploding over my head which I couldn't dodge' was his reaction. Despite an increased work load, he was far from displeased; hitherto only Kaunitz had been accorded such an honour. (In 1824 Francis would offer him in addition the post of lord chamberlain, which he would decline, commenting, 'Better die a natural death than be killed by pinpricks.') He was already so busy that he frequently compared himself to 'my friends the spiders whom I love because I have admired them so often'. He was forced by lack of power and resources to remain in the centre of his webs—'beautiful to behold, artfully spun and able to stand up to occasional shocks but not to a gust of wind'.

The title 'chancellor' has given some historians an inflated idea of Metternich's role in the Monarchy. The office added very few substantial powers to the control of foreign affairs; it did not make him prime minister—he remained only one minister among many, even if he was Francis's favourite. 'There is a general impression, especially in foreign countries, that Prince Metternich had unlimited influence over the Emperor,' Count Hartig (his colleague for many years on the *Minister-konferenz*) recalled in 1849. 'Such an impression is completely without foundation since the prince's views were seldom heard in the government's home departments and he was deliberately kept at a distance from them.'

He still mourned for his dead daughters and, trying to forget them, sold his house at Baden outside Vienna, 'the place where I lost half my life'. He wished that it could be razed to the ground —'I want to see the entire site covered by tall grass and brambles like a wilderness, the only landscape which bears any resemblance to my heart.' Yet he could still joke. Visiting his mother, who lived not far from the capital, 'I got into my carriage at eight o'clock in the evening. By nine o'clock there were rumours that I had dashed off to meet Tsar Alexander. It was therefore assumed that a very grave crisis indeed was threatening, and by eleven o'clock that evening twenty-five of my closest friends had gathered at my house.'

In October 1821 he went to Hanover, where the King—otherwise George IV of England—his fat person crammed into an Austrian hussar uniform and covered in Austrian orders, welcomed Metternich as a dear friend. 'I don't remember ever being hugged so warmly or having such nice things said about me.' Indeed, the King sang the chancellor's praises so effusively that he embarrassed even Metternich. He went on to declare his devotion to the Emperor ('Our Emperor') before making violent personal attacks on the Tsar and Capo d'Istria, ending with 'a frightful explosion against his own ministers'. Castlereagh alone was excepted—'He understands you, he's your friend, and that says everything,' said the King.

More important, Castlereagh had come to Hanover with King George, he and the Austrian chancellor reforging their old partnership to their mutual satisfaction. 'Metternich's visit went off miraculously,' he wrote to his brother. 'We never understood each other so well. It was a great treat to me, I am convinced to both.' The reason for it being a great treat was that Britain was no less alarmed than Austria at the prospect of Russia invading Turkey, an invasion which could mean Russian control of the Mediterranean and the Near East. For a time the British foreign secretary had even suspected Austria of planning to divide Turkey-in-Europe with Russia. Very relieved, he agreed with Metternich in seeing Capo d'Istria as a most dangerous man but, like the chancellor, felt confident that together they should be able to stop Tsar Alexander; all that was needed was to persuade the Sultan to treat his Christian subjects better and withdraw his troops from the Danubian principalities.

Castlereagh also accepted that the Alliance was 'actually existing in full force'. It seemed as though he was underwriting the concept of a European union, of a universal guarantee. He reported on 22 October 1821 that under no circumstances would the Tsar 'ever separate himself from the conservative principles of the Alliance . . . We believe that it would be sufficient, both in the general and in the particular interests of the Powers, to regard this basis as existing in fact.' A week later he wrote to the British ambassador at St Petersburg that the nature of Turkish power had been 'fully understood when the existing state of Europe, including that of Turkey, was placed under the provident care and anxious protection of the general Alliance'. This was the language of Metternich, and the same concept of European unity.

At the same time, no less than Metternich, the British foreign secretary saw the Jacobins as the ultimate enemy. When the uproar over Queen Caroline's divorce had subsided, he had written to Metternich on 6 May 1820, 'Your Highness will observe that, although we have made immense progress against Radicalism, the monster still lives, and shows himself in new shapes; but we do not despair of crushing him by time and perseverance.'

Darya Lieven was at Hanover too, by herself, so that she and her lover were able to resume their affair, if only for a week. Despite royal approval of his foreign secretary's politics, relations between King George and Castlereagh were cool; Lady Castlereagh had gravely insulted George's mistress, Lady Conyngham. 'We set to work together to restore his fortunes with the King,' Darya records. They succeeded so well that George IV wanted to make Castlereagh his prime minister. Should this happen, in Metternich's opinion, 'Our political situation would certainly benefit from England taking a more vigorous role in world affairs.' Castlereagh was the only man who might have overcome British insularity.

From Hanover the new chancellor went to Frankfurt, to attend the *Bundestag*. Everywhere he was received with wild enthusiasm, welcomed obsequiously by the 'humming bird kings' and their little courts, cheered even at the universities. He reported with satisfaction that in retrospect the 'student business' which had had to be settled by the Carlsbad Conventions was beginning to look ridiculous. Correctly, he ascribed his popularity to smashing the Carbonari in Italy—'merely a band of ragamuffins', he disclaimed modestly. He was now playing almost as important a role in German life as he did in Austrian.

Nevertheless, he was worried by Greece and Spain. Opponents hoped to weaken his grip on Tsar Alexander. After all, the Orthodox Christians of Greece were the Russians' coreligionists and the Tsars had been their Protectors for half a century; it had always been Russian policy that one day New Byzantium should liberate the Old. During the previous summer Baroness Krüdener had written to Alexander preaching a new Crusade, promising that he would attend the Christmas Liturgy at the Church of the Holy Sepulchre in a liberated Jerusalem. Just before Metternich's meeting with Castlereagh, Russia had very nearly declared war on Turkey.

Capo d'Istria bombarded the Tsar with hideous tales of Turkish atrocities. The Austrian chancellor countered with reports of revolutionary plots all over Europe, claiming that the western leaders of the Greek rising were Carbonari whose real aim was a general European revolution. His correspondence shows complete confidence. 'Just now I'm fighting Tatischev,' he wrote of the Russian ambassador in March 1822. 'The good man is just like an eel.

Luckily I'm an experienced old fisherman.' He compared the battle between himself and Capo d'Istria to a conflict between positive and negative, believing that 'two parties are fighting each other all over the world, the Capo d'Istrias and the Metternichs. Since the Tsar is a Metternich, his opponents will have to be abandoned to their fate.' He knew that his hold over the Tsar was almost unbreakable—'Tsar Alexander is of all children the most childish.'

However, Metternich realized that, with his restless army, Alexander might well try to compensate himself for prestige lost in the East by increased Russian activity in the West. The Tsar revived a scheme for an Allied invasion of Spain to evict the liberals. Metternich knew that the British would oppose it even more strongly than they had intervention in Naples, and feared it might destroy his reconciliation with Castlereagh. Early in June he wrote to ask the British foreign secretary for support against the Russians at the next congress, which would meet at Verona in the autumn, begging him to come to a preliminary congress at Vienna if he could not be at Verona. 'Should you fail me, I shall be alone,' he pleaded, 'and the battle will be unequal.'

'Sometimes Capo d'Istria behaves like a mouse in a hole, sometimes like the cat outside,' he observed on 19 June. 'If things don't go the way he wants, he squeaks in his hole. If it gets really difficult the cat shows her claws.' But a week later Capo d'Istria was sent on leave, never to set foot again on Russian soil. He had been finally outmanoeuvred by a promise of Austrian support for the Tsar should Turkey refuse any Russian demands which were specifically guaranteed by treaty. Accepting that he must pay a price for Allied cooperation, Alexander dismissed the minister whom Metternich considered an 'evil element of perpetual dissension'.

Meanwhile, the chancellor felt 'a hundred years old'. He was cheered by his new sculpture by Canova, *Amor and Psyche's First Kiss*. 'The two children kiss as if they had never done anything else. When the very pure and innocent visit me, however, I have to hang a dressing gown round Amor and throw a sheet over Psyche.' He enjoyed Barbaia's new Italian opera at Vienna, attending rehearsals. 'Rossini himself is in charge, with an orchestra and chorus which amaze everyone.' He liked only *bel canto*. 'This evening I went to a German opera for the first time—a German voice is pitiable compared to an Italian.' He grumbled at his work load. 'My office is just like a headquarters. Every minute someone comes in to interrupt me . . . There are times when my poor head is so tired that I long to lie down alone and sleep.' He hated his wife and children leaving him to go to the country. 'I have no family life, which is my main pleasure,' he complained. 'I have my two gardens, the sun and Italian opera, which are well worth having but don't add up to happiness.' He would read himself to sleep with two or three chapters of Livy, in Latin.

In July 1822 the Marquess of Londonderry, as Castlereagh had been known since his father's death, confirmed that he would be coming to Verona accompanied by the Duke of Wellington. Only a month later Metternich was informed that the British foreign secretary had gone off his head and cut his throat with a penknife. During his last, deranged meeting with George IV he had told the King, 'It is necessary to say goodbye to Europe; you and I alone know it and have saved it; no one after me understands the affairs of the Continent.' Metternich was distraught:

> The man is not to be replaced, not where I am concerned. He was devoted to me, heart and mind, not only because he liked me, but out of conviction. Most of what would have been easy with him will be hard work with his successor, whoever he is. I was waiting for him here as if for my other self.

Darya Lieven was fully aware that it was a disaster for her lover:

> Besides mourning Lord Londonderry as a friend, you have to mourn him as a minister—perhaps the only man in England who understood European politics, and whose principles as well as his inclinations urged him towards friendship with Austria. What a loss for us all, but above all for you!

Metternich asked the British government to send Wellington to Verona, as 'the only man who, up to a point, can replace him.'

The partnership of Metternich and Castlereagh had been a vital element in the Congress System. Both had believed in it, if in different ways; where Castlereagh thought that Britain should take military action only if war threatened the continent's equilibrium —'We shall be found in our place when actual danger menaces the system of Europe'—Metternich was more positive. Yet each had respected the other's position. Castlereagh assured Darya in March 1822, 'We are in perfect agreement, Prince Metternich and I, on the fundamentals of every question; but in the application of our views on the Eastern Question, I find a shade of difference which makes me anxious to bring him round to my own point of view.' Such an approach explains why they worked so well together.

Britain's new foreign secretary was George Canning, determined to appeal to British xenophobia. 'He is no more capable of conducting foreign affairs than your baby,' George IV told Mme Lieven. 'He doesn't know the first thing about his job; no tact, no judgement, no idea of decorum.' The King had appointed him with the utmost reluctance. Three years later Darya would answer Tsar Alexander's inquiries about Canning with, 'The distinctive mark of his policy is to be the enemy of Prince Metternich.'

In the meantime, the Spanish question was growing still thornier. In July the problem was to find some means of dissuading the Tsar from marching across Europe to Madrid to reinstate King Ferdinand as absolute monarch. The situation had since been altered radically by France's ambitious new foreign policy, inspired by the Vicomte de Chateaubriand, French ambassador at London. The Bourbon army wished to replace memories of Napoleonic glory with battle honours of its own and relished the prospect of rescuing a Bourbon King from his subjects. By autumn 1822 a French 'army of observation' had taken up position in the Pyrenees. When the Duke of Wellington arrived in Paris at the beginning of October on his way to Vienna, the head of His Most Christian Majesty's government, the Comte de Villèle, informed Wellington that the army might conceivably be poised for invasion; hitherto it had been disguised as a *cordon sanitaire* against an epidemic of yellow fever just across the frontier. The Duke at once sent to London for instructions on how to deal with this new development. Castlereagh wrote back insisting that he oppose any form whatever of intervention in Spain—depriving him of any scope for manoeuvre at Verona.

At Vienna Wellington realized that nothing but Spain would be discussed during the Congress of Verona. Before the Duke left the Austrian capital, Tsar Alexander, who had also gone there, told him that he was in favour of intervention but by a Russian, not a French, expeditionary force. Since Metternich's new influence over the Tsar was by now well known, Wellington felt that the Austrians should be able to defuse the issue. He reported that in his view there was going to be 'an unanimous decision to leave the Spaniards to themselves'.

The congress which met at Verona in October 1822 recalled the splendours of that of Vienna. The Austrian Emperor and the Empress Charlotte (his fourth consort) were accompanied by Metternich and Austria's ambassadors to London, Berlin and St Petersburg, with Gentz discreetly in attendance. The King of Prussia brought his chancellor Count Bernstorff. The Tsar's suite included not only Nesselrode (now sole foreign secretary) and his envoys to London and Paris, but General Prince Volkonsky, chief of the Russian general staff, with five other generals. Wellington was supported by the British ambassadors to Vienna, Berlin and Constantinople. Among France's representatives were the Vicomte de Montmorency, foreign minister, and M de Chateaubriand.

All the Italian sovereigns were present, including the Duchess of Parma—Napoleon's widow. Chateaubriand teased her, saying that he had seen some of her Parmesan soldiers at Piacenza but that once upon a time she had had many more of them. Marie Louise, who was enjoying the festivities after missing those at Vienna in 1815, replied simply, 'I don't think about that sort of thing any more.' Everyone was amused when she repeatedly defeated Wellington at whist.

The royal personages and their entourages attended a notably spectacular state banquet given by Emperor Francis in the great Roman amphitheatre. Metternich had invited Rossini, who long remembered the chancellor writing to him that 'since I was "The God of Harmony" would I please come to where harmony was so badly needed'. Night after night the maestro—whom Metternich now called 'my good friend Rossini'—conducted performances of his operas in Verona's little theatre.

Nevertheless, in many ways the congress was run on surprisingly modern lines. Metternich had what would nowadays be termed a keen sense of public relations and was particularly concerned about coverage by the press. Chateaubriand (who later published a book, *Le Congrès de Vérone*), recalls seeing him rush into a corner with Gentz to compose a counterblast to some hostile article.

The chancellor did not anticipate any trouble over Greece, and indeed the congress would swiftly condemn the Greek War of Independence as 'a rash and criminal enterprise'. However, from the very beginning he realized that Spain was going to be a different matter altogether. He was deeply opposed to intervention; his plan was to present invasion as the only possible course and then to show that it was impractical, after which all five powers would send letters of protest to the Madrid government—Russia and Prussia might make the tone as stern as they liked, Britain as mild. He hoped that this would be sufficient to frighten the Spanish liberals into reaching a compromise with King Ferdinand. He genuinely feared that intervention here might upset the equilibrium throughout Europe, telling Lord Londonderry, the British ambassador to Vienna, that the Tsar wanted the French to take their 'gangrened armies' into Spain simply because he expected a revolution to break out in their absence, which would enable him to send '200 to 300,000' Russian troops into France.

Just as Wellington had predicted, the Spanish question dominated discussions. The Tsar wished to send an army of 150,000 men into Piedmont, where a base would be set up from which it could easily invade Spain or put down revolutions in France or Italy; he fancied the idea of Cossacks in Andalusia. A Russian military presence in Western Europe was totally unacceptable to Metternich. Nor did he want French intervention, proposed by Montmorency and Chateaubriand; they were exceeding their brief, since Villèle's intention was for France to threaten, not to invade.

Far from favouring military intervention, the chancellor saw it as a last resort; Austrian interests were not endangered in Spain as they had been in Naples. On 19 November a protocol was signed by Austria, France, Prussia and Russia in which they pledged co-operation in the event of 'a war declared or provoked by the present government of Spain'. Intentionally, it was a vague and inconclusive document.

Alone, the Duke of Wellington refused to sign. Metternich tried desperately to persuade him. After all, during the Neapolitan crisis the Duke's advice had been 'Prince Metternich must march.' But he thought himself bound by Canning's directions which, in his soldierly way, he obeyed blindly. As George IV put it afterwards, 'He had the great, great disadvantage of being incapable of flexibility or of making a diplomatic approach.' At one meeting with the chancellor he clapped his hat on his head to show that his decision was final. 'We have passed but a stormy week,' he reported. It was the second time Britain had fallen out with the Alliance. Even so, few at Verona can have guessed that it meant the end of the Concert of Europe. In the same month Canning declared 'for Europe, I shall be desirous, *now* and *then*, to read *England*'.

Wellington did not realize that his refusal had been Canning's first shot in a campaign to destroy the Alliance. However, the Duke soon regretted his hard line. 'He said he quite understood that his visit had had worse results than those which had first appeared,' Darya recorded two months later. 'That every day the separation of England from the great Alliance became, and would become, more noticeable; that it was certainly a misfortune for everyone and a very great misfortune for England; and that he did not know to what to ascribe it. Was it Londonderry's death, or his own behaviour at Verona?'

In another letter of January 1823 Darya describes how all too many people felt about Metternich, relating Lady Grenville's opinion:

> What she finds particularly remarkable about you is the hatred, the enthusiasm, the distrust, that pursue you in turn.

> She sees you as both god and devil; and I can understand her perplexity; for I have not a very clear idea of you myself.

Yet Darya had seen him only recently, having been at Verona, though this time accompanied by her husband. It was the last time that she and Metternich would meet as lovers. He wrote to his wife, telling her how he spent his evenings at the Lievens' house with Wellington, the Duc de Caraman (the French ambassador to Vienna), Prince Ruffo (the Neapolitan ambassador) and Count Bernstorff. 'Princess Lieven's *salon* in Verona is just like ours in Vienna.'

Darya had not enjoyed herself, however. She complained of being 'the sole representative of my species', that all the other ladies were 'thorough barbarians'. There was too much competition. Not only had M de Chateaubriand brought his beautiful mistress, Mme Récamier, but Lady Londonderry (wife of the British ambassador to Vienna and Castlereagh's sister-in-law) had captivated Tsar Alexander despite her plumpness. 'I have had some good scenes with her,' Lady Londonderry wrote of Mme Lieven from Verona. 'The other day I received a note from the [Russian] Emperor during dinner, and her curiosity was so excited that after repeatedly asking who it was from, she put out her thin red paw to snap at it, but Metternich, who was sitting between us, interposed and said "*Ce serait une indiscretion impardonnable pour une jeune femme de produire ses billets.*" She was not to be pacified, and as I took care she should not see the note she turned sulky.' Darya's unhappiness was compounded by Nesselrode refusing her request to transfer her husband to Vienna as ambassador.

Metternich was very pleased with his son Victor, by now nineteen, who had come with him to the congress and who wanted to follow in his father's footsteps. 'Victor enjoys his work as much as his friends and comrades in Vienna do the *Prater.*' He was proud of the way in which the boy translated an important English despatch.

Altogether, it seemed that Metternich had achieved a good deal in those few weeks. Perhaps he had not forged closer links with Britain, as he had hoped to do before Castlereagh's tragedy. But he had stopped the Tsar from overrunning Europe with his troops, delayed the French and kept the Alliance in being. He did not despair of Britain playing a larger role in European affairs, reassured by George IV's enthusiasm; the King's diplomatic service in Hanover communicated His Majesty's views to 'his beloved Metternich'—Canning's phrase. Metternich believed Wellington to be basically well disposed, for all his stubborn contrariness at Verona. But he failed to appreciate the powerlessness of a British monarch and the Duke's mediocrity as a statesman.

Moreover, the congress demonstrated triumphantly Metternich's domination of the Tsar. Not only had he routed Capo d'Istria, but, as Wellington observed, he was almost Alexander's prime minister. He had achieved this by his flood of correspondence on the subject of imminent revolution. An undated memorandum which he sent to the Tsar at about this time gives some idea of his arguments. He told the former disciple of Baroness Krüdener that 'one of the weakest aspects of the human mind has been an inclination down the ages towards the shadowy domain of mysticism'. Men who joined the clandestine societies which now threatened Europe, 'dupes of their own imagination', were—so he claimed—coordinated by a secret committee at Paris. Luckily, 'the world has never seen such an example of unity and solidarity among great polities as that by Russia, Austria and Prussia during recent years'.

He left Verona in excellent humour. He would not have understood the satire of his favourite English poet Lord Byron, in 'The Age of Bronze'.

Strange sight this Congress! destined to unite
All that's incongruous, all that's opposite.

Even Gentz did not see that anything disastrous had happened at Verona. 'God holds his hand over Austria,' he assured his friend Pilat. 'So long as the Emperor and Prince Metternich live, no storm can destroy us.' Yet Byron had underlined the congress's weakness.

After Verona, the chancellor went to the Emperor's 'good city of Venice' for the Tsar's visit. He was amused by Alexander's raptures—'He thinks the Giudecca is like the Neva and the Doge's

Palace like some of the Moscow palaces.' He himself did not care for Venetian palazzi, finding them too large and cold. 'However, I have good accommodation, plenty of sun and even stoves; also a splendid state-bed, which seems more suited for a Danaë than to me, so I've had my little camp-bed put up.' What he liked was not the canals but the little streets with their pretty shops. He went to Cimarosa's *Il Matrimonio Segreto* at the Venice theatre—'the story of a marriage so secret that I'm hanged if I understood it'. Rossini called on him, complaining of his first tenor, an Irishman who had been learning Italian, and of 'an English ambassador who thinks he's a *maestro di capella*'—a reference to the musical Lord Burghersh.

On the Emperor's orders Metternich returned to Vienna by way of Munich, to give the Bavarian King an account of what had happened at Verona. His visit gave rise to absurd rumours; the King of Württemberg was to have Poland in exchange for his kingdom, which would be annexed by Bavaria; Bavarian troops were to be sent to fight the Turks; and the Bavarian constitution would be suspended. These fantastic stories demonstrate the extent of his hold over Germany.

He may have seemed all-powerful but the Alliance was doomed. Early in 1823 he received the unwelcome news that Réné de Chateaubriand had become France's foreign secretary, an appointment as ill-omened as that of Canning. A famous writer, not even a politician let alone a diplomat, and inordinately vain, Chateaubriand saw his 'ministry' in terms of personal and national glory. He was supremely indifferent to the Alliance. 'I was faced by an anti-Bourbon France and two great foreign ministers, Prince Metternich and Mr Canning,' he would recall in *Mémoires d'Outre-Tombe*. His country was burning to avenge the humiliations of the previous decade. He saw the chance of a dramatic gesture which would demonstrate that the French were still the *Grande Nation*. Accordingly, on 6 April an expeditionary force under the Duc d'Angoulême crossed the Bidassoa and by August had crushed all liberal resistance, freeing Ferdinand VII from his rebellious Cortes. So swift a success showed that Metternich had been correct in thinking the

Spanish liberals weak and unpopular, that all that was needed to remove them was diplomatic pressure, not invasion.

Liberal historians of Metternich have described gleefully how he was 'trapped' by his conservatism into depending on Russia. No doubt many High Tories in pre–Reform Bill Britain had vague reservations about intervention, but these were due to Olympian insularity, not to a rejection of the old order; they agreed with Metternich more than they disagreed—had he lived, Castlereagh would have papered over the cracks instead of widening them. Indeed, some cabinet ministers openly approved of the French invasion of Spain, as did the King. They were deeply concerned by the growing rift between Britain and her continental allies, a rift which Canning was now making unbridgeable. The Austrian chancellor did not trap himself; he was left in the lurch by two chauvinist foreign ministers, Canning and Chateaubriand.

His diplomacy cannot be faulted. Henry Kissinger gives a professional assessment, defining Metternich's outstanding gifts in this field as tact and a sensitivity to nuance; Kissinger also credits him with a knack of identifying the fundamentals of a situation together with a psychological insight which enabled him to dominate opponents—'And because the end result of Metternich's policy was stability and Austria's gain was always intangible, his extraordinary cynicism, his cold-blooded exploitation of the beliefs of his adversaries did not lead to a disintegration of all restraint, as the same tactics were to do later in the hands of Bismarck.' It was this desire for stability which made him so effective.

Yet Kissinger is far from uncritical:

> Whenever Metternich operated within a fixed framework, when an alliance had to be constructed or a settlement negotiated, his conduct was masterly. Whenever he was forced to create his own objectives, there was about him an aura of futility . . . Because he never fought a battle he was not certain of winning, he failed in becoming a symbol. He understood the forces at work better than most of his contemporaries, but this knowledge proved of little avail, be-

> cause he used it almost exclusively to deflect their inexorable march, instead of placing it into his service for a task of construction.

This is too subjective a judgement. It begs the entire question of Metternich's conservatism, damns him for not being a man before his time. He 'created his own objectives' for the Congress System and, as has been seen, was clearly far from futile in doing so.

No one can query his industry. Throughout his career he shouldered a huge work load, paying meticulous attention to detail. As far as possible he made close friends with every foreign ambassador to Vienna, entertaining each one by himself at the Ballhausplatz or at the villa on the Rennweg, asking each one to stay at his country houses, holding interminable conversations. He built up dossiers on all foreign ministers, their qualities and views, their strengths and weaknesses. His own envoys received exact instructions, minutely detailed but of the utmost clarity; much of his working day was spent in drafting dispatches. There were three types: the official dispatch, which might be shown to the foreign minister of the power concerned, and published if necessary; the 'reserved' dispatch, whose contents might be communicated privately; and the secret letter, which identified aims and laid down what tactics were to be used. He was interested only in achieving clearly identified objectives, never in showy diplomatic 'triumphs'; he took immense pains to avoid humiliating opponents, always trying to leave them a way out. Few foreign ministers can have been more successful. Yet in 1819 he had written wearily to Darya Lieven, 'The great game of diplomacy leads to more disappointments than successes, to more trouble than glory.'

His Europeanism has been queried. In 1824 he would tell the Duke of Wellington, 'For a long time now Europe has had for me the value of a mother country (*patrie*).' 'By this he simply meant that as an aristocrat he could fit into aristocratic society anywhere in Europe,' observes Dr Sked, with too much cynicism. Some other historians (A. J. P. Taylor and Paul W. Schroeder) dismiss his Europeanism as a smokescreen for Austrian self-interest. Here, however, Sked disagrees, stressing that Metternich saw Austrian and European interests as identical, citing his comment, 'There exists in Europe only one issue of any moment and that is revolution.'

Metternich's own version of how he had seen the Alliance carries conviction. 'I never thought that it had any purpose other than to give solidarity to the leading European powers in maintaining the common peace,' he would confide in 1830 to Count Ficquelmont, one of his most trusted men. 'The basis of the Alliance, its watchword and daily concern, was respect for the genuine independence of all states, the preservation of friendly relations between all governments, the plea for an open explanation . . . whenever some grave problem endangered the maintenance of peace, and finally emphatic respect for all rights, for everything which has a legal existence.' There is no need to doubt his sincerity.

Like Winston Churchill, Clemens von Metternich considered 'jaw-jaw better than war-war', and he always believed that the Alliance had offered the best means of ensuring peace. Until the end of his career he would strive to resurrect the Concert of Europe.

13

The End of the Alliance: The Congress of St Petersburg

That miserable Eastern Question is again coming to the fore.

METTERNICH, October 1824

'Neither the Turks nor the Greeks want us to intervene: very well then, we withdraw' . . . if one considers that the withdrawal breaks the last bond uniting England to the policy of the Continent, then the matter takes on a different complexion. It means a complete revolution in the political system of Europe; it means the breaking up of the Alliance; in a word, it means that Mr Canning gets his own way.

PRINCESS LIEVEN, November 1824

Prince Metternich began the New Year of 1823 with less cause for optimism than at any time in the last decade. George Canning had replaced a British foreign secretary who was his friend, while at Paris Chateaubriand was equally antagonistic. He would soon see the Triple Alliance sundered inexorably by the 'Eastern Question'. It was to be a period of failure and discouragement, compounded by ill health and bereavement.

He would be fifty in May. Although his hair had turned white and his face was thin and lined, he remained young for his age, full of energy and enthusiasm, despite an air of cynicism, of world weariness. He was still handsome, just as much an '*homme à femmes*' as ever, delighting physically and mentally in women's company. But he was approaching a species of midlife crisis. An alarming work load, together with constant travel and a demanding social life, was taking its toll.

The first great problem was the invasion of Spain. Unlike the Duke of Wellington, who prophesied that '300,000 men' could not subdue the Spaniards, Metternich never had any doubts about the outcome. At the end of April he noted that the Viennese were applauding the French troops' triumphant advance across the Bidassoa as if they were Austrians. He felt a certain pleasure at the rage of the British; the French were reconquering the peninsula less than ten years after Wellington had ejected them. 'My first priority amid the upheaval must be to save the principle, and that principle is the Alliance,' he wrote to Prince Esterházy in London. But he was nervous about Chateaubriand's grandiose ambitions.

Chateaubriand was no less uneasy about Metternich, if for very different reasons. In 1821 the Duc de Caraman had reported from Vienna that the Austrian chancellor was 'a dangerous enemy, a subtle intriguer . . . he controls a thousand levers, which he operates very cleverly, circulating rumours . . . destroying statesmen.' More than one Gallic historian has shuddered at his supposed skill in ruining opponents with libel and slander.

Darya Lieven sent a steady stream of letters from England, dwelling on Mr Canning's enormities. It has been generally thought that she had no ulterior motive, yet as a top-flight Russian agent who was far subtler and far more intelligent than her country's foreign minister, let alone her sovereign, she realized that it was no bad thing for Russia if the Austrian chancellor and the British foreign secretary should be on bad terms; the close links between Metternich and Castlereagh had always worried St Petersburg. If Russia was to have her way in the Eastern Question, it was wholly desirable that Metternich and Canning should detest each other. Nor is it inconceivable that she depicted Wellington as a bumbling idiot from the same motive; it was expedient that Austria should despair of her last real friend in Britain. She certainly tried to discredit Esterházy, making out that he was a fool and that the King disliked him. At the same time she was careful to pass on much accurate and extremely valuable information. She was in an excellent position to do so, being on almost amorous terms with George IV, frequently staying with him at Windsor and Brighton, a friend of the Duke of York (heir presumptive to the throne) and of Lord Grey, the Whig leader; even Mr Canning himself danced attendance on her.

It was not hard to widen the rift with Canning. In August Canning told the prime minister that the British government must reconsider 'how we stand towards the Alliance' and 'the part which we will, or will not, take in these periodical sessions of legislation for the world'. Eager to restore the prestige of a Britain humiliated by France, and in any case antipathetic towards the Congress System, he believed she could benefit from a disunited rather than a united Europe; individual countries would be easier to deal with. A convinced Tory, in no sense a sympathiser with revolution, he was not averse to other nations adopting a constitution modelled on that of Great Britain. His policy enjoyed widespread popular support, whipped up by his rousing speeches—which made gloomy reading at the Ballhausplatz.

In March Canning had formally acknowledged that the Greeks were belligerents. Metternich regarded this as tantamount to recognising revolutionaries; Gentz complained bitterly that Britain had never really been committed to the European Concert—it was vital to counter her baneful influence. However, in the summer Canning announced that Britain would remain neutral in the struggle between Greeks and Turks. Meanwhile, Russia was sabre-rattling, having broken off diplomatic relations with the Porte in August the previous year. But by September 1823 Turkey had met all the Russian demands, apart from withdrawing Turkish troops from the Danubian principalities. Then the Sultan refused to evacuate his garrisons in Moldavia and Wallachia under any circumstances.

In August Metternich had observed, 'Turkey doesn't worry me, only France and Spain.' Yet he was very relieved when the Tsar invited the Emperor to meet him on the border to discuss the Turkish situation.

The meeting was to take place early in October at the Austrian town of Czernowitz (today Chernovtsy, capital of Soviet Moldavia).

In Metternich's view, 'Quite apart from the importance of its agenda, the meeting itself will make an impact like firing heavy guns.' He set out on 20 September, admiring the road through the mountains to Galicia and the wooded Galician plain, if shocked by the poverty of landowner and peasant alike. At Przemysl he awoke with an attack of rheumatic fever. He insisted on being driven back to Lemberg (Lvov), where he collapsed. It was the same illness which had plagued him so often before; he thought that it had been brought on partly by cold, partly by worry at the meeting ahead. He was laid up for a fortnight, unable to sleep. Emperor Francis came and sat by his bed, later in his sickroom when he was convalescing, chatting amiably but avoiding politics to stop him fretting. When Count Mercy arrived from Vienna to take his place, Francis laughed and told Mercy, 'We ought to make a fine job of it—I know very little about the subject, while you knew nothing till yesterday!'

Dr Jäger rushed out to tend the invalid, who was frantic with worry. 'Just imagine my position,' Metternich wrote to Eleanor. 'The only man who understands the business at all left in bed at Lemberg while the two Emperors are at Czernowitz with only two possible outcomes: immediate war between Russia and the Porte or immediate peace. And here I am, peace in my grasp and knowing just how to get it, lying ill in bed!' Then he learnt it was to be peace—'everything is arranged in marvellous fashion, the triumph total'. In his absence the Tsar had paid him every possible compliment. He travelled back slowly at the end of October, orders having been left for him to be housed en route 'like the Emperor himself'. When he reached Moravia he was struck by the contrast with Galicia:

> Two days ago I saw peasants working in the fields with no clothing save a shirt, children as old as four sitting naked in the fields their parents were tilling. The first little Silesian I met had on a nice cap and frock, and was carried by a mother in a good coat with thick red worsted stockings and stout shoes. I could have cried over the first and hugged the others.

But as soon as he got to Vienna he collapsed. Jäger told him it was due to worry and that he must give up work. His lungs were still affected. He was depressed by news from England and about Canning's behaviour. 'He's certainly a very awkward opponent but I've faced much more dangerous.' (A few weeks later he observed, 'What irritates me about the English is that they're all slightly mad, something we have to put up with, pretending not to notice the ridiculous side.') Deep despondency set in just before Christmas —'It's a sad fate for a statesman always to have to battle his way through never ending storms.'

He was irritated by news of the Monroe Doctrine. In his Message to Congress of 2 December 1823 President Monroe—inspired by Secretary John Quincy Adams—had declared that America was for the Americans and that intervention by the Alliance to recover Spain's former American colonies would be seen as 'the manifestation of an unfriendly disposition towards the United States'. Metternich wrote to Baron Lebzeltern that there had come to pass what he had long feared:

> The New World has announced that it has broken with the Old, a break which is neither optional, temporary nor conditional but a real break which separates the states of Europe from the Republic of North America, just as natural incompatibility causes a break between bodies of a rather different sort.

Ironically, although Canning was largely responsible for the attitude of Americans such as Monroe and Adams, privately he shared some of Metternich's regret; he once defined 'the line of demarcation which I most dread—America versus Europe'.

Optimism returned with improving health. In January Metternich commented, 'At St Petersburg everything goes very well, very well.' He was especially pleased by Nesselrode's promotion to privy counsellor, since he regarded Nesselrode as pliable. He seems to have been fully restored by 2 February because we know that when he visited the secret police's headquarters at Vienna that evening he was on his way to a ball.

At 7.00 p.m. the 'Grand Inquisitor of Europe', as his enemies were now calling him, entered the cell of Count Federigo Gonfalonieri, who had requested an interview. A leader of the Milanese Carbonari, the Count had been arrested in 1821 and condemned to death, his sentence being commuted to fifteen years imprisonment; he was about to leave for the Spielberg, the prison-fortress in Moravia. Metternich hoped to learn details of the 'European conspiracy' to which Confalonieri had claimed to belong; here, at last, might be a clue to that 'grand revolutionary committee' at Paris. However, the Count could tell him nothing, since the 'European conspiracy' had been a mere piece of boastful rhetoric. Sir Llywellyn Woodward, if admitting that the chancellor had made no 'deliberate attempt to take advantage of the nervous strain which had been put upon a delicate and gently nurtured man', blames him for taking no interest in what happened to prisoners at the Spielberg. Their fate was touchingly described by Confalonieri's fellow Carbonaro Silvio Pellico, in *Le mie Prigioni*, which was intended to arouse sympathy for the Risorgimento. The Austrian chancellor is portrayed as a relentless persecutor.

In 1846 a French historian, Jacques Crétineau-Joly, began work on a study of the Carbonari and an Austrian official presented him with a parcel sent by Metternich. He was astonished to find a copy of *Le mie Prigioni* with a written dedication to the chancellor 'in homage, with the respectful gratitude of the author, Silvio Pellico'. There were also letters from various inmates of the Spielberg, all of them political prisoners—including Confalonieri—thanking Metternich. Crétineau-Joly called on the chancellor to ask for an explanation. He was told:

> I was anxious that the Imperial government should not lose dignity. You must be aware of the sort of life led by political prisoners. I might as well tell you that when the Spielberg had the honour of housing the Carbonari's leaders I literally did the best I could, so far as was in my power, to give them an existence which was at least bearable, materially and spiritually. Men with imagination, the absence of books, writing paper and lighting deprived them of all intellectual

> activity. They were fastidious and found the rough if nourishing prison food revolting. As persons of a certain social standing, life in the cells was torment for them. After obtaining the Emperor's permission, I ordered that they should be given books, candles and writing materials. I also ordered that they should have the sort of food to which they were used, and be allowed to talk to each other. But I would not make any concessions on prison uniform, which sent Count Confalonieri nearly mad. The soul of this noble conspirator recoiled at the touch of prison garb.

All these men had their sentences reduced.

Although many Carbonari were caught plotting to murder both Emperor and chancellor, not one was executed. In England, by contrast, the Cato Street conspirators were hanged in public, after which they were quartered, their bodies being cut apart by medical students. Time and again Metternich interceded for political prisoners.

Yet he despised his opponents, and not just Carbonari who offered to betray accomplices in return for a bounty—'heroes at ten louis d'or'. He held all liberals in contempt. 'I should have liked Robespierre much better than the Abbé de Pradt, Attilla better than Quiroga.' (The Abbé, who had been one of Napoleon's less effective diplomats, was now a liberal pamphleteer, while General Quiroga was a leading Spanish liberal.) 'Tyrants don't frighten me. I should know how to survive their wrath or at any rate how to endure it honourably. But the lunatic Radicals and boudoir philosophers nauseate me.' He was equally contemptuous of those who compromised. When informed by a Portuguese that the King of Portugal was contemplating a constitution on French lines, he told his informant, 'You're faced with death so you take poison—our ancestors' attitude was "If you're poisoned, take an antidote." '

M de Chateaubriand was a particular *bête noire*. It gave Metternich real pleasure when Villèle, whom he respected, sacked his eccentric foreign minister in June 1824. 'I know a "bonnet man" when I see one, and I don't care if the bonnet's red or white' was Metternich's comment. 'In fact I prefer the demagogue to the royalist version of Jacobin; one attacks the monarchy from the front, the other ends by strangling it.' Later he observed of Chateaubriand that 'unbalanced by excessive vanity and wild ambition, he worked under M de Villèle for just as long as he thought that he could control the prime minister.' When Chateaubriand attacked Villèle, the chancellor commented, 'No one, in my opinion, ever prostituted himself in the way that the *vicomte* has done. More of a revolutionary than any real revolutionary, falser than any of them, and more extreme than the men of the Terror . . .'

When Metternich heard of Chateaubriand's imminent downfall he was at Johannisberg. 'My table is generally laid for twenty-five, though often I entertain forty or fifty,' he wrote to Gentz. His guests must have been discussing the renewal of the Carlsbad Decrees—that 'vindictive act of a frightened despotism', as a liberal historian has described them. No doubt much to the chancellor's satisfaction, a group of revolutionary students from the university of Erlichingen were being tried in Munich; the horrified Bavarians heard of a plot to overthrow their monarchy and establish a republic after subverting the army. He had no trouble whatever in persuading the *Bundestag* to renew the decrees, since the German rulers with liberal tendencies, those of Baden, Württemberg, Hesse and Weimar, offered no resistance. A new law banned the press from reporting the *Bundestag*'s debates. Metternich had already written to Baron Lebzeltern at St Petersburg in February that 'the Restoration is progressing [in Germany]', arguing that constitutions were unpopular in the states which had them because of the increased taxation needed to pay the deputies.

At Ischl, where Metternich went to take the waters in July, a crowd mobbed him, all trying to shake his hand—'from the same sort of curiosity which impels a mob to run after a camel or an ape', he commented. He returned to Johannisberg in excellent spirits. 'Finishing all one has to do, overcoming all the difficulties which accompany it, to be wonderfully fit, breathing pure, wholesome air and living in a heavenly place, these are what make the brighter side of life,' he wrote to Floret at the beginning of August.

Later that month the Emperor asked Metternich to his personal retreat, Schloss Persenburg, a clifftop castle which overlooked the

Danube. He had not seen 'my Imperial master' for nearly four months, for the first time in his fifteen years as a minister. 'Prince Kaunitz had the longest ministry,' he reflected. 'He held office for forty years and reached the age of eighty-four. I should have had as long a career at seventy-four but I shan't live to see it.' He was struck by his host's simple way of life at Persenburg, that of a little country squire. He was bored when he came back to Vienna—'My one amusement is the opera . . .'

In September, King Frederick William wrote to Prince Metternich to congratulate him on his success in renewing the Carlsbad Decrees. It had 'confirmed the most perfect unity in the views and interests of Prussia and Austria'. The chancellor replied that he based his policy 'on complete unity between two states whose regrettable mistakes [in the past] had resulted in a mutual rivalry which had seemed almost insurmountable . . . As long as Prussia and Austria are united, and the unity is obvious to all, then every benefit is possible for Europe.' Undoubtedly he believed sincerely in partnership with Prussia in dominating Germany—as long as he could dominate Prussia. He considered that at present he enjoyed a decisive moral superiority over its government.

In October 1824 he wrote 'I feel wonderfully well', laughing at Dr Jäger's comment that good health made him look 'less like a scholar'. But only a few days before, he had written apprehensively that the 'miserable Eastern Question' was once more demanding attention, and that he might even have to contact Mr Canning.

The situation had been worsening since Byron's death at Missolonghi in April, which captured the imagination of all Europe. Tsar Alexander found himself in an increasingly difficult position. While agreeing that the Ottoman Empire should be allowed to survive, and that many of the Greeks' supporters were dangerous revolutionaries, he was uncomfortably aware that the Greek cause was popular in Russia; not only were the Orthodox clergy eager that he go to the assistance of persecuted Christians, but his troops were restless. 'Your Emperor does not know what to do with his army to stop disaffection,' George IV had pointed out to Darya Lieven the previous year. 'It's to his advantage to use it.' In May

1824 the Tsar proposed that a conference take place at St Petersburg, followed by a full-scale congress. He sent a memorandum to European governments, suggesting that Greece be divided into three autonomous principalities on the model of Moldavia and Wallachia. Plainly Russia hoped to establish a protectorate over them, as it had over the Danubian principalities. It was equally clear that no great European power was going to tolerate such an extension of Russian influence.

Metternich accepted an invitation to the conference, but no firm date was fixed. Nor did he reply to the memorandum for three months, and then with a Sybilline note stating that its 'fundamental arrangements' accorded with 'essential conditions for a generally acceptable pacification.' He was playing for time, hoping that Mehemet Ali, Pasha of Egypt, who was laying waste the Morea, would bring the Greeks to heel. Unexpectedly, Mehemet Ali failed. At the end of October, Metternich wrote gloomily to Esterházy that he doubted 'whether the pacification of Greece could be brought to a satisfactory conclusion by negotiation since all elements for success are lacking'. The situation worsened when Canning refused to send a representative to the conference on the grounds that the Greeks themselves objected to Russia's proposals, a refusal which angered Austria as much as Russia; Metternich knew very well that the British foreign secretary was determined to prevent any revival of the Congress System. The conference assembled at the Russian capital at the close of the year—in practice several discussion groups—and achieved nothing. Metternich could see no point in the two other partners of the Triple Alliance, Austria and Prussia, attending a full-scale 'Congress of St Petersburg' and Austria was only represented by the Austrian ambassador, Lebzeltern. It was a grievous disappointment for the Tsar.

What made the Eastern Question nerve-racking was Alexander's unstable temperament. 'He will feel, as his people will wish him to feel, the ignominy of being ruled by an Austrian minister,' Capo d'Istria had prophesied to Darya Lieven in 1823. However, Metternich never lost his nerve. 'One's hair need not grow grey because of the views or idiocies of the Russian Cabinet, since it's so impractical that these can never take a practical form,' he would comment in April 1825 after receiving alarming reports from Lebzeltern.

For some time Eleanor had been spending part of the year at Paris, as the climate seemed to suit her delicate constitution. On 12 January Metternich wrote, 'I begin to have serious fears for my wife's health'; on 30 January, 'My anxiety about my wife's health grows greater and greater'; and on 8 February, 'The news I have of my poor wife from the physicians has made up my mind to go to Paris.' When he reached her, he saw there was no hope; the tuberculosis she had passed on to her children was killing her. 'I am troubled to the very depths of my heart and just now am good for nothing,' he confided on 14 February. 'Face to face with a catastrophe, the thought of which fills me with sorrow, after thirty years of undisturbed married life I find myself reduced to a fearful loneliness. How am I going to look after my daughters?' She died a Christian death on 19 March. He commented, 'It was the leave taking of a beautiful soul.'

George IV and Wellington invited Metternich to England, but he did not want to meet Canning. 'Wellington came to tell me that he was going to write to you suggesting a new plan of travel, which is this; you would embark at Dieppe and come to Brighton, where I should be and Wellington also,' Darya wrote enthusiastically on 25 March, after her first letter of sympathy. 'From there you would go to Windsor, and you could leave England without going to London and consequently without seeing Mr Canning. He thinks it an admirable plan, as it would please your friends and infuriate your enemy.' However, her lover was much too diplomatic to accept such a scheme, although it had King George's warm support.

Restoration Paris gleamed with prosperity and elegance. The court was even more imposing than before 1789, while the new King, Charles X, was dignified and charming. France was richer than at any time for a hundred years, administered more efficiently than ever before. The prime minister, the Comte de Villèle, had stabilised the franc at the value which it kept until 1914; the machinery of government installed by Napoleon was run by noblemen genuinely loyal to their sovereign. The morale of the Bourbon army was excellent after its triumph in Spain. Even men of letters tended to be convinced royalists—at this date Victor Hugo, Lamartine, Alfred de Vigny and Balzac were all legitimists.

At bottom, Metternich, for all his cosmopolitan outlook, was too Teutonic to sympathise with the French. He had always been uncomfortably aware that their régime's foundations were unsound. 'There was only one Frenchman who ever understood how to master the Revolution, and that was Bonaparte,' he had observed in August 1823. 'The King's government inherited the Counter Revolution from him, not the Revolution . . . today France is like a ship in a storm steered by inexperienced pilots.' As for the King, 'Charles X is frank, loyal, amiable, chivalrous and religious but at the same time weak, too open to suggestion, self-willed and even violent in his prejudices.' In the chancellor's view the régime was fatally flawed as a consequence of Bonaparte having granted a constitution in 1815, undoing everything he had achieved—'The power which France possessed under the Empire was totally destroyed by the ruinous concessions Napoleon had to make during the Hundred Days.' Some may disagree with his analysis, but no one can deny his accuracy in predicting the Revolution of 1830.

When he was received by King Charles at the Tuileries, he recalled tactfully how, in the very same room fifteen years before, Napoleon had told him, 'If ever I disappear as a result of some catastrophe no-one but the Bourbons could sit here.' The King was at his most amiable, investing him with the Order of the Saint-Esprit (the *Cordon Bleu*) and inviting him to dinner, 'a distinction which, I believe, has since the establishment of the monarchy been accorded to only two other private persons, the Duke of Wellington after the battle of Waterloo and Lord Moira as a personal friend of the late King', he reported proudly to the Emperor. 'The dinner was quite *en famille,* with only the King, the Dauphin, Madame la Dauphine and the Duchesse de Berry. The royalists praise the gesture to the skies while the revolutionists believe that all is over with freedom of the Press.' Everyone made him welcome. Visitors came flocking—'Ultras, Bonapartists, Jacobins and Jesuits, a complete valley of Jehosaphat,' he told Gentz. Even the Archbishop of Paris, Monseigneur de Quélen, called on him, a prelate famous for preaching that not only did Our Lord come from a very good family indeed on His father's side, but there was good reason to believe that through His mother He was the rightful legitimist Prince of Judea. He enjoyed meeting the conservative thinker Louis de Bonald, one of the 'Prophets of the Past'. 'I see a great deal of Bonald,' he reported. 'He interests me very much and is far more down to earth than I had expected.'

Nonetheless, the France of 1825 made Metternich thoroughly uneasy. 'My feeling of a dreadful state of affairs here is so strong that I cannot possibly express it,' he informed the Emperor. 'Everything sacred has been undermined . . . It is a society ruined by conflicting passions.' One third of the population was unbaptised, there was a flood of antireligious and pornographic literature. The upper classes were greedy for money and titles.

Yet he was impressed by the prime minister, Joseph de Villèle, a charmless nobleman from Toulouse, former naval officer and sometime slave trader. 'The present ministry is definitely the best since the Restoration,' he confided to Gentz. 'But it consists of only one man . . . Villèle's strength lies in something he said to me the other day. When I asked him bluntly "Are you going to stay or will they turn you out?" he answered "I'm determined to stay and a determined man isn't easily put on one side" '—words which might easily have been spoken by the Austrian chancellor, who was also reassured by the eagerness with which his views were sought. 'People look on me as a kind of lantern to light up a dark night . . . Villèle is always running in and out with questions which, God knows, are easy enough to answer.' Although full of foreboding, he was more than satisfied with his visit, telling the Emperor, 'It would be difficult for me to give Your Majesty any idea of the good effect which my stay here has had on all political matters.' He was able to report that 'in the Eastern Question France goes along with us entirely'. At the beginning of April he learnt that, at the conference still dragging on at St Petersburg, France had joined Austria and Prussia in rejecting armed intervention in the Balkans. The 'English-Spanish Question'—the future of Spain's former colonies in Latin America—proved more complicated, but before leaving Paris on 20 April the chancellor had a last meeting with Villèle, after which he wrote to the Emperor, 'Now there is not a single dark area here in diplomatic affairs.'

His visit to Lombardy was made memorable by the offer of a Cardinal's hat from Leo XII. This unwordly but impeccably conservative pontiff believed that he wished to enter the Sacred College, an illusion which had arisen from his often expressed preference for the colour red. It was one of the few honours ever declined by Metternich. If a ludicrous episode, it shows the position which he now occupied in Europe.

Undoubtedly he was vain, though his conceit has been exaggerated. He would have been inhuman not to take pride in his achievements. His real weakness was excessive optimism. At the end of June he assured Gentz that the Eastern Question could be solved to Austria's satisfaction, stressing that an envoy sent by Canning to Nesselrode (to see if Russia and England could settle the Greek problem between them) had been told that Alexander would never desert his allies. Austria must go on temporising, 'wade through the mud . . . If we get past September and October safely, we shall have won.' His reason for thinking so was that Ibrahim Pasha, Mehemet Ali's son, looked to be winning the war in the Morea. He was also convinced that the Tsar would never unleash his troops because he did not trust them. (Lebzeltern had got wind of the liberal officers who would launch the Decembrist coup at the end of the year.) Metternich's warnings to Alexander about worldwide Carbonarism had been based on more than cynical alarmism.

Yet the Tsar was on the point of making a volte-face. The St Petersburg conference had adjourned without reaching a decision; it was quite clear that the Austrians had been playing for time. And during his visit to Paris, in a rare moment of indiscretion, Metternich had boasted that he knew how to handle the Tsar. His words were reported to Alexander, who ordered Nesselrode to reconsider Russia's relations with Austria.

Darya Lieven played a key role in the ensuing realignment. She was fully aware that her husband, a very limited man, only kept his embassy because of her astonishingly close links with the men who ruled England. Even so, she lived in constant dread of

Lieven's recall. That summer she had gone back to St Petersburg alone to ingratiate herself with the Tsar and Nesselrode. In the meantime she had learnt of the growing rift between Alexander and her Austrian lover.

The Duke of Wellington once observed of Darya, 'She can and will betray everybody in turn if it suits her plans.' As soon as she saw Tsar Alexander, she informed him that he was the dupe of Metternich, who had tricked him by inventing imaginary difficulties. She suggested that the time had come to break with Austria over the Eastern Question, denied that Canning was a 'Jacobin' and proposed an alliance with England. Anxious to preserve her valuable relationship with 'my Clement', she tried to cover her tracks by warning Lebzeltern that Russia might declare war on Turkey if Austria was not more cooperative. To her astonishment, the ambassador replied that the Tsar dared not go to war—he would be in more danger from his own troops than from the Turks.

On Darya's last morning in St Petersburg, Nesselrode brought her instructions from the Tsar; she was to contact Canning and tell him that Russia wanted an alliance with England but it was up to him to make the first move. In October she and her husband called on the foreign secretary at his house at Seaford near Brighton. It is not known what was said, but Lieven had further talks with him at the end of the month during which the ambassador stressed Russia's break with Austria and France over the Eastern Question. Again Darya dissembled, writing to Metternich that 'there is a certain coldness towards you at St Petersburg'. He wrote back that he was well aware of it. 'What have I to fear? The noise?' He joked that 'thick mists lie on the Neva but they will soon clear'. The Russians would realize that they had taken the wrong road. Privately he may have been thinking that they were likely to see a coup by the army.

There were problems to worry the chancellor nearer home. As Apostolic King of Hungary, the Emperor summoned the Hungarian Estates to meet at Pressburg (Pozsony). 'On 11 September the Hungarian Diet, one of the most tiresome constitutional *divertissements* in the world, will be opened,' he told Gentz. 'I shall have to speak Latin and dress like a hussar.' As a Hungarian magnate (he had been created 'Lord of Daruvár'), clad in dolman, high boots and plumed kalpak, he attended the Empress's coronation as Queen. The Diet was a less cheerful business. It had not been called since 1812, Hungary being ruled by Imperial rescript, but he had advised the Emperor-King to summon it to approve new taxes. Much to his alarm, there was an unexpectedly fierce outburst of Magyar nationalism, one demand being that Hungarian should replace Latin as the language of the Diet. A parliamentary opposition emerged, led by Count István Széchenyi, a rich young magnate who was a cousin of Eleanor.

Széchenyi was the first great Hungarian noble to insist on speaking Magyar during debates in the Diet, and he gave a year's income towards founding an academy to study the language. A Hungarian Whig (who during visits to London had fallen under the spell of Lord Holland), he wanted his country's constitution to become more like that of England, urging fellow magnates to surrender their exemption from taxation. He also produced a whole portfolio of plans for economic and industrial development, of which the most successful was an iron bridge across the Danube linking Buda and Pest, the *Lánchíd*—modelled on the Hammersmith Bridge. In addition, he inspired a chain of debating clubs. Metternich recognised a formidable opponent, 'a political spitfire', and tried, unsuccessfully, to convert him to absolutism, warning of the peril in which overassertive nationalism placed the Monarchy. 'Pull out a single stone and the whole structure will come crashing down.' Ironically, in future years Metternich was forced to ally with Széchenyi's disciples, adopting many of his economic and industrial ideas. Looking back, Metternich described the Count as 'a heated but high minded patriot', admitting that he had always stayed loyal to the Monarchy.

He began to worry about the revolutionary threat in England, of all places. In September he sent Esterházy an odd instruction about the project to establish a university of London. 'I authorise you to tell His Majesty that I am perfectly certain in stating that should the scheme be accepted, it will be the end of England.' This has caused much amusement among English historians and admittedly it is difficult to understand what inspired the warning

—perhaps a memory of his experiences at Strasbourg as a young man. Yet he was justified in suspecting that the framework of English government and society was far from secure, as would be seen in the years before the passing of the Reform Bill.

Tsar Alexander I died suddenly and unexpectedly on 1 December 1825. Metternich genuinely regretted his passing. He was one of the few men who ever understood the Tsar. In 1829 he wrote a 'Portrait' of him for what he called his *Gallery of Celebrated Contemporaries*. It is a study which tells one a good deal about Metternich's genius for psychological domination:

> He was as easily led astray by excessive mistrust of erroneous theories as by a natural weakness for them. His judgement was always under the sway of some new idea which had caught his fancy; he seized on them as if by sudden inspiration and with the utmost enthusiasm. Soon he was ruled by them, making the subjection of his will an easy matter for their originators.

The analyst continues that, 'after long observation', he had discovered that Alexander's thought went in cycles of about five years. An idea

> grew in his mind for about two years until he regarded it as a system. During the third year he stayed faithful to the system he had adopted and cherished, incapable of estimating its true value or any dangerous consequences. In the fourth year awareness of these consequences began to diminish his enthusiasm. In the fifth there was a confused mixing of the old, nearly worn out system with the new idea. This new idea was often the exact opposite of the one which he had just abandoned.

In his view the Tsar died 'from weariness with life . . . his character was not strong enough to keep a balance between contradictory inclinations'.

Metternich informed Darya Lieven that 'fiction has come to an end and now we're starting history'. ('*Le roman est fini, nous entrons dans l'histoire*'.) It was a fair comment. Alexander's enthusiasms and vacillation had thrown the foreign policy of almost every European country into confusion. Yet he had been the original begetter of the Alliance, even if he had thrown it over at the last. Darya wrote with unintentional irony, 'He gave me a new interest in life.'

But would Metternich be able to cope with the new Russian ruler?

14

War?

The system of union known as the Alliance has for long been nothing more than a sham.

METTERNICH in 1827

We should have to declare war if Russia tried to expand her territory in the Levant since it would increase her frontiers with us . . . Those territories, if left in Turkish hands, benefit both our frontiers and our political position.

METTERNICH to Baron Lebzeltern, 1816

The Eastern Question was about to become the greatest threat to European peace since the Hundred Days. Metternich would suddenly find himself faced by the spectre of war in the Balkans. At the same time a series of harrowing personal tragedies devastated what had already been an unusually sad middle life.

Confusion over the succession to the Russian throne resulted in an abortive revolt at St Petersburg by the Decembrists—'Russian Carbonari', as the chancellor called them—who demanded a constitution. Metternich's warnings to Alexander about secret societies had not been so very wide of the mark—the conspiracy was 'an exact copy of those at Madrid, Naples and Turin', he wrote. 'Had Tsar Alexander lived, the same thing would have happened, and he and the Imperial family would have been massacred.' As for the present Tsar, the thirty-year-old Nicholas I, he commented, 'It would be impossible to cast the new reign's horoscope.'

In any case, Metternich was desperately worried by the grave illness of his friend and patron, Emperor Francis, who in March 1826 hovered between life and death. 'I needn't tell you that these last six days have been full of terrible anxieties for me,' he confided to his son Victor. 'Besides the uneasiness I felt from the very beginning of His Majesty's illness, I had to think about the future—or how to arrange it.'

He was taken aback by the news that Wellington was being sent by Canning to bring the new Tsar formal condolences and congratulations from King George. However, he sent a message to his old friend. 'Metternich is quite prepared to enlist under your banners and to leave the interests of Europe in your hands, satisfied that they cannot be placed in better.' He might not have said it had he known that Christopher Lieven (about to be created a Prince) had wept with joy on hearing that Wellington would go to St Petersburg and that Darya was seeing Mr Canning every Sunday afternoon. Metternich was very angry when he learnt that on 4 April 1826 a protocol to work together to secure Greek autonomy had been signed by Britain and Russia; he described the protocol as 'an abortion which in a few weeks will be disowned by those who formed it'. The Alliance was indeed a thing of the past.

Lady Georgina Wellesley, wife of the British ambassador at Vienna, told one of the protocol's secret architects that Prince Metternich was paying daily visits to a Fräulein Antoinette von Leykam, 'Whom some say is your future wife, others your present mistress,' Darya wrote furiously on 16 May. 'So much for the constancy of men. Don't you think my reproaches are rather lukewarm? If I were to take revenge—Heavens, no I shan't take revenge.' She had heard that while the girl was very pretty, she scarcely belonged to the great nobility; her great-grandfather had been a coachman at Wetzlar, her grandfather an ennobled civil servant and her mother a Neapolitan opera singer. Metternich's own mother remonstrated when she heard that marriage was in the air. But Antoinette Leykam was twenty-one, small and blonde, very attractive, with a taste for the arts, and apparently in love with a man thirty-three years older than herself.

Although he was in his fifties, there seems to have been a cult of Metternich among Viennese young ladies. Mélanie Zichy-Ferraris was the daughter of the acknowledged queen of the capital's society, Countess Molly Zichy-Ferraris—a bosom friend of old Princess Metternich. Twenty-one, tall and striking, with a voluptuous figure, raven-black hair, and one blue eye and one green, she is said to have told her friends that one day she would marry the chancellor; she wrote him a letter of sympathy when Eleanor died. Her parents were eager for the match. But Metternich wanted the socially impossible Antoinette.

'In the French newspapers Mr Canning is beginning to be called "the accomplice of the abominable head of the Holy Alliance," ' he noted with amusement in June. 'I hadn't expected it, but we always get what we least expect.' In reality Canning was working tirelessly to widen the rift between Austria and Prussia.

After 'that detestable Eastern Question' Portugal was the main diplomatic irritant. There had been coups and countercoups in Lisbon since 1822. Its throne was disputed between Dom Miguel, the conservative leader, and his seven-year-old niece Maria, supported by the liberals, a struggle which continued for a decade. The previous monarch had granted a constitution in 1822, much to Metternich's annoyance. By the summer of 1826, full-scale civil war was looming, Miguelista guerillas raiding from Spain, where King Ferdinand gave them shelter. Naturally, Canning supported Queen Maria and the constitutional party. In August Austria proposed that a full-scale congress should meet as soon as possible to discuss the situation, but the Russians refused to attend it. In September Canning went over to Paris—where he too was invited to dinner by Charles X—and persuaded the French government to bring pressure on the Spanish King to curb the Miguelistas. Secretly the Austrian chancellor continued to encourage them.

Despite her anger—perhaps simulated—over Antoinette von Leykam, Darya went on writing to Metternich once a fortnight till 22 November, when she thanked him for his letter 174 and begged him to keep on writing. 'We should be hard put to it, you and I, to find in the whole world people of our own calibre. Our hearts are well matched, our minds too; and our letters are very pleasant.' But the correspondence ceased. Gentz had deduced that the protocol, at first thought to be the result of Wellington's ineptitude, must have been inspired by the Lievens.

In August Metternich visited his country estates. He wrote to his mother that Königswart 'still bears traces of your kind nature and good taste'. He also told her that their new family vault at Plass would soon be finished, Plass being an abandoned but magnificent Bohemian abbey which he had bought recently and was converting into a *Schloss*. He wrote to her from Johannisberg too, boasting of his magnolias and azaleas—'All the neighbours come to see my garden.' Among his visitors was the Marquess of Hertford (the model for Thackeray's Marquess of Steyne in *Vanity Fair*), 'the most decided Tory in England'. He told Gentz, 'I haven't met so independent minded, thoughtful and clever an Englishman for years.' What pleased him greatly was Hertford agreeing that Canning was 'the scourge of the world'.

As the chancellor had seen immediately, the protocol between Britain and Russia made war more, rather than less, likely should the Porte not accede to their demands. Admittedly, in May 1826 at Akkerman in Bessarabia the Sultan's envoys gave every indication of wishing to cooperate; but when a convention was signed there in October which gave the Danubian principalities increased independence, they did not yield an inch over Greece. Nevertheless, the Lievens convinced Canning that the protocol could be implemented without going to war. An unexpected development was the sabre-rattling philhelenism of Charles X, who informed Canning during his visit to Paris that he wanted Russia and Austria to threaten Turkey into compliance by land, while France and Britain did so by sea. Metternich could do nothing to stop the slide towards war; in November he acknowledged ruefully that the Tsar obviously disliked him. In January 1827 Russian, British and French delegates began formal negotiations in London to replace the protocol by a tripartite treaty.

The Austrian and Prussian ambassadors represented their countries. On 25 March Metternich sent Eszterházy precise instructions; the powers must agree unanimously on action to be taken; an armistice and a cease-fire should be obtained from the Porte; and Turkey-in-Europe should be divided between Moslems and Christians, under a guarantee by the powers. He stressed that 'the Kaiser is, from conviction and feeling, unwilling to admit the chances of a war with the Porte'. This time Metternich was not optimistic.

He ended his instructions with: 'The disorder which reigned for six years in the Eastern Question will not yield easily to a preconceived idea of Tsar Nicholas, which moreover is not quite clear to anyone.' In May the Russian ambassador to Vienna conveyed a message from the Tsar: 'The Emperor sees with the most lively regret the court of Austria bringing forward proposals on the Eastern Question which differ from those of His Imperial Majesty.' Metternich remained unshaken. Yet he hinted at his bitterness in a despatch of 11 June to Count Apponyi, the new Austrian ambassador to Paris: the Emperor preferred to remain true to his principles rather than 'sacrifice them in the hope of saving by his agreement the appearances of an Alliance which one of its principal members constantly disowns'—a hit at Britain, where Canning was now prime minister. On 6 July 1827 the plenipotentiaries of Russia, Britain and France signed the Treaty of London. By it they agreed, in a secret clause, to use their joint navies to intervene forcibly if the Porte did not give way over the Greeks; such intervention would be aimed primarily at preventing Mehemet Ali sending reinforcements from Egypt to the Morea; in effect, it would be a blockade. Even Wellington saw the danger of war, going down on his knees (if he is to be believed) to ask Canning to omit the secret clause.

When the French ambassador to St Petersburg, the Comte de la Ferronays, stayed with Metternich at Königswart en route to Russia, Metternich suggested to him that the 'present difficulty' between the Russian and Austrian governments was 'a kind of game designed to make us give in—a game which will end soon enough if we keep our nerve.' Moreover, 'The absurd Triple Alliance is only in its first stage.' As for Austria, 'Our isolation in the affair stems solely from the unconquerable aversion of our august master to violate what he regards as a principle.' Metternich instructed Baron Ottenfels at Constantinople to persuade the Turks to defuse the situation by making timely concessions. 'Knowing your zeal and devotion to the service, I need not beg you to use all the promptitude of which the forms of Ottoman diplomacy admit.'

Metternich was much encouraged by Canning's death on 8 August. His valediction was: 'the man whom Providence hurled upon England and Europe like a malevolent meteor . . . England is delivered from a great scourge.' By then Wellington had come to share his opinion—Canning had 'done as much mischief in four months as it was possible for a man to do. God knows how it is to be remedied.' The chancellor had high but misplaced hopes of the Duke as a friend of Austria.

Meanwhile, there was his marriage. He wrote in October to Countess Molly Zichy-Ferraris, Melanie's mother, to complain of gossip. (Every princely drawing room in Vienna talked of nothing but his *mésalliance,* including his own mother's.) 'Tittle-tattle is the peculiar characteristic of Viennese society,' he grumbled. The Emperor had been his only friend in the matter, his only confidant, the 'surest guide and kindest of fathers'. Francis was sympathetic; notoriously uxorious, he had buried three wives. Antoinette was obviously a most attractive girl; rumours circulated that Victor Metternich had wanted to marry her himself, but his father forbade the match as being beneath him. In a gesture of support, the Emperor created Antoinette Countess of Beilstein in her own right.

All this time the situation in the Levant was deteriorating. The Allies had now blockaded the Turkish and Egyptian fleets in the bay of Navarino in the Morea. Vice-Admiral Sir E. Codrington, commanding the British squadron, sent an insulting message to the chief of the Austrian flotilla in the Archipelago, accusing him of aiding the Ottoman fleet; Codrington warned him that he would not make any distinction between Austrian and Turkish vessels.

Metternich's wedding took place quietly on 3 November 1827 at Hetzendorf outside Vienna, at a palace lent by the Emperor. As his carriage was leaving the Ballhausplatz it was stopped by an equerry with an urgent summons to the Hofburg; here Francis gave him the news that on 27 October the Allies had blown the Turkish fleet out of the water at Navarino. The chancellor then went on to his wedding, so late that his mother and sister were beginning to hope that he had changed his mind.

The marriage meant the loss of a supremely valuable contact for Darya, whose brother had just been appointed head of Tsar Nicholas's secret police, the Third Section. Furious, she quoted Mme de Coigny's pun with relish—'*Le chevalier de la Sainte Alliance a maintenant fini par une mésalliance.*' Antoinette was certainly an odd choice for someone credited (wrongly) with thinking 'mankind begins with barons'.

Metternich lamented 'the terrible catastrophe of Navarino', telling Apponyi that he had always known the Treaty of London could end only in complete inaction or war; he described Constantinople as 'defenceless against a combined invasion by [Russian] land forces supported by reinforcements echeloned along the Black Sea, and provisioned by a fleet'. The Emperor was so alarmed that he wanted to mass 100,000 troops in Hungary; there were rumours, reported by the Russian ambassador, that Austria intended to occupy Serbia, and perhaps Moldavia and Wallachia as well—the last two being regarded in normal times as Russia's preserve. The chancellor succeeded in dissuading his master. Not only were the Imperial finances too vulnerable, but the Carbonari in Germany and Italy would take advantage of the situation. Metternich continued urging the Porte to conciliate the Tsar by making peace with the Greeks. If war between Russia and Turkey did not come immediately, it was made inevitable by the obstinacy of the Turks, who even tried to reassert their grip over the Roumanians.

By now the British were beginning to appreciate the unsoundness of Canning's policy. The last thing they wanted was Russia in possession of Constantinople. 'Goody' Goderich, Canning's successor, was correctly seen by Metternich as 'feeble'—George IV called his prime minister a 'blubbering fool'. However, the chancellor was reassured when Wellington became premier in January 1828. Unfortunately, like so many great soldiers, the Duke would scarcely prove a distinguished statesman.

Metternich had other worries. 'For France there is nothing but the Republic or the Empire,' he observed to Victor in the same month. 'It is possible France may have to go through anarchy once again to reach order.' In February he repeated, 'The country that is most seriously ill is France . . . the country with the least promising future.'

In a memorandum of March 1828, designed to be shown to Wellington, he expressed his fear of a religious war breaking out in the Near East which might engulf Europe, threatening 'the foundations of the peace so gloriously established and so happily maintained for fifteen years'. Yet 'measures which six months ago might have been considered more than rigorous may now be the Porte's salvation and expedient for Europe'. Metternich proposed that the Morea and the Greek Islands should be given autonomy, a realistic acceptance of the facts very similar to the solution eventually adopted. Nevertheless, both Wellington and the Tsar rejected it out of hand. At the end of the year the chancellor proposed a congress to discuss the entire Eastern Question, again to meet with a refusal.

Russia invaded Turkish territory in April 1828, 'all that we have dreaded and foreseen'. Yet conciliatory approaches were made by Tsar Nicholas to the new Austrian ambassador at St Petersburg, Count Zichy. 'I shall always be the Holy Alliance's warmest supporter,' said Nicholas. 'I repeat that I abhor and detest the Greeks . . . I look on them as subjects in revolt against their legitimate sovereign.' But the losses inflicted on Russian commerce by the closure of the Bosphorus (and of the Black Sea ports), together with the refusal to evacuate the Danubian principalities, had forced him to go to war—no obstacle would stop him, even if the campaign meant the collapse of the Ottoman Empire.

Metternich neither liked nor trusted Russians. He speaks of no other race with such detestation. 'That dung-heap of semi-humans, made up of the filthiest elements but gilded from top to bottom, totally ignorant and puffed up like balloons, aping fashion in such a way as to look ridiculous, that swarm of effeminates who try to push their way into every salon . . .' was his opinion in a despatch to Lebzeltern of February 1826. At about the same time he told a French statesman, the Duc de Damas, that if Russia's 'so-called civilised class' had a veneer of civilisation, it penetrated none of her institutions. She might have to pay dearly for this veneer, 'which creates two peoples out of a single empire, one belonging in the drawing room, the other tied to the soil'. As for the Russian army, it was 'a species of infernal machine [ie a bomb] placed halfway between the two extremes'. While Metternich thought that Russia was a strong and potentially very dangerous neighbour, he was convinced that many of her institutions were structurally unsound.

By the end of September, with winter approaching, the Russian advance into the Balkans—directed by the Tsar in person—was grinding to a halt. Nicholas had expected the Turks to be overcome by fear and rise in revolt against the Sultan Mahmud II. Instead, they were fighting back with the utmost gallantry while, overextended, the Tsar's own troops were starving and disease-ridden. The Austrian chancellor was nonetheless extremely worried. 'If the war should be renewed in 1829, then Europe will have to face a dreadful prospect of troubles and revolutions.' What was at stake was 'the survival of the old political order or its fall'.

A harrowing year of bereavement began for Metternich with the death of his mother in December 1828. Although resigned—the old princess had been ill for some time—he was saddened. 'If my mother had not been my mother, she would still have been a life-long friend,' he wrote to Molly Zichy. 'Our minds had so much in common.' Much to his joy, in January 1829 Antoinette gave birth to a son, Richard; twelve days later she died of puerperal fever. He was shattered. 'The Emperor, who is certainly my best friend, wants me to go to the palace,' he told Victor. (He declined, since he would have to come back to his house anyway.) 'Adam Müller heard of the death,' he recounts in the same letter. 'He looked up to heaven and said solemnly "Now, for the first time, I know man's fate" and fell, struck dead by an apopleptic fit.' He ended, 'After this tale of death and mourning what more can I say. You are my nearest friend, and you must share my only too natural sorrow. May God keep you and my other children and help me drag out the rest of my miserable existence as He sees fit.' Antoinette had been not quite twenty-three. He had a portrait of her painted posthumously, keeping it in his study for the rest of his life.

His relationship with his first son was an unusually close and happy one. They corresponded regularly. 'I take refuge from myself in the troubles of Europe,' he told Victor three weeks after Antoinette's death, and related how he was at his desk by nine o'clock in the morning, often working a fifteen-hour day. 'I hope we shall come to an end in the East, but what are we going to see in the West? Poor France is in a very, very bad way!' By contrast he was delighted by the passing of the Catholic Emancipation Bill in England in April, prompting Emperor Francis to send 'His Britannic Majesty sincere congratulations on the issue of an affair which will add a fresh flower to the glory of his reign'. (George IV had given his assent with the utmost reluctance.) During the same month he noted that the Russian army was having to recruit sixteen-year-old boys. He was uneasy, however, at the number of spies in the Balkans—'Serbia and Albania are full of Russian agents.' He was also concerned about who would become King of Greece. In his opinion Leopold of Coburg (later to become King of the Belgians) 'must have been stung by a tarantula to want the job'.

Victor had never been strong, having inherited his mother's tuberculosis. In the latter part of 1828 he had been coughing so much that his father made him leave the Paris embassy and spend the winter in Italy. In July 1829 he returned to Vienna, where the doctors' treatment produced a temporary improvement so that in August the chancellor was able to visit his new château of Plass. He wrote to his son about the hordes driving out from Marienbad to inspect it: 'Thirty or forty carriages are parked round the little inn every fine afternoon . . . Among visitors in 1829 were the Queen of Haiti and the Princesses Amethyst and Athenaïs, her august and very black daughters.' He spoke with melancholy about his new chapel and family vault but joked about Gentz, who had accompanied him—'Gentz is more innocent in the country than in the town'—and how fascinated Gentz was by Metternich's iron foundry.

When the chancellor returned to Vienna in September, he found Victor much better. Suddenly the young man's condition deteriorated. During his final illness he would not let his father leave his bedside. 'I have seen many men die, in various ways—I have never seen one depart as my poor son departed,' he confided in Molly Zichy. 'Death itself was for him, and for us all, a deliverance.' Victor died at the end of November, aged twenty-six. Within twelve months Metternich had lost his mother, his wife and his son.

Despite problems with supplies and sickness, the Russian army in the Balkans regained the initiative in the spring and summer of

1829. The Tsar's chief-of-staff, General Count Diebitsch, routed Hussein Pasha's troops, reaching Adrianople with a small force early in August. 'The future existence of the Ottoman Empire is in doubt,' Metternich warned Eszterházy in a despatch of 21 September. 'No power is more interested than Austria in preserving what is left of this empire.' He was relieved by the mild terms secured by the Turks in the same month at the peace of Adrianople; they had to complete their withdrawal from Moldavia and Wallachia, leaving the entrance to the Danube under Russian control, and accept a Greek state. But Turkey-in-Europe remained and the Russians did not, as feared, annex large areas of the Balkans. 'The end of the Turkish monarchy could only be survived by Austria for a short time,' Gentz had written in 1815. He called the peace of Adrianople 'the greatest piece of luck Europe might hope for'. The Austrian chancellor informed the Emperor that the peace was 'to be regarded as a moment of repose'.

In the same report of 9 October he lamented that the Alliance no longer existed; otherwise the crisis of 1827–9 might have been avoided. He was still confident that, sooner or later, the European powers would join Austria in rebuilding the Alliance which alone could ensure peace.

Initially Metternich (and Gentz) welcomed the appointment of Prince Jules de Polignac as head of the French government in November 1829. In August the chancellor had written that a reform in the electoral laws or the press laws was essential for France but very difficult, in October that there would be either a revolution or a new and more effective restoration. But he was disturbed by Polignac's ambitious foreign policy and preference for Russia as opposed to Austria. Nor did he like the announcement in March that France was sending an army to conquer Algiers, though later he contemplated the possibility of a congress assembling there to recreate the Alliance.

Clearly with the unpleasant possibility of a Franco-Russian axis in mind, but also with real sincerity, in May 1830 he had lectured the French ambassador at Vienna, the Comte de Rayneval, about the danger of 'bilateral' alliances. 'Europe's salvation depends on general, not partial alliances,' he explained:

> I'm not thinking in terms of the Holy Alliance, which in any case was never anything more than a pious fiction; nor in terms of the Treaty of Chaumont which was for a single special occasion; nor in terms of the Congress of Aix-la-Chapelle. What I want is a moral understanding between those five powers whose strength and standing make them the natural arbiters of Europe's fate. I only ask that they take no important step, do nothing which might put the general peace at risk, without first reaching a joint understanding. I want them, before all else, to be guided by the reflection that nowadays ideological considerations are not always the most important, that each country has to take its own particular domestic circumstances into account. The tranquillity of every state is menaced by a spirit of innovation, though a better name for it would be disorder. We must oppose it, with a determination to preserve, and we have to try to strengthen and stabilise all our existing institutions. It makes no difference whether they are old or new—if they are institutions with proper legal standing, then they deserve our support.

In part this was intended to warn Rayneval that, if the French government meant to increase its power, it should do so on the basis of the Charter of 1815, much as Metternich disliked constitutions. Yet the outburst was also a good summary of both his European philosophy and his conservatism.

Throughout the first half of the year 1830 the chancellor had been growing increasingly uneasy. In his eyes Wellington was just as ineffectual as Polignac and he saw grave disorders ahead in both their countries; on 15 June he described London and Paris as 'madhouses'. The only hope lay in a revival of the Alliance.

15

The New Restoration Europe, 1830–35

The present state of Europe is disgustful to me.
METTERNICH to George Ticknor in 1836

For, since Austria was a European necessity, Europe was an Austrian necessity. Austria could not follow a policy of isolation, or even of independence; she had always to be justifying her existence.
A. J. P. TAYLOR, *The Habsburg Monarchy*

Restoration Europe gave every sign of coming to an end during the early 1830s. In France the Bourbons fell, through their own folly. In England revolution was only averted by the Reform Bill. Poland and Belgium rose against foreign masters, while liberal monarchies were established in Spain and Portugal. It looked as though the Vienna settlement had been smashed. 'The gaze of the impartial and informed observer rests at the present time on a world in ruins,' Metternich commented during the last months of 1830. Yet Austria, Germany and Italy were unaffected, and the Triple Alliance was reforged, while most of the 1815 frontiers survived. The Restoration proved to be far from dead.

On 31 July 1830 Metternich informed Emperor Francis that August was going to be a landmark in European history. 'Whatever happens, one will be able to say that a whole new order has been born.' He was referring to French ordinances altering the electoral system and abolishing freedom of the press. While he thought them 'the most important thrust at Liberalism since the Carlsbad Decrees', he had grave misgivings about Polignac's capacity to stage such a coup when the French army was away in Algiers.

On the evening of 4 August a French newspaper, sent posthaste to him by the Austrian ambassador at Frankfurt, who had been given it by the Rothschilds, arrived at Königswart. It contained a report of the July Revolution ('*Les Trois Glorieuses*', the *Three Glorious Days*) and the fall of Charles X, commenting, 'Any return of the Bourbons would seem difficult since, to judge from public opinion in Paris and the surrounding departments, the nation is ready to be cut to pieces rather than let itself be ruled by them again.' When he read it, Metternich fainted. Dr Jäger, summoned to revive him, heard him mutter, 'My entire life's work has been destroyed.' His despair is understandable. A cleverer man than King Charles could have survived. Now it looked like 1792 all over again, as if anarchy and then dictatorship would follow, spreading the Jacobin creed throughout Europe in the wake of appalling wars.

On 7 August the Duke of Orleans, the son of Philippe Egalité and head of the younger branch of the Bourbons, was proclaimed King of the French. If, as Gentz puts it, King Louis Philippe I at least represented the monarchical principle, the Austrian chancellor thought that 'a royal throne surrounded by republican institutions' was quite meaningless. Indeed, his view of the July monarchy in France is of the utmost importance for an understanding of his opposition to liberal democracy. Metternich did not oppose long-established constitutions, such as that of the British; what he feared were *new* constitutions which, he believed, must inevitably lead to chaos. He was convinced that the Orleanist régime was a repetition of the French constitutional monarchy of 1791–2, no more than a halting place on the giddy downward slope into full-scale revolution—in modern terms, that liberal democracy would swiftly be replaced by totalitarian democracy. As late as May 1832 he wrote to Apponyi (who remained as Austrian ambassador at Paris) that 'France in 1832 resembles France in 1792'. He was always certain that Louis Philippe could not last, and ultimately events would prove him right.

He was soon on his feet again, writing to the Emperor at midnight on 4 August that he was going to see Nesselrode—providentially, the Russian foreign minister was taking the waters at Carlsbad, only a few hours drive from Königswart. Two days later they agreed on what to do, written down by Metternich on a small sheet of paper which became known as the *chiffon de Carlsbad*, 'the scrap from Carlsbad'; Austria and Russia would not intervene unless the new French government threatened the rest of Europe. The chancellor hoped it would be 'a basis of union between the great powers and in particular the old Quadruple Alliance'. However, the Tsar wanted to take military action, calling Louis Philippe 'a vile usurper'. (Even in England the new monarch, William IV, referred to the King of the French as an 'infamous scoundrel'.) Russian troops in Western Europe were one of Metternich's nightmares, so Austria and Prussia recognised the Orleanist régime, forcing Nicholas to follow suit.

'The extraordinary influence exercised by the Revolution of July over men's minds, far beyond the boundaries of France, is shown by what happens every day,' the chancellor wrote in October. The Belgians had risen at the end of August, demanding independence from their Dutch rulers. In November the Poles threw the Russians out of Warsaw. In the same month Wellington resigned, refusing to have anything to do with parliamentary reform, and a Whig government came in with Lord Grey as prime minister; an increasingly violent period of political agitation began in England. Revolt threatened in Germany and Italy.

Chaos in the world of diplomacy, let alone the menace of revolution, required strong nerves. Metternich wisely took steps to ensure feminine support, proposing to Mélanie Zichy-Ferraris in October 1830. He was fifty-seven, she twenty-five, but she accepted with alacrity. They were married in Vienna on 30 January 1831 by the Papal Nuncio, 'all Vienna making an appearance' at the reception, according to the bride's diary. Next day she was received in audience by the Emperor at the Hofburg. 'Make him happy' said Francis. 'He forgives all his enemies and never bears a grudge'—an odd compliment for the Grand Inquisitor of Europe. He praised his chancellor again and again. Despite discrepancy in age, and despite her overbearing temperament, the marriage

The young Metternich, by Anton Graff. (*Ullstein Bilderdienst, Berlin*)

Metternich's father, Count Franz-Georg Karl von Metternich-Winneburg, later Prince of Ochsenhausen, an underrated diplomat and statesman. (*Private collection*)

Metternich's mother, born Maria-Beatrix-Aloisia von Kagenegg, by Franz Lieder. (*Private collection*)

Metternich's first wife, born Princess Eleanor von Kaunitz—'Laure'—in middle age during the 1820s, by Franz Lieder. (*Private collection*)

Wilhelmine of Courland, Duchess of Sagan, an unfaithful mistress who made Metternich very unhappy. (*Bild-Archiv der Österreichischen Nationalbibliothek, Vienna*)

Duchesse d'Abrantès, Napoleon's 'little pest', whom Metternich seduced for political reasons. (*Bibliothèque Nationale, Paris*)

Napoleon in 1814 after hearing that the Allies had entered Paris—'Prince Metternich . . . has destroyed me systematically,' he commented later—by Paul Hippolyte Delaroche. (*Archiv für Kunst und Geschichte, Berlin*)

Metternich in 1818, one of three portraits by Thomas Lawrence; the prince disliked this version because of its sardonic expression. (*Bild-Archiv der Österreichischen National-bibliothek, Vienna*)

Bust of Metternich in 1819, by Bertel Thorwaldsen. (*Bild-Archiv der Österreichischen Nationalbibliothek, Vienna*)

Bust of Alexander I, by Bertel Thorwaldsen. At first Metternich's opponent, the Tsar eventually became his political disciple. (*Private collection*)

Princess Lieven—'Darya'—Metternich's mistress and a Russian agent who betrayed him, by Thomas Lawrence. (*Tate Gallery, London*)

ABOVE: Metternich's third wife, twenty-two years younger, countess Mélanie Zichy-Ferraris. (*Ullstein Bilderdienst, Berlin*)

ABOVE: George Canning, the British statesman who wrecked Metternich's plans for European cooperation, by Thomas Lawrence. (*National Portrait Gallery, London.*)

RIGHT: Metternich at sixty-three, still the most powerful man in Europe, by Giuseppe Molteni. (*Bild-Archiv der Österreichischen Nationalbibliothek, Vienna*)

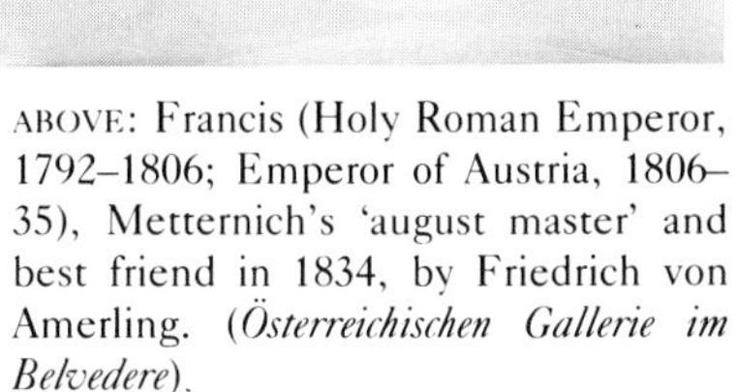

ABOVE: Francis (Holy Roman Emperor, 1792–1806; Emperor of Austria, 1806–35), Metternich's 'august master' and best friend in 1834, by Friedrich von Amerling. (*Österreichischen Gallerie im Belvedere*).

ABOVE: Metternich in 1837 as senior Knight of the Golden Fleece, by Johann Ender. (*Bild-Archiv der Österreichischen Nationalbibliothek, Vienna*)

RIGHT: Emperor Ferdinand (1835–48) and the Empress Maria Anna Carolina, as King and Queen of Hungary. (*Bild-Archiv der Österreichischen Nationalbibliothek, Vienna*)

Metternich in his eighties, from a photograph of about 1855 by Mylius. (*Bild-Archiv der Österreichischen Nationalbibliothek, Vienna*)

proved a great success. The couple's physical relations were clearly most satisfactory, resulting in four children.

Catholicism formed another strong bond. After the terrible months during 1828–9, Metternich had installed a private chapel at the Ballhausplatz. His cult of St Paul was by now so strong that he would insist on calling one of their sons after him, although Mélanie—no less devout—disliked the name.

He even told her about his work. 'Today I breakfasted alone with Clemens for the first time since my marriage,' she records in her diary for 17 February. 'He spoke a great deal about business and explained to me all his views and plans.' She adds, 'Gentz interrupted our conversation.'

One day in 1831 she found the Grand Inquisitor and his henchman blowing soap bubbles with Richard, his three-year-old son by Antoinette. Gentz was part of the Metternich household, despite frequent arguments. Often a waspish critic of the chancellor's policies, he continued to breakfast with them almost every morning (although he had a beautiful and devoted mistress, Fanny Elssler, the ballet dancer). 'I love hearing them talk together since the former [Gentz] has tremendous wit, for all his oddities,' Mélanie observes. She adds, 'Things seem to be going rather badly in England. Worst of all, my poor Clemens, having taken vast pains on a plan which is the only safe way out for us can find no-one to support him but is constantly frustrated.' She writes with rather less affection for Gentz in November. 'Clemens showed me a letter from Prince Wittgenstein to Gentz from which it is quite obvious that the latter is in the habit of telling all his friends abroad that Clemens no longer does any work, and that he [Gentz] has to attend to business of every kind single-handed . . . I am astonished at Clemens who, although well aware of it, remains friendly.'

Gentz was desperately frightened by the prospect of hostilities with France. There was a vociferous war party at Vienna, led by Prince Albert Schönburg (Austrian envoy to Württemberg) which he feared was beginning to win over the chancellor. In February 1831 Gentz believed that war was inevitable. However, Metternich was always aware of the fragile condition of Austria's finances, an awareness which induced caution. Even so, at the end of March his wife noted, 'I found Clemens sad and thoughtful. Affairs in France give him great anxiety and he is expecting war.' He had decided that Austria and Prussia should intervene in France to restore Charles X, but Archduke Karl refused to command the Imperial army on the grounds that the Monarchy's finances could not take the strain; the campaign had to be called off when it was learnt that Austria could find only 170,000 men for the purpose, as opposed to Prussia's 250,000. The atmosphere continued to be explosive for several months. Mélanie reveals how much Metternich worried beneath that imperturbable exterior. 'In spite of a fearful storm, Clemens and I set out for Baden,' she records on 1 July 1831. 'My husband wanted to speak with the Emperor. Everywhere he finds cause for anxiety in foreign affairs. One cannot conceive how things can get any better. We are faced by terrible crises and I see no way out. Clemens was with the Emperor till three in the morning.'

Meanwhile, the Belgians were in revolt against their Dutch King. The Prussian army prepared to march in and restore him, but it was clear that the French would go to the aid of the Belgians. While sympathising with the Dutch King, Metternich had no wish for a full-scale European war. A conference met at London in November 1831, attended by envoys from all the great powers, and concluded that the only viable solution would be an independent state of Belgium. Austria and Prussia disliked upsetting the 1815 settlement but accepted that it was better than war, the conference deciding that the frontiers should be those of the old United Provinces as they had been under Austrian rule. Many Belgians would have liked union with France and in February, as a compromise, the Belgian assembly chose Louis Philippe's son, the Duc de Nemours, to be their King. Britain then threatened to declare war. Austria's candidate was Archduke Karl, who had briefly been governor-general at Brussels in 1793–4. The ultimate choice was Leopold of Saxe-Coburg (the widower of Princess Charlotte of Wales). Even then, the Dutch invaded the country in August, to be swiftly driven out by a French army with the approval of the London conference.

During the Belgian crisis a new—and, from Metternich's point of view, malevolent—figure entered the stage of European politics, in 1830. This was the British foreign secretary, Lord Palmerston, a xenophobic Whig with a taste for popularity, who would pander to the most chauvinist instincts in the British character. A politician more skilled and far tougher than Canning, he liked to pose as a champion of liberal causes. His biographers emphasise his desire for peace, which is beyond question. They are less convincing when they infer that Palmerston was Metternich's rival rather than opponent; they suggest that both were competing for the leadership of Europe, which is why each tried so often and so unsuccessfully to stage a peace conference he hoped to dominate. Continental historians (such as Jacques Droz) disagree, arguing that Palmerston considered a divided Europe beneficial to British interests. 'Everywhere, indeed, by stirring up national feeling and liberal agitation, she [Britain] prepared to overthrow the Europe established by the 1815 treaties' is how Droz interprets his policy. Certainly Talleyrand had understood Palmerston's aims in this way before leaving the French Embassy in London in 1834. So did Metternich.

Two months after the Polish uprising of November 1830, the Seym (Diet) deposed the Tsar as King of Poland. Austria and Prussia agreed on joint action to deal with revolts in their own Polish provinces. Metternich warned Trauttmansdorff, Austrian ambassador in Berlin, that the crucial factor would be the Russian army's morale. In the spring heavily outnumbered Polish forces brought to a halt General Diebitsch's advance on Warsaw, and went on to win further victories. Volunteers from all over Europe joined them, including many Napoleonic veterans. But in September 1831 the Russians stormed their way into Warsaw and the war was over. The Poles had offered the throne to an Archduke, but a restored Kingdom of Poland was scarcely welcome to Austria, fearful that disaffection might spread to its Galician provinces. In September, Metternich told a Polish envoy, Count Zamoyski, that his countrymen's only course was to surrender. 'We are putting a stop to much bloodshed, and saving the Russians from losing a battle, a defeat which might affect all Europe,' Mélanie wrote proudly, reflecting her husband's view. Not many Poles would have agreed with his comment in March that 'Tsar Nicholas displays the greatest calm and gentleness'.

It is unlikely that Metternich obtained a true picture from Prince Esterházy's despatches of what was happening in England during 1830–32 when the country was disrupted by the agitation for the Reform Bill. It was sufficient for him that his old friend the Duke of Wellington had his house in Piccadilly stoned by a mob. It seemed as if France's '*trois glorieuses*' might be repeated across the Channel; there were even rumours that William IV and the Duke were planning a coup like that attempted by Charles X and Polignac. When the bill was passed, in Metternich's opinion the old British constitution had been replaced by something similar to the French *Charte* which he so much despised. He was justified in believing that it opened the way for the middle classes to supersede the aristocracy as Britain's rulers.

As he had expected, there was some serious trouble in Italy. Lombardy-Venetia was too firmly under control for the Carbonari to attempt a rising, but in February they rose in the Duchies of Parma and Modena, establishing 'governments'. Austrian troops chased them away early in March. A revolutionary government was also set up at Bologna in the Papal States, its leaders intending to march on Rome. This rising too was swiftly crushed by the Austrians, who maintained a garrison at Bologna until 1838. Metternich attributed the risings to the 'Paris Committee', that great central revolutionary committee which his agents never quite succeeded in tracking down; he believed it had assured the rebels that the Austrians would not intervene. 'The passage of the Po by our troops having dispelled the phantasmagoria, panic seized the conspirators,' he told Apponyi. He added that the 'Italian Revolution' was the result of French propaganda, and that whenever a village rose in revolt it was led by a Frenchman. He grew surer than ever that the French were behind Italian disaffection when, in a melodramatic and futile gesture, a French expeditionary force occupied the Papal port of Ancona in February 1832 as a protest against 'intervention'.

Sometimes he treated the French with the utmost gentleness. 'A young Frenchman, editor of the *Journal des Débats*, has arrived here,' Mélanie recorded on 20 June 1831. 'He is a bitter opponent of my husband and his policy. Clemens at once invited him to dinner. That is so like his way of revenging himself!' He could be more brutal, if as subtle. In February he had used the presence in Vienna of the Duc de Reichstadt, the son of Napoleon and Marie Louise, as a threat to bring Louis Philippe to heel. 'What we ask is not to declare war against us by helping the Italian Revolutionaries.' He stressed the extent to which the Bonaparte family were intriguing and enclosed a letter from Joseph Bonaparte written in October 1830; it urged Metternich to place Napoleon's son on the French throne as the one man who could stop the Orleanists. He had already instructed Apponyi to remind the French how extraordinarily tactful he was being about '*Napoleon II*'.

Metternich seems to have felt genuinely uneasy about the young man. Gentz's friend Count Prokesch von Osten noticed that whenever his name was mentioned the chancellor's expression was that of someone swallowing a pill, yet it may have been sheer pity. The Eaglet died at Schönbrunn from phthisis in July 1832, still only twenty-one. No doubt he was something of a political embarrassment, but despite Bonapartist attempts to portray Francis and Metternich as his gaolers, he is known to have been very fond of his grandfather, while the chancellor sent a message—'apart from France, access to which doesn't depend on me, he can go to whatever country suits him. The Emperor puts the restoration of his grandson's health before all else.' He visited the Eaglet just before he died and reported to Francis that 'it was a heart rending spectacle of decay'.

At the end of June 1831 Metternich confided in Count Apponyi, 'We are very busy with German affairs at the moment. The country is a prey to frightful disorder. Through listening to Liberals, and under the delusion they are ruling democratically, its Princes have reduced their powers to zero. Luckily the Confederation exists and we're about to use it.' He waited another year until he had a pretext. In May 1832 a journalist named Philipp Jacob Siebenpfeiffer assembled some radical students at Schloss Hambach in the Bavarian Rhineland, ran up a German tricolour of black, red and gold—the flag's first appearance—drank the health of Lafayette as architect of the July monarchy and demanded a German republic. Shortly after, German republicans in Paris gave a banquet in his honour at which Lafayette presided. At Frankfurt a month later the Bundestag passed the 'Six Articles', banning political rallies still more rigorously, further restricting the freedom of the press and imposing stricter university discipline; above all, they empowered the confederation—meaning Austria and Germany—to intervene in any state which introduced a new constitution. As the chancellor explained, the question was 'whether Germany remains an independent country or whether she is to be absorbed into the French Revolution'.

Exactly a month afterwards Palmerston attacked the Six Articles in the House of Commons as a champion of European liberalism. On 7 September he sent a despatch to the president of the *Bundestag,* protesting that intervention by Austrian and Prussian troops 'might produce a general convulsion in Europe'. Metternich wrote to him, complaining that this was gross interference in German affairs. Even Palmerston's sovereign William IV was outraged as King of Hanover. What made the foreign secretary seem more than a little hypocritical was his refusal to condemn the Tsar's savagery in Poland—he was hoping to revive Canning's Anglo-Russian alliance.

As if this maelstrom of foreign policy were not enough trouble, the Metternichs had their private sorrows. 'Clemens came to me with the news that our old friend had passed away at nine o'clock,' Mélanie records of Gentz's death on 9 July 1832. 'He feels deeply the fresh loss he has sustained. All those whose company he really enjoyed are gone and he finds himself sadly desolate.' Metternich arranged and attended a Protestant funeral and, since Gentz had left only debts, paid for the tombstone himself. He also had a street in Vienna named after Gentz. 'A rare combination of the most marked talent and true genius has gone down into the grave with the dead man,' the chancellor wrote a week later to Count Prokesch von Osten. 'His place can never be filled, and though for the last few years Gentz worked for me only nominally, I feel his loss in so many important ways.'

Fortunately another friend, still more valuable, survived. 'Clemens described a really touching conversation he has had with the Emperor,' Mélanie noted in her diary on 13 November 1832:

> The latter said he prayed to God, above all, to preserve Clemens for him since 'without you I don't know how to undertake anything'. Clemens explained to the Emperor that he couldn't continue without him, that his strength would fail. He also said that the Emperor was doubly necessary to him, since he was always influenced by his probity and judgement.

The loyal wife adds, 'May God preserve them both because truly one without the other cannot save the world.'

Something of the reason for the undoubted affection in which Emperor Francis was held by many of his subjects may be learnt from a story recorded by Princess Mélanie:

> During his stay at Schönbrunn, as he was walking through Hietzing he saw them burying a poor man who was accompanied to the grave by only the two men carrying the coffin and a priest. The Emperor said to his adjutant Appel 'We will follow this fellow, he is so deserted.'

No similar tale could be told of any other monarch of the period.

Yet for all his kindness, Francis was a harder man than his chancellor. In 1848 Metternich would tell Count von Hübner that if the Emperor had taken his advice on foreign affairs, he had not done so on internal matters. 'As chancellor I had the right to speak but I did so very moderately, and only during real crises when vital principles were at stake.' Surveillance of writers, artists and musicians was encouraged by Francis, not by Metternich. Nor would he take any notice when the chancellor spoke of the need to reorganise the Monarchy. 'His basic benevolence towards his subjects did not make Francis want to improve their lot by bringing in a programme of rational reform,' says the French historian Victor-Louis Tapié. 'In his view it was enought for them to be given the right to live in peace and order—in "*Ruhe und Ordnung*".'

In April, Mélanie gave birth to her first son, whom she insisted on calling after his father. 'I never saw Clemens so pleased,' she writes. On 15 May Metternich was sixty. But on 10 June the baby died. His wife begged him not to grieve so much, since it might injure his health. He answered that he was far too accustomed to sorrow to have any fear of it making him ill. They went off to Königswart, always his favourite refuge.

Meanwhile, foreign affairs were as threatening as ever, even if war seemed less likely. The most extraordinary development was an *entente* between France and Britain. As early as August 1830 the chancellor had remarked on the resemblance of the upheaval in France to the English Revolution of 1688, a resemblance stressed enthusiastically by the July Monarchy which welcomed the Reform Bill of 1832 as a kind of British *Charte*. Louis Philippe had many influential English friends, while in 1832 his daughter married King Leopold of the Belgians, still much liked across the Channel. His new foreign minister, appointed the same year, was the Duc de Broglie, hailed as a French Whig. More important, Talleyrand, France's ambassador in London, had charmed Palmerston. Metternich was more realistic: 'In England revolution only begins as yet to threaten' was his comment. 'If it has made some progress in men's minds it has not so far overturned the existing order of things, whereas in France there is nothing left for the Revolution to destroy.'

In 1832 the Eastern Question reemerged, in a different form, when Mehemet Ali, the Pasha of Egypt, rebelled against the Porte, wiping out Sultan Mahmud's armies in both Syria and Anatolia. The Tsar intervened to protect the Porte against invasion, landing 14,000 men on the shore opposite Constantinople, which was further defended by the Russian navy. On 26 June Count Orloff signed the Treaty of Unkiar-Skelessi with the Turks, a document which had been drawn up personally by Tsar Nicholas. The Russians promised to defend Turkey-in-Europe against any aggression; in return, by a secret clause the Porte promised to forbid entry into the Dardanelles to all foreign warships while allowing those of Russia free passage. An indirect Russian protectorate had been established over the Ottoman Empire.

Britain in particular was outraged. It meant the end of Lord Palmerston's scheme for reviving Canning's alliance with Russia; he would never again trust the Tsar. Broglie was no less angry; since Napoleon's conquest of Egypt, France had taken an almost proprietary interest in Egyptian affairs. Like the French, Metternich was taken completely by surprise at the news of Unkiar-Skelessi, at first refusing to believe it; unlike them, however, he welcomed it, seeing not only a long-desired chance of meeting the Tsar and negotiating face-to-face, but also a possibility of reviving the Triple Alliance.

A conference was arranged, to meet at Münchengrätz (now Mnichovo Hradiste) in Bohemia early in September. It would be attended by the Tsar and the Austrian Emperor, with their foreign ministers. First, however, Metternich went to discuss the problems of Germany with his old friend the King of Prussia, and also to let Frederick William know just what he hoped to achieve at the conference; he never took anyone for granted, especially when the Prussian chancellor, Ancillon, was covertly hostile. According to Mélanie, her husband came back well satisfied from his talks with the King at Teplitz in August.

Münchengrätz, 'a very small and filthy town' in Princess Mélanie's opinion, was to be the scene of one of Metternich's greatest triumphs. He was aware that he had influential enemies in Russia, such as the ambassador at Paris, General Pozzo di Borgo—'After England, it is Austria for whom he has born the most active and long standing hatred,' the chancellor had observed in 1826. He knew that the foreign minister, Nesselrode, had great confidence in Pozzo. However, he was not in the least worried about his ability to handle Nesselrode, that 'poor little fellow' whom in the past he had so often brought round to his way of thinking.

The Russian whom Metternich regarded as most formidable was Nicholas I, the 'Nebuchadnezzar of the North', who was a very different man from Alexander. 'This new Tsar has succeeded in enveloping himself in a system of fear, and rule by fear suits the Russians,' he had written. 'His policy will be Russia first and foremost.' Metternich realized that Nicholas was only interested in the Alliance as long as it profited Russia, that 'empire on the frontier of civilisation, with no resemblance to other European states'. He had no fear of Tsarist Russia; it was the thought of a non-Tsarist Russia, a revolutionary Russia, which frightened him. 'What would happen to Europe if 30 million slaves and an army of 800,000 were let loose?' he once asked. 'Where we and every thinking European see a vista of death they [the revolutionaries] see life and triumph.' No one can deny the clarity of his vision of a 'Jacobin' Russia. He had every reason for wishing that Tsar Nicholas's régime should prosper.

The Tsar did not like what he had heard of Prince Metternich, who had manipulated his elder brother Alexander so cunningly. Moreover, the chancellor was not a soldier, the only type of man with whom Nicholas felt at ease, but a polished and supremely Western bureaucrat. No doubt like the Comte de Falloux, the Tsar expected to see an overdressed survival from the eighteenth century; if so, as Falloux puts it, he would have been surprised at beholding 'one of the most handsome and distinguished men of his day, in no way antique or foppish, very well informed and thoroughly up to date in his conversation'.

The Metternichs dined with the Emperor and Empress every day at Münchengrätz, usually playing billiards afterwards. When Tsar Nicholas arrived on 10 September he told the chancellor, 'I have come to place myself under the orders of my chief—tell me my mistakes.' He called on Mélanie, who had at first thought him cold and stiff, and was very friendly, later revealing that he too played billiards. He confided his private opinion of Metternich in a letter to the Tsarina: 'Every time I go near him I pray God to deliver me from the Devil.' (In 1839 he referred to Metternich as 'a cohort of Satan'.) Even so, during the conference he succumbed to Metternich's charm, admitting that he was very amusing. Moreover, even before the 1830 revolution, Nicholas had decided that the survival of Turkey-in-Europe was in the best interests of European stability and of Russia.

The chancellor knew at once that he was going to get what he wanted. He told General Benckendorff (Darya Lieven's brother), 'At meetings like this they used to discuss matters and scribble papers for months on end. But your Tsar has another method.

Everything is decided and settled in an hour.' In Mélanie's words, her husband 'was shut up with Nesselrode'. On 18 September 1833, Austria and Russia signed an agreement that they should do everything in their power to save the Ottoman Empire, and to decide together on what action should be taken if despite their efforts it showed signs of disintegrating. They also agreed on joint action in case of future Polish risings. In addition, there was to be a declaration by Austria, Russia and Prussia (signed at Berlin the following month) reaffirming the three powers' support for legitimacy and for nonintervention—unless invited by a legitimate sovereign. Münchengrätz had not only settled the Polish and Eastern Questions—at any rate while Metternich was chancellor—but it had revived the Triple Alliance.

No less hostile a critic than A. J. P. Taylor has to admit his success:

> To keep the peace between Russia and Austria and yet to prevent any further advances in the Near East was Metternich's greatest diplomatic achievement, all the greater for his rating it less high than his struggle against the 'revolution'.

Not everyone saw it in that light at the time.

As Metternich had commented earlier in 1833, 'In short Lord Palmerston is worrying about everything.' When Palmerston heard of the conference at Münchengrätz he was convinced that Austria and Russia had agreed to divide up Turkey between them. The French were no less alarmed. The '*entente*' responded by creating what it hoped would be a power bloc to counter the Triple Alliance. They saw their opportunity in the Iberian Peninsula. Supported by the arch-reactionary Ferdinand VII of Spain, King Miguel and his traditionalist followers had been in complete control of Portugal for some years; the liberals who supported Queen Maria held only one small island in the Azores. The situation changed when Ferdinand died in September 1833, the same month as the Münchengrätz conference. Spanish liberals soon took over Spain in the name of Ferdinand's daughter, Queen Isabella, and ousted the legitimist claimant, Don Carlos, the late King's brother; to preempt a Carlist-Miguelist axis, they then undermined Don Miguel's régime so effectively that he was quickly replaced on the Portuguese throne by Queen Maria. England and France supported the new governments with enthusiasm, the four countries forming a 'Quadruple Alliance' in April 1834 to preserve the Spanish and Portuguese constitutions; Palmerston wrote exultantly to his brother, 'I should like to see Metternich's face when he reads our treaty.'

Although thoroughly in favour of Don Carlos and Don Miguel, the Austrian chancellor had made a point of recognising neither, restricting himself to a threat of intervention in both Iberian countries if revolution ensued as a result of the altered successions. He tried to defuse the situation by urging a return to the Concert of Europe; in July he suggested a pact between the 'Northern Powers' on the one hand, and Britain and France on the other, with the declared intention of guaranteeing European peace. Britain rejected the proposal.

In November 1834 Lord Palmerston sent a letter to the British chargé d'affaires at Vienna, Mr Fox-Strangways, to inform him that the Whig government had resigned and he was leaving office. He added, 'Lose no time in taking this note to Prince Metternich. I am convinced he will never in his life have been more overjoyed than when he reads it, and that I shall never have seemed so agreeable to him now that I am bidding him "goodbye".' The chancellor replied with a letter to Fox-Strangways, commenting, 'If instead of the word "joy" he had used "hope" he would not have been far wrong.' But Palmerston returned as foreign secretary within a very few months.

Quite apart from the danger of going to war over Belgium or the Iberian Peninsula, there was the constant menace of the Italian secret societies. After the rout of the Carbonari in 1831, from his lair at Marseilles Mazzini had formed *Giovine Italia*, whose objective was a united socialist republic of Italy under what he termed 'a species of Comité du Salut Publique'. Most menacing if even more ineffectual were Buonarotti's *Veri Italiani*.

Filippo Buonarotti (1761–1837) had a history of the sort which aroused Metternich's worst suspicions. He had been in Paris during the Terror, when he was a member of the Jacobin Club and an enthusiastic Robespierrist; later he played a prominent role in the abortive 'communist' rising led by Babeouf, the 'Conspiracy of Equals'. His society of 'Sublime Perfect Masters' had three levels of initiation: members of the first were told simply that they must strive to achieve Deism and the Sovereignty of the People; of the second that their aim was a republic; and of the third that they were working for a communist society. When the July Revolution had made it possible for him to return to Paris in 1830 he was hailed by the left as a ghost from the glorious past, becoming a living embodiment of 1793 to whom every revolutionary flocked, and had reorganised what was left of the French Carbonari, the *Charbonnerie Démocratique Universelle.* Needless to say, Austrian agents reported whatever they could learn of his activities to the chancellor at Vienna. If his organisation was not the *Comité Directeur,* which supposedly controlled all Europe's secret societies from Paris, Metternich must have been convinced that Buonarotti's organisation was very close to it. The involvement of this Terrorist of '93 in the societies strengthened Metternich's belief that the real struggle was not between conservatism and liberalism but between conservatism and red revolution.

Soon entire regions of Piedmont were disaffected as a result of Mazzini's activities, and remained so until purged in 1833. Other cells were discovered in Tuscany and Naples. Like the Carbonari, their members plotted ceaselessly to assassinate both Emperor Francis and his chancellor. There were Mazzininians from Italy among the men who attempted a coup at Frankfurt in April 1833; the free city was promptly occupied by 'federal' troops—in practice mainly Austrians and Prussians. The invasion of Piedmontese Savoy from Switzerland by a band of Italian and Polish revolutionaries in February the following year, during which a steamboat was seized on Lake Geneva, failed disastrously when its leaders quarrelled. 'The enterprise in question is the work of *Giovine Italia,* which looks on the law of the land as a mere dream in comparison to where it has undertaken to lead the human race' was Metternich's comment on hearing the news. 'The dregs of the entire population of Europe are the promoters of the great work.'

A hundred took refuge in Switzerland but the chancellor forced the Swiss to expel them, moving Austrian troops up to the frontier. (Palmerston protested about the occupation of Frankfurt and warning to Switzerland, a piece of arrogant interference which irritated every German government.) The society Young Italy collapsed, whereupon Mazzini established another society, Young Europe, whose members numbered not only Italians but French, Germans, Swiss, Poles and even Austrians, their object being the creation of a socialist, republican Europe—after they had destroyed the Metternichian system. These bitter young men, forerunners of the anarchists of the last quarter of the nineteenth century, were feared throughout the continent.

However, Metternich was a happy man, very fond of his high-spirited Hungarian wife. Jäger warned him to curb his 'conjugal excesses', angering Mélanie, who refused to speak to the well-meaning doctor. Jäger loathed her, claiming in his memoirs that 'she brought a spirit of arrogance into the house', although Prince Metternich himself was 'a simple, sincere, good natured man'. She was amazed at the easy way in which her husband spoke to lesser mortals. (She is confirmed by Marshal Marmont, who comments on Metternich's manner 'never varying towards great or small'.)

The chancellor was blind to Mélanie's faults, telling his friend August Vernhagen von Enser, 'I met her very late in life and now I couldn't do without her.' She helped with his work, reading despatches to him. He confided in her, even what would now be termed top-secret information—as in 1834 when his agents learnt that Don Carlos had left London secretly to start a civil war in Spain. She took a keen interest in foreign affairs, sometimes questioning Metternich's judgement. 'It is not known who will succeed Lord Grey and Lord Palmerston,' she commented in July 1834. 'Clemens dreads the [English] government falling into still worse hands. I on the contrary think it's the beginning of better times.' (They were both wrong, since the Whigs came in again.) But there is no evidence that she influenced her husband's policies in any way.

If the chancellor insisted 'I've never been a Richelieu', he was indisputably the second man in the Monarchy. In his *Souvenirs* the

Comte de Sainte-Aulaire, the French ambassador, recalls the Archdukes' deferential manner when they met Metternich at the Hofburg, taking off their hats, standing with backs to the wall and behaving 'like corporals before their captain', while he responded with a curt bow and a few words. He was the main topic of gossip at the capital among all classes, and a familiar figure on state occasions—each Corpus Christi (18 June), as senior Knight of the Golden Fleece he walked at the Emperor's side in robes of purple and gold.

He possessed a strong if discreet link with the great families—Schwarzenberg, Furstenberg, Schönburg and Lobkowitz, Clary, Czernin, Dietrichstein, Esterházy, Apponyi, Palffy, and Czartoryski. All aspired to join the orders of chivalry, of Maria Theresa, the Golden Fleece and Malta. No one could do so without the Emperor's permission, which meant Metternich's permission. He was chancellor of the Maria Theresan Order, whose Knights were the Monarchy's greatest heroes, and doyen of the Golden Fleece, whose Knights were its greatest nobles. He controlled admission to the Austrian Knights of Malta, the Grand Priory of Bohemia, regarding it as one of the last bastions of pre-1789 Europe; in 1838 he encouraged it to erect a new priory in Lombardy-Venetia, with an Archduke as Grand Prior. (He saw that the Emperor accorded its Lieutenant Grand Master at Rome full diplomatic status as a reigning sovereign, receiving his resident envoy at Vienna, although the Knights had no hope of regaining Malta.)

The Metternichs' supremacy in Viennese society was absolute. Every member of the great families who could obtain an invitation flocked to their balls and routs, their dinners and receptions. In her diary Mélanie writes of rooms filled to overflowing, of staircases crowded to the point of suffocation—'I could scarcely push my way into my own drawing room.' Nonetheless, she enjoyed herself thoroughly, sometimes waltzing till four in the morning, after her husband had stolen back to his despatch boxes.

The Princess describes an entertainment she gave in May 1834, at their villa on the Rennweg (then a suburb of Vienna). The party was for the plenipotentiaries of the Princes and free cities of Germany, assembled at the Imperial capital to discuss ways of combating the revolutionary spirit. (The chancellor had been warning them that its adherents were by now 'questioning the claims of the middle classes to privileges or property rights while simultaneously wooing the lower classes by encouraging them to hope that all types of property would sooner or later become theirs'.) Mélanie tells us:

> On the grass a Turkish tent had been put up, with tea-tables on either side, the beautiful dresses [and uniforms] making the scene very gay. Two military bands were stationed near the house, playing in turn . . . In the tent a very pretty theatre had been erected and comic tableaux were performed by Scholz, Nestroy and Fritz Furstenberg, which were very funny and earned loud applause. Good music was being played in the *salon* . . .

There was a gypsy camp with gypsy dancers, lighted by Bengal fire, a 'charming military dance by children' and fireworks. One suspects that the part of the entertainment which pleased Metternich most were his conservatories, lighted by different-coloured lamps—'We lingered for a moment, to look at the pelargonium which were just in full bloom.'

Occasionally Mélanie's vivacity caused problems. On New Year's Day 1834, M de Sainte-Aulaire congratulated her on her diamond tiara, saying amiably, 'It looks like a crown.' 'Why not?' retorted the chancellor's consort. 'It belongs to me—if it wasn't my property I wouldn't wear it.' Louis Philippe's envoy blenched at this all too clear jibe at his sovereign's usurpation. He complained to Metternich, who is said to have replied, 'You must forgive me but I am not responsible for my wife's upbringing.' Sainte-Aulaire called on her to extract an apology, without success.

Their entertainments were not restricted to the great princely families or ambassadors—even if the Viennese middle class was ruthlessly excluded. Distinguished writers and scientists were made welcome. Balzac came on at least two occasions, a fat and ludicrously overdressed little man. The chancellor shook the novelist's hand warmly. 'I haven't read any of your books,' he told Balzac somewhat disconcertingly. 'But I know all about you—you're obviously mad, or at any rate you amuse yourself at the expense of other madmen, in trying to curse them with a madness even greater than your own.' Balzac, as much a snob as he was a legitimist, pretended to be amused, and the two men undoubtedly took to one another. Metternich even suggested a plot for a play, '*L'Ecole du ménage*', which Balzac actually wrote, though it never reached the stage.

In April 1835 Princess Mélanie had written in her journal, 'We had a sort of dinner party for the learned. Among the merry-makers were Mme von Goethe, the poet's daughter-in-law, and Mme Jameson, a blue-stocking in every sense of the word . . . As it was, these two persons, of whom I had been really frightened, talked in the easiest and most agreeable way, so that one is completely at ease with them.' (Mrs Jameson, born Anna Murphy and a former governess, was the author of the highly fashionable *Diary of an Ennuyée.*)

Another British writer who met the Metternichs was Anthony Trollope's mother, the novelist Frances Trollope, who recorded her impressions of them in *Vienna and the Austrians* (1838). 'The Prince is of medium height and slim.' He 'normally has a gentle and kindly expression, but his pale blue eyes give the impression of a profoundly thoughtful man. He is gracious and dignified, both innately and in manner; he imparts by his whole bearing an air of tranquility, of philosophic calm'. She was struck by his love of poetry and much admired 'a felicitous choice of words and a clarity which stamped all his thought with a remarkable precision'. He told her that 'political science can be reduced to terms as exact as those of chemistry; if only men would refrain from theorising and take the trouble to note the similar nature of results traceable to identical causes'. As for Mélanie, 'She is young and full of charm. Her humorous and animated expression is not entirely without a touch of disdain. But one can pardon a pretty young woman, especially when she tempers it, as does this seductive creature, with a deliciously sweet smile that plays around her lips at the very moment of her most outrageous sallies.' Mrs Trollope was moved by the affection which the couple showed for each other—'that conjugal affection more often encountered in novels than in life'.

Like some modern politicians, the chancellor was only too well aware of the value of a flattering profile in print and prepared to pay the price for such gushing testimonies as that of Frances Trollope. For once one has the impression made by the interviewer on the interviewed. 'Clemens, Hermione and I dined at the English ambassador's,' Mélanie writes. 'Among the guests was mistress [sic] Trollope. She is a worthy woman, very simple and straight-forward, who listens to one attentively and is grateful for the least hint of sympathy. She must be between forty and forty-five and has a slightly vulgar look, although her conversation suggests she has been impeccably brought up. She made a conquest of my husband while for his part he gave me the feeling that he had done the same with her.'

'He was the sort of man that nowadays would be equally a favourite with the ladies in the drawing-room and with the men in the smoking-room,' an Edwardian biographer suggests. 'The former he would probably have delighted with descriptions of the dresses worn at the Court of Napoleon in 1809 and at the Congress of Vienna in 1815; the latter with anecdotes of Napoleon and perhaps a vivid account of the famous interview in the Marcolini Palace.' Even so, he had at least one disconcerting trait, according to Baron Meyendorff, who was the Russian ambassador to Vienna during the 1830s. After paying tribute to his distinguished bearing and good looks, to his 'stiff grace', the baron tells us how all this changed if Metternich laughed. 'There was something Mephistophelian in the grimace, while the prince's voice, normally a drawl, grew harsh and high pitched when he joked.'

The couple went out a good deal, enjoying the pleasures of Biedermeier Vienna to the full. They saw Schuster at the Leopoldstadt Theatre, the comic genius Nestroy at the Wieden (once 'in a new, very pretty little piece called "Lumpazivagabundus" ') and heard the first Viennese performance of Hérold's *Zampa* at the Kärntnerthor. They walked in the Helenenthal, listening to the elder Strauss's orchestra and a regimental band greet Emperor Francis with the *Gotterhalte* and then serenade him. Occasionally they drove out into the country in the evenings, visiting Dommayer's Restaurant at Hietzing, where they danced to an excellent band.

Despite such relaxations and his wife's unfailing support, Metternich suffered a good deal from strain caused by worry and too much work. Even in the first weeks of their marriage Mélanie noted, 'Clemens is overwhelmed by business and his nerves are affected—he is sick of finding so much work mount up because of his ambassadors' mistakes.' In January 1834 she records that he has had to stay in bed and how she has read him an article from the *Révue de Paris* about Bonny Prince Charlie. He told her that he had persuaded George IV to erect a monument to the Prince (Canova's in St Peter's?). And then he burst into such a violent fit of weeping that she was very frightened. He had other nervous crises of the same sort.

He lived in constant fear of revolution, relying heavily on police intelligence and censorship. This is frequently cited as the darkest side of the 'Metternich System'—a misused phrase—and has been consistently exaggerated. Admittedly he worked closely with Count Josef Sedlnitsky, who was head of the *Polizeihofstelle* (Imperial Police Department) from 1816 until 1848 and did exactly what the chancellor told him. Indeed, in 1817 Metternich boasted, 'In me you behold Europe's chief minister of police.' Beyond question Austria was a police state. The *Polizeihofstelle*, founded by Joseph II, had been expanded by Francis during the wars with France and had bureaux all over the Empire, together with agents and informers. In 1801 it took over the censorship, including the *Geheime Zifferkanzlei* (Cipher Office) in the Hofstallburg. Not only were books, plays and newspapers censored, but letters too.

Foreign as well as diplomatic correspondence was intercepted by the *Geheime Zifferkanzlei*. One expert claimed to have cracked 85 codes; the French cypher was broken by 'borrowing' it from the ambassador's son while he slept. Opening, copying and resealing took the *Postlogisten* under two hours, between a letter's arrival at the central post office in Vienna at 7.00 a.m. and its return in time for the mail, which left at 9.00. Code experts accompanied the chancellor everywhere, even to Johannisberg or Königswart.

Metternich created a species of 'Interpol' to combat international revolution. Intelligence reports reached him from every Austrian embassy and consulate. There was an 'Investigation Centre' at Mainz for Germany, aided by the Rothschilds' information service. The Italian states were helpful, especially Parma and Modena. If Prussia and Bavaria were not always so cooperative, General Benckendorff's Third Section at St Petersburg was in constant touch. France assisted sometimes until 1830, while even Britain occasionally sent in reports about Mazzini. In addition, embassy staff in every European capital gathered information about the opinions and weaknesses of public figures and the whereabouts of revolutionaries and political refugees. A British observer had commented in 1819, 'Nothing can surpass Prince Metternich's activities in collecting facts and information upon the inward feelings of the people.'

All this gave the chancellor a sinister reputation, which was magnified out of all proportion by his liberal opponents. But, as he saw it, he was defending not just Austria but all Europe from revolution and war. There were very few political prisoners in the Empire and certainly no torture. The total police force in Vienna was 700 (including a mounted detachment and a 'civic guard'), which was less than a quarter of the number of regular constables in London. There were only 22 *Postlogisten*. (Even in Britain the Home Office censored the letters of dangerous radicals, albeit on a smaller scale.)

A very modern feature of Metternich's approach to politics was his attitude to the press, at home and abroad. As has been seen, the *Österreichischer Beobachter* was the government's mouthpiece. The British ambassador reported, 'Every day the editor of this journal, Josef-Anton von Pilat, comes to the Chancellery and, after receiving the master's orders, settles down in the antechamber to write the article for the next day, the text of which is immediately submitted to the Chancellor.' Metternich suggested many of the articles, continuing to provide some himself; they dealt with current affairs, internal and external, from his own special point of view. Gentz was sadly missed, as to a lesser extent were Adam Müller and Friedrich von Schlegel, who had both died before Gentz. To some degree Gentz's place was filled by another Prussian, Karl Ernst Jarcke, the 'mini-Gentz'; born in Danzig, a former professor of criminal law at Berlin University who became a fanatical Catholic and Ultra, Dr Jarcke joined the chancellery at Vienna in 1838 when he was thirty-seven, advising Metternich on publicity for the next decade. Intellectual journals, such as the *Wiener Zeitung*, also published articles on lines suggested by the Ballhausplatz in return for secret subsidies.

Ambassadors had the task of making Austria's views known abroad by infiltrating articles into the foreign press. Editors often helped without realizing, by publishing unsigned copy of mysterious provenance. Sometimes these contributions contained blatant untruths so that the Austrian government could then refute them—as in London in 1827 when Esterházy succeeded in placing several such pieces in the *Morning Chronicle*. The Ballhausplatz provided all its embassies with suitable material. The *Journal de Francfort*, a French language publication financed by Vienna which covered international affairs, circulated in every European capital and its articles were always available for copy—like syndicated articles today. Ironically, Metternich despised journalism. He once said of a French lawyer, who seems to have been a journalist, 'You might say that he was born from dung, just as Venus was born from sea-spray.'

Metternich's relations with his ambassadors and diplomatic staff were unusually warm. He liked envoys to stay *en poste*, sometimes for over twenty years. He was not bothered by sexual or financial peccadilloes, by bad manners, even by inefficiency. He let Baron Vincent remain at Paris so that he could reach retiring age and not be disgraced, despite his unpopularity with the embassy as well as the French. Such an attitude earned the chancellor genuine loyalty while his men gained a deeper understanding of local conditions. Vincent, Apponyi, Esterházy, Neumann, Zichy, Ficquelmont, Mercy, Floret, Wessenberg, Lebzeltern, Ottenfels, all did him remarkable service. The Austrian diplomatic corps was the most professional and the most dedicated in Europe.

Sometimes Metternich sent someone like Floret to find out just what was happening in the embassies. If shortcomings emerged, he reacted tolerantly. He was sympathetic. Bertier de Sauvigny cites Metternich's reply of March 1846 to the Austrian minister at Florence, Baron Neumann, who had asked for permission to visit Rome:

> Go or don't go, depending on whether you feel you can do so without harming the service. You are much too reliable and experienced a diplomatist to need advice, particularly advice from 300 leagues away. I authorise you to do what you want, and at whatever time you think proper or convenient.

Clearly he was a pleasant man to work for—'His manner towards colleagues was always charming,' Prokesch-Osten tells us.

However, all Metternich's envoys were swamped by reams of verbose advice. In despatches he was alarmingly garrulous, a failing of which he was well aware; he once said that he knew how to bore men to death. But the essence of what he had to say was invariably to the point.

The chancellery at the Ballhausplatz was not only the centre of Metternich's official life but his principal home. 'You cannot think how beautiful my rooms are when the sun shines through them,' he wrote once. Always careful about the impression he made on visitors, there was a vast antechamber in which they waited for their audience. 'It is a really magnificent room, eighteen foot high, the walls covered with books up to the ceiling. There are some 15,000 volumes in fine mahogany bookcases without glass.' As for his study, it too was large—'I like to be able to move about'—with three windows and huge chests-of-drawers. During May and June he worked at his villa on the Rennweg, luxuriating in its beautiful garden.

Ironically, in view of his love of the Czech countryside, Metternich's principal rival at this time was a Czech, Count Anton Kolowrat-Liebsteinsky, former *Burgraf* (Governor) of Bohemia. This bad-tempered, aggressive nobleman, a curious combination of great landowner and bureaucrat who became what in effect was minister of the Interior, has been mistakenly claimed as a liberal because of his sympathy for all Slavs and dislike of Metternich.

Admittedly he told the chancellor that his policies amounted to no more than 'a forest of bayonets' and 'leaving things as they were', that he was playing into the revolutionaries' hands. But on the same occasion he assured Metternich, 'I am an aristocrat by birth and conviction and agree totally with you that one must strive for conservatism . . . We differ only about methods.' From 1828–48 Kolowrat was head of the *Staatsrat*'s political and financial departments. He had found favour with the Emperor by sending in a list of Bohemian freemasons with his own father's name at the top; he confirmed this good impression by balancing the Monarchy's budget for 1829. Quite apart from natural antipathy, Kolowrat undermined Metternich by a ruthless paring of the defence budget; he described the Imperial army as 'a shield which weighed down the rider'. The chancellor had a chance to demand Kolowrat's dismissal at the end of 1829, after he had been insufferably rude, but refrained, telling the Emperor that Kolowrat was 'a useful tool'. Metternich had nothing to fear from him while Francis lived.

Meanwhile, Austria's position in Germany was threatened by a new phenomenon, the *Zollverein*. This had originated in a number of separate customs unions which grew up within the confederation after Prussia made her territories a tariff-free zone in 1818. Her new possessions in the Rhineland and Westphalia had given her control of many of Germany's most important trade routes and waterways, and in 1828 she began a trade war to force the other unions to join her in a single union. Six years later, the *Zollverein* was formally inaugurated; by 1836 the only German states outside it, apart from Austria, were the Hanseatic ports and the Hanoverian customs union. Metternich warned the Emperor of the danger of economic domination by Prussia. If no economist, Metternich was eager for Austria to accept the *Zollverein*'s repeated invitations to lower her tariff barriers and join. But Kolowrat and Austrian business interests refused to allow any reduction in tariffs.

The winter of 1834–5 was a bitter one. 'I was terribly upset this morning to hear from Clemens that the Emperor was dangerously ill,' Mélanie recorded on 23 February. Francis had caught a chill after going to the *Burgtheater* which turned into pneumonia. Five days later, Mélanie wrote, 'We see death approaching.' The

Emperor was conscious until almost the last moment. His chancellor persuaded him to sign a document, addressed to the heir to the throne, which had been drafted by Gentz for just such a crisis; it was taken in to the dying man by his confessor, in case Metternich's opponents should try to prevent it reaching him. The key sentences read, 'Give to Prince Metternich, my most faithful servant and best friend, the confidence which I have shown him over so many years. Do not take any decision concerning public affairs or about people without first hearing what he has to say.'

During Francis's last agony, two days after signing the document, Metternich took the Archdukes and Kolowrat into an adjoining room and told them, 'In future the throne will be occupied not by a man but by a symbol, as on an altar. We must serve it like priests in order to fulfill our duty. The Emperor Ferdinand will be a species of Dalai Lama.'

Emperor Francis died on 2 March 1835. There is no need to doubt the chancellor's grief. However, he assured Count Apponyi in Paris that 'no innovation in policy or principle will take place during the new reign'.

16

'A Continuous Chain of Rearguard Actions,' 1835–43

. . . a continuous chain of rearguard actions to delay, to cover, and to argue away the breakdown of the Concert of Europe and all it stood for.

R. A. KANN, 'Metternich, a Reappraisal of his Impact . . .'

Metternich is only a shade of his former self.

TSAR NICHOLAS I in 1845

His Royal, Apostolic and Imperial Majesty Ferdinand I was a physical and mental defective, known popularly in Vienna as Ferdy the Fool—*Nandl der Trottel.* Yet he spoke several languages fluently, performed ceremonial roles adequately and possessed a naïve charm which inspired affection. He was touchingly supported by his beautiful and saintly wife, Maria Anna of Savoy. As he was childless, there had been talk of replacing him by his younger brother, the Archduke Franz Karl (father of the future Emperor Francis Josef) but Franz Karl was almost as ineffectual. Baron von Kübeck, a senior official in the financial department, wrote gloomily that Austria was now a monarchy without a monarch. This did not worry Metternich. He had always supported Ferdinand's succession, partly from respect for the legitimist principle of primogeniture, and had urged his coronation as King of Hungary. No doubt too he hoped that someone so amiable and so easy to manage would enable him to control Austrian policy more completely than he had under Francis. Indeed, on seeing his employer return from the

Hofburg, flushed and with glistening eyes, to announce, 'The Rubicon has been crossed—Ferdinand is Kaiser,' Dr Jäger asked himself, 'Had I before me, I wondered, a new Richelieu, or a new Mayor of the Palace of the sort there used to be in the time of the Merovingian Kings?'

Francis I had bequeathed a species of triumvirate. In his will he stipulated that, besides the chancellor, his brother Archduke Ludwig should advise on 'important matters of domestic administration', and for the moment it would be difficult to remove Kolowrat. Even so, for a time it really did seem as if Metternich had a chance to make himself all-powerful. He reckoned without Ludwig's elder brothers. Archduke Karl, the hero of Aspern-Essling, and the Liberal Archduke Johann (who had married Fräulein Plochl, daughter of a Styrian postman), were mortified by their exclusion from power. At first, however, they did not appreciate that they had an ally in Kolowrat.

Metternich's entire policy after 1822 has been described with some truth as a series of rearguard actions to conceal the end of the Concert of Europe. Admittedly, he had at least succeeded in reviving the Triple Alliance. However, from 1835 onwards his power base grew steadily weaker, and he was to be threatened increasingly on all fronts. Nonetheless, regardless of advancing years and growing discouragement, he fought on with undiminished skill and determination.

There was another meeting of the sovereigns of the Triple Alliance at Teplitz in September 1835, as if to emphasise that nothing had changed. Poor Ferdinand was overwhelmed and would never attend such a meeting again. Yet although Ferdinand made an unhappy impression on the Russians, who knew a madman when they saw one, the chancellor was able to build on the sound relationship which had been established at Münchengrätz. When Francis died, Nicholas had assured Vienna that he saw the 'internal tranquillity' of the Austrian and Russian empires as a matter of mutual concern, promising to safeguard it with 'all the resources and all the power with which Providence had endowed him'. He now repeated these assurances. (In 1837 he would inform Metternich, through Count Tatischev, his ambassador, that 'in any eventuality Austria can count on Russia, for the Tsar will never forget what he promised at Münchengrätz'.) There was full agreement on every aspect of international policy, and on questions nearer home. The Third Section at St Petersburg appointed an officer to liaise with Count Sedlnitsky's *Polizeihofstelle* at Vienna. Russia, Austria and Prussia sent an ultimatum to the tiny Polish Republic of Cracow that unless it at once restrained the activities of revolutionaries who had taken refuge there, they would send in troops to do so—as they did in 1836.

Tsar Nicholas also insisted on visiting Vienna. 'Write to your wife and let me bring your letter to her,' he told Metternich. When he arrived, he made a point of calling on Mélanie as well as on the Empress, treating the Princess 'with the most exquisite tact and the most perfect propriety'. His visit was undoubtedly intended as a gesture of support for the chancellor.

Metternich was encouraged by overtures from Louis Philippe. While he never ceased to distrust the 'royalty of the barricades' or the land of the *Comité Directeur*—where Buonarotti was training a no less terrible successor in Auguste Blanqui—he now realized that the King of the French was secretly a conservative. 'He only uses the cast-off clothes of liberalism as a covering,' he observed to Count von Hübner in July 1833. 'Having seized the throne, Louis Philippe wants to stay there,' he told Apponyi the following September. He tried to influence the King by sending him notes through the Paris embassy; even if he could not persuade him to go further right, he hoped that a closer link might make for smoother international relations. Eager for respectability and acceptance by other European dynasties, the July monarchy sought the hand of an Austrian Archduchess for the heir to the French throne. In the summer of 1836, with his brother the Duc de Nemours, the Prince Royal—the handsome and charming Duc d'Orléans—arrived in Vienna to seek a bride. When his eye lit on Archduke Karl's daughter Teresa she was horrified, saying that such a match was a death sentence, since she would undoubtedly be murdered in the next French Revolution; no one in Austria had forgotten the fate of Marie Antoinette. The entire Imperial family opposed the marriage. So did the chancellor, despite Orléans calling at the Ballhausplatz to beg Metternich not to stand in the way of his happiness. Metternich was confirmed in his view by news from Paris of an attempt to assassinate Louis Philippe.

Meanwhile, Metternich's quarrel with Kolowrat came to a head when the chancellor took charge of the arrangements for Ferdinand's coronation as King of Bohemia at Prague on 7 September. As the minister responsible for internal affairs, and as former Grand Burgrave of Bohemia, Kolowrat was outraged by the 'Rhinelander' interfering in a matter which meant so much to his homeland. He threatened to resign but instead went off to his estates on sick leave; Metternich commented that the minister was suffering from 'piles which had mounted to his head', a reference to his love of desk work.

The chancellor would regret that he had not insisted on Kolowrat proceeding with his resignation. Kolowrat blocked Metternich's policies in too many fields. The adjutant-general, Count Karl Clam-Martinitz, head of the army department in the *Staatsrat,* and General Radetzky, commander-in-chief in Italy, were constantly complaining of his economies with the military budget; inevitably an underfunded army must weaken Austria's international standing. Kolowrat's fellow Bohemian magnates, farmers on a vast scale, had persuaded him to resist any reduction in duties on imported beet sugar, a refusal which ended any hope of entering the *Zollverein.* Worst of all, Kolowrat stood in the way of the chancellor's plan for reforming the Empire's administration.

What Metternich proposed was that the *Ministerkonferenz* should be replaced by a ministerial cabinet in the modern sense, with the chancellor as 'prime minister'. It would be detached from the *Staatsrat,* which was to become a purely advisory *Reichsrat* with members from the regional *Landtage;* this too would be under the chancellor's presidency. The new system meant an end of the old *Kabinettsweg* or loose ministerial council, now rudderless in the absence of a firm ruler. Had the plan been adopted, Metternich would have become effectively regent of the Empire. Yet his object was not so much personal power as efficiency—to put an end to the confusion between the consultative and executive spheres of government. In retirement he wrote, 'One of the great obstacles with which I have had to battle during my ministry has been the lack of energy in the internal administration.' Indeed he considered Kolowrat 'fundamentally honest'; his real objection to Kolowrat was that the latter was at bottom no more than a hidebound bureaucrat.

Similarly, there was more to Kolowrat's hostility to the chancellor's plan than mere personal dislike. He was not just a dull bureaucrat who disliked change but a convinced centralist in the tradition of Joseph II. He genuinely feared that Metternich's foreign policy might endanger Austria, through spending too much on 'the forest of bayonets' or by embarking on a war. He was certain that he himself was far better qualified to run the Monarchy.

After learning at the end of October 1836 that Archduke Ludwig had approved the plan, Kolowrat contacted Archduke Johann, who hastened to Vienna. There began a partnership between the two men which would survive until 1848. They had the tacit support of Archduke Karl, who was very angry at Metternich's refusal to let him become commander-in-chief in place of his lunatic nephew. Johann swiftly rallied the chancellor's many enemies and won over Ludwig, after which he confronted Metternich in a three-hour meeting at the Ballhausplatz. Abandoned by all save Clam-Martinitz, the chancellor gave way.

Johann and Kolowrat then produced an alternative scheme, which was adopted. A *Ministerkonferenz* was established, but with a committee of four at its head instead of the chancellor—Archdukes Ludwig and Franz Karl, Kolowrat, and Metternich. Ludwig was nominally president, while Kolowrat remained effective head of the *Staatsrat,* with control of the treasury and official appointments.

Many observers were surprised that the chancellor did not resign. Some historians suggest that he could not afford to do so because of his extravagant private life. Yet if a severe blow, both for himself and the Monarchy, it was far from being total defeat. Kolowrat had not emerged as a 'prime minister', even if he succeeded in dominating Archduke Ludwig. 'It is true that he [Kolowrat] held control of the purse-strings in the Monarchy just as before 1835, but the man who really controlled the higher imperial police was Metternich, who likewise had the leading voice in the affairs of Italy and Hungary' is the verdict of the Austrian Empire's latest historian, Alan Sked. 'There is a strong case to be made out, therefore, that, given his control of defence and foreign affairs also, Metternich's position was stronger than Kolowrat's.'

Even so, after 1836 the chancellor gave up hope of reforming the Austrian administration. He had placed great hopes on his plan; Mélanie records sleepless nights during the negotiations. The new régime was still slower and less enterprising than that of the Emperor Francis in his last years. Ludwig, who presided over the *Ministerkonferenz*, was too limited and indecisive to offer any sort of leadership, insisting on the submission of written reports on almost all items on the agenda, while Franz Karl could barely understand the proceedings at all. The chancellor and Kolowrat were frequently at loggerheads.

Nevertheless, Metternich had survived Francis's departure with much of his power intact. Outside observers received the impression that nothing had changed, that he was still the most powerful man in Europe. Even his critics among the Archdukes and the bureaucrats still considered him indispensable for Austria's well-being. The exception was Kolowrat, who nursed an implacable hatred for the chancellor. However, this was not reciprocated by Metternich, who tried to work with Kolowrat as best he could. He knew very well that the Monarchy's finances were unsound, admitting that economies in the army were unavoidable. He was thinking of finance when he confided to General Clam-Martinitz in the summer of 1838, 'We cannot sack Kolowrat—he would only come back as a ghost.' (One reason for the chancellor's seeming serenity during this difficult time may have been the birth of his youngest son, Lothar, in 1837, forty years after the birth of his first child.)

The menacing figure of Buonarotti left the scene in September 1837. The republican demonstration at the old Robespierrist's funeral was a chilling reminder of the continuing hold of Messianic socialism, of the threat of revolution. A thousand French and Italian workers followed the cortège of 'the friend of equality'. (Blanqui, under police surveillance, was prevented from attending.) Yet 'Buonarettism' was split. Metternich had observed shrewdly in

1834, after Young Italy's abortive invasion of Savoy, that the 'head of the committee'—Buonarotti—did not approve of the plans of 'this bold conspirator'—Mazzini. 'The old conspirator [Buonarotti] could not conceive the Day of Judgement without fire and gnashing of teeth,' says J. L. Talmon. 'Dictatorship and terror were, in his opinion, the inescapable necessity of the Revolution.' Buonarotti had therefore 'excommunicated' Mazzini, who believed that a wave of brotherly love would accompany the revolution in Italy, making terror unnecessary. Nor had Buonarotti approved of his unruly disciple's recruitment of members of the Italian aristocracy. But in January 1837 Mazzini had gone to London, where he would spend a decade in exile.

Since Ferdinand had performed so well during his crowning at Prague, the chancellor decided to have another coronation at Milan. The Emperor was crowned as King of Lombardy in September 1838 with the hallowed Iron Crown (hammered out of a nail from the True Cross. Save for Napoleon's gaudy usurpation in 1805, the ceremony had not been performed for centuries). There was an amnesty for political prisoners and the occasion typified the chancellor's strategy of giving the separate peoples of the Monarchy an illusion of independence and national identity. For a week the Metternich *salon* was the centre of social life in the northern Italian capital, Rossini playing the piano while the great tenor Prince Belgiojoso sang his songs.

The Kingdom of Lombardy-Venetia was ruled as an Austrian province, not as a separate state. The Viceroy's role was basically ceremonial, his powers negligible. Nor did the 'Aulic Council' at Vienna have any real independent existence. The Kingdom was administered from the Imperial capital by Austrian government departments. Moreover, Metternich had a special official stationed in Milan whose function was to provide a direct link between the chancellor and the governor, as well as reporting on the political situation—especially on any symptoms of popular unrest. Metternich had scant respect for Italians. 'Italy is full of idlers and proletarians who pour out words in cafés and the other public places which customarily pass for home among them,' he commented to Apponyi in 1831. As for the northern Italians, he told a Milanese at about the same time, 'The Lombards have never been more pro-Austrian than when they were under the [Napoleonic] Kingdom of Italy, and they have never been more opposed to Austria than when under our government.'

Even so, his attitude was very far from being hostile. Many Italian as well as Austrian officials were employed. He was most anxious to develop the Kingdom's economy, and in 1841 urged the building of railways to link it to Vienna. His purpose was not just to integrate Lombardy-Venetia more closely into the Empire, but to demonstrate to other Italian states that its government was the most efficient and beneficial in the entire peninsula. He was optimistic that after a period of 'quarantine' from revolutionary politics, and the rooting out of secret societies, there would be no more need for excessive police surveillance or for Marshal Radetzky's garrisons to be quite so watchful.

Unfortunately, although Metternich loved Italy, he never understood any of its inhabitants. In Lombardy-Venetia he antagonised not so much the professional classes, who benefitted from what was undoubtedly the most efficiently run and most prosperous economy in the peninsula, as the aristocracy. He insisted on the vetting of all titles and pretensions in nobility, applying strict Austrian standards to what had always been a much more easygoing system. No one except those with sixteen quarterings was admitted to the Vice-Regal court at Milan (and only after the quarterings had been checked), while many a duke or prince found himself demoted to a mere count. In the end, most of the northern Italian aristocracy boycotted the Metternichs' receptions, and the Jockey Club of Milan, the younger Lombard nobles' favourite meeting place, bristled with hostility. Another irritation was the Austrian civil law code, in itself excellent but which required a working knowledge of German if precedents were to be cited. In addition, there were frequent grumbles at the arrogance of the military, although this contained many Italian officers.

In June 1839 Metternich had once more to attend the opening of the Hungarian Diet at Pressburg, which had had to be summoned because of the Empire's financial problems. The Magyars had a genuine constitution, however archaic—a larger percentage of the population possessed the vote than in Orléanist France. Magyar had replaced Latin as the language of debates, which were frequently noisy, the lesser nobility which provided most of the deputies being especially aggressive. The Diet's formal consent had to be obtained before taxes could be levied or troops conscripted, and it was often vociferous in criticising the policies of the Palatine's Council—which in practice meant attacking the Hungarian Chancellery at Vienna. There were formidable opposition leaders, such as Barons Wesselényi and Eötvös, Count Batthyányi, Déak and Lajos Kossuth. The latter, a half-Slovak petty noble turned journalist, advocated a programme of reform which included everything most dreaded by Metternich; if implemented, it would create a liberal Hungary all but independent of Austria. The chancellor considered Kossuth and his followers to be subversives, telling the Palatine Archduke Joseph that 'the Hungarian polity is a monarchical-aristocratic one; it cannot be accommodated to democratic institutions'. He foresaw civil war and in 1837 had secured from the Tsar a written guarantee that he would intervene if there was a revolt—'At all costs Austria could depend on Russia.'

The situation in Hungary had been made still more difficult by Kolowrat, who in 1836 had used his control of official appointments to make his son-in-law Count Pálffy head of the Hungarian Chancellery. Although Pálffy bore one of Hungary's greatest names, he could not speak a word of his native language. For a time, Metternich lost control of Hungarian affairs—which was one of Kolowrat's motives for making the appointment—and under Pálffy's inept and brutal handling the situation grew critical. Kossuth and Wesselényi were arrested, accused of treason and sent to prison. However, by then everyone realized that Pálffy had lost his head and would have to go.

By 1841, the chancellor had accepted that Hungary could only be ruled through the Diet. When Pálffy's successor had been appointed and Metternich regained control, he began to work with the conservative party, while he had Kossuth and Wesselény released from prison under a special amnesty for political prisoners which he had introduced in 1840. He recognised that a 'quarantine' of the sort employed in Italy was out of the question, that a subtler approach was needed. Throughout he kept in touch with Isztvan Széchenyi, although rejecting his offer to mediate with the Diet. Széchenyi led a group of deputies who saw themselves as Hungarian Whigs and whose political position was between those of the conservative Count Dessewffy and Kossuth; they were dedicated to administrative and economic reform—their aims being well symbolised by the new suspension bridge inspired by their leader, which was to join Buda to Pest—but they never had any hope of winning power. The future lay with the fiery Kossuth and his Magyar gentry.

In June 1839 the Eastern Question flared up again, when Mehemet Ali's troops under their French officers inflicted a total defeat on the Ottoman army at Nisib in Syria. Sultan Mahmud II, who had sent the expedition to reconquer Syria for him, died of drink just before news of the disaster reached the Porte. The entire Turkish fleet defected to the Egyptians, who were now in a position to attack Constantinople. Once again Metternich fell back on the Concert of Europe. He had already proposed a conference of the five great powers, to meet at Vienna and discuss the problems of the Porte. This time even Palmerston accepted. No reply was received from Russia, but Austria, Prussia, Britain and France sent a note to the Turks, guaranteeing the survival of their empire. However, in August Tsar Nicholas—always suspicious—sent word that Russia would not be represented at the Vienna conference. He implied that the chancellor had deserted him in order to ally with France.

In mid-August, worn out by work and worry at the prospect of the end of the Triple Alliance, Metternich had a total physical and nervous breakdown. He collapsed—a stroke was feared. He was forced to rest completely for six weeks. Count Fiquelmont, ambassador at St Petersburg and a man whom he regarded as the ablest of his subordinates, took over while he convalesced at Johannisberg.

During his absence there was a new and astonishing alignment, between the Tsar and Palmerston. A new conference was to take place at London early in 1840. It was hoped that the five great powers would reach an agreement and settle the problem of Egypt and Turkey once and for all.

Before the conference met, Palmerston was to cause Metternich trouble elsewhere. The Neapolitan government had declared its sulphur mines a state monopoly, selling them to an international cartel. It had every right to take such a step. However, in April 1840 the foreign secretary sent the British Navy to blockade Naples, demanding the abolition of the monopoly together with compensation for British sulphur merchants. Metternich complained that the blockade might very well cause a revolution and that if it did, Austrian troops would have to put it down; he begged Britain to save him from such an embarrassment. Palmerston then asked France to mediate, the end of the affair being that King Ferdinand was bullied into submission and the monopoly was revoked.

Adolphe Thiers became head of the French government in March 1840. A hot-tempered little adventurer, the model for Balzac's ruthless hero Rastignac in *Le père Goriot,* he lacked any sense of moderation. Metternich considered him to be totally unscrupulous, without beliefs or principles. Nevertheless, Metternich knew that Louis Philippe, despite distrusting the man, would be forced to appoint him. The chancellor had written of M Thiers early in 1839: 'Travelling light and being decidedly agile, he is one of those men who slip, like a draught, through every crack.'

Hungry for popularity, Thiers arranged for Napoleon's body to be brought back from St Helena for reburial at the Invalides. In the Bonapartist tradition he took a passionate interest in Egypt and Syria, being determined to help Mehemet Ali and his son Ibrahim. Both men were extremely popular in France for having given employment to so many French ex-officers, while it was widely hoped that a strong Egyptian-Syrian state would buttress France's North African empire. Thiers intervened on his own without bothering to consult the other powers; he attempted to arrange a settlement between the Porte and Egypt which would leave Mehemet Ali and his son in undisputed possession of Syria—he was convinced that he could force it through in the face of Palmerston's preference for a partition of Syria. Nor would he send a French representative to the conference in London.

Palmerston took advantage of the absence of French representation to induce Russia, Austria and Prussia to sign the London Convention of July 1840 which offered Mehemet Ali Egypt to bequeath to Ibrahim with the Pashalik of Acre for his lifetime only. Palmerston felt no qualms about breaking the *entente,* the Northern Powers being delighted to help him do so. The French received the news with fury. 'A wave of anger swept the entire country,' the Bonapartist historian Victor Duruy recalled. 'The government gave the appearance of associating itself with this understandable outburst of national pride and France had her hand on her sword hilt.' To the French it seemed as if all Europe was against them. Thiers lost his head, declaiming 'an army ready and well armed, that's our policy'—he threatened to invade the Rhineland. Germany erupted, every local newspaper printing Becker's fierily patriotic verses, '*Sie sollen ihn nicht haben, den freien deutschen Rhein*' ('They're not going to have it, the free German Rhine'). The situation grew even worse when the British, Russian and Austrian fleets shelled Mehemet Ali's garrison at Beirut into surrender after he had tried to crush an uprising by Syrian Christians. However, France recalled her own fleet, although it outnumbered the British, and Mehemet Ali ceased to be a threat to Turkey. King Louis Philippe had had enough, Thiers being forced to resign in October. Metternich, who had genuinely feared that war might break out in the West, commented, 'The man was wrong in every way'—he had 'taken no nationality into account apart from the French'.

Thiers was succeeded by François Guizot. Surprisingly, this austere Protestant intellectual soon showed in his foreign policy that he had more in common with the Austrian chancellor than any other European statesman, even if they did not always agree. Both learnt to trust and even like each other. Guizot too possessed a 'philosophical' approach to conservatism while, ironically, his mistress was Princess Lieven, still pursuing her taste for love and power politics. In 1841, France rejoined the Concert of Europe, signing the Straits' Convention together with the other powers; this put an end to Russia's right of passage through the Dardanelles, closing the straits to warships of every nationality.

The chancellor appeared to be isolated when his great ally Clam-

Martinitz died in 1840. However, he found that he had much in common with Karl Freiherr von Kübeck, who became president of the *Hofkammer* (Imperial Exchequer) the same year and joined the *Ministerkonferenz*. 'Hans' Kübeck, the son of a Moravian tailor, had worked his way up through the civil service and had been the real architect of Kolowrat's widely acclaimed balancing of the budget estimates in 1829. He concentrated on improving the monarchy's economic resources and, largely due to Salomon Rothschild's support, gave Austria excellent railways. Flattered by Metternich's friendliness, he was in any case sympathetic towards his proposals that Austria should either enter the *Zollverein* or else take over southern Germany's commerce by exploiting the rail link between Austria and the Adriatic.

During his visits to Germany, the chancellor received the distinct impression, only too well justified, that Austria was lagging behind economically. 'I observed [industrial] forces in operation, and the direction they were taking; I felt strongly that we are in a position of inferiority because we have no commercial policy of our own, no policy which was specifically Austrian, and which answers to the situation,' he reported. 'I felt that our policy was negative in contrast with the unceasing activity I could see elsewhere.' He was determined to redress the balance.

By 1841, the South German states, growing nervous at unmistakable signs of Prussian expansionism, were ready to welcome Austria into the *Zollverein*. Metternich dreamt of creating a customs union in the centre of Europe, which would include not only Germany and the Habsburg lands but the Italian states as well, a *Zollverein* of seventy million people, extending from the Baltic to the Mediterranean, and from the Rhine to the Russian border; it would enable Austria to reassert her domination over Germany and make possible the formation of a *Lega Italica,* bypassing the misgivings of Italian sovereigns. Kübeck supported the plan warmly. When put to the *Ministerkonferenz* in November 1841, it was received with no less enthusiasm by Archduke Ludwig and Kolowrat, a commission under Count Hartig being appointed to examine its feasibility. However, Hartig's commission decided against it, on the grounds that the integration of the Hungarian and Austrian customs which must first take place would cause such resentment in Hungary that it might lead to demands for secession. The chancellor was bitterly disappointed. 'Austria is on the point of seeing herself to some extent excluded from the rest of Germany', he told Kübeck, 'and treated as a foreign country.' Metternich's alternative scheme of developing the Adriatic outlet was also rejected, because it would cost too much to build the railways.

If he failed over the *Zollverein,* Metternich was far more successful in his encouragement of railways. For once the *Ministerkonferenz* was less obstructive than Emperor Francis, who had feared that railways might be used to bring revolution into the Habsburg lands. After Francis's death, Metternich had been swiftly converted to the idea by Salomon Rothschild, who obtained concessions to build lines from Vienna to Galicia and to Brünn (Brno) in 1839. Soon there were lines to Budapest and Trieste. When further expansion was threatened by mismanagement and corruption, the state took over the task. It is perhaps surprising that Metternich was so keen a supporter of the railroads' construction. 'Generally speaking, I am against [such] enterprises being promoted by the state,' he was to write in 1844—in words which sound strangely modern today. 'They should be left to private individuals, though I speak only of those which require a great amount of capital. Nonetheless I would like to keep a government's right to exercise protection and control.'

He made a further attempt to take the Monarchy into the *Zollverein* in 1843, producing a workable scheme for the abolition of tariffs between Austria and Hungary. As before, it was supported by Kübeck. However, Metternich was absent when the plan came up for discussion by the *Ministerkonferenz.* Unexpectedly, Kolowrat decided to oppose it and made certain that it was rejected.

The 1830s and early 1840s had seen the autumn of Metternich's dominance. Despite the July Revolution, and despite the death of Francis, he still towered over every other statesman in Europe. In 1836 he had some unusually revealing conversations with an American scholar. In June that year Mr George Ticknor of Boston, sometime professor of modern languages at Harvard and a close friend of Nathaniel Hawthorne, called on Metternich at the Ballhausplatz with a letter of introduction from Alexander von Humboldt. It was the first of four meetings. 'Prince Metternich is now just sixty-three years old,' Ticknor wrote, 'a little above the middle height, well preserved in all respects, and rather stout, but not corpulent, with a good and genuinely German face, light blue eyes that are not very expressive, and a fine Roman nose . . . His hair is nearly white, and his whole appearance, especially when he moves, is dignified and imposing; but his whole appearance is winning.'

At the second meeting (on 1 July) the chancellor spoke with remarkable frankness about himself and about his political attitude. 'I am myself moderate in everything, and I endeavour to become more moderate. I have a calm disposition, a very calm one,' he assured his guest. 'Monarchy alone tends to bring men together, to unite them into compact and effective masses; to render them capable by their combined efforts, of the highest degrees of culture and civilisation.' Ticknor objected, arguing that individuals were of more importance in a republic, since a republican government had less power.

'I am aware that your country could never have made so much progress in so short a time under any other than a democratic system,' answered Metternich, 'for democracy, while it separates men, creates rivalships of all kinds, and carries them forward very fast by competition among themselves.' Democracy was natural to Americans. But:

> In Europe it is a lie, and I hate all lies . . . I have always, however, been of the opinion expressed by Tocqueville, that democracy, so far from being the oldest and simplest form of government, as has so often been said, is the latest invented form of all, and the most complicated. With you in America it seems to be *un tour de force perpetuel.* You are, therefore, often in dangerous positions, and your system is one that wears out fast . . . You will go on much further in democracy; you will become much more democratic. I do not know where it will end, nor how it will end; but it cannot end in a quiet, ripe old age.

Metternich then asked who would be the next President of the United States. Ticknor, a Whig, replied that to his regret it would be the Democrat, Martin Van Buren. The chancellor commented:

> Neither should I be of Mr Van Buren's party were I in America. I should rather be of that old party of which Washington was originally the head. It was a sort of conservative party, and I should be conservative almost everywhere, certainly in England and America. Your country is a very important one. This government is about to establish regular diplomatic relations with it. You have always managed your affairs with foreign nations with ability.

'The present state of Europe is disgustful to me' was a remark which Metternich made over and over again. 'England is advancing towards a revolution . . . has no great statesmen now, no great statesmen of any party, and woe to the country whose condition and institutions no longer produce great men . . .'

France, on the other hand, had the Revolution behind her, though she too lacked able men—'Louis Philippe is the ablest statesman they have had for a great while.' Yet:

> The influence of France on England since 1830 has been very bad. The affair of July, 1830, is called a revolution: it was no such thing; it was a lucky rebellion, which changed those at the head of government, nothing else. But when Louis Philippe said, at the famous arrangement of the Hôtel de Ville, '*The Charter will become a reality*', he uttered a falsehood . . . there existed no Charter at the moment when he spoke, for that of 1814 was destroyed, and what became of the Charter afterwards he knew as little as anybody in such a moment of uncertainty. The elements of things in France are very bad . . . there is a great deal of talk about a constitutional government like the English, which they can comprehend as little as they can our German theories or your practical democracy.

He told the man from New England, 'I do not like my business—*Je n'aime pas mon métier* . . . the present state of Europe disgusts me' and how at the turn of the century he had thought of emigrating to America but had been held back by his inheritance. Curiously, after so many years, he explained, 'I did not make the peace of 1809, for I did not choose to make it. When a minister begins, under such circumstances, as I began under then, he must have a clear ground—*un terrain net* . . .'

The conversation lasted for about an hour and a half. The chancellor spoke throughout with great earnestness and eloquence, sometimes striking the table, but, Ticknor tells us, 'He was always dignified, winning and easy in his whole air and manner.'

When they rejoined Mélanie and the rest of the party, the conversation was about the legal action brought against the British prime minister by the husband of his mistress, Mrs Norton. 'If Lord Melbourne had been convicted he must have gone out, and perhaps the Ministry would have been entirely dissolved—an event which would have diminished, I am sure, the Prince's disgust at the present state of Europe,' says Ticknor. (Palmerston was Melbourne's foreign secretary.)

Ticknor was impressed by the dinner, 'as delicious, I suppose, as the science of cookery could make it, and extended through from ten to fourteen courses, with many kinds of wines, and among the rest Tokay'. He adds:

> We had good Johannisberg, of course, and the Princess made some jokes about *her* selling it to the Americans, to which the Prince added, that *he* had an agent in New York for the purpose, and that we could buy there as good wine as he gives to his friends in Vienna.

Metternich was still immensely proud of Schloss Johannisberg, where he spent a few weeks every year, entertaining so lavishly that on one occasion his wife compared it to a hotel. Yet his favourite country houses were those in Bohemia and Moravia, where he now had extensive estates. According to the *Almanach de Gotha* for 1836, in Bohemia he owned 'the seigneurie of Plass joined to the domains of Katzerow, Biela and Kraschau' and 'the seigneurie of Königswart joined to the domains of Miltogau, Amonsgrun and Marensgrun'; in Moravia 'the seigneurie of Brzezowitz and the domain of Kowalowitz'. He liked Königswart best. He told Ticknor that no part of Europe had prospered more than Bohemia during the last twenty years.

The two men genuinely respected each other. 'I take him to be the most consummate statesman of his sort that our time has produced' was the American's verdict on the chancellor. The latter's friend Humboldt told Ticknor, 'Prince Metternich, whom I met at Teplitz, was delighted by his meeting with you. You seem much more rational in his eyes than what he calls my liberalism.'

However, the dialogue had taken place when the chancellor was still in his self-confident sixties. The septuagenarian Metternich would be a very different man—and in very different circumstances.

17

Metternich at Seventy

Metternich is only a shade of his former self.
TSAR NICHOLAS I in 1845

A final victory of this policy of pure monarchism was an impossibility.
SRBIK, *Metternich, der Staatsmann und der Mensch*

Metternich reached the age of seventy in 1843, despite a conviction that he would die young. He was less vigorous and Mélanie worried about his health, but his mental energy was unimpaired. He kept pace with events—it has been said that he was never ahead of his time or behind it—and could cope with any crisis. There was no apparent threat to Restoration Europe; Orléanist France had been contained, while the Triple Alliance remained intact. The Italian societies had been broken, their leaders chased into exile. If he had been checked over the *Zollverein*, it looked as though he had found a solution to the Hungarian problem. When the first hint of disaster appeared in 1846 it came from a most unlikely quarter.

The political situation at Budapest began to improve during the Diet of 1843–4. A new and effective conservative leader emerged, Count György Apponyi, with whom Metternich established a cautious alliance. The chancellor encouraged a programme of economic reforms (an investment bank, new roads and railways) very like that advocated by Széchenyi, so that 'hollow theories and sterile polemics would go up in smoke'. It was his answer to Magyar nationalism and separatism, 'a saving operation'. He warned that 'though the fire of revolution has not broken out, it smoulders on and if the elements are not halted they will transform the old structure into a heap of cinders'. Since emerging from prison in

1841, Kossuth had been rabble-rousing through his paper *Pesti Hirlap*, which blamed Hungary's woes on Vienna instead of on the 'plum-tree' nobles' refusal to pay taxes. Metternich took some of the wind out of Kossuth's sails in 1844 by accepting Magyar as the Diet's official language; Ferdinand would open the 1847 Diet by reading out a speech in Magyar. The chancellor had fully accepted that Hungary could only be governed through its constitution.

If Hungary was the centre of nationalist debate within the Monarchy, Metternich saw the problem as a whole. He still intended to build an all-embracing central government behind a constitutional façade. (In 1847 Count Ficquelmont would define it neatly when complaining of the problems of attempting to 'go on running the Kingdom [of Lombardy-Venetia] as a province but organise and above all govern it in such a fashion that we might present it as an Italian state'.) The chancellor continued to encourage local languages and traditions, looking with a benevolent eye on provincial Diets as long as they did not try to discuss politics, and dreamt of Ferdinand being crowned as Emperor of Austria at a coronation to be attended by representatives from every Diet. After 1848 and the attempt to build a *Grossdeutschland,* he was to write that he had never seen Germanisation as an option for the Monarchy, since Austria was 'a Magyar-Slav state' and that even its German-speaking provinces had no bond with Germany.

Originally Metternich had favoured the Czech revival. But Frantisek Palacky, once a conservative, began to seem threatening when his great *History of Bohemia* displayed nationalist undertones in those volumes which appeared in the 1840s, with their glorification of the Czech heresiarch Huss. Palacky's friend, the journalist Pavel Havelicek, was a liberal who stridently demanded a constitution for Bohemia. Metternich declared that 'Czechism is a tendency which, if things take their ordinary course, only leads to small aberrations, but in an epoch of general excitement it works like bean-salad in a cholera epidemic'.

The Croats were a special case, since he hoped to play them off against the Magyars. When it was purely linguistic and literary, he had encouraged Ljudevit Gaj's 'Illyrian' revival (which enjoyed the backing of Croatia's greatest magnate, Count Draskovich of Trakostjan), allowing him to publish a newspaper called *Illyrian News*. But Gaj developed into a pan-Slavist, seeking a Kingdom of Croats, Slovenes, Serbs and Bulgars within the Monarchy; it implied just the sort of destabilisation of the Balkans most dreaded by Metternich, who remained totally convinced that Austria had reached saturation point and could not absorb any more territory. In 1840, Gaj tried to persuade the Bosnians to rise against the Turks; he had been largely financed by Russian agents in Serbia, whose Prince looked to St Petersburg rather than to Vienna. In 1841 the chancellor ordered Gaj to stop his activities, whether political or cultural. Two years later he relented, to some extent, while in 1847 the Croat Diet was permitted to use the 'Croatian-Slavonian' tongue.

The years 1843–5 were comparatively peaceful for Metternich as far as foreign affairs were concerned. The Eastern Question had died down for the moment, while Germany and Italy remained more or less tranquil. The only cause for concern was the new King of Prussia. The chancellor's old friend Frederick William III, who during the latter part of his reign took Vienna's advice on liberalism almost reverently, had died in 1840. If charming and kindly, Frederick William IV was also vain and unstable, a fervent romantic whose fantasies would ultimately drive him insane. Inspired by his vision of medieval Germany, he had a sneaking sympathy for nationalists; Arndt had been allowed to resume his lectures at Bonn while, more ominous, Jahn had been released from police surveillance. For the moment, despite the anti-French outburst which had convulsed Germany in 1841, the mischief went no further. Even so, it grew increasingly clear that the King was turning his back on conservative advisers and was toying with the idea of a constitution.

In August 1845 King Frederick William IV came to Stolzenfels in the Prussian Rhineland, very near to Johannisberg. He had a long and revealing conversation with Metternich, who afterwards observed bitterly, 'Prussia's greatest weaknesses lie in having a King who, while wanting the best, is eccentric and in the undeniable fact that the old Prussian political machine has been demolished. Meanwhile a new machine still remains to be constructed . . .'

Queen Victoria and Prince Albert were also staying at Stolzenfels, together with the King and Queen of the Belgians. Metternich had hoped Victoria would prove a good conservative, though he feared the influence of her uncle, King Leopold. The chancellor considered that if the King's advice to her about Britain's internal affairs might do no damage, his meddling in foreign affairs could be very unhealthy indeed:

> Leopold will support revolutionary principles in the [Iberian] peninsula and he's going to fuel the fire in any business which involves Russia. He won't be exactly anti-Austrian but on the other hand he won't support our particular brand of politics.

These had been Metternich's views in 1837. He was irritated by Leopold's dynastic ambitions. The Coburgs had married the Queen of Portugal and the English Queen, as well as the Duke of Orléans, heir to the throne of France. 'This is a family produced by our times, which mirrors their spirit,' Metternich observed disapprovingly to Neumann at the embassy in England in 1843. 'During an epoch when so many thrones are tottering an association has emerged to cast a speculative eye over them. The Coburgs constitute the association . . .' He expressed ironical surprise that they did not have designs on the Ottoman succession. He grumbled that Victoria's 'species of cult' for her husband's family was really too much—she was 'not at all English but totally Coburg'. He dined with her informally in her private apartments at Stolzenfels, finding her rather childish, shy and seemingly a little bored; with hindsight we know that for her part the Queen thought him prosy but pleasant enough. Her reserve was almost certainly due to her beloved Uncle Leopold having warned her to say little. The chancellor was at least able to have a lengthy conversation with Prince Albert, who expressed his deep uneasiness about what might happen in Prussia.

In December 1845 the Tsar came to Vienna to discuss the proposed marriage of his daughter, Grand Duchess Olga, to Archduke Stephen, the Palatine of Hungary's son; the Austrians insisted that the girl should abandon her Orthodox faith and become a Catholic, which at once put an end to the match. Metternich may well have wished to prevent it taking place; he had no desire to see a Hungarian pretender-in-waiting who could count on Russian support. Mélanie found Tsar Nicholas very much altered when he called on her. 'His features wear an even harder expression while the terrible severity of his glare is in no way softened by the set of his mouth.' The Tsar was still talking to her when the chancellor entered the room. As soon as Metternich changed the subject and began discussing foreign affairs—the Tory Cabinet in London—Nicholas broke in, 'Not a word about politics! I'm only here to talk to your wife.' However, he agreed to have a meeting with Metternich next day, during which he appeared to be much more relaxed.

The Tsar's grim manner may have been due to seeing the Emperor Ferdinand at the parade which he had just left; the Tsar had watched Ferdinand being hoisted onto the saddle of his charger 'with all the precautions normally taken to help a frightened woman'. The poor lunatic gave Nicholas the impression that the Habsburgs and their entire Monarchy were completely finished. He wrote to the Tsarina, 'I have to tell you that everything here goes very badly. Metternich is only a shade of his former self; Kolowrat too is old; the Archduke Ludwig is more irresolute than ever . . . Hungary is sullen, Galicia on the point of bursting into flames.' Even so, he paid the chancellor a grudging, backhanded compliment: 'This régime will only survive as long as you do.'

Mélanie worried more than ever about her husband's health. He was now seventy-two, yet he still worked for fifteen hours a day. His face was increasingly lined, while he was growing very deaf. Partly to keep him away from his place of work, and no doubt partly to have an equally imposing home when his death should cause her departure from the Ballhausplatz, his wife persuaded him to build a palace on the Rennweg, designed, as she put it, 'to shelter the whole family when he who is the sole reason for our existence has been taken from us'. Metternich enjoyed telling the architects precisely what he wanted. It was to be on a suitably grand scale, with a frontage containing forty windows. Work began in 1846.

In January of that year he had realized a lifelong ambition, presiding over the foundation of an 'Imperial and Royal Academy of the Sciences' at Vienna. His old enemy Archduke Johann became its principal trustee. He assured the Archduke that he was 'much considered in the learned world', which did not make Johann any fonder of him.

The chancellor had grown increasingly worried about Galicia, where the *szlachta*—landowning nobles, great and small—still dreamt of a new Kingdom of Poland, while on the border the Republic of Cracow continued to be a hotbed of conspiracy. His agents in Paris discovered that émigré Poles were organising a coup at Cracow and revolts in Poznan and Galicia, to take place in 1846. On 17 February news came that an uprising in Poznan had been forestalled, the Prussian authorities arresting the leaders. But next day revolutionaries seized Cracow and declared a 'socialist' republic. General Wrbna marched in swiftly to occupy the city.

What now took place is among the gravest charges ever levied against Metternich. Undeterred by what had happened at Poznan, the *szlachta* tried to revolt on 17 February. The traditional Polish version of what ensued has been given recently by Count Adam Zamoyski:

> Premature action in Galicia alerted the Austrian authorities, who reacted with speed and perfidy. They appealed to the mainly Ruthene peasantry, explaining that the Polish lords were plotting a rising which would enslave them and offering cash for every 'conspirator' brought in dead or alive. The result was a terrible night of butchery in which bands of peasants attacked over 400 country houses, killing about a thousand people, few of them conspirators.

While admitting that 'nobles had been slaughtered in their thousands by the local peasantry, apparently under the illusion that this had been ordered by the Emperor', Dr Alan Sked is convinced that 'the Habsburg authorities—despite later charges of connivance—knew nothing about what was going on, and were appalled at the results of the blood-lust'. Yet if there is not a shred of evidence to implicate the chancellor, there is plenty which points at petty officials on the spot.

Some of the leaders of the would-be uprising seem to have promised the peasants, poor even by Eastern European standards, that if they joined in the uprising they would be given the property of all Austrians and Jews—whom they must first murder. As Sked points out, 'The description of the Gallician serfs as "work-animals" goes a long way to explain what happened in 1846.' A mob armed with scythes and flails informed the Austrian *Kreishauptmann* (town governor) at Tarnow, Baron von Breinl, of what it had been told to do; almost certainly he ordered it to defend the Emperor's government and attack the *szlachta.* In consequence, 1,458 members of the landowning class were murdered or seriously wounded, together with 80 priests in the Tarnow area; for three days carts came into Tarnow filled with mutilated bodies, the peasants being under the impression that there was a price on the heads of their victims. The official Prussian gazette printed a letter emanating from Polish exiles in Paris; it claimed that the Austrians had connived at the massacre and rewarded its perpetrators.

Metternich gave his own version of what happened in a letter to Apponyi of 18 March. When a number of Polish landlords had appeared in Polish national dress, armed and bearing the flag of Poland, and ordered their peasants to join in the rising, the men had refused, saying that they would not commit a crime:

> The plotters then had the most stubborn bastinadoed, and when it did not have the desired effect, pistolled several. This lunatic behaviour acted like a signal to the mob. They rushed at their aggressors and struck them down . . . News of what had taken place in the [Tarnow] region spread to other regions, brought by the fugitives themselves, resulting in scenes scarcely less bloodthirsty.

Although horrified as a landowner, he was not entirely displeased. Significantly, Breinl was ennobled *after* the rising. In the same letter to Apponyi, Metternich writes:

> It was not the government which crushed the attackers: the local population took it on themselves . . . Two facts stand out in this story. One is the quite incomprehensible frivolity with which the Polish emigration embarked on a scheme as vast as it was fantastic. The other is the resistance which the united aristocratic and democratic parties have met from our people. *What is a democracy without the people?*

'An event of extraordinary significance has just occurred,' he informed Marshal Radetzky in Lombardy. 'The attempt by Polish émigrés to start a second Revolution in former Polish territories has been frustrated. The attempt was crushed by the Polish peasantry.'

Even so, he had no intention of relying on peasants to keep order in Galicia. His panacea was 'Develop the German element.' He did not dislike Poles as Poles. What he feared was 'Polonism':

> Polonism is only a formula, a word behind which hides the Revolution in its most brutal form . . . Polonism declares war not only on the three powers occupying the territory which was once Poland, it declares war on every existing institution . . .

Even if the chancellor exaggerated, undoubtedly a fair number of Polish émigrés subscribed to the ideals of Buonarotti or Mazzini.

Just as he had tried to arm the Belgian peasants against the French Revolution fifty years before, Metternich now saw new allies for the Monarchy throughout the Empire. He was convinced that 'the ordinary man' distrusted liberalism and nationalism, and 'the uncertainties of abstract ambitions'. After the Galician *jacquerie* he observed, 'The masses are conservative and always will be.' He advised using peasants against Hungarian and Italian nationalists. In consequence, Radetzky made a real effort to enlist the Lombard country people against the upper classes, promising reforms which would benefit them at the landowners' expense. Threats of a Galician-type upheaval in Italy were made in the Austrian press. (The theory was not altogether groundless—the 1848 Revolution would fail throughout Europe partly because of its inability to recruit the peasantry.)

The old man was showing surprising stamina. 'Clemens took charge of the affair at once,' Princess Mélanie records after the Polish insurrection. 'The chancellery quickly began to look like a military headquarters.' She adds, 'My poor Clemens, who had to take all the strain during the crisis, was additionally afflicted by a heavy chest cold which ended by exhausting him completely, so that he ran a high temperature for three days, but it didn't stop him working.' It was an impressive performance by a man of nearly seventy-three, whom the Tsar had just dismissed as 'a shade'.

Music meant as much to him as ever, the operas of Donizetti being a fresh enthusiasm. In March 1842 the composer called on him, with a letter from Rossini, and was promptly asked to dinner. In May, Metternich gave a supper party in his honour. Donizetti was enchanted, writing:

> I found Princess Metternich the most amiable woman you could imagine so far as I was concerned, though others may say the reverse. She said she didn't like me because I had made her cry too much in *Linda* [*di Chamonix*], but that's a compliment.

The Metternichs also invited him to their annual party at the Rennweg on the Emperor's birthday, where he was overwhelmed by his reception. He wrote a romanza for cello or horn specially for the chancellor, '*Più che non m'ama un angelo*'. In February 1843, he conducted a concert at the Ballhausplatz performed by an orchestra of aristocratic amateurs.

In 1846 the chancellor was saddened at hearing of Donizetti's mysterious illness (probably undiagnosed syphilis), telling Apponyi, 'Donizetti is much liked here and everybody wants to know what has happened to him.' He asked the ambassador to look after the composer, as there were rumours that he was in a lunatic asylum and being robbed—'in any case the loss of Donizetti is a sore blow to opera.' An Austrian agent visited the asylum at Ivry almost every day, sending reports on the patient's health to Vienna until his death in 1848.

Some idea of the septuagenarian Metternich's pleasures may be learnt from an entry in Mélanie's diary for May 1846:

> For six weeks Viennese society has been busy applauding a Swedish singer whom we've already heard in Germany, and who turned many heads at Berlin. Mlle [Jenny] Lind . . . sings very well, which means there are moments when she's charming, and she could become a great singer. She is incapable of expressing passion but she knows how to convey sentiment . . . The one artist who in my opinion deserves the prize for the [opera and ballet] season is Fanny Elssler, who danced the part of *Esmeralda* with incomparable grace and irresistible talent. Liszt too had his moments of brilliance . . .

They often went to see Fanny Elssler, a close personal friend of whom they were very fond and who visited them frequently. As for Liszt, Mélanie was once worsted in an exchange with him, when he was playing at the Ballhausplatz. 'You must make a lot of money,' she observed in her loud, carrying voice. 'No Madame, I merely make music,' he replied. Another composer whose operas they enjoyed was Bellini; there are references to visits to the *Kärntnertor Theater* to hear *Norma*. They listened to a good deal of Schubert at musical evenings, though Metternich's favourite song always remained Rossini's '*Mira la bianca luna*'. Johann Strauss the Elder dedicated a '*Grazien-Tanze*' for the piano to the Princess.

There was music throughout Vienna in the Biedermeyer heyday. 'To any sensible observer the Viennese look as if they're permanently intoxicated,' wrote a critic of the régime, Franz Schuselka, in 1843:

> Eat, drink and be merry, are the virtues and pleasures which count most here. For them it's always a Sunday, always Carnival. There's singing everywhere. The many, many taverns are full of revellers all day long and all night long. Everything, whether ordinary every day life, art or literature, is dominated by sly, clever, joking. For a Viennese what matters most about any important event is to be able to make a joke of it.

What angered this particular observer was that revolution appeared to be so unlikely. Metternich's policy of 'repose' still seemed most effective.

His family was his own principal pleasure. Watching his great-granddaughter, aged eighteen months, playing at the feet of his granddaughter Pauline, he exclaimed, 'What I was really meant to be was a children's nurse.' 'I can't imagine anyone more easy and more pleasant,' Pauline recalls. 'It isn't given to everybody to understand instinctively, as he did, how to be at home with children, young people and simple, even humble, folk in general.' She describes how they spent Christmas evening at the Ballhausplatz:

> At seven o'clock, after the family dinner which, as the custom was in those days, began at five o'clock, the doors of the great reception room in the State Chancellery, with a superb, gigantic Christmas-tree in the middle, were flung open, and we rushed in, to revel in the countless lovely toys with which the huge room was crammed. The most beautiful toys came from old Salomon Rothschild . . .

She remembered her grandfather in spring at the Rennweg, and his delight if the lilac was in blossom. 'He was a passionate lover of nature and of flowers and would go into such raptures over the loveliness of spring as I have never, or hardly ever, heard from the lips of anyone else.'

It was a peculiar irony that one of the most savage blows which Metternich received during his entire career should be dealt by the

Catholic Church. In June 1846 Gregory XVI died and a 'liberal' Pope was elected, the fifty-four-year-old Cardinal Mastai-Ferretti, Bishop of Imola, who became Pius IX—better known to history, even among Anglo-Saxons, as 'Pio Nono'. The Church had tried to come to terms with the ideas of the French Revolution as early as the election of Pius VII in 1800, but when Bonapartism and then the Restoration were seen to be more powerful, as always she had opted for what seemed to be the stronger ally, in the partnership of 'Throne and Altar'. (Only in the 1960s did the ideas of the Revolution finally penetrate Catholicism and the Papal monarchy become a totalitarian democracy, the people of God the people of the social contract.) The new pontiff was scarcely a liberal, simply a naïve and warmhearted priest who wanted to please everybody; he would have to learn painfully the truth of the chancellor's definition of liberal aims—'Get out, so that we can take your place.' To begin with, he seemed harmless enough. If Mélanie could write in her diary for June that year 'Politics look as though they're taking on a more menacing air in Italy and the Holy Father's death may have been the signal for the long planned revolution', a few weeks later she would write of Pio Nono's amnesty for political prisoners and exiles, 'It's an act inspired by just the same ideas as those of my husband.' The chancellor too saw no cause for alarm as yet.

In November Austria annexed the 'Free Republic of Cracow'. The absence of an Anglo-French *entente* enabled Metternich to do so without France objecting, even if there were loud protests in the English press. It was not a step he liked taking, since it meant a further departure from the Treaty of Vienna, but, as he stressed, the purpose of that treaty was to guarantee peace, not to create trouble centres; the little state had certainly been troublesome enough, a sanctuary for Polish revolutionaries intent on destabilising Austrian Galicia. Metternich emphasised that Cracow had not mended its ways despite many warnings, and that if Austria had not taken it over, Russia would have done so.

At the end of 1846 the chancellor realized that the reign of Pius IX was going to be very dangerous indeed. While he approved of the Pope's intention to reform the ramshackle administration of the Papal States, he was alarmed by the expectations of nationalists all over Italy. Pius had appointed the reputedly liberal Cardinal Gizzi secretary of state, while his amnesty was filling Rome with agitators. In Lombardy-Venetia, priests were already showing open hostility towards Austrian troops.

18

The Storm, 1846–48

> A spectre is haunting Europe—the spectre of Communism. All the powers of old Europe have entered into a holy alliance to exorcise this spectre: Pope and Tsar, Metternich and Guizot, French Radicals and German police-spies.
>
> KARL MARX,
> *Communist Manifesto,* January 1848

> To make a revolution is to subvert the ancient state of our country; and no common reasons are called for to justify so violent a proceeding.
>
> EDMUND BURKE,
> *Reflections on the Revolution in France*

In retrospect the abortive uprisings at Cracow and in Galicia would be seen as the start of the landslide which destroyed Restoration Europe and the Metternich system. The chancellor thought he was witnessing what he had watched at Strasbourg sixty years before, that the Revolution was coming again and the Terror would soon be in full swing—though convinced that this time it would break out in Italy, not in France. He and his wife revealed in their papers—he in his despatches and letters, she in her diary—their increasing bewilderment and horror.

No one really knows why the 1848 Revolution happened, least of all why at Vienna, and nobody can explain exactly why Metternich fell. If opposed to change, he was far from being out of touch with popular opinion; he read the extremely perceptive police reports, while the jibe that he saw everything from the windows of aristocratic drawing rooms is belied by his cultivation of scientists, artists and men of letters. All one can say is that his 'system' was bound to go in the end. Viktor Bibl, the harshest of his modern critics, is convincing when he credits the chancellor with believing that revolutions 'came not from economic misery or dissatisfaction with the political structure but were the work of secret societies, dreamers and unbalanced doctinaires'. For Metternich, liberalism and nationalism were no more than spectres, which should disappear of their own accord.

For once, Srbik agrees with Bibl. 'No one questions his [Metternich's] judgement in seeing destructive forces at work in all the heady currents from the Reformation to Liberalism, in "Prussianism" or "Teutonism", or in the politics of the industrial proletariat,' he writes. 'His great weakness was an inability to identify forces in the new climate which were genuinely creative and deserved encouragement.' Even the chancellor's admirers are forced to admit that, apart from promoting industrial development, he had no social policies whatever. As Srbik puts it, 'If Metternich understood the limits of the possible in foreign affairs, as an ultra-conservative he invariably hoped for the impossible where internal matters were concerned.' Nevertheless, his world ought to have lasted at least until his departure from the scene. When the revolution came, it ended so quickly, and in such abject failure, that one may be forgiven for wondering sometimes why it ever broke out at all.

Metternich knew that the world was changing but did not realize quite how much. Between 1819 and 1843 the Monarchy's population increased by a quarter to over 36 million; Vienna's inhabitants, who at the end of the previous century had numbered 235,000, were now nearly 400,000. One could travel to Prague, Budapest or Trieste by train and there were a thousand miles of track. (By tradition every Archduke was apprenticed to a trade and the young Francis Joseph chose that of engine driver.) Steamships plied the Danube, while Hungarian and Polish grain was exported from Trieste by the Österreichischer Lloyd Line, which owned 26 vessels in 1848. Steam looms had transformed textile production in lower Austria and Bohemia, and the output of Bohemian iron and steel trebled between 1820 and 1846. However, steam-driven machinery caused the layoff of thousands of old-style journeymen. During the

1840s a series of bad harvests and potato blights—especially in 1846–7—caused soaring food prices and a credit slump, which made unemployment still worse. (During 1847, 10,000 factory workers were laid off in Vienna alone.) The streets were full of beggars.

As Srbik shows, Metternich had recognised the threat to his world posed by capitalism—and the pauperism which frequently accompanies it—but had hoped to avoid any trouble by the increased profits accruing to both state and private business. An industrial recession was something altogether new in his experience.

At the same time, the enormous growth of a new middle class, who resented their exclusion from government, increased criticism of him. They joined noblemen and intellectuals in the '*Juridischer-Politischer Lesverein*' (Juridical-Political Reading Circle) founded at Vienna in 1842, a similar *Lesverein* being founded at Prague. The *Landtag* of lower Austria, whose assemblies met in Vienna, voted to admit members of the bourgeoisie. Dissatisfaction with the régime grew. In 1842 Freiherr von Andrian-Werburg (in an anonymous pamphlet printed in Germany) had warned of disunity among the various peoples of the Empire; ironically, his solution was that of Metternich—more power for provincial Diets and a *Reichstag* at Vienna with deputies from all the Habsburg lands. In 1847 the *Landtag* of Lower Austria demanded the publication of the treasury's accounts.

Looking back from June 1848, Palmerston was to accuse Metternich of being 'the ruin of an age . . . he succeeded for a time in damming up and arresting the stream of human progress.' Metternich has also been blamed for doing nothing to halt the régime's slide into crisis. Yet there was little he could do. In exile he admitted that its worst failings had been the pettyfogging interference in minor administrative matters, which crippled the machinery of government, and neglecting to provide central representation for the Monarchy's different regions:

> Should I have made the government take a different direction? I did not have the power to do so. Should I have derailed it? But stopping it that way would have resulted in revolution.

He emphasised that his job was to represent Austria abroad and safeguard its political interests. What he did not say is that he had been blocked, first by Emperor Francis, then by Kolowrat and the Archdukes.

Afterwards the playwright Franz Grillparzer decided that the régime's essential decency, its reluctance to use harsh measures, had been the real cause of its fall. Certainly Francis I's death had been followed by a relaxation which was largely due to the chancellor. 'Were it not for the order and security everywhere prevailing, a stranger might hardly suppose, beyond the walls of the cities, that any police existed only at the frontiers,' wrote Mr Turnbull, a visitor from England in the 1830s. 'In no continental country have I ever travelled, in which, except in the provincial capitals, is so little of it either seen or felt.' This was an authoritarian régime too tolerant for its own good.

Another mistake was not to woo the middle classes—the financiers, lawyers, professors, writers. 'Separate by reasonable concessions the moderate from the exaggerated, content the former by fair concessions and get them to resist in resisting the insatiable demands of the latter' was Lord Palmerston's remedy. If Metternich did this, he 'would find his crop of revolutions . . . soon die away on the stalk'. Yet if the chancellor distrusted 'the monied interest' and intellectuals, the alienation of the bourgeoisie was not due to any personal prejudice—many of his right-hand men and allies came from the middle classes.

Such people were increasingly frustrated by their exclusion from government, irritated by a censorship which would not leave them alone. Not only journalists and playwrights were affected, but theologians and scientists. Academics and professional men complained constantly. At first Grillparzer had been inclined to support Metternich, and in 1848 he would be a supporter of the counter-revolution. He respected the chancellor's love of literature and was deeply impressed by his reciting from memory a hundred verses from *Childe Harold*. Yet he rejected Metternich's 'system', damning him as the 'Don Quixote of Legitimism'. (Unknowingly he echoed Palmerston's comment that censorship in a land swarming with professors and newspaper men was a quixotic notion.) In 1845,

Grillparzer and a delegation of writers asked the chancellor to ease the censorship. Metternich refused, explaining politely that to do so might hamper the government's 'good intentions'. What he did not say was that his colleagues would never allow it.

There was a flood of hostile literature, censorship evaded by printing in Germany. Andrian's was the most influential of such books; in the second volume, which appeared in 1847, he attacked the bureaucracy and the censors, demanding that Diets should have burgher and peasant members. Karl Beidtel's jeremiad about Austria's financial future came out the same year, warning that soaring inflation and state bankruptcy lay ahead, urging the calling of a national assembly to deal with the impending catastrophe. Karl Moering's *Sybilline Books from Austria*, published in January 1848, was a blistering attack on the régime's ineptitude. Similar opinions had been voiced since 1841 by the liberal periodical *Die Grenzboten*, produced in Brussels and read in every café in Vienna. All these publications demanded more power for provincial Diets, an Imperial Diet and an end to censorship. They would have been surprised to learn that privately the chancellor was not entirely opposed to these demands, perhaps because there was so far no movement within Austria for a liberal monarchy of the French or Spanish sort.

'He has no strength left for a fight as he used to,' Mélanie lamented in 1840. In reality her husband retained astonishing energy and was still able to achieve a great deal in defending his world until the end came. He would never lose the will to govern.

Even before Pio Nono's election, Metternich had been deeply suspicious of Charles Albert of Sardinia, fearing that the King hoped to use liberalism to acquire Lombardy. And, as he told Apponyi on 1 March 1847, 'Behind Liberalism marches radicalism.' A fortnight later, Cardinal Gizzi relaxed press laws and censorship. Political journals and clubs sprang up in Rome, all nationalist and liberal.

Palmerston's attitude was a constant irritation to the Ballhausplatz. During this crucial period the British foreign secretary's approach to Italian politics was based on the grossest misconceptions and wishful thinking, as was that of many British diplomats. In August 1847 Palmerston wrote to Lord Ponsonby at Vienna:

> The accounts which Her Majesty's Government receives from Italy, and of which copies are sent to you, show that the apprehensions of Prince Metternich are extremely exaggerated; and that whatever may be passing in the minds of some few enthusiasts, nothing has yet happened which can justly be called a revolution, or which can indicate any, the most remote, probability of an attempt to unite Italy under one authority.

In December he informed Ponsonby, 'With regard to the events which are now passing in Italy, Her Majesty's Government do not apprehend therefrom danger to the internal tranquility of the Peninsula.'

In October Mr Henry Howard of the British Embassy in Berlin had commented in a despatch to the foreign secretary:

> Prince Metternich, as your Lordship is aware, lives in the past and in illusions which he sedulously keeps up, not listening to others of a different opinion from himself, or rather listening only to his own voice and only attending to such of his agents as report in his own sense. He compares the present movement in Italy to that which took place in the years 1820 and 1821, and represents it in the light of a revolution, the work of secret societies and Radicals, with Republican and Communist objects.

Most British observers considered the Austrian chancellor to be a fossilised reactionary who was hopelessly out of touch with reality.

Metternich was on more sympathetic terms with Guizot, if in 1839 he had suggested that the French prime minister 'confused doctrines with principles'. (By contrast, Guizot wrote of Metternich in his memoirs, 'One saw in him a rich, complex, deep intelligence unfold itself, zealous to seize and utter general ideas and abstract theories and at the same time a supremely sharp, practical sense.') The reason for growing closer was concern about Prussia. The chancellor's German policy had always been based on cooperation with the Prussians, but both he and Guizot were uncomfortably aware that, unlike the Habsburg monarchy, the Prussian state had not yet reached the point of 'territorial saturation'. Yet even Guizot did not share Metternich's fears over Italy. However, events were going to show only too soon that Metternich's predictions had been astonishingly accurate.

By the spring of 1847 the palace on the Rennweg was almost ready. Underneath the balcony of the huge house were the words '*parvus domus, magna quies*' ('small house, great rest'), usually cited as an example of the chancellor's vanity but more likely to have been a wry joke. It seemed that he would know little rest there. Princess Mélanie had written in January, 'The King [of Prussia] has promulgated a constitution, without teeth or merit, which means nothing today but which could burst into flames tomorrow and destroy the kingdom.' In March she confided to her diary her worries about their prospects in the new palace:

> Clemens is very taken by it, but I only tremble when I think of it. The future is so dark and the present so sad for me that I scarcely dare think further ahead than tomorrow . . .

Clearly she was desperately alarmed by the political situation:

> Attempts at reconciliation between France and England are a source of great embarrassment for Louis Philippe and his cabinet. Furthermore, there is the condition of Spain and Portugal, countries which are a prey to the greatest confusion. Italy is boiling over, while Prussia with its clever constitution is a cause of grave concern to the French cabinet. Kings and ministers are crying out to be rescued since they can no longer control movements which never cease to challenge them . . .

In April she was writing 'our hearts are profoundly troubled and full of apprehension for the future', that 'in Italy matters are taking a troublesome turn, and in particular at Rome'.

'The general situation in Europe is very dangerous, my dear count!' Metternich himself wrote to Apponyi in June 1847. 'I await

M Guizot's reply about affairs in Switzerland, which have taken the most detestable road possible.' Swiss liberals, who dominated the federal Diet, were trying to replace the constitution of 1815 by a more centralised state. The situation was complicated by religious disagreements. In 1845 the *Sonderbund*, a league of seven staunchly conservative and Catholic cantons formed two years earlier, had become an armed confederation ready to defend itself against a federal decree expelling the Jesuits. Austria demanded that religious rights should be respected, fearing that should the federal government at Berne triumph, Switzerland would become the first victim of the coming revolution. (The federal president, Ulrich Ochsenbein, was said to be a foaming radical.) Guizot proposed that the powers should intervene, a proposal which Palmerston thwarted by playing for time—he hoped for a civil war which the liberals would win.

In July 1847 Mélanie recorded in her diary how Rome seemed from the perspective of the Ballhausplatz:

> My poor husband is very much absorbed by Italian affairs. Rome is in total revolution. They have set up a citizens' guard and chased out the city governor; at all the street corners there are stuck up the names of those whom the population want to see outlawed, and among their number, naturally enough of course, are those of the better-class-people and right-thinking persons . . . Daggers are sold publicly in the streets with their hilts made in the shape of the Papal arms and bearing the motto '*Viva Pio Nono*'! So now the people are going to commit murder under his patronage. The garrison at Ferrara has been reinforced but it looks very much to me as though the Pope is quite openly opposing any steps which are being taken to stop the evil spreading. There is talk of his abdication.

On 17 July, Metternich had ordered not only the reinforcement of the Austrian garrison at Ferrara but the occupation of all key points in the city after anti-Austrian demonstrations—as Austria was entitled to do under the Treaty of Vienna. The Pope protested, as did King Charles Albert and also Lord Palmerston, who at once put the entire British fleet in the Mediterranean on the alert. Garibaldi wrote from South America offering the services of his 'Italian Legion' to the Church. (A former member of *Giovine Italia*, he was precisely the type of revolutionary adventurer whom the chancellor expected to take over the Papal States.) The reports of disaffection in Lombardy-Venetia were by now so alarming that Metternich contemplated visiting Milan and Venice to inspect the situation on the spot.

The British ambassador at Vienna, Lord Ponsonby, sent a despatch to Lord Palmerston on 30 July. The chancellor had told him that there was a full-scale revolution in progress at Rome. When Ponsonby demurred and inferred politely that he was exaggerating, Metternich—clearly very agitated—replied, 'A revolution is made when the government of a state is deprived of all its powers, of all governmental action.' He informed the ambassador that 'the chief object of the party now successful at Rome is to establish the union of all Italy under one government. It could only be achieved by conquest, and conquest effected either by a monarchical or a republican force could not be permitted by the powers of Europe.' (In the event, all Italy would be conquered by Piedmont in 1860.) 'The Kaiser is determined not to lose his Italian territories,' he added. 'This empire may fall, but if it falls, it shall be on the field of battle.'

'The Pope shows each day that more and more he is losing all sense of what is practical,' the chancellor observed sadly to Count Apponyi on 7 October. 'Warm of heart and weak in understanding, since assuming the tiara he has allowed himself to be caught and tied up in a net from which he has no idea of how to disentangle himself, and if matters take their natural course he will be chased out of Rome.'

Amazingly, Metternich was able to find time in which to tutor the seventeen-year-old presumptive to the throne. 'Each Sunday afternoon Clemens gives lessons on diplomacy to the young Archduke Franz,' Mélanie recorded in October. 'He examines important events in contemporary history with him and shows him their real significance.' (Francis Joseph may have been putting these lessons into practice as late as 1916.)

There was trouble everywhere. In Switzerland on 11 November federal forces attacked the *Sonderbund*, whose cantons surrendered one by one; the Swiss civil war was over within less than three weeks, at a cost of twenty-eight killed on both sides. The chancellor expected the Swiss 'to place at the disposal of the Italian Radicals a rescue-party of 30,000 brethren and friends . . . We are going to reinforce our army in Lombardy heavily.' The Duchess of Parma, Marie Louise, died in the following month, depriving him of a dependable ally.

The defeat of the *Sonderbund* humiliated Metternich. Yet it is unlikely that diplomacy could have prevented the federal authorities from triumphing over the Catholic cantons, while military intervention was out of the question. 'Whatever happens, we'll think of a means of repairing the damage,' wrote Mélanie. 'Clemens hasn't let himself be discouraged. Danger only increases his energy, in spite of all the obstacles that Palmerston thinks up to stop the powers settling the problem by joint action. Unfortunately Clemens is quite isolated.'

He accepted that there would have to be change, in the Monarchy and in Germany. He did not object to reforms, if he could initiate and control them. He secured decrees which lightened the Galician peasants' labour obligations (the *robot*) and allowed them to appeal against decisions by manorial courts. He proposed that representatives of the Bohemian Diet should come to Vienna to discuss taxation, but was blocked by Archduke Ludwig and Kolowrat. In Hungary his alliance with György Apponyi's conservatives prospered, and he aroused considerable interest in the abolition of customs barriers; only the economic crisis saved Kossuth. He persuaded the *Ministerkonferenz* to set up a commission to explore closer links between Vienna and the regional Diets. He prepared new press laws. He stopped King Frederick William IV from cancelling the constitution he had recently granted and restrained the Grand Duke of Hesse from confronting the liberals.

Understandably he began 1848 in no very optimistic spirit. 'I shall start this letter by wishing you a happy New Year, without committing myself to guaranteeing that it will be a very good one,' he told György Apponyi at Paris on 2 January.

Mélanie echoes his gloom. 'This year is not beginning in a very reassuring way. At Milan great disturbance and uproar about cigars. Sadly, the civil government is weak and feeble. One would have said they wanted to blame Radetzky for letting his soldiers smoke cigars. They issue feeble proclamations which encourage the revolutionaries.' What had happened was that the Milanese, led by the young noblemen of the Jockey Club, had tried to enforce a boycott of tobacco, which was an Austrian state monopoly, in the belief that it would reduce the Imperial revenues. In retaliation Radetzky's men smoked liked chimneys, causing fights in the streets. The clergy were so hostile that the troops were ordered not to confess to them. Much of the opposition stemmed from the frustration of the nobility and the upper bourgeoisie at being excluded from the administration. However, in Italy Metternich was inflexible, convinced that even modest concessions would be taken for signs of weakness.

Metternich's irritation at the situation must have been deepened at news of the Milanese singing, on every possible occasion, Bellini's '*Guerra! Guerra!*' from *Norma*, surely the silliest of all songs of war. He had no reason to expect an armed rising in Lombardy, which had a most formidable garrison commander in Field Marshal Radetzky. 'If the Lombards had been Poles, we would have had at the beginning of 1848 the same scenes south of the Alps which we deplored in Galicia at the start of 1846,' he told Ficquelmont on 8 January. (Ficquelmont, his most trusted colleague, had been at Milan since the previous year.) The chancellor favoured harsh measures, for him a sign of extreme uneasiness:

> We must make some examples, and the most fruitful will unquestionably be among those who aspire to the most gangrenous class of the Lombard population, that of the loiterers, the 'lions', that bastard race of decayed aristocracy, and after or with them the briefless barristers and letterless litterati.

This uncharacteristically bad-tempered tone betrays his anxiety.

He was relying more and more on his wife. 'Clemens has told me to file his papers,' she noted in January. 'It's a labour of Hercules.' Her testimony grows increasingly alarmed:

> The news from Parma and Naples is very bad. Felix Schwarzenberg thinks that the King of Naples is so frightened that he won't put up a fight. What is certain is that royal troops have been repulsed at Palermo and there's no more army properly speaking. A few days later a constitution was proclaimed, although it didn't stop Sicily seceding. The King of Sardinia is following suit: he has granted a constitution too; the Grand Duke of Tuscany is doing the same. Italy is breaking up.

She was proud of her husband's steady nerve—'Clemens is admirable. Fear has no place in him, though sometimes he gets very excited.' She was very bitter at England's behaviour—'It is totally incomprehensible how an entire nation can be so infatuated with such a man as Palmerston, who makes Great Britain look like the great power of shiftiness and intrigue.' (Some historians agree with her about Britain: 'Whether, as in Palmerston's day, she allied herself with the revolutionaries, her aim was always to divide and weaken the Continent,' says Jacques Droz.) 'One thing is clear to me,' continues Mélanie, 'which is that a general hatred has been unleashed against us, and that our enemies' strength, together with the unbelievable weakness of our friends, will end by destroying us.'

Metternich began to suspect that the French Revolution might be repeated in Italy. On 29 January, writing to Ficquelmont at Milan, he quoted a letter from the Grand Duchess of Tuscany to her sister. (No doubt intercepted in the post.) 'We are in an unspeakable position here. Everything is lost and we are at the people's mercy. We await the fate of Louis XVI and his family.' However, the most immediate danger came from Piedmont. Would the Piedmontese army attack? Yet if Austria could hold out long enough, Italian liberalism was bound to fail. 'So, let us *govern* in the Kingdom of Lombardy-Venetia!' he exhorted Ficquelmont.

On 22 February Count Josef von Hübner, a young attaché at Milan, breakfasted with the chancellor and Princess Mélanie at the Ballhausplatz, the day martial law was declared in Lombardy-Venetia. He was instructed to ensure that the press made clear to every Italian state that the Austrian army would not hesitate to restore order as it had once done in Naples. On the evening of 28 February, Hübner discussed Guizot's troubles with Mélanie. 'If he falls,' she cried, shaking, 'we're all lost!' They did not know that Guizot had fallen four days earlier and that Louis Philippe had fled.

On 29 February, copies of the *Augsburger Zeitung* reached Vienna with news of a revolution at Paris. Financial panic ensued, with a heavy run on the banks. Metternich went white when he read that a republic had been declared in France. He telegraphed Berlin, asking that Prussian officials be sent to Vienna to discuss means of containing the upheaval.

On 1 March Hübner spent the morning at the Ballhausplatz, where the chancellor gave him an analysis of the situation. 'Everyone tells me "something must be done." But what?' He explained how Emperor Francis had rejected his proposals for reform in 1817, 1826 and 1835. He went on:

> Certainly it's essential to adapt our provincial diets to the needs of the time and increase their powers. But that's not enough. There will also have to be a central body sitting at Vienna (leaving Hungary aside for the moment), composed of delegates from the diets. It should be a chamber of provinces, not a chamber of deputies, a *Volkshaus* whose members will be elected in the same way as those of the provincial diets . . . We must be careful not to destroy the separate identities of the provinces. That would mean an end of the personal bonds which join them to the dynasty and with them the most effective way of supporting the Crown by preventing enmity and quarrels between the different races which comprise the Monarchy.

Metternich was not indulging in an idle fancy. Kübeck had already proposed summoning an Imperial Diet to Vienna, to discuss financial problems. 'Such a move would have been of incalculable importance and might have paved the way for constitutional change within the Monarchy,' observes their colleague Hartig, writing at the end of 1849. But while the *Ministerkonferenz* was favourable in principle and the plan was under serious discussion, nothing had been done. 'Save for this delay the régime could have faced the impending revolution with far greater confidence,' says Hartig. 'It could no longer have been accused of ignoring the wishes of the Diets, whose members wanted to play the role of representatives of the people, and the transition from absolute to constitutional monarchy would have been less hasty and destructive.'

As for censorship, the chancellor went on to tell Hübner that he blamed it on the late Emperor:

> Kotzebue's assassination in 1819 by a fanatical young German bigot influenced him deeply. Ascribing too much importance to the secret societies, which were then undermining Italy and to a lesser extent Germany, he believed he had found a cure for the evil by keeping the so-called intelligent classes under meticulous police surveillance . . . The result has been a covert irritation with the government, as well as vague yearnings for political reform on the model of the Liberal constitutions in some minor German states.

He had often pointed this out to Francis, who had remained obdurate.

'The Emperor's death altered my position profoundly,' continued Metternich. 'From the accession of the present Emperor I have felt myself paralysed.' However he could not resign without wrecking the structure of which, together with the Emperor Francis during his reign and, since the latter's death, by himself, he had been the main prop:

> Remove the column and the vault it supports will collapse. If in 1817, or later, in 1826, the Emperor had adopted my ideas on reorganising the Diets, we might perhaps be in a position to face the storm. Today it's too late . . . But I can tell you something which I want you to remember. My resignation will mean the Revolution.

On the same day that he saw Hübner, the chancellor wrote an anguished letter to György Apponyi at Paris:

> France has returned to the follies of the first Revolution . . . What has happened has thrown out all my calculations, if impressions deserve the name of calculations. Europe has been put back to 1791 and 1792. Will 1793 be absent? Austria is no longer alone in having to face the Revolution. But the peril which we share is enormous. There is good reason to despair of the social fabric's survival!

What was happening confirmed only too brutally his conviction that the political stability of Europe was indivisible.

On 3 March, Kossuth made a fierce speech in the Hungarian Diet, demanding that Hungary should manage her own finances and that similar Diets should be set up in every province of the Monarchy to control what he termed Vienna's 'extravagance'. On 7 March, news reached Vienna of riots at Frankfurt, Karlsruhe and Stuttgart. 'They want to dissolve the Germanic Confederation and chase away the Kings' was Mélanie's comment. 'Everywhere there is upheaval and madness.' Yet it still seemed as if Vienna would stay quiet. However, on 10 March Baron Sieber, a chancellery official, advised her to deposit her diamonds in a secure place, as they would not be safe in her own house. Another official warned her to be on her guard 'because hatred for Prince Metternich has reached its peak'. Nevertheless, Sedlnitsky told them on the following day that nothing would happen. The situation began to deteriorate on Sunday. Members of the Diet of lower Austria drew up a petition for debate the following morning; it complained of being cut off from the Emperor by his advisers—a thinly veiled reference to the chancellor. Also on Sunday, students at the university drew up their own petition, which they handed in at the Hofburg the same afternoon; this demanded more representative government and an end to censorship—clearly they had read Andrian.

On Monday 13 March, the *Landtag*—the Diet—met at the Landhaus in the Herrengasse, where further demands for reforms of the sort urged by Andrian were debated noisily. Hundreds of students gathered outside, joined by a growing crowd. It then moved on to the Ballhausplatz. Watching from a window, Mélanie joked that all it needed to be happy was a sausage stall. It was far from menacing and Metternich was unalarmed. As Hartig pointed out, while Metternich had long realized that an explosion of some sort was unavoidable, he did not think that it would occur quite so quickly or so spontaneously, since the supposedly all-seeing police gave him no warning.

Yet there was very serious financial unease, expressed in an accelerating run on the bank—all too many had been frightened by Beidtel's alarmist book. If the government went to war with France, it might cause a state bankruptcy—as might the looming campaign in Italy. 'Gentlemen from aristocratic circles joined the revolutionary movement and on the morning of 13 March appeared at my grandfather's with the deputation which informed him in the most brutal manner that he must resign,' Pauline tells us. They were fearful of being ruined, remembering the bankruptcy of 1811. Their concern had spread to court circles. The old man was unshaken, but this fear of general financial disaster played a crucial part in his downfall. He had become a liability.

Meanwhile, the crowd outside the chancellery went on growing. Escorted by soldiers, Metternich walked over to the Hofburg at midday to discuss the situation with Archduke Ludwig. They agreed that it should be announced that a commission would study ways of increasing the Diets' powers, and that troops should be brought in to clear the streets. When the troops arrived, fighting broke out. Order was restored, but at 5.00 p.m. officers of the Civic Guard, led by a wine merchant named Scherzer, together with a delegation from the Diet, went to the Hofburg; they warned Ludwig that unless the troops returned to barracks at once and the chancellor resigned, Vienna would erupt.

Metternich was summoned to the Hofburg. He seemed calm enough, in a bottle-green coat and black stock, carrying a gold-topped cane—he wore a noticeably sardonic smile. He brought with him his friend Field Marshal Prince Alfred Windischgrätz, commanding officer at Prague, who happened to be staying with him; Windischgrätz was ready to fight, and went home to change into uniform when the chancellor told him he would have to take command in Vienna. Leaning against a windowsill, Metternich then addressed the *Ministerkonferenz*, the entire Imperial family being assembled in an adjoining room. He spoke of the common peril facing Europe and it was plain that he had no intention of yielding. At about 7.00 p.m. his old enemy Archduke Johann interrupted, seconded by Kolowrat. Was he aware that his resignation had been demanded by representatives of the people? It became clear that everyone present wanted him to go. Another delegation had got into the palace and was shouting for his resignation in the corridors outside.

If the *Ministerkonferenz* had supported the chancellor, he would almost certainly have weathered the storm. Afterwards Grillparzer wrote that two battalions would have been quite sufficient to disperse the demonstrators. No doubt Metternich was old, but Radetzky, who eventually triumphed in Italy, was eighty-four. The chancellor was prepared for the struggle, the army was loyal and Windischgrätz was a most capable commander. But the Archdukes and Kolowrat had lost their nerve.

Archduke Ludwig took Metternich by the hand and told him the safety of Vienna depended on his going. Abandoned by all, he answered that he did not want to be the cause of any bloodshed or embarrass the government, and would therefore resign. However, he insisted that each Archduke must release him from the oath in which he had sworn to Emperor Francis to serve Ferdinand. (The significance of the oath has been overlooked by historians, yet it illustrates Metternich's essentially feudal attitude to his sovereign, explaining much about his conservatism, why he never forced through his reforms.) The Archdukes released him. Then he went into an anteroom and wrote out his resignation:

> My sentiments, my ideas, my solutions have never altered. Throughout my whole life those have been forces which can never die within me. I embodied them in the motto I have left for my descendants so that they will never forget them. That motto is 'strength through right'.

He announced his resignation personally to a fresh deputation at 9.00 p.m. and then strode impassively through the hostile crowd in the corridors, to return to the chancellery.

Mélanie greeted him. 'Well, are we all dead?' she asked. 'Yes, my dear, we're dead,' he replied. He told her that he was relieved to have no more responsibility:

> The overthrow of the existing social order is now inevitable. I could not have stopped it because I was alone today, supported by no-one. I could not have avoided making concessions which must inevitably lead to disaster, and I have escaped the shame of signing them.

He had no illusions; he knew that his resignation alone was enough to precipitate revolution. He went to bed and, so his wife tells us, slept 'the sleep of the just'. It was his last night at the Ballhausplatz.

Next day Vienna was still more disturbed. Pauline, who was in the chancellery with her mother Leopoldine, remembered gangs of men throwing stones at their windows and jeering at the sentries. In the afternoon the Metternichs fled, on foot through the gardens, to Count Taafe's house in the Löwenstrasse a quarter of a mile away. Baron von Hügel, whose brother had once been engaged to Mélanie, found them there. 'I could not desert the old man with the broken frame and the broken heart,' he recalled. Count Rechberg took the younger members of the family to safety by train, but the ex-chancellor had to be more cautious. Escorted by Hügel, after dark Metternich and his wife left the Löwenstrasse by cab to where a carriage stood waiting to take them to a castle of Prince Liechtenstein at Feldsberg, near what is now the Czech border. They arrived in the small hours of the morning, Metternich collapsing from nervous exhaustion. On 22 March, they were informed that the *Ministerkonferenz* wished them to leave within twenty-four hours. They thought of going to Plass, since the peasants and foundryworkers there had written offering to protect them. However, Leontine—who, with Richard, had rejoined them—argued that England would be safer.

The little party travelled as inconspicuously as it could, by train and coach (their two vehicles being put on board the train when necessary) for nine days throughout Bohemia and Germany, under assumed names. They would have been penniless but for Hügel, till the Rothschilds came to the rescue with a large loan. Mélanie was terrified, trembling every time she saw a student. Eventually they reached Arnhem in Holland, where Metternich again collapsed; he was suffering from kidney trouble, in agony from the jolting of the carriage. There were rumours of revolution in England, so they waited at Arnhem for confirmation.

The Prince was distressed by reports in the newspapers of uprisings all over Europe; Mélanie confided to her diary, 'Our Monarchy is in the process of falling apart.' She was moved by her husband's stoicism—'his calm, his magnanimity, his patriotism, which makes him reject any thought of Austria having been ungrateful'. He was cheered by letters from the Empress and the Archduchess Sophia, mother of the heir to the throne. The former wrote that he would always be a great man, whatever happened—'*é sempre grande nella prosperità è nella tribolazione.*' Sophia told him how much Austria owed him, including '*mon pauvre Franzi*'—'I have to thank you for all the good you have done my son this winter, shaping his ideas.'

News reached them of the ignominious failure of the great Chartist demonstration in London on 10 April. They left from Rotterdam on Wednesday 19 on board the mail ship *Rainbow,* crowded with sheep and cattle, and steamed up the Thames the following morning—colliding with a sailing vessel which smashed one of the paddlewheels. According to *The Times,* there was no one to meet them when they disembarked at Blackwall Pier, but the stationmaster placed a railway carriage at their disposal which brought them into London. From Fenchurch Street Station they took a cab to the Brunswick Hotel in Hanover Square, where accommodation had been reserved, arriving at 11.00 a.m. They learnt that the Duke of Wellington had already called. Mélanie wrote in her diary, 'I thanked God for our safe arrival and asked myself if what had happened had only been an awful dream.'

19

The Sage of the Rennweg

I was a rock of order.

METTERNICH to Baron von Hübner, 1859

For God's sake, no ultimatum to Italy!

METTERNICH to Emperor Francis Joseph, 1859

The fair wind which brought the Metternichs to London never left them. As far as any exile could be, theirs was a pleasant one. Financial needs were met by the Tsar and the Rothschilds, while society lionised them. In a surprisingly short time the revolutions collapsed all over Europe—within three years the Metternichs would be able to return to Vienna and a dignified retirement on the Rennweg.

Metternich liked England immediately. He was flattered by the attention paid to him despite his fall from power. *The Times* chronicled his movements; as soon as he arrived it reported that he was 'looking well and appears to have suffered but little from the anxiety he has recently undergone'. Nearly every day the Duke of Wellington rode from Apsley House to 44 Eaton Square, which the Prince rented from Lord Denbigh. (It is still there.) There was a stream of visitors, including such friends from the past as Aberdeen and Londonderry, together with public figures like Lord Brougham or Lord Lyndhurst. They attended Wellington's annual Waterloo banquet, went to a masked ball at Londonderry House. They met Guizot, who had also taken refuge in London, and their old enemy Palmerston.

An old acquaintance who called at the Brunswick Hotel the day after their arrival was Luigi Lablache, the great *basso* of the operas of Rossini and Donizetti, the original Don Pasquale. His voice could shatter a window. Metternich had first heard him at Vienna in 1824 with Barbaia's company. *The Times* reported that 'the celebrated singer, who had enjoyed the friendship of Prince Metternich for many years, was honoured by His Highness with an interview'.

Metternich at once made friends with Benjamin Disraeli, leader of the Parliamentary Opposition, with whom he had much in common. He advised him to rename his fragmented Tory party the 'Conservatives', advice which was taken. Deeply impressed by his political genius and kindly, amusing personality, Disraeli told him, 'You are the only philosophical statesman I have ever encountered.' Mélanie noted in June that Disraeli was attacking the government violently, blaming them for all the upheavals on the continent. Her husband may well have given him ammunition.

By May 1848, European affairs seemed to be going from bad to worse. The Imperial family fled to Innsbruck and a Committee of Public Safety was set up in Vienna. Prague and Budapest were in the hands of liberal extremists, while Milan had been lost. Northern Italy expected 'freedom' at any moment, to be brought by Piedmontese troops. Then suddenly the tide began to turn; in the second half of June Prince Windischgrätz shelled his way into Prague and the Czech revolution was over. In the following month the Piedmontese withdrew from Lombardy after being heavily defeated by Field Marshal Radetzky, who reoccupied Milan, while Croats loyal to the Emperor rose under their viceroy Jellačić against the Hungarians.

Mélanie, who in June had been writing 'there is no madness, no crime, left uncommitted', began to cheer up in August. The Metternichs went to a reception given by the Palmerstons at which 'Palmerston pretended to be glad at our success in Italy'. (Disraeli again attacked the foreign secretary in Parliament; Palmerston was enraged when he recognised turns of phrase which could only have come from Metternich.) 'The revolution seems to be losing ground,' Mélanie noted in September. However, she was very upset to learn that her cousin Isztván Széchenyi had gone mad. In

October, not without a certain satisfaction, her husband told Disraeli:

> Count Széchenyi suddenly got to the point where truth which had hitherto eluded him appeared naked before him. He went mad and is at present in a mental home outside Vienna. The doctors have not given up all hope of curing him and I share their optimism in view of his current condition. He has moments of lucidity when he looks back into the past. 'Prince Metternich has always told me how wrong I have been. He has warned me not to interfere with the foundations of a building lest it collapse. I have failed to profit from his advice. I have destroyed my own country.' Then he lapses into madness again.

In Mélanie's words, Eaton Square proved 'horribly dear'. The *Brighton Guardian* was therefore able to announce under 'Fashionable News' that on 15 September 'Prince Metternich and suite arrived at 42 Brunswick Terrace'. They were met at the station by Colonel Eld, the town's master of ceremonies, and escorted to the house, which turned out to be superior to Eaton Square in every way. (A pleasant, cream-washed Regency building on the front, it is now the Alexandra Hotel.) 'Brighton is a charming town,' Metternich wrote two days later. 'Our house doesn't face the harbour, since Brighton doesn't have one, but it faces the beach.' He wrote and received countless letters, read the newspapers, accepted an invitation to join the Brighton Conservative Club. Otherwise he lived a very quiet life. He enjoyed watching the ships in the distance, describing the Channel as 'a species of maritime *Corso*': since his arrival there had never been less than twenty-eight vessels in sight, sometimes as many as forty. He commented on the deserted state of his old friend George IV's Pavilion, which was falling into ruin because no one wanted to buy it. Exactly two months later, after a spell of unusually fine weather, he was writing, 'I know of no place better for the health than Brighton.' He was delighted at finding in a garden not far from their house a huge magnolia tree finer than any he had ever seen, even in Italy.

'Our three saviours, Windischgrätz, Radetzky and Jellačić, will, I hope, raise up our poor Monarchy again,' Mélanie confided to her diary in October. Her husband said that only one word described the condition of Europe—'anarchy'. Yet he saw a certain logic in the way in which order was undoubtedly being restored. He was amused by the shift in English public opinion which he discerned in *The Morning Post*—'Radical only a few months ago, this paper is now conservative.'

At the end of October in a battle near what is now Vienna Airport, Jellačić's Croats prevented the Hungarians from reinforcing the Viennese revolutionaries. Windischgrätz was able to fight his way in and recapture the city, before dealing with the Hungarians. On 21 November the iron-willed Prince Felix Schwarzenberg was appointed first minister; on 2 December the Emperor Ferdinand abdicated in favour of his nephew, the eighteen-year-old Francis Joseph. It was only a matter of time before the full reestablishment of the Monarchy.

Meanwhile, Prince Metternich was living a vigorous social life. The Brighton season began in November. The Duke of Devonshire gave splendid balls at his house in Lewes Crescent, all attended by the Metternich family. The Duke took the Prince to the French opera in his private box. The Metternichs' old friend from Vienna, Jenny Lind, sang at concerts in the town hall, conducted by another old friend, Johann Strauss the Elder. Lord Aberdeen came down from London to see the Prince, while those members of the Royal Family who remained faithful to Brighton (the Duke and Duchess of Cambridge, and the Duchess of Gloucester) visited him. At the Bedford Hotel he met the historian Lord Macaulay—who shocked Mélanie by suggesting that the Pope should retire to a flat in Paris.

Another old friend was staying at the Bedford, Princess Lieven, accompanied by her lover Guizot. Pauline Metternich, who saw her a few months later, describes her as looking like a family portrait. 'She always dressed in black, wore an enormous hat, had a green shade over her eyes, and carried a gigantic fan,' Pauline recalls. 'She paraded before us, stately and imposing, without so much as deigning to glance at us poor earthworms.' Neither of the former lovers were keen to see each other again, but Mélanie insisted on bringing them together.

Darya gives a characteristically acid vignette of husband and wife:

> She is plump, vulgar, natural, kind, easy-going; he is serene, pleased with himself, and never stops talking, very tedious, slow and deaf, very intellectual indeed, boring when he talks about himself and his infallibility, charming when he speaks of the past, especially about the Emperor Napoleon.

He told Darya how when he had gone to Pius VII with the Emperor's bribe of a pension of twenty million francs if he would obey, the Pope answered that fifteen sous a day were enough for him to live on. 'I was never so proud as when I brought this reply to Napoleon.'

In December the Metternichs were Wellington's guests at Stratfield Saye. Metternich was touched by the Duke's warm welcome, enjoyed the comfort and luxury, and was intrigued by the strict timetable of a great English country house. 'If I have a criticism of this way of life, it is that one eats too much.'

Lord Palmerston called at Brunswick Terrace. (In February the then Austrian chancellor had spoken of the foreign secretary as 'placing himself at the heart of every disturbance in Europe . . . a demented leader . . . a mixture of sour feeling with a weakness for bad jokes and a facile grasp of foreign affairs combined with unequalled frivolity in action'.) Palmerston questioned him closely about Austria's new leaders. When he came to Baron Jellačić, the Croat paladin who had helped to regain Vienna for the Monarchy, Metternich—who tells the story himself—replied:

> 'I never saw him, which is scarcely surprising since the *canaille* never came near me and I had no desire to go looking for him. All I know about the man is that he was a man of letters and a Jew.' 'A Jew'? asked Palmerston, who almost

fell off his chair. 'Yes, a Jew, but that isn't why he's been shot' I answered.

Eventually the misunderstanding was cleared up; very deaf, Metternich had heard 'Jellinek' for 'Jellačić'.

Metternich may have reflected on Palmerston's smug insistence in 1847 that the Pope's reforms would bring stability. A fortnight before Palmerston's visit, the pontiff's 'prime minister' had been stabbed to death, Pio Nono fleeing in disguise; Mazzini's men would shortly set up a Roman republic in the Eternal City. Metternich had predicted all these developments.

A more welcome visitor was the MP for Buckinghamshire, who travelled down by train in January 1849 to ask advice. 'I never heard such divine talk,' Mr Disraeli told his wife. 'He gave me the most masterly exposition of the present state of European affairs, and said a greater number of wise and witty things than I ever recollected hearing from him on the same day.' His host, who knew a political genius when he saw one, was encouraged by the future leader of the Conservative party being so well disposed towards Austria and towards the traditional order in Europe as a whole.

Although the train to London took less than two hours, Mélanie wanted to be nearer the capital. They could not afford Eaton Square again, but she found a house at Richmond, into which they moved in April 1849 after spending a few nights at Mirvat's Hotel in Brook Street (soon to be renamed Claridges). The garden ran down to the towpath besides the Thames. 'A magnificent cedar of Lebanon on the lawn beneath our windows takes the place of the big lime tree in my garden at Vienna,' he wrote happily. 'They live in a most charming old house on Richmond Green, called the Old Palace,' Disraeli informed Lady Londonderry. 'Nothing can be conceived more picturesque.' Yet he was worried by Metternich's appearance—'much altered, very extenuated'. He had been attacked by a species of anaemia and began to have fainting fits. No doubt the shock of 'March '48' was partly responsible. Fortunately, his mind was unimpaired.

In April Hungary declared herself an independent republic, but in July Tsar Nicholas would keep the promise he had given long ago, Russian troops joining with Austrian to crush the Magyars. The Monarchy had survived. Yet there was no question of Prince Metternich returning to Austria. For in June the Viennese press had accused him of taking bribes from St Petersburg amounting to 750,000 ducats a year and of 'squandering state funds'; a commission of enquiry was set up, his palaces and estates being confiscated until its findings should be announced. He was totally dependent on the generosity of the Tsar and of the Rothschilds.

Despite his poor health Metternich was not unhappy at Richmond. The house was full of young folk, his last child, Lothar, being only twelve. The stream of visitors continued. Among them was Darya Lieven; in July she told a friend that Clemens had a fainting fit every day—'Those close to him are worried and certainly they are bad symptoms at seventy-six.' Another visitor was Princess Bagration, once the 'Naked Angel' of the Congress of Vienna and the mother of his illegitimate daughter (Countess Blome, who had died in 1828). She was still as scantily dressed as ever, despite being nearly seventy and having aged very badly. 'It was a sight for the gods to watch my grandfather, always so dignified and patrician in appearance, towing this poor shrivelled mummy on his arm to the table,' Pauline tells us unfeelingly. Princess Bagration still flirted desperately with him. Johann Strauss the Elder came too, telling Princess Mélanie that the Viennese were beginning to realize they had made a mistake. 'It's a bit late now,' was her comment.

Metternich genuinely liked what he saw of England and the English. 'What makes this great country so strong is its unshakeable conviction of the value of law and order, and of liberty, which can really function on such foundations,' he had written only a few days after his arrival. Moreover, 'I meet all my old friends and that hospitality which is not just an empty phrase but a special quality of this nation.' If he was deeply hurt by Queen Victoria ignoring him, what would nowadays be called the Establishment went on fêting him, including the Whig prime minister Lord John Russell (although Lady John was very rude to Mélanie, telling her that she supported the Hungarians). He was always treated as the greatest living expert on European affairs, and he could count on his views on any subject being well aired in *The Times* whenever he chose—apparently by 'inspiring' a friendly journalist. 'I couldn't have been better received if I'd been John Bull himself,' he observed. Strangers would come up to him in the street and insist on shaking his hand. He credited the English with 'a vast amount of common sense', together with 'calmness of a sort which has long been forgotten on the Continent and for which it ought to rediscover a taste, for its own good'. He even approved of the political system, 'diametrically opposed to that sort of Liberalism which is doing such harm elsewhere in Europe'. When discussing English parliamentarism, he made a comment worthy of Bagehot: 'In old England only things have value, while men have value simply as the representatives of things.'

He began to dress like an Englishman, very plainly, wearing black or dark blue frock coats, a habit which he retained for the remainder of his life. Since Richmond was clearly going to be too cold and damp for him to spend the winter there, he looked forward to spending it at Brighton.

He was cheered by a letter from Francis Joseph at the end of July. The Emperor expressed concern at rumours about Metternich's health, insisting that his services to the Monarchy would never be forgotten. 'I shall be very happy to repeat my assurances of unaltered feelings if, at a time which I hope is not too far off, kindlier circumstances should bring you back to your native soil . . .' It acted as a tonic, the fainting fits becoming much less frequent. He began to go out for drives and to visit friends.

Mélanie did not like England as much as her husband did, persuading him that Belgium would be cheaper. King Leopold replied to his request for permission with a warm invitation—'The climate is gentler, life easier, than in the beautiful island where you now live.' They went to Mirvat's to prepare for the journey. 'Our dear Duke of Wellington came up from the country expressly to say goodbye and the Duke of Cambridge from Kew,' wrote Mélanie. They steamed out of Charing Cross Station in one of Queen Victoria's personal railway carriages, Lord Brougham and the Duke of Mecklenburg-Strelitz being among the party which travelled with them as far as Dover. The ship's captain gave up his cabin, Metternich sleeping on the bed, Mélanie on the deck.

They had difficulty in finding accommodation at Brussels, finally renting the small Hôtel Bériot in the Boulevard de l'Observatoire from a famous violinist. Later they moved to an old house in the Place du Grand Sablon, which belonged to the Duc d'Arenberg. Metternich calculated that the cost of living was 60 per cent cheaper than in England, a Belgian carriage costing a quarter the price of one across the Channel. They spent eighteen months here, treated with as much interest and respect as they had been in England; there was the same stream of visitors, King Leopold calling frequently. 'My grandfather considered him one of the best diplomatists he ever met,' says Pauline Metternich, 'very wary, very far-seeing, and crafty to the highest degree.' Another visitor was Thiers, seeking first-hand information for his monumental study of Napoleon.

Mentally Metternich remained as energetic as ever. He read all the major European newspapers every day, conducted a vast correspondence, and sent reams of advice to Kübeck and to Schwarzenberg at Vienna. It is probable that Schwarzenberg did not want him back at the capital for fear he might meddle. Schwarzenberg abandoned both constitutional government and what may be termed Metternich's 'cultural federalism' for a centralised tradition of Joseph II. The former chancellor had very mixed feelings about his successor, at first praising him as a man of courage and vision but later blaming him for always asking too little or too much. He cannot have approved of Schwarzenberg's aggressive attitude in his dealings with the French.

He was far less happy in Belgium than he had been in England. Francis Joseph's letter had thoroughly unsettled him. Early in 1850 he told his daughter Leontine how deeply he missed his garden at Vienna. 'My own flowers please me so very much more than those of other people,' he wrote to her. 'Go and see the palace when the lilacs are in blossom, and give them my greetings.' The fainting fits went on, as embarrassing as they were alarming; he would fall out of his chair and then be very angry at attempts to help him to his feet, quite unaware that he had briefly lost consciousness. He had to wait for the commission of enquiry to clear him of the charges of financial misconduct. It issued a number of meaningless interim reports without reaching any conclusion. Undeniably his personal expenditure had been astronomic, but there was no evidence whatever of dishonesty; inevitably, his diplomacy on the grand scale had been very expensive indeed, especially when he was entertaining kings and emperors. He had accepted valuable gifts from foreign governments, but in no sense could these be considered bribes, while it was plain that he had never misappropriated state funds. At the end of 1850 the commission dissolved itself. If there was no formal acquittal, its dissolution was a tacit declaration of his complete innocence.

At last, in March 1851—prompted by Mélanie—Metternich wrote to Schwarzenberg asking him to sound out Francis Joseph: 'Would my return to the Empire be an embarrassment for the government?' He reminded Schwarzenberg that he was nearly seventy-seven, that his only real home was Vienna. There was a prompt reply; the Emperor would be very happy to see him back in the capital.

On 9 June the Metternichs left Brussels, not for Vienna but for Johannisberg. The last part of the journey was by paddle steamer down the Rhine. They remained at Johannisberg until September, being visited in August by Frederick William. 'The King embraced my husband with touching warmth,' Mélanie records. A bottle of the best of their wonderful hock was produced in which to drink Francis Joseph's health. No doubt the wine had also been brought out for Prussia's new envoy to the federal Diet: 'M de Bismarck . . . had a long conversation with Clemens and appears to have the best political principles.

They reached Vienna at 4.30 p.m. on 24 September, having travelled down the Danube from Linz. Crowds were waiting on the bank to welcome home the frail old man. 'We found the villa just as we had left it,' wrote Mélanie ecstatically of their palace on the Rennweg. 'The flowers seemed to greet our return.' Schwarzenberg called on them next day, and spoke at length with Metternich, making himself equally amiable to the Princess. Visitors, who included the entire Imperial family, continued to call for weeks to congratulate them on their return.

Not everyone was pleased to see him back. A newspaper announced that in gratitude for his homecoming the ex-chancellor would redeem all pawn tickets under twenty gulden; in consequence, crowds of ticket holders besieged the Metternich palace for several days. This typically Viennese joke was the only unpleasantness.

The Emperor had been away in Galicia, but as soon as he returned to Vienna he went to the Rennweg. On 3 October Mélanie recorded how the twenty-one-year-old Francis Joseph, looking very handsome and serious, had told her 'he was happy to see Clemens back at Vienna after the horrible time we had been through'. He then spent two hours with the Prince, in private conversation behind closed doors; he assured him that he was going to ask his advice on many matters. He did indeed consult the ex-chancellor frequently. Schwarzenberg did not, though remaining on the friendliest terms. They were invited to balls at the Hofburg and Schönbrunn, Mélanie dancing with great enjoyment. She did not enjoy a ball at the Ballhausplatz quite so much. On seeing her in her old home, Archduchess Sophia exclaimed, 'What Mélanie, *you*'ve come? You really are admirable!'

Metternich now possessed all the money he needed, his estates and revenues having been restored, even the pension for his years as chancellor. The Rennweg became, so Pauline tells us, 'a rendezvous for all the diplomatic world, as well as for the whole of Viennese society'. Among the most frequent guests were Prince Windischgrätz—who alone had stood by the chancellor in March 1848—the poet Baron von Zedlitz, and the British ambassador the Earl of Westmorland with his wife. Metternich tried to secure better relations between Austria and Britain. He showed Schwarzenberg a letter from Queen Victoria to a German relation, which complained that the chancellor was unbearable, 'Austria's Palmerston'. Alarmed, Schwarzenberg adopted a much more tactful tone in his dealings with Britain, so much so that Westmorland thanked Metternich for his intervention.

Prince Schwarzenberg died suddenly in April 1852, still only fifty-two. During a mere three and a half years in office he had completely restored the Monarchy's authority and the Emperor always remembered him as 'the greatest minister I ever had at my side'. Yet his unified state was not going to last, as he had begun the alienation of Prussia, which from a partner in Germany became a rival.

The office of chancellor remained unfilled, but Count Karl Ferdinand von Buol-Schauenstein, ambassador to London, was appointed foreign minister. He was the son of an old colleague of Metternich who at the time approved of the appointment, though privately he thought Buol quick-witted but shallow. Mélanie noted with satisfaction that as soon as the new minister took office, 'He at once came to see Clemens and treated him with the most perfect deference.' At first he consulted the master, who was only too pleased to give advice, including how to handle the British; Metternich sent him an analysis of Palmerston's address to the electors of Tiverton, besides explaining that the names of Whig and Tory had lost their meaning in the days of 'Mr Canning of ill-omened memory'. A flood of paper continued to arrive from the Rennweg until the end of Metternich's life. After a year or two Buol began to ignore his advice, though he never forgot to treat him with the deepest respect.

The man who had persuaded Schwarzenberg and Francis Joseph to bring back absolutism, the octagenarian Baron Kübeck, retired but nonetheless remained extremely influential in government circles. Still a warm friend of Metternich, he was always ready to listen to his opinions. However, he would die within three years.

In the spring of 1852, Mélanie recorded a visit to Vienna by Tsar Nicholas, who called at the Rennweg twice. On the first occasion Nicholas 'showed us really touching affection'. On the second 'he begged us to go on thinking of him as one of our most devoted friends'—a rare display of feeling by one of the most terrifying men in nineteenth-century Europe. Significantly, he did not forget to have a long conversation with Metternich; clearly he was convinced that the ex-chancellor knew what was really happening in the Austrian Empire. Bismarck too came once or twice, to see what a modern historian has called 'the tremendous old man'.

The Crimean War revealed the limitations of Metternichian diplomacy when practised by someone else. Tsar Nicholas's determination to carve up Turkey-in-Europe and Napoleon III's ambition to emulate his uncle's military glories had made a major conflict extremely likely. Russia declared war on Turkey in October 1853, ostensibly to protect the Christian shrines of Palestine, France and Britain declaring war on Russia in the following March. At stake was not what Thiers described as 'giving a few miserable monks the key of a grotto', but whether or not the Tsar should have Constantinople. Austria's problem was to remain neutral without alienating Russia; she had no wish to divide the Balkans with her or to fight anyone. Metternich's view was that she should adopt the position she had used during the Greek War of Independence in the 1820s, staying aloof from both sides. Although admitting that he was alarmed—in July 1853 he declared that the situation was 'like a bad dream'—he was reasonably optimistic, writing that Francis Joseph's mind was in tune with his own and moving 'towards universal peace'. The situation was complicated still further by the Tsar's conviction that Austria was bound to repay him for saving the monarchy in Hungary in 1849—many Austrian officers thought that the Imperial and Royal army should fight at the Russians' side.

Nicholas tried to preempt Austria, by invading the Danubian principalities on 3 July 1853 without warning, and by suggesting that Francis Joseph should take Bosnia and Herzegovina. The Emperor argued for nearly a year. Then, without consulting Metternich, Buol persuaded Francis Joseph to let him send an ultimatum to St Petersburg—to demand that Russia evacuate Moldavia and Wallachia. When the Russians left, Austrian troops marched in. On the same day as the ultimatum was delivered, the ex-chancellor had written to Buol, warning him that Austria must never let herself be used as 'the East's advance guard against the West, or the West's against the East.' After the ultimatum had gone, he commented, 'The fatal consequences of any and every action are hidden from Count Buol. He can see what is just in front of him; of what is coming he sees nothing.' Buol compounded his folly by allying with Britain and France in December 1854 but then refusing to commit Austrian troops, although a year later he threatened to declare war if Russia did not make peace. He had already destroyed the counterrevolutionary alliance by the ultimatum of 1854. When the war ended, Austria did not have a friend in Europe. The last vestiges of Metternich's Vienna settlement had disappeared forever.

Moreover, Buol ignored the need to restore Austria's understanding with Prussia. Schwarzenberg had destroyed it by thwarting Berlin's plans for a single German state and then humiliating her, but the relationship might still have been reforged. Instead of reviving Metternich's tactful approach, the new foreign minister allowed Austrian officials to behave with insulting arrogance towards Berlin's envoys at Frankfurt. This neglect of Prussian susceptibilities would have disastrous consequences.

Metternich was distracted from foreign affairs by Mélanie's increasingly serious illness. Ever since the birth of her last child in 1837, she had suffered from stomach pains and fever which frequently prostrated her. These had grown worse in 1848. At the very moment when Russia was invading Moldavia, in June 1853, she began to go downhill but lingered for over six months. She died on 3 March, only forty-eight. Mercifully it was a peaceful death; the only sign she gave of sensing its approach was to ask for the Last Sacraments—her husband told Hügel that she never once complained, never showed any fear. Ironically, she had always dreaded outliving Clemens and dragging out a lonely old age. It was a shattering blow for a man of nearly eighty-one.

Hermine, his youngest child by Eleanor, looked after him for the remainder of his life. Characteristically, he once observed of her, 'She is very like my mother and therefore possesses some of my charm.' Despite this tribute she had never married.

A daguerreotype taken during these last years shows a face of great if weary nobility, curiously ascetic—that of an aged abbot rather than an elder statesman. 'Every evening, after the theatre, people flocked to my grandfather's drawing-room, and often it was so full that one could barely find a place to sit down,' Pauline remembered. 'Since my grandfather had grown deaf he could not take part in a general conversation so that anyone who spoke to him had to talk very loudly, which deeply embarrassed those who were shy.' However, he no longer went into society, never attending levées and seldom visiting the Emperor. He was delighted when in 1856 his son Richard, about to become the Austrian minister at Dresden, married his granddaughter Pauline. (As she was the bridegroom's stepsister a dispensation had to be obtained from the Church.) He insisted on giving half his silver to the couple, for them to use at the legation.

He continued to spend midsummer at Johannisberg and most of August at Königswart. He was visited at Königswart in 1857 by Albert Edward, Prince of Wales. At fifteen, the future Edward VII was not very interested. He remembered that Metternich, who reminded him of the Duke of Wellington, spoke a great deal about Napoleon.

Pauline describes his life in the country. He rose at eight and dressed immediately with the utmost care, as if expecting visitors at any moment. He had a cup of tea, then sat down at his desk, where he read the newspapers and wrote letters. (As late as April 1859 he sent a letter to Rossini, inviting '*mon cher maestro*' to come and stay with him at Johannisberg before it was too late.) 'His handwriting was still clear and beautifully formed,' she tells us. His mental faculties were unimpaired. In the afternoon he went for a stroll in the gardens and in evening played whist, but most of his time was taken up by reading—according to his granddaughter, he devoured every important new book.

After the end of the Crimean War in 1856, he grew very worried about Piedmont's designs on Lombardy-Venetia. He realized that Cavour, the Piedmontese prime minister and a political genius, hoped to embroil Austria in a war with France, where Napoleon III was posing as a friend of Italian nationalism. In 1859, the Piedmontese goaded Buol into declaring war. A worried Francis Joseph arrived at the Rennweg on 20 April to ask for the master's advice. It was, 'For God's sake, no ultimatum!' The Emperor replied, 'It went off yesterday.' At the beginning of May before going to the front, he again came to ask for advice, having sacked Buol.

Metternich did what he could, advising that Count Rechberg —with whom he had worked for many years—be appointed foreign minister. He suggested seeking help from Prussia and Russia, though they had been alienated by Schwarzenberg and Buol. 'My grandfather followed the news from the front with unflagging interest but owing to constant bad news with a growing sense of pain and sorrow,' Pauline tells us. 'His mental faculties had not weakened in the slightest, so we found it impossible to keep anything secret from him. He read the newspapers every day and had a complete grasp of the situation, describing it on the very eve of his death as a desperate one.'

On 21 May the Emperor came to the Rennweg, asking Metternich to draft the necessary documents for a regency should he be killed in the war. He also asked Metternich to draw up a will for him. But Metternich did not have enough strength for the task. When he received Francis Joseph he was so frail that he had to stay in bed during the audience, which lasted for three hours. Hübner, who was back from Paris, where he had been ambassador until the war broke out, took the tottering old man round the gardens of the Rennweg. He told Hübner, 'I was a rock of order' (*'ein Fels der Ordnung'*). When he said goodbye, he repeated, as if to himself, *'Ein Fels der Ordnung.'*

It is the measure of his reputation that even now he was consulted by the new foreign minister, Rechberg. Metternich could not help him. The nucleus of that Concert of Europe which he had maintained for so long had vanished. Schwarzenberg had alienated Prussia, Buol Russia.

On 5 June Count von Rechberg was with him when the report of the Austrian army's defeat at Magenta arrived—Milan lay at the mercy of the French and Piedmontese, who marched in two days later. He fainted. It was said that the battle of Magenta killed him.

Metternich paid his last visit to his garden on 10 June, carried in a chair, but was unable to get out of bed the following morning. His valet summoned the family and Dr Jäger. He was given the Last Sacraments by the Franciscan friar who had been saying Mass daily in his chapel. When the priest left Metternich smiled at Jäger, waving his hand feebly to show that his heart had almost stopped beating. He died just before noon.

For three days his body lay in state. His farewell was worthy of one who remembered the pomp of the Holy Roman Empire. The huge hearse bearing his coffin to the Karlskirche was emblazoned with the arms of Metternich quartering Austria, while on top were four black cushions on which lay his orders—Malta, St Stephen of Hungary, the Golden Fleece, the Saint Esprit, St Anne of Russia, San Gennaro of Naples, the Black and the Red Eagle of Prussia. The hearse was escorted through the streets by rows of friars carrying tapers. Archdukes, Princes of the Empire and Knights of Maria Theresa were waiting for him in the vast church, which was draped in black. After a great Mass for the Dead with the *Dies Irae* and ending with the *Götterhalte,* the coffin was taken to the *Nordbahnhof* for his last journey. He was interred quietly at Plass beside the three wives and eight children who had gone before him.

20

After Metternich

Der Weg der neuern Bildung geht
Von Humanität
Durch Nationalität
Zur Bestialität

FRANZ GRILLPARZER

The Austro-Hungarian Empire still looks better as a solution to the tangled problems of that part of the world than anything that has succeeded it.

GEORGE KENNAN

Metternich's worst fears came true. Germany was unified under Prussia in 1870. If it seemed for half a century after his death that he had been wrong to think revolution marched behind liberalism, he would be hideously justified. The conflict of 1914 destroyed the 'Northern Powers': Rousseau's totalitarian disciples took over Russia, and very nearly Western Europe as well, while nationalism poisoned Germany.

'The most celebrated statesman in Europe has lived just long enough to see all the objects of his life frustrated, or if not yet wholly frustrated, still in such jeopardy that their doom cannot be long averted,' *The Times* pronounced when he died. Historians considered him a failure. Treitschke, the 'Apostle of Prussianism', accused the chancellor of placing 'the foot of the House of Austria on the neck of the German Nation'—Metternich had been 'filled with black hatred of a law abiding people'. His reputation declined still further after the publication in 1880 of a collection of his diplomatic and personal papers, which included an 'autobiographical fragment'. The historian Paul Bailleu published an attack on the fragment the same year, showing that occasionally the chancellor's vanity had made him rewrite history.

Disraeli always remained a firm admirer. When he met Pauline Metternich in London in 1879, just after a war over the Eastern Question between Britain and Austria on one side and Russia on the other had been narrowly averted, he at once began to talk about her grandfather. 'All his predictions have come true,' said the prime minister. 'He really did have the gift of prophetic insight.'

During the early 1920s hope in the League of Nations revived interest in the Congress System and in Prince Metternich. His ideas attracted considerable attention, especially his attitude to Europe. His ally Gentz had written in an essay famous in its day:

> Because of their geographical position, and the similarity of their customs, laws, requirements, way of life and culture, the states of this continent form naturally a great political league, which with good reason has been called 'The European Commonwealth' . . . The members of this natural league of nations are in such constant close contact that none of them can remain unconcerned by what is happening in one another. It is not enough to say that they live side by side. If they are to survive, then they can only survive because of one another and through one another.

The words may be those of Gentz, but it is the chancellor's voice.

An Austrian, Heinrich von Srbik, was the first historian to defend him, in *Metternich, der Staatsmann und der Mensch* (1925). While admitting Metternich's shortcomings—wishful thinking and inability to see any good in the new forces—Srbik argued that he had nonetheless been 'one of the very greatest masters of international politics in the history of modern Europe'. Even liberals were impressed by Srbik's book. Sir Llywellyn Woodward conceded that the chancellor's 'care for European peace, his refusal to take the loud-spoken claims of nationalists at their own valuation, or to think in terms other than those of the well-being of many millions of men of different nationality and place and language, may redeem much of his narrowness and some of his mistakes'.

However, the renewed interest died away when the world grew disillusioned with the League of Nations. Ironically, at the very time that Metternich's views on European unity were being reexamined, the Monarchy's successor states were embarking on aggressively nationalist policies and demanding the revision and enlargement of their frontiers—a scenario which may well recur before the end of the present century.

In the 1930s European Jewry had reason to regret that the world was no longer ruled by men such as Clemens von Metternich. If opposed to much of what he stood for, Heinrich Heine had written of his respect for him. The poet also shared his distrust of German nationalism, approving of the '*Demagogenverfolgung*', which had bridled Jahn and the *Burschenschaft*. 'Although I am a radical in England and a carbonaro in Italy, I am emphatically not a demagogue in Germany, purely and simply because if such men were triumphant several thousand Jews would die.' Heine prophesied:

> Should the subduing talisman, the Cross, break, then will come roaring forth the wild madness of the old champions, the insane Berserker rage of which the northern poets sing. The talisman is brittle and the day will come when it will break pitifully. The old stone gods will rise from their long-forgotten ruin and rub the dust of a thousand years from their eyes; and Thor, leaping to life with his giant hammer, will crush the Gothic cathedrals.

Even the Nazis accepted the accuracy of Heine's prophecy.

New admirers of Metternich arose in the aftermath of the Second World War, arousing the wrath of A. J. P. Taylor. He sneered at them as 'renegade American liberals' seeking a hero with which to inspire the 'Western Union' in the Cold War. His anger did not dissuade Henry Kissinger from expressing deep (if far from unqualified) admiration of the chancellor in one of the best of all books about him.

While one can chart fluctuations in Metternich's reputation, it is not so easy to assess his achievements. 'It was the greatness and the strength of Metternich during these fateful years [of the French Revolution and Napoleon] to have foreseen that human contrivances, however clever and beneficial, would not endure, and to have understood the peculiar elasticity with which men would finally revert to former habits,' writes Sir Lewis Namier. 'The failure of struggling, striving men brings the heir of ages back into his own.' That is the measure of the chancellor's one unalloyed triumph, outwitting Napoleon.

The positive and negative elements in Metternich's later career are far harder to judge. Certainly he knew how to identify his enemies. 'In Germany the attack still comes from the middle class against the throne and the upper class; in France, where these two latter elements have disappeared, the mob is now rising against the bourgeoisie,' he observed in 1831. 'That is the logical sequence.' There were later nineteenth century conservatives who, like Metternich, saw liberal régimes as phases acted out by dupes. In Dostoyevsky's opinion too, the revolution was undoubtedly going to be millennarian and anti-Christian. (The chancellor would have recognised Buonarotti in Dostoyevsky's Piotr Verkhovensky [in *The Devils*] and his views—'The need for culture is an aristocratic need. As soon as you have family or love you acquire a need for property . . . Everything must be reduced to complete equality.') In the next century Weimar Germany, Third Republic France, Republican Spain and Giolitti's Italy confirmed Metternich's fears, while Russia took Buonarotti's ideas to their logical conclusion—just as Nazi Germany realized the aspirations of Jahn and the student 'martyrs' of the Carlsbad Decrees.

What is beyond dispute is that Metternich enabled the Habsburg Monarchy to go on being what it wanted to be for over three decades. He convinced the world that Austria was the successor to the Holy Roman Empire and the pivot of Europe, even if she was always too poor to wage war; Russia and Prussia thought her indispensable. Dominating Germany and overawing Italy added to the appearance of strength. For thirty-three years he preserved the Monarchy from revolution.

He has been castigated for offering no alternative, no hope of change. Kissinger portrays him as a victim of the 'conservative dilemma', citing his own word: 'I claim to have recognised the situation, but also the impossibility to erect a new structure in our Empire.' Admittedly, whether the plans for constitutional reform rejected by Emperor Francis would have made very much difference is questionable. However, Metternich's 'system' did at least prolong the life of what he regarded as the best of all possible worlds; as Namier puts it, 'Metternich was sincerely attached to the Habsburg Monarchy because, like no other State, it was bound up with the time and world in which he would have chosen to live.'

Yet he refused to despair of the future. 'Quibbling, whether called theology, philosophy or politics, when it usurps the role which belongs to principles and practicality, brings down societies,' he wrote in 1850. 'It may dissolve empires but it does not kill the human race. Principles are imperishable . . . after the crisis they come back into their own. The process is slow but sure.'

It has been suggested that he saw stagnation as the sole alternative to chaos. He sometimes gives this impression: 'The late Abbé de Pradt thought he had said everything in announcing "Mankind is on the march"! I permit myself to ask the question "Towards what"?' But here he was simply reacting to Pradt, one of the most superficial if widely read political writers of the day. Undoubtedly he believed in progress, as he made clear in December 1849: 'There are two sorts of men in the world; those of the past and those of the future. The second sort, and I claim to be among them, are the only ones who matter, since yesterday no longer exists—one must be involved with tomorrow, with what's going to happen.'

Personally he disliked the term 'Metternich system', calling it a '*fausse dénomination*'. In 1852 he defined it as 'not a system but the application of the laws which rule the world.' Stripped of its verbiage, this means that it was a strategy rather than a system, to ensure the survival of the traditional social order and the 1815 settlement. 'From his own perspective it is difficult to see where Metternich went wrong' is Alan Sked's verdict. 'What is really amazing is how much he achieved . . . The Europe of his day came closer to his ideals than to those of his opponents or his rivals.'

It can be argued that Metternich's grandeur lies in accepting the possibility of failure. Bertier de Sauvigny prefaced his remarkable study of the chancellor with a quotation from an unfashionable philosopher of the right, with whom Metternich had little in common. 'Nothing is easier than Revolution,' wrote Charles Maurras. 'What is splendid and difficult is to avoid the shock, to guard against upheaval. To sail and reach port, to endure and make others endure is the miracle.' If the chancellor never reached port, he endured for astonishingly long.

His greatest historian, Srbik, insists that he was a political thinker in the grand manner. In Srbik's opinion, Metternich's significance at the deepest level lies in his 'constant and consistent opposition throughout the world of European civilisation to the levelling by democracy and the rule of the mobilised masses, which threatened the historical order of state and society as well as individual culture'. He has sometimes been compared to Disraeli. While he shared that eccentric Englishman's timelessness—he would have been home at the siege of Vienna or in modern New York—he lacked Disraeli's cynicism and pessimism. If he too looked back, Metternich's vision of history had much more hope in it. In some ways it was akin to that of Giambattista Vico, who, in the *Scienza Nuova*, divides history into cycles (an age of gods, an age of heroes and an age of barbarians), arguing that each cycle passes on its skills.

'The mistake was in accepting the would-be philosophic and scientific character which Metternich gave to his harangues' is how Namier explains the decline in the chancellor's reputation. 'These were songs in which the music mattered and not the text.' The emergence of a united Europe in the 1990s, together with the crumbling of the Russian Empire in Central and Eastern Europe, gives Metternich fresh relevance today. For he always looked beyond mere national interest. (Viereck stresses his rejection of what Nietzsche calls 'atavistic attacks of soil attachment'.) He believed in national traditions contributing to a joint heritage, as opposed to nationalism. A modern Austrian admirer, Hugo Hantsch, singled out the federal system as his most creative concept: Austria was to be a federation of its historic lands; Central Europe a federation of sovereign states; and Europe as a whole a federal system based on the principle that great powers are equal. 'It was an approach pointing to the future,' says Hantsch, 'and it sets Metternich among the ranks of truly great statesmen.' Even Sked, who sees Metternich as a centralist, admits that he 'viewed the Empire as a European microcosm'.

His advice to Kübeck at the end of 1849 is undeniably topical. At Frankfurt the German nationalists whom he had always distrusted were trying to create a single *Grossdeutschland*, a state which would contain every German-speaking land, including Bohemia and Prussian Poland; some Frankfurt deputies even wanted the German community at Paris to be represented. Metternich totally rejected *Grossdeutschland*. 'There is only one way in which Germany can make good her nationhood, which is by forming a confederation of states,' he told Kübeck. 'Prussia proposes a single state instead of a confederation . . . Should Prussia succeed in implementing her plan, a very skilfully constructed plan—and she has an excellent chance of doing so—the consequences will of necessity be incalculable, in view of the danger it will create not only for Prussia herself but for the entire European community.'

No less topical, in the context of the new Russian revolution, is his dictum that 'once it has taken the first step, revolution tends to run the whole course', and his conviction that political strife is an inevitable consequence. 'When anarchy comes to a head in any state, it invariably ends in civil wars or in foreign, and often in both at the same time.' He saw no peaceful solution—'In a great social crisis the people cannot be both sick man and doctor.'

Metternich's formula of legitimacy (minus the dynastic element) and tradition may still be helpful in Central Europe, where, as in post-1815 Europe, unless secured by peaceful negotiation any changes in the 1945 frontiers could spell disaster. Kissinger has rephrased legitimacy as depending on 'acceptance, not imposition', while tradition (cultural nationalism instead of the linguistic and racial sort) is equally capable of redefinition. Nor is it inconceivable that Metternich's Austria may reappear, in the form of a loose Danubian federation (Austria, Hungary, Czechoslovakia, Poland and northern Yugoslavia), as a counterweight to the economic might of the new Germany.

If chauvinist nationalism still lingers on viciously, it looks as though Metternich's other great enemy, Messianic socialism, is all but moribund, the most significant development in political thought since the French Revolution; the great Utopian movement to reconstruct the world which began in 1789 finally collapsed in 1989. There has been a return to the policy of conserving existing frontiers and constitutions, albeit liberal constitutions. One cannot deny that the great chancellor was himself overtaken by history. Yet his hatred of war and chauvinism, his faith in the old Christian Europe and his diplomatic genius are worth remembering at a time when Europe is striving for unity.

Sources and Bibliography

Since Metternich was in power for nearly thirty-nine years and lived to be eighty-six, the documentary material is on a scale scarcely surpassed by that on Napoleon. The most important sources are the archives of the *Staatskanzlei* and the *Kabinettsarchiv*, both in the Haus-Hof-und Staatsarchiv at Vienna. (In 1959 the Haus-Hof-und Staatsarchiv published a catalogue of the documents concerning his life.) There are also the personal papers and Princess Mélanie's diary—forty volumes—which were discovered at Plass in 1949 by Dr Marie Ulrichova and transferred to the Czech State Archives at Prague. Additional material is to be found in the archives of almost every foreign ministry in Europe. Needless to say, he figures prominently in countless contemporary memoirs and collections of correspondence. A study which makes full use of all this is beyond the capacity of the most industrious historian. Those who have consulted it to greatest effect are Srbik, whose monumental *Metternich der Staatsmann und der Mensch* has not been superseded since its appearance in 1925, and Bertier de Sauvigny, whose *Metternich et son Temps* came out thirty years ago but remains indispensable.

The foundation for any book on the chancellor is the collection of Metternich's papers, which he intended to take the place of a biography and which were published at Vienna in 1880. Admittedly, the autobiographical fragment is not always reliable. The account of his duel with Napoleon in 1813–15 was written fourteen years after, and that of his later career was written in 1844 and 1852; his memory is sometimes at fault, while sometimes he distorts the facts so as to flatter himself—notably in the account of the famous interview with the French Emperor at the Marcolini Palace in 1813. Albert Sorel's comment on the fragment is sometimes quoted by very superficial historians: 'He makes himself the light of the world; he dazzles himself with his own rays in the mirror which he holds perpetually before his eyes.' But, as Pieter Geyl showed in *Napoleon: For and Against,* Sorel's intention was to discredit the chancellor in support of his thesis. ('In Sorel's reading,' says Geyl, 'all Metternich's negotiations [in 1813] had no other aim than to win time and to put Napoleon in the wrong with Europe and with France. One has only to look at the realities of Austrian conditions and of Metternich's policy to understand that the mediation was meant seriously, at any rate at first.') Moreover, the material in these eight volumes consists mainly of letters, memoranda, and despatches, with extracts from his wife's journal, the autobiographical fragment amounting to less then a single volume. In Bertier de Sauvigny's view the collection 'has always been and remains, in spite of its imperfections, the basis of every study of Metternich.'

Among English biographies, that by Alan Palmer (1972) is the most thorough and, as far as possible, is based firmly on the sources, but it is unsympathetic in tone. Some historians have admired the chancellor (Viereck and Kissinger), others have execrated him (Bibl and Taylor). The debate is summarised in Schwarz's *Metternich, the Coachman of Europe* (1965) and Kraehe's *The Metternich Controversy* (1971). A more detached approach has recently emerged, expounded by academics such as Dr Alan Sked of the London School of Economics—who has inherited the mantle of C. A. Macartney. His *Decline and Fall of the Habsburg Empire* (1989), reflecting the latest research, is surprisingly favourable in its interpretation of the chancellor.

Both English and American historians of the Monarchy tend to ignore the work of such fine French scholars as Victor-Louis Tapie or Jacques Droz. Not only do their books contain much original research, but they often approach topics from a different standpoint—for example, when examining the Metternich-Palmerston confrontation.

BIBLIOGRAPHY

Contemporary works:

Abrantès, Duchesse d', *Mémoires*, Paris, 1905–13.

———, *Histoire des salons de Paris*, Paris, 1836–38.

Andrian-Werburg, Viktor Freiherr von, *Österreich und dessen Zukunft*, Hamburg, 1842–47.

Angeberg, Comte de, *Le Congrés de Vienne et les Traités de 1815*, Paris, 1863–64.

Anon., *Tablettes Autrichiennes, contenant des faits, des anecdotes et des observations sur les moeurs, les usages des autrichiens et la Chronique Secrete des cours d'Allemagne, par un témoin secret*, Brussels, 1830.

Anon., *The State of the Nation at the Commencement of the Year 1822*, London, 1822.

British Diplomacy, 1813–1815. Select Documents dealing with the Reconstruction of Europe (ed. Sir C. K. Webster), London, 1924.

British and Foreign State Papers, London, 1841.

Buonarroti, F. M., *Conspiration pour l'égalité dite de Baboeuf*, Brussels, 1828.

Burghersh, Lady, *Letters from Germany and France During the Campaign of 1813–14* (ed. Lady R. Weigall), London, 1893.

Castlereagh, Viscount, *Correspondence, Despatches and Other Papers of Viscount Castlereagh, Second Marquess of Londonderry* (ed. 3rd Marquess of Londonderry), London, 1853.

Caulaincourt, Marquis Auguste-Louis de (Duke of Vicenza), *Mémoires*, Paris, 1933.

Chateubriand, Vicomte François-René de, *Mémoires d'Outre-Tombe*, Paris, 1849–50.

———, *Congrés de Vienne*, Paris, 1838.

Consalvi, Cardinal, *Mémoires du Cardinal Consalvi* (ed. J. Cretineau-Joly), Paris, 1864.

Correspondence respecting the affairs of Italy 1847–49, presented to both Houses of Parliament, London, 1849.

Fain, Baron Agathon-Jean, *Manuscrit de Mil Huit Cent Treize*, Paris, 1825.

———, *Manuscrit de Mil Huit Cent Quatorze*, London, 1823.

Falloux, Comte Alfred-Pierre de, *Mémoires d'un Royaliste*, Paris, 1888.
Garde-Chambonas, Comte A. de la, *Souvenirs du Congrès de Vienne, 1814–1815*, Paris, 1904.
Gentz, Friedrich von, *Tagebücher, auch dem Nachlass Varnhagen von Ense*, Leipzig, 1873.
———, *Briefe von und an Friedrich von Gentz* (eds. F. C. Wittichen & E. Salzer), Munich, 1909–13.
———, *Dépêches inédites du Chevalier de Gentz aux Hospodars de Valachie, pour servir à l'histoire de la politique européenne* (ed. Graf A. Prokosch von Osten), Paris, 1876.
George IV, *Letters 1812–1830* (ed. A. Aspinall), Cambridge, 1930.
Goethe, Wolfgang, *Aus meinem Leben. Dichtung und Wahrheit*, Leipzig, 1903.
Grillparzer, Franz, *Sämtliche Werke*, Munich, 1862–65.
Guizot, Francois, *Mémoires pour servir à l'Histoire de mon Temps*, Paris, 1859–61.
Hartig, Graf Franz, 'Genesis or details of the late Austrian Revolution', in *History of the House of Austria* by Archdeacon Coxe, vol. IV, London, 1853.
Heine, Heinrich, *Sämtliche Schriften*, Munich, 1868–76.
Hübner, Graf Joseph, *Neuf ans de souvenirs*, Paris, 1904.
———, *Une année de ma vie*, Paris, 1891.
Kübeck, Freiherr Karl von, *Tagebücher*, Vienna, 1909–10.
Laborde, A. J. de, *Précis historique de la guerre entre la France et l'Autriche en 1809*, Paris, 1823.
Las Cases, Comte Dieudonné de, *Mémorial de Sainte-Hélène*, Paris, 1951.
Lebzeltern, Ludwig, *Mémoires et papiers de Lebzeltern, un collaborateur de Metternich*, Paris, 1949.
——— (ed. Grand Duke Nicholas Mikhailovich), *Les rapports diplomatiques de Lebzelfern*, St. Petersburg, 1913.
Liedekerke Beaufort, Comte Hilarion de, *Le Comte Hilarion: Souvenirs et biographie du premier Comte de Liedekerke Beaufort* (ed. C. de Liedekerke Beaufort), Paris, 1972.
Lieven, Princess, *Letters of Princess Lieven to Lady Holland, 1847–57* (ed. E. A. Smith), Oxford, 1956.
———, *The Private Letters of Princess Lieven to Prince Metternich* (ed. P. Quennell), London, 1937.

———, *Unpublished Diary and Political Sketches of Princess Lieven* (ed. H.Temperley), London, 1925.

Metternich-Winneburg, Prince Clemens Lothar Wenzel von, *Memoirs*, New York, 1980.

———, *Clemens Metternich–Wilhelmine von Sagan: Ein Breifwechsel, 1813–1815* (ed. M. Ullrichová), Graz & Cologne, 1966.

———, *Aus Diplomaten und Leben, Maximen des Fürsten Metternich* (ed. A. de Breycha-Vautier), Graz, 1964.

———, *Briefe des Staatskanzler Fürsten Metternich-Winneburg an Grafen Buol-Schauenstein, 1852–59* (ed. C. J. Burckhardt), Munich & Berlin, 1934.

———, *Une Dernière Amitié de Metternich, d'après une correspondance inédite* (ed. Boyer d'Agen), Paris, 1919.

———, *Lettres du Prince de Metternich à la Comtesse de Lieven* (ed. J. Hanoteau), Paris, 1909.

———, *Correspondance du Cardinal Hercule Consalvi avec le Prince Clément de Metternich, 1815–1823* (ed. C. van Duerm), Brussels, 1899.

———, *Mémoires, documents et écrits laissés par le Prince de Metternich* (ed. Prince Richard Metternich), Paris, 1880–84.

Metternich-Sandor, Fürstin Pauline, *Geschehenes, Gesehenes, Erlebtes*, Vienna, 1921.

Muenster, Graf Ernst von, *Political Sketches of the State of Europe, 1814–67*, Edinburgh, 1868.

Napoleon, Emperor, *Correspondance de Napoléon Ier*, Paris, 1858–70.

Nesselrode, Graf Karl-Robert von, *Lettres et papiers du Chancellier Comte de Nesselrode*, Paris, 1904–7.

O'Meara, Barry, *Napoleon in Exile: or, a voice from St Helena*, London, 1822.

Palmerston, Viscount, *Life and Correspondence of the Hon John Temple, Viscount Palmerston* (ed. E. Ashley), London, 1876.

Pellico, Silvio, *Le Mie Prigioni*, Turin, 1832.

Pezzl, Joseph, *Skizze von Wien unter der Regierung Joseph II*, Vienna, 1789.

Rémusat, Comtesse Claire-Elisabeth-Jeanne de, *Mémoires, 1802–8*, Paris, 1880.

Rosenkrantz, Niels, *Journal du Congrès de Vienne, 1814–1815*, Copenhagen, 1953.

Sainte-Aulaire, Comte Beaupoil de, *Souvenirs, Vienne, 1832–41*, Paris, 1926.

Sealsfield, C. (Carl-Anton Postl), *Austria as it is*, London, 1828.

Talleyrand-Périgord, Prince Charles-Maurice de, *Mémoires de Talleyrand*, Paris, 1891.

———, *Correspondance inédite du Prince de Talleyrand et du Roi Louis XVIII pendant le Congrès de Vienne*, Paris, 1881.

Ticknor, George, *Life, Letters and Journal of George Ticknor*, Boston, 1876.

Trollope, Frances, *Vienna and the Austrians*, London, 1838.

Turnbull, Peter Evans, *Austria*, Edinburgh, 1840.

Villeneuve, Marquis Pons-François de, *Charles X et Louis XIX en exil: mémoires inédites*, Paris, 1889.

Wellington, Duke of, *Dispatches, Correspondence and Memoranda of Field-Marshal Arthur, Duke of Wellington*, London, 1867–73.

———, *Supplementary Dispatches, Correspondence and Memoranda* (ed. 2nd Duke of Wellington), London, 1858–76.

Later Works:

Alison, Sir A., *The Lives of Lord Castlereagh and Sir Charles Stewart*, London, 1861.

Anderson, M. S., *The Eastern Question, 1774–1923*, London, 1966.

Andics, E., *Metternich und die Frage Ungarns*, Budapest, 1973.

Bailleu, P., *Die Memoiren Metternich*, Munich, 1880.

Balfour, Lady F., *The Life of George, Fourth Earl of Aberdeen*, London, nd.

Barany, G., *Stephen Széchenyi and the Awakening of Hungarian Nationalism, 1791–1841*, Princeton, 1968.

Bartlett, C. J., *Castlereagh*, London, 1966.

Bertier de Sauvigny, G. de, *Metternich et la France après le Congrès de Vienne*, Paris, 1968–72.

———, *Metternich et son Temps*, Paris, 1959.

———, *Metternich et Decazes d'après leur correspondance 1816–1820*, Paris, 1953.

Bibl, V., *Kaiser Franz, der letzte-römisch-deutsch Kaiser*, Vienna, 1937.

———, *Metternich, der Dämon Österreichs*, Leipsig & Vienna, 1936.

———, *Metternich in Neuer Beleuchtung*, Vienna, 1928.

Bortolotti, S., *Metternich e l'Italia nel 1846*, Turin, 1945.
Buckland, C. S., *Friedrich von Gentz's Relations with the British Government, 1809–12*, London, 1933.
———, *Metternich and the British Government from 1809–1813*, London, 1932.
Cecil, A., *Metternich*, London, 1933.
Corti, Count E. C., *Metternich und die Frauen*, Vienna & Zurich, 1949.
———, *The Rise of the House of Rothschild*, London, 1928.
Coudray, H. du, *Metternich*, London, 1935.
Cresson, W. P., *The Holy Alliance*, New York, 1922.
Deák, I., *The Lawful Revolution: Louis Kossuth and the Hungarians, 1848–49*, New York, 1979.
Droz, J., *Europe between Revolutions 1815–1848*, London, 1967.
———, *L'Europe centrale: évolution historique de l'idée de Mitteleuropa*, Paris, 1966.
———, *Histoire de l'Autriche*, Paris, 1961.
———, *Restauration et révolutions (1815–1871)*, Paris, 1953.
———, *L'Allemagne et la Révolution Française*, Paris, 1949.
Emerson, D. E., *Metternich and the Political Police. Security and Subversion in the Habsburg Monarchy, 1815–1830*, The Hague, 1968.
Ferrero, G., *The Reconstruction of Europe: Talleyrand and the Congress of Vienna, 1814–1815*, New York, 1963.
Goldstein, R. J., *Political Repression in 19th Century Europe*, London & Canberra, 1983.
Good, D. F., *The Economic Rise of the Habsburg Empire, 1750–1914*, Berkeley & Los Angeles, 1984.
Grimsted, P. K., *The Foreign Ministers of Alexander I*, Berkeley, 1969.
Grunwald, C. de, *Tsar Nicholas I*, London, 1954.
———, *Trois siècles de diplomatie russe*, Paris, 1945.
———, *La vie de Metternich*, Paris 1938.
———, *Stein, l'ennemi de Napoléon*, Paris, 1936.
Haas, A. G., *Metternich, Reorganisation and Nationality, 1813–1818*, Wiesbaden, 1963.
Hales, E. E. Y., *Mazzini and the Secret Societies*, London, 1956.
———, *Pio Nono*, London, 1954.
Hannah, C., *A History of British Foreign Policy*, London, 1938.
Hantsch, H., *Der Geschichte Österreichs*, Graz & Vienna, 1951–3.
Hinde, W., *Castlereagh*, London, 1981.

———, *George Canning*, London, 1973.

Hobsbawm, E., *The age of revolution 1789–1848*, London, 1964.

Kann, R. A., *A History of the Habsburg Empire, 1526–1918*, London, 1974.

———, *The Multinational Empire, 1848–1918*, New York, 1950.

Katzenstein, P. J., *Disjointed Partners, Austria and Germany since 1815*, Berkeley, 1976.

Kissinger, H., *A World Restored*, New York, 1957.

Kraehe, E. E., *Metternich's German Policy. The Congress of Vienna, 1814–1815*, Princeton, 1983.

———, *The Metternich Controversy*, New York, 1971.

———, *Metternich's German Policy. The Contest with Napoleon, 1799–1814*, Princeton, 1963.

Langer, W. P., *Political and Social Upheaval, 1832–52*, New York, 1969.

Lefebvre, G. *Napoléon*, Paris, 1935.

Lincoln, W. Bruce, *Nicholas I, Emperor and Autocrat of All the Russians*, London, 1978.

Macartney, C. A., *The House of Austria: The Later Phase, 1790–1918*, Edinburgh, 1978.

———, *The Habsburg Empire, 1790–1918*, London, 1968.

———, 'The Austrian Monarchy, 1792–1847', in *New Cambridge Modern History* (ed. C. A. Crawley), vol. IX, Cambridge, 1968.

Malleson, G. B., *Life of Prince Metternich*, London, 1888.

Mann, G., *Secretary of Europe: The Life of Friedrich Gentz, Enemy of Napoleon*, New Haven, 1946.

Marriott, Sir J. A. R., *Castlereagh, The Political Life of Robert, Second Marquess of Londonderry*, London, 1936.

———, *The Eastern Question*, Oxford, 1917.

Masson, F., *L'Impératrice Marie Louise, 1809–1815*, Paris, 1902.

Mathy, H., *Franz Georg von Metternich*, Meisenheim, 1969.

May, A. J., *The Age of Metternich*, New York, 1963.

Mazade, C. de, *Un Chancellier d'Ancien Régime*, Paris, 1889.

Mikhailovich, Grand Duke Nicholas, *L'Empéreur Alexandre Ier*, St Petersburg, 1912.

Milne, A., *Metternich*, London, 1975.

Namier, Sir L., *Vanished Supremacies*, London, 1958.

———, *The Revolution of the Intellectuals*, London, 1945.

Neue Österreichische Biographie, Vienna, 1923–35.
Nicholson, H., *The Congress of Vienna*, London, 1946.
Paléologue, M., *Alexandre I, un tsar énigmatique*, Paris, 1932.
———, *Romantisme et diplomatie*, Paris, 1924.
Philipps, W. A., *The Confederation of Europe*, London, 1913.
Pirenne, J. A., *La Sainte Alliance*, Neuchatel, 1946.
Radvany, E., *Metternich's Projects for Reform in Austria*, The Hague, 1971.
Rath, A. J., *The Viennese Revolution of 1848*, Austin, 1957.
Redlich, J., *Emperor Francis Joseph*, London, 1929.
Reichenberg, F. von, *Prince Metternich in Love and War*, London, 1938.
Roberts, J. M., *The mythology of the secret societies*, London, 1972.
Robertson, *Revolutions of 1848*, Princeton, 1952.
Rolo, P. J. V., *George Canning*, London, 1965.
Sandeman, G. A. C., *Metternich*, London, 1911.
Schenk, H. G., *The Aftermath of the Napoleonic Wars*, London, 1947.
Schroeder, P. W., *Metternich's diplomacy at its Zenith, 1820–23*, Texas, 1962.
Schwarz, H. F. (ed.), *Metternich, the 'Coachman of Europe'*, Lexington, 1962.
Sked, A., *The Decline and Fall of the Habsburg Empire 1815–1918*, London, 1989.
——— (ed.), *Europe's Balance of Power, 1815–48*, London & Basingstoke, 1979.
———, *The Survival of the Habsburg Empire: Radetsky, the Imperial Army and the Class War, 1848*, London & New York, 1979.
——— (ed. with C. Cook), *Essays in Honour of A. J. P. Taylor*, London & Basingstoke, 1976.
Sorel, A., *L'Europe et la Révolution Française*, Paris, 1904.
———, *Essais d'Histoire de Critique*, Paris, 1883.
Srbik, H. Ritter von, *Metternich, der Staatsmann und der Mensch*, Munich, 1925 & 1954.
Stearns, J. B., *The Role of Metternich in Undermining Napoleon*, Urbana, 1948.
Stiles, W. H., *Austria in 1848–49*, New York, 1852.
Sweet, P. R., *Friedrich von Gentz, Defender of the Old Order*, Madison, 1941.
Talmon, J. L., *The Origins of Totalitarian Democracy*, London, 1952.

Tapie, V-L, *Monarchie et peuples du Danube*, Paris, 1969.
———, *La révolution de 1848 dans l'empire d'Autriche (1848–1851)*, Paris, 1954.
———, *L'Europe centrale et orientale de 1689 à 1796*, Paris, 1952–57.
———, *Le monde slave de 1790 à 1850*, Paris, 1950.
Taylor, A. J. P., *Europe: Grandeur and Decline*, London, 1967.
———, *Englishmen and Others*, London, 1956.
———, *The Habsburg Monarchy*, London, 1948.
———, *The Italian Problem in European Diplomacy, 1847–49*, Manchester, 1934.
Temperley, H.W.V., *England and the Near East*, London, 1936.
———, *The Foreign Policy of Canning, 1822–27*, London, 1925.
Treitschke, H. von, *Deutsche Geschichte in Neunzehnten Jahrhundert*, Leipzig, 1880.
Troyat, H., *Alexandre Ier, le Sphinx du Nord*, Paris, 1980.
Tulard, J., *Napoléon ou le mythe du sauveur*, Paris 1977.
Vandal, A., *Napoléon et Alexandre I*, Paris, 1897.
Viereck, P. *Conservatism Revisited*, New York, 1949.
Walker, M. (ed.), *Metternich's Europe, 1813–48*, New York, 1968.
Ward, D., *1848, The Fall of Metternich*, London, 1970.
Ward, Sir A. W., *The Period of the Congresses*, London, 1919.
Webster, Sir C., *The Foreign Policy of Palmerston, 1830–41. Britain, the Liberal Movement and the Eastern Question*, London, 1951.
———, *The Congress of Vienna*, London, 1934.
———, *Palmerston, Metternich and the European System, 1830–41*, London, 1934.
———, *The Foreign Policy of Castlereagh, 1812–15. Britain and the Reconstruction of Europe*, London, 1931–35.
———, *The European Alliance*, Calcutta, 1929.
Woodward, Sir L., *War and Peace in Europe, 1817–70*, London, 1931.
———, *Three Studies in European Conservatism*, London, 1929.
Woolf, S., *A History of Italy, 1700–1860*, London, 1979.
Zamoyski, Count A., *The Polish Way*, London, 1987.

Index